Crossing the bridge

Also by David Wake

NOVELS
I, Phone
The Derring-Do Club and the Empire of the Dead
Hashtag
The Derring-Do Club and the Year of the Chrononauts
The Derring-Do Club and the Invasion of the Grey
Atcode

NOVELLAS
The Other Christmas Carol

ONE-ACT PLAYS
Hen and Fox
Down the Hole
Flowers
Stockholm
Groom

NON-FICTION
Punk Publishing (*with Andy Conway*)

Crossing the Bridge

DAVID WAKE

WATLEDGE BOOKS

First published in Great Britain by
Watledge Books
Copyright © 2017 David Wake

This paperback edition 2018
3

ISBN: 978-1911310983

Cover art by Smuzz
www.smuzz.org.uk

CONTENTS

1. The Battle of Culloden Moor 3
2. The Drive to England 21
3. The Battle of Derby 33
4. The Chellaston Campaign 51
5. The Swarkestone Stratagem 61
6. Prisoner of War 75
7. The March South 89
8. The Propaganda War 113
9. Encampments 127
10. Rules of Engagement 143
11. Intelligence 166
12. Insurgency 180
13. Insurrection 208
14. The Cost of War 221
15. Shock and Awe 232
16. Trouble and Strife 250
17. A Calm before the Storming 273
18. The Walls around the City 286
19. Tunnels beneath the River 299
20. Police Action 307
21. The War on Westminster 323
22. Air Supremacy 335
23. Exile 351

There is no **Bonnie Prince Charlie Society**, but there is a **Charles Edward Stuart Society**.

For legal reasons, the two organisations have no similarities whatsoever, honestly, and the characters in this novel don't bear any resemblance to any of them, of course; nor is any implied, nor should any be inferred, obviously – except for their warm welcome and their sense of fun.

♦

"It's going to be a happy ending – though he still gets hung, drawn and quartered."

Mel Gibson on "Braveheart"

THE BATTLE OF CULLODEN MOOR

Seventeen Forty Five.

Across a green and pleasant land, a scarlet regiment formed up: *Redcoats!*

They'd primed their muskets.

I tugged my borrowed targe hard against my left shoulder, comforted by the shield's heavy, leather protection, and tested the balance of my claymore. You are never more alive than when you are about to die.

"For Scotland!"

"For Scotland!!!"

Rabbie raised his blade and we Jacobites, knee-deep in heather, followed his example – our steel flashed in the sun and our dirty tartan flapped in the chill breeze.

"For Bonnie Prince Charlie!"

"For Bonnie Prince Charlie!!!" The thunderous response contained some truly appalling Scots accents.

A dreadful calm settled all that time ago...

♦

...and I sit here now, trapped in this prison cell, and remember, wondering at the path that led down here. There are times when you can reflect, pop your head above the battlements of your routine, and ask yourself where did it all go pear-shaped? For me, there's a clear route, a southerly direction that fixes that battle at Culloden on Square One and this day of reckoning at the journey's end. I suppose you can look back on your life from any point to any other point; from maternity ward to execution chamber; from cradle to shallow grave; from that battle in the heather to the coming slaughter on the streets of London.

Somewhere, I took a left instead of a right.

I must figure it out. I must know. I need to know.

But there's not much time left.

I owe it to the others to atone, but how can I, without knowing where I went wrong?

At the Battle of Culloden Moor, in that quiet before the storm, I remember looking at my watch...

♦

Seventeen Forty Six.

"Charge!"

"Charge!!!"

The unstoppable force of colourful tartan and blunt swords surged towards the unbreakable wall of shining buttons and bayoneted muskets. There's nothing like a Highland charge and this was nothing like a Highland charge: forty mad men and women running at full pelt with a bouncing gait across the springy foliage, screaming at the top of their voices. Such was our enthusiasm that the first Scots went down before the English fired a shot.

"Present!"

Here it comes, I thought, here it comes.

With a few exceptions, the Redcoats levelled their guns. Between the blur of running figures, I saw an English dandy giving orders, the cutting wind flapping his foppish white cuffs. I recognized him: for goodness sake, it was Ross – what was he doing with the English?

He hammed it up: "Wait for it! Wait for it!"

4

We were close, close enough for them to see the whites of our eyes and the stains on our teeth.

"Fire!"

The English line seemed to explode – a devastating volley of flame, noise and smoke. Men fell, thrown back by the imagined lead balls, with screeches bursting from their throats. Too many – far too many – had fallen in the first volley and we realised at once. So Jacobite after Jacobite staggered to their feet and charged on into the growing confusion. Our line was broken; the fog of war spread in the white cotton wool of musket smoke, as soldiers ran in odd directions.

Desperately, the Redcoats reloaded, ram-rodding charges of fresh gunpowder down their barrels.

"Fire at will."

"Who's Will?"

"Bollocks!"

Another volley detonated across the field at almost point blank range. The screams of dying men mingled with the growing undercurrent of laughter.

"I'm hit, I'm hit," screamed the Scot to my left, "I'm going down."

I reached the English line at a full run, slowed a few yards away and nodded to an opposing Redcoat, a young man, twenty-something like myself. Anxiously, he levelled his musket. The bayonet flashed forward and I glanced it aside with my targe, a drumbeat of steel against studded leather. We fought for a moment, and then I tapped him on the shoulder with my claymore.

"Oh right," he said before he hollered in agony and fell over, careful to keep his musket and powder bag out of the damp heather.

I was killed then, struck from behind by some murderous Englishman. I crumpled to my knees and pitched forward into the cold clammy clutches of death.

"Oi!" said the dead man at my side, "careful of my sarnies."

5

"Sorry."

I shifted off his bag and rolled onto my back. The heather sprung up around me to hide the battle and dull the musket fire. It was peaceful. The sky above was blue, and two planes had crossed their white contrails to make a huge St. Andrews cross as if to celebrate a great Scottish victory.

Rabbie hove into view.

"Keep going! Keep going!" he yelled. He leaned over to pull me up.

"We're supposed to lose," I said.

"You give up too early, Guy."

Behind the rope cordon, spectators booed and hissed at the dreadful display of cowardice. I smiled and waved back.

"He killed me," said the Redcoat next to me. "Dashed bad luck."

"How many times have you been killed?" Rabbie asked.

"Oh... at least, four or five times," said the Redcoat.

"At least," I said. "Anyway, you're supposed to be shot too."

"Oh yes, sorry, I got carried away," said Rabbie, then he shouted: "Will someone shoot me?"

So Rabbie went off in search of death and glory.

"Thanks for backing me up, old chap," said the Redcoat, rolling over to face me.

"Old chap?"

"With... er..."

"Rabbie. He's the old chap, thirty–"

A shot rang out: "Thanks," Rabbie shouted, and then, "Arrgggghhh!"

A ripple of applause rewarded Rabbie's practised death throes.

"Liam," said the Redcoat.

I rolled over and shook the offered hand: "Guy."

"Pardon?"

"I'm Guy."

"Jolly good battle – wot?"

"Not bad," I said, smiling at Liam's phoney posh accent. "Not as good as the one before lunch."

Liam got out a smartphone.

"Oi," I said, looking around in panic, "don't let Rabbie see that."

"What?"

"He'll do his nut. It's anachronistic."

"You're wearing a watch."

"Oh... shit!" I pushed it further up my arm.

We laughed and Liam put his smartphone away.

A tannoy squawked over everything: *"Let's hear it for the Redcoats."* There was clapping from the crowd. *"And for the Jacobites!"*

This evoked applause and even whoops. The English tourists always prefer the underdog.

Liam helped me up. I brushed down my plaid and then flicked a few bits of moss off the back of his Government uniform. He adjusted his wire-framed glasses.

"Computer programming," Liam said.

"Pardon?"

"I'm a computer programmer at a bank."

"Right."

"This is great, much better than..."

"Than?"

"Nothing."

Another volley of musket fire and Rabbie's distant shrieks pierced the air yet again. Clearly, he had survived his previous fatal wound, and so won another bout of clapping at this second, or possibly third, death.

The distorted voice cut across the banter: *"I can see some of the Jacobites fleeing the scene towards the beer tent and its selection of fine ales. And there are cakes and coffee in the refreshment area as well as ice cream and doughnuts. Please enjoy yourselves and thank you for coming."*

The tannoy switched to music and some indie rock drifted over the battlefield.

"And you?" Liam asked.

"History," I said. "I'm doing a doctorate."

"On the Jacobite Rebellion?"

"God no! Early twentieth-century politics. The causes of the world wars. I do this for fun."

"Right."

"Fancy a pint?"

"You're asking an Irishman if he wants a drink?"

"But I thought that English accent was genuine."

"Begorra and bejesus," Liam stressed, "is Britain being a land of teetotallers now?"

"I sincerely hope not."

We ambled across the field towards the source of the music, weaving our way between the intermingling clumps of red and tartan. I homed in on one uniform with a particularly shiny collection of brass buttons.

"Ross," I said, ready to start the banter. "What's with the red coat?"

"Och, the English were short of officers, so I filled in."

"But we were short of men."

"Aye."

"If you'd been on our side," I said, "then we might have won."

The clump of soldiers around us all laughed, although I think I'd used the same line the year before. Re-enactors are nothing if not traditionalists.

"It's really difficult walking on this stuff," said Liam. "It's like a springy mattressy thing."

"Surprised health and safety haven't had words," I said. "You could easily turn an ankle in this stuff."

"Lucky it's no too wet," said Ross.

"It is wet," Liam insisted.

"Nah, that's no wet. Two years ago..."

"Three," I insisted.

"It pissed it down and we were sliding everywhere. Covered in mud, we were. It was like Glastonbury."

We reached the beer tent, a canvas structure jutting out from a truck. The high bar and sullen serving wenches decorated with facial piercings were already besieged by soldiers from both sides.

"What do you fancy?" Liam said.

"Are you sure?" I asked.

"The man offered of his own free will," said Ross.

"It's no trouble, I've a city job and you're a student."

I scanned the beer taps: "Eighty Shillings, please."

"Same for me."

Ross was... is – *God, I hope he's all right* – he's a big man, red-haired, and a drinker. He's Scottish, as he will no doubt tell you, and that it's nothing to do with geography, it's a state of mind. Or after several pints of heavy, it's a state of mindlessness; but he is someone you can depend on. I like that, a straight talker who always tells you when you're talking pish. He's a teacher, his directness being a positive asset, I'd have thought. I met him, I think, at another re-enactment event, five or six years ago now, or longer. He must be nearly in his thirties now. During the re-enactment season, you meet the same people, year after year, all wearing the same costumes, and the dates merge into one continuous time-stream: fight-drink, fight-drink, fight-drink... like Valhalla – *Oh God, I don't want to die.*

Liam's the opposite: black-haired, wiry and nervous, with a bizarre habit of pushing his glasses back up his nose every two minutes when he's had a few. He'll talk (and boy can he talk) about the city, money and programming, even though he hates all three. There's always something in his hands – always fiddling is our Liam – and he's hardly built to jostle his way through the red and tartan lines to the front of a beer tent 'queue'. We first met that day at the last battle at

Culloden. Hard to believe it was only a few months ago – so much water under the bridge.

And I'm Guy Wilson.

A student of sorts, I guess. I studied in Plymouth and then moved up here to Scotland to do my doctorate. I've a girlfriend, Mandy... had a girlfriend.

That's all...

Oh God, please God someone help me. I can't face this. I'm torturing myself remembering this. It's like I missed so much the first time round, so I need to rewind and rewatch it all again.

In Edinburgh, I share a flat with three other postgraduates, when I'm not staying over at Mandy's. I have a reasonably full social life. I like films, music, beer – the usual stuff. What have I got to show for it all? Just a partial thesis at almost 17,500 words and a half-full bottle of single malt tucked behind the telly. I don't suppose I'll get to finish either.

Anyway, there we were, the Three Musketeers together for the first time: an Englishman, an Irishman and a Scotsman walked into a bar.

"He's a long time getting the drinks in," Ross said.

"You should have patience," I said.

"If only she'd let me."

"If only who'd let... oh, Patience."

The music over the tannoy finished and the news took over. It started with a piece about some financial pig's ear before moving on to the usual twaddle about the day's events in Parliament. The Speaker of the House of Commons was soon shouting: *"Order, order."*

"I wish he would order," said Ross.

"What's this?" I asked.

"I wish he'd order, I'm parched." Ross raised his voice. "Man dying of thirst here!"

"No, the news?"

"Westminster's messing up our country."

"What country would that be? Kent?"

"Och aye, shame on you, yer Sassenach."

In the distant debating hall, an MP shouted over the cacophony: *"...we will never give up. One sees violence and disorder at every turn..."* (as if on cue, a few muskets fired a loud volley behind us) *"...this must be checked, contained, controlled..."*

There were the cries from the other Members of Parliament, *"Shame! Shame!"*

"Oh, it's bloody Trudie," said Ross over the Speaker of the House calling for order yet again.

"...there is only one way to control this anarchy..."

"Who?" I asked.

"Och, Guy, what planet have you been living on? Do ye no know what's going on? He's an MP... Och, I forgot, he's post-1939, so you won't have heard of him. I forget historians know nothing of modern politics."

"...we must give the forces of law and order the right tools, the same defence as all the other first world modern police forces..."

"Guy!" Liam passed a pint over the heads of those behind him in the queue. I took it, the plastic container distorting in my grip, and passed it to Ross. Liam brought the other two over himself, by which time Ross had half-finished his.

"...we must arm the police!"

The Right Honourable John Trudie, MP, finished his speech (the *'boo-hisses'* outnumbered the *'hear-hears'*) after which the newsreader told us to expect showers tomorrow – a storm was brewing.

"Cheers," said Liam.

"Cheers."

"Sláinte."

The beer tasted good, though there was a slight tang of slops. Still, at least it wasn't lager.

"You coming to Derby?" I asked Ross.

"Och, I don't know."

"Come on, Ross!"

"What's Derby?" Liam asked.

"Only the greatest re-enactment in the Jacobite calendar, isn't it, Ross?"

Liam's face lit up: "Really?"

"How come you don't know that?"

"I've not been in this re-enacting lark long."

"How long?"

"My first time," Liam said, laughing. "So Derby's good?"

"We go every year, don't we, Ross?"

"Aye." Ross finished his pint.

"It takes the whole weekend. There's a battle like this on the Saturday," I explained, "and then on the Sunday, we do the same thing at Swarkestone."

"Swarkestone?"

"Swarkestone is where–"

"Och, you silly Southerner," said Ross to Liam. "You've only gone and asked a historian to give us a lecture."

"I'm not a Southerner," Liam complained. "I'm from Belfast, Northern Irish to the core and–"

"I think you'll find Belfast is south of Gretna," Ross said.

"First I've heard that Shropshire has been moved north of Hadrian's," I said.

"Telford is north of the Watford gap," Ross insisted. "I was brought up in Aberdeen, so I am a true Scot."

"No, you weren't," I said, playing my role. "You were born in Kent."

"Aye, but being born in Kent means never having to say you're from Surrey."

"Tell me again, Ross, is Kent in the hard north or the soft south of the Home Counties?"

"'Tis your round."

I showed him my half-full pint; Liam did the same.

"Daylight robbery," said Ross, and he went off for three more pints of Eighty Shillings.

"Are you back to work on Monday?" I asked.

"No," said Liam. He looked at his damp shoes. "I'm sort of taking a sabbatical."

"For the summer?"

"Er... yes."

There was an odd hesitation in his voice. I didn't think much of it at the time. Perhaps, because I didn't know him then, I just thought he spoke like that. He pushed his wire-framed glasses up his nose.

"You should join us for Derby," I suggested.

"Well... I'd like to."

"It's in a couple of months' time. Ross drives us in his van. We share the cost of the diesel."

"No problem."

We finished our drinks having seen Ross coming back with two pints. He always gets served quickly – big man.

"Ross?" I said, taking the fresh ale and placing it in the now empty first pint, so that the double plastic 'glass' bent less.

"Och, I need my pint."

As Ross went back for his pint, a couple approached. You only had to look at the sharply ironed and mismatched tartan to know they were from the US. The Americans lollygagged too.

"Ross," I said when he got back, "is it all right for Liam to join us in the van to Derby?"

"I've not said... aye, the more the merrier."

The American woman cut in: "You're one of the Scottish clansmen?"

"Och aye," said Ross, laying it on. The woman was momentarily taken aback to have the Redcoat answer in such a thick brogue.

"We're confused," she said. "The Scottishmen–"

"Jacobites."

"They seem to have won."

"Och, aye, the noo, they always win. Did ye no ken that?"

"But," the American insisted, "didn't Bonnie Prince Charlie lose?"

"Och, he wins now."

The man piped up: "Is that because they resent the English for destroying their revolution?"

"Och, no," said Ross. "'Twas the fault of the Americans."

"Americans?"

"Och aye. Yon Yanks came and fought wi' the Sassenachs."

"I don't see the stars and stripes."

"Weren't invented. See yon Union Jack." Ross pointed to where a Union *Flag*, properly missing the red 'X' of St. Patrick, fluttered. "That was ye colours back then."

"No, I think not," said the woman's husband, "we declared our independence."

"In 1776, which was thirty years after Culloden," I ventured.

"Aye," said Ross, "so long before you lot were the insurgents."

The Americans blanched.

"The Jacobites were true revolutionaries," he added. "At the time, your future Americans were still English, so you were the despots. Ye ken?"

"Ross," I warned.

"English despots, who kicked out thousands of true Scots in the clearances–"

"A lot of Scots settled in America," I said.

The Americans nodded in reply, or in apology, and beat a hasty retreat.

"It was the Scots who organised the clearances," I said to Ross.

"Turncoats acting under the orders of their English lords and masters."

"The Scots were doing it for at least fifty years *before* Culloden and most went to America, so those two there are probably the descendants of the true Scots. The ones that call themselves Scots were probably... what? Collaborators?"

"Och, that explains the independence vote."

We moved away from the beer tent, making our way towards the public area with its ice cream vans and doughnut stalls. A vendor went around selling helium-filled balloons, which bobbed and danced above small children, and spread out amongst the crowds as they funnelled towards the car park. The day was nearly over.

"Och, you're in trouble now."

"I am?" I said.

"What is it?" Liam asked.

"Guy. He's always being stopped by the polis," said Ross. "Ninety-nine?"

A clutch of red balloons parted and I saw two police officers approach, a six-five giant and a WPC, each swaggering in their stab jackets and utility belts. They came straight towards me. I downed the remainder of my pint and dropped the plastic into a bin.

"Excuse me, Sir," said the WPC. "Is that a weapon?"

"I'm just pleased to see you," I replied.

Ross looked heavenward and dragged Liam away towards the serving side of an ice cream van.

The policeman stepped to one side, checking the crowd, but the WPC came right up to me.

"If you wouldn't mind, Sir?" she said, pointing to a space away from any observers, where the refrigeration unit chucked out a dry heat with a headache-inducing throb. I went and, as soon as we were out of public view, the WPC pushed me back against the metal panel. It moved in and out: *lub-dub*.

"I'll have to search you, Sir," she said, already feeling down my white shirt and further to where the plaid was folded and wrapped into a kilt. Her hand reached the hem... and then started to come up inside.

"Are you going to make good on that?" I asked.

She looked round: "Maybe not. It is a bit public." She stood upright and kissed me. I responded. It was very pleasant, our tongues jousting to–

"Polis brutality!"

It was Ross resplendent in his uniform, every inch the picture of an English Officer, except for the ice cream with a chocolate flake set at a jaunty angle.

"Ross," the WPC said, not looking round: "Go away!"

"You carry on snogging, Mand. Don't mind me." Ross stuck out his tongue and licked his ice cream suggestively.

Mandy took my arm and pulled me away. Her police training meant it wasn't the nice romantic gesture she intended. She sort of twists, and I'm a macho bloke so I don't say anything, but it can be painful.

"Pervert," said Mandy to Ross as we passed.

"Arrest me!"

"You're not her type," I said as she tugged me along.

We disengaged as soon as we reached the crowd, so we looked just like any other policewoman walking with a helpful citizen.

My girlfriend has a clean and antiseptic look in her black and white livery, just a hint of blonde hair wisping to escape from under her cap. She's the same age as I am, but looks much younger. It's what they say about the police, isn't it? Younger every year. Women in uniform, what can I say?

I miss her, which is a strange thought now.

"Did you see the battle?" I asked.

"No. We were over there," she said, and vaguely indicated the other side of the field towards the Culloden monument. I could see the turret of stones concreted around a plaque. I knew the inscription from memory.

**THE BATTLE
OF CULLODEN**
WAS FOUGHT ON THIS MOOR
16TH APRIL 1746

THE GRAVES OF THE
GALLANT HIGHLANDERS
WHO FOUGHT FOR
SCOTLAND & PRINCE CHARLIE
ARE MARKED BY THE NAMES
OF THEIR CLANS

As well as the Irish, French, Dutch, Germans and so on – the battle had been positively cosmopolitan. Scotland and a European union against the English. Of course, it excluded all the Scots killed on the Duke of Cumberland's side, and the English killed fighting for Bonnie Prince Charlie.

"It was OK," I said.

"Good."

"You'll be at Derby?"

"I don't have to work the whole weekend."

"Great," I said.

Mandy bit her lip as she nodded... *oh God, she had known back then!*

♦

I feel a prickling cold despite the airless heat of the cell and I swear the hairs on my neck are standing on end. She had known all that time ago at Culloden, and I hadn't realised until this moment. I can remember her expression, I can see it in front of me now, and it's obvious. Hindsight is the great magnifying glass of the historian, but at the time, standing on the trampled heather, I hadn't a clue.

What an idiot!

And before then, if you think about it, when we'd leant against the back of the ice cream van and kissed, and I had felt the heat of passion as well as the pumping exchanger of the refrigeration unit. She had known, hidden it away in the freezer compartment of her heart, and I'd had no idea at all, not the slightest inkling – *oh bollocks!*

I pace the empty cell again, three yards by eight, wanting to escape not just from the concrete and steel, but from my thoughts as well. But I can't. It all goes round and round as I walk up and down.

I think I'm underground. The echoes seem to sound underground somehow. I came down in a lift, I'm sure. I think I'm sure. How deep? Mandy, why did you–

I check my watch and find myself looking at my blank wrist again. And, of course, my watch isn't in my sporran – there's just the box - *that damn box!*

I must have been in here for hours, but it could be ten minutes that only seems like years, or two days that have gone by in a blink. I just want it all over.

No, I don't want it to be over, I don't want my friends to be dead.

I sit down again, stare at the white wall, and wonder whether it's already too late.

Or, God help us all, is it happening now? Beyond this silence is everything shouting and screaming, bloodshed and dying, a real battle instead of harmless make-believe?

Back at Culloden that day, Mandy and I would have held hands, but for the uniform. She'd joined the police force eighteen months before we met. She had weird shifts, but I could avoid writing my thesis any time, so it worked well. She was living in some flat and then, when she finished her probation (funny expression for the police when you think about it), we'd been within a whisker of moving in together. Unfortunately, a colleague, Fiona, split up with her husband and the two of them ended up sharing a flat.

I left a toothbrush at hers, she deposited a whole washbag at mine, and gradually we both ended up with two sets of the essentials. She was very organised, and fit, and I liked her smile.

She smiled at me back then too, and gave me a peck on the cheek before she double-timed across to join her colleague, jogging with her hand on her baton. They went off to patrol the car park leaving Ross, Liam and me to plan Derby.

Life isn't just sudden changes; there are gradual forces that shape you. A toothbrush here, a washbag there, the endless stupid tights on the floor, and suddenly, without any noticeable transition, you're living together in two flats. We had an understanding that we'd move in with each other as soon as Fiona got her life back together.

That's not going to happen, is it?

I sit on this concrete bed and look at my fingers, and through them I can see my boots, the laces confiscated so I don't hang myself. The irony of that.

It's been a long walk and it'll be over soon. Not long now before they come back: a bullet in the head, a shallow grave waiting or my body floating down the Thames, and then what? I'll become a footnote in history.

Not even that, a question mark.

Whatever happened to Guy Wilson?

"Have I Got News For You"
21:00 BBC1 (except Scotland)

Although the Home Secretary, Timothy Dorrington, MP, has had to cancel at the last moment, Ian Hislop and Paul Merton are joined by other celebrity panellists and a new guest host for another episode of the popular satirical news quiz.

THE DRIVE TO ENGLAND

Ross had this transit van to lug stuff all over the place. Battered was an understatement. The bodywork was white, except for a wing, which was blue, and third gear always complained bitterly in the cold. We were the army's baggage train packed full of re-enacting gear, tents and general luggage and some – *click, fizz* – cans of beer.

Ross and I shared the driving, and we collected Liam from a street corner, where he'd been standing with his suitcase. We'd only met him once, weeks back, but we were soon ribbing each other like old friends. We had the "did you get my text saying I was early?" conversation, and then my phone beeped to say his text had arrived.

Anyway, soon enough we were heading south. The great lumbering vehicle bounced along the inside lane of the M74 at 60mph, and occasionally, downhill, it reached a dizzying 75, which prompted Ross to bellow: "The engines canna take it!"

We reached that section of the motorway where it splits into two. The whole landscape, deep green and battle grey, stretched out with only the southbound three lanes visible, just as the three-day weekend stretched before us.

We'd planned some sight-seeing, a couple of battles in Derby with all our mates and some serious drinking – and some frivolous drinking as well. I, of course, had a whole weekend with Mandy to enjoy too. She hadn't fancied staying in the van with three blokes – what a surprise! – so she was coming down in her own car and had booked the Lawn's Hotel. There was something quite filthy about booking a hotel room for the two of us.

In the van, we were talking about... I've no idea. I said, "When I was young–"

"Ah diddums, Guy, did yer mother take away yer rubber duck?"

"I was just saying–"

"Canna do this, canna do that, yer getting to be such an old maid." Ross turned to Liam sitting in the passenger seat. "It's him having a polis woman for a lassie."

"So?" Liam asked.

"We can't do anything... no joints, no drinking at all, not even a pint, when driving... it's terrible."

I wasn't going to stand for this: "It's–"

"The nanny state, that's what it is," said Ross. "Soon we'll all have personal polis women checking up on us. Privatised, probably G4S, of course."

"Honestly, Ross."

"Although those bulletproof jackets–"

"Stab vests."

"Whatever, they do nothing for their figures."

"I give up!"

I sat back and watched the scenery zip by. It seemed brighter, greener, the sky bluer and the clouds fluffier somehow. The sun beamed down through the canopy in that exciting dappled fashion that creates shadows that swim across the landscape like shoals of fish. I closed my eyes: the light shining on my face such that an orange curtain filled my vision. The future was bright, the future was... I'm thinking in adverts. Let's try: the light flickered across my eyelids like a movie. Does your life really flash before your eyes just before you die?

Good God, this is exactly what I'm doing: sitting in this cell replaying my life.

"So, every trip somewhere," Ross continued, "we break the law."

"Break the law?" said Liam.

"That's it," said Ross. "Nothing major like murder, treason and the like. Something minor, trivial, but none the less an act of defiance. Although parking offences are a wee bit expensive and I'm not risking getting any points, so I reckon we should try something else."

I interrupted: "I'm morally against littering."

"It's quite hard to find a law to break without an ethical issue raising its ugly head."

"How about Class-B drugs?" Liam suggested.

"Aye, but not in the van. Pongs the place rotten."

"Fair enough," said Liam. "What's that noise?"

"What noise?" said Ross.

"The... knocking."

"It's the engine."

"Is it a problem?"

"No, I'll turn the radio up."

"I had a squeaky shoe once," I said.

"And?" Liam asked.

"I turned my mp3 player up."

It was great to be together, doing all the Jacobite re-enactments, but I knew even then that this would be the last season. These long summers would be over. I'd finish my thesis, Ross would get another job and Liam... but I didn't know Liam's situation when we were driving to England – that came later.

I suppose I genuinely thought it would last; we'd all keep in touch, the odd reunion here and there, friends for life. You never think you'll drift away from your mates. Of course, I didn't know that the Three Musketeers, as we were to become, wouldn't fade away, but go out in a blaze of glory.

Or, in my case, just disappear.

But I never thought that Constance – I'm stretching my metaphor here because I wasn't d'Artagnan and he was the Fourth Musketeer anyway – would... you know, that my Constance would be so in*constant*.

"Och, there's a sorry sight."

"What?" Liam asked Ross.

"England."

We looked and just caught the sign before we hurtled past. Liam and I broke into *Rule Britannia* at the top of our voices.

"Och, will you no stop that pish," said Ross. "It's all about beating up the Scots."

"That's the National Anthem, verse four – 'rebellious Scots to crush'," I said.

"So, my National Anthem is about beating myself up," said Ross.

"'Fraid so."

"And this is what we voted 'yes' for," said Ross. "And then you ninnies go and vote to leave the EU."

"I didn't–"

"Post-Brexit, there'll be passport control here. Did you no ken there's an alternative verse written by the Jacobites."

"No."

"Oh yes," said Ross and he cleared his throat in readiness.

"Oh no," said Liam and I in mock horror.

"God bless the Prince, I pray," Ross began in full flow. "God bless the Prince, I pray, Charlie I mean;

That Scotland we may see. Freed from vile Presbyt'ry,
Both George and his Feckie, Ever so, Amen."

"Amen," Liam and I finished.

We sounded terrible, but it passed the time and it was better than listening to *I Should Be So Lucky*, *The Loco-Motion* and so on yet again.

None of us had the heart for song when the road became the M6 and the inevitable roadworks ground everything to a crawl. It wasn't for long as we'd planned a little diversion. The year before, Ross and I had been to Gretna Green, but this year we promised ourselves Hadrian's Wall and so it was that we turned left at Carlisle.

As the saying goes: a diversion, it's the way forward.

Thinking about it, it must have been around this time that the Home Secretary, the Right Honourable Timothy Dorrington, MP, was interviewed on television. We didn't see it, we didn't even see the famous gag on *Have I Got News For You*, but it became part of the zeitgeist.

"We must work with the community," he'd said.

"What happens when a particular community doesn't work with you?" said the interviewer.

"Community policing: it's the way forward. Certain MPs–"

"That would be John Trudie."

"I wouldn't like to single out anyone in particular, but certain MPs would prefer a more... draconian system."

"Perhaps that's necessary when a particular community doesn't want to play ball with Community Policing."

"Community policing: it's the way forward. This is why this Government is so keen to reduce all the red tape. We're committed–"

"But will reducing red tape, useful though that is, do enough to allay public concerns?"

"We have already nearly 150,000 police, so a saving of 15 seconds to fill in the arrest form is like putting an extra 1,000 bobbies on the beat. People want bobbies on the beat. But it isn't just pure numbers, it's the number of man-hours on the street—"

"Or woman-hours?"

"Police hours on the beat. That's what this Government stands for. That's what we promised at the last election. And that's what we're going to deliver. Community policing: it's the way forward."

"But what if a particular community doesn't respond to community policing."

"Community policing: it's the way forward."

And so on.

'Community Policing' as a policy buzzword replaced 'Neighbourhood Policing' and 'Bobbies on the Beat'. They'll come round again: it's the way forward.

I think he said it seven times.

That's one more than Jeremy Corbyn asking David Cameron about Tax Credits and not getting an answer. This isn't the record by any means. On *Newsnight*, Jeremy Paxman asked Michael Howard the same question "Did you threaten to overrule him?" an insistent twelve times. Still, as Winston Churchill once said, if it's worth saying once, it's worth saying twice. Or something like that. I'm not sure exactly, which probably means he said it after 1939.

Misquoting: it's the way forward.

There's a theory that the roots of the Second World War lie in the failure of the Roman Empire to conquer Germania. It was the Battle of the Teutoburg Forest in 9 AD when Varus lost three legions to Arminius and Roman expansion in that direction stopped. Emperor Augustus drew a line through the forests. Germany was not conquered and, while the rest of Europe developed a taste for wine, underfloor heating and decadence, the myth of Aryan Supremacy was born – cue Hitler.

The northern extreme of the Roman Empire was Hadrian's Wall, at least according to the picture books on Ancient Rome. The huge fortification snakes across England from Carlisle to Newcastle, and separates England's green and pleasant land from Pictish Scotland's drab and rainy glens: it kept the unruly Scots at bay. It's nonsense really because Scotland was conquered by the Roman Governor, Agricola. It was just that the Scots never took to the aforementioned wine, underfloor heating and decadence.

Eventually, Hadrian built a wall to say: 'This far and no further.' The Romans never went north again, except when they built the Antonine Wall, various forts, roads, aqueducts, wine cellars, underfloor heating and all the other things that the Romans ever did for us.

You can walk along Hadrian's Wall today, particularly the stretch half-way between the White Cliffs of Dover and Sherwood Forest, or so it suggests in that Kevin Costner film about our heritage, *Robin Hood: Prince of Thieves*.

All this was pretty much the topic of conversation when we got there, parked and walked up towards the line of stone.

Ross held his arms aloft and–

♦

Fuck! Shit, shit, shit.

That was a cell door slamming, close by. I stand, tense, and I can feel the adrenaline flooding my veins. Yes, there's a corridor outside and that was definitely the door at the end. I listen, straining on tiptoe, as if that's going to help. I can hear... footsteps. Can I hear footsteps? Shouldn't they be getting louder? Please let them get quieter... *shhh, shhh...*

I clench my fists as if I'm going to fight my way out of here. *What's that?*

I can't hear a damn thing, my heart pumping away, my breath shallow and rapid. I'm hyperventilating – calm down, calm down, calm down.

Ross held his arms... *please, please, I don't want this. Christ, God, Allah, anyone, please no. This is sweat, actual cold sweat on my palms and it's horrible. My fingers glisten, and my hands are shaking. They must belong to someone else. I can't feel this trembling that I see in front of me. Beyond them is the iron door to this prison cell. It's closed. It's opening.*

♦

Ross held his arms aloft. We got out of the van to stretch our legs, get some fresh air and enjoy the view. He said: "This is mine, and that's yours."

"You're giving us Scotland?" I said.

Ross turned to face the other way: "This is yours, and you're welcome to it," he said.

"England belongs to the people," said Liam.

"A Republican, are you?" said Ross. "It all belongs to the Queen."

"It belongs to the National Trust," I said. "Anyway, it's England on both sides of the wall."

"No," said Ross.

"Yes," I insisted, "Scotland's not for another twenty miles or so to the north. Didn't you see the signs?"

"So, Hadrian's Wall separates England from another bit of England," said Liam.

"Och, the Sassenachs nicked our land," Ross insisted. "It's really Scotland. We'll get it back."

"What?" I said. "By marching on Derby?"

"Don't talk pish."

"The Romans built this to keep your kind out of civilisation," I said.

"That's a fallacy," said Ross. "We Celts built it to keep the Europeans in their place."

"You Celts want to remain in Europe. It's Britannia that wants to leave... actually Britannia begged the Romans to stay. Voted 'Remain', but were 'Left'."

"And we got the Romans to pay for the wall too."

"Did you now?" said Liam. "And I suppose you got them to guard it for you as well?"

"Best way. Delegation: it's the way forward. It was obviously that way round, because who'd want to live in England?"

"Not me," said Liam. "The Irish can only live in countries that make whiskey."

"You can't call that peat bog water whisky."

"I've never seen a peat bog any more than you've seen heather."

"I've seen Heather," said Ross. "Back of the bike sheds."

We laughed.

Who indeed would want to live in England? It had gone to the dogs, post-Brexit.

Mandy did, for one, I thought. I knew she'd looked into the transfer options. She'd mentioned it. She'd also mentioned that I never listened. I mean, come on, I never thought she was serious.

I sat down on the cold stones, those discarded blocks of the wall, and felt the wind through my shirt. The constant gales had pushed the trees to one side and it did look like a god-forsaken place. Imagine what the Romans must have made of the cold... and this was the height of summer. The IXth Hispana had been stationed here: Hispana, as in Hispanic, and it was a long way from Spain, a long way from anywhere, a long way from Londinium.

Mandy wanted to move south. She couldn't. It was just silly. All our friends lived in Edinburgh, for goodness sake. It still had a proper NHS too. We were going to stay and that was that. "What do you mean 'more than I've seen heather'," said Ross. "This is heather, all this here."

"That's bracken."

"Rubbish... Guy, what is it?"

"I was just thinking about the wall," I said. "It's humbling, isn't it, to think that this was built by a Roman soldier nearly nineteen hundred years ago?"

"I bet he got his mate to help," said Liam.

"They forced us Scots."

"They make whisky in England, you know," I said.

"No way!" said Ross.

"Somewhere in Norfolk. And there's that Welsh one too."

"Nonsense, there's only Scotch."

"It's windy," said Liam. "I'm not sure I like being outside."

"We'll find a nice cosy pub, don't you worry," said Ross. "They have them in England, I believe. It's not completely civilised."

Ross and Liam set off down the hill.

Liam called back: "Guy?"

"Och," said Ross. "He's missing his woman."

"Love's a terrible thing," said Liam. "Worse than drink. Ross, now, would you swap a bottle of single malt for a woman?"

"I'd swap one for Heather behind the bike sheds."

"For me, it would be Siobhan. Guy?"

"I think Mandy wants to move to London," I said.

"Sweet Jesus!"

"She canna do that," said Ross. "You've got roots, family, friends. The local's only just learnt yer usual."

"I can't move," I said. "But, you know..."

"Got it bad?" said Liam.

"Yeah."

And I had. Funny how you know, but you can't act on it until it's stated. It's not real: stocks may go down as well as up; there might be another World War; your girlfriend might move away; but until it's said aloud, it's only in the realm of insurance salesmen. Historical trends need a defining moment: Archduke Franz Ferdinand must die; someone has to invade Poland; a girlfriend must say she's going... then, and only then, is a decision made.

◆

The cell door is still closed. It only looked like it was opening because everything became brighter, more real, as my eyes dilated. I hear a sob, and I'm breathing again.

I get to live a little longer – false alarm.

It's quiet and you'd hear boots on a concrete floor in a tiled corridor outside – surely?

I don't like how I'm slick and clammy. I want a wash, clean my teeth and drink a pint of warm beer somewhere with oak beams, brasses and a roaring fire. I want red patterned carpet with antique knickknacks on high, dusty shelves. I want a packet of ridge-cut smoky bacon crisps, and, above all, I want my friends.

We were just three blokes having a good time without a care in the world. All right, lots of cares, but trivial. We didn't mean any harm. It didn't amount to anything. It shouldn't be about to go to hell.

◆

On that windswept archaeological site, Ross grabbed me by the shoulder and hauled me to my feet.

"Come on, Guy, let's be going," he said. "We'll find a pub, get plastered, and then tomorrow, when the hangover's gone, we'll get to Derby. Things'll look better in Derby."

"I suppose," I said.

We walked down the hill. I stopped briefly to look over my shoulder towards Scotland. 'Forlorn' is the word, but I expect I just looked like a pillock.

Welcome to DERBY

The centre of the UK geographically, culturally and historically

Just south of the Peak District, with some of the most beautiful countryside in England, the city mixes the traditional and the contemporary.

We can trace our history back to the Roman camp of "Derventio".

Bonnie Prince Charlie visited in 1745 and the Industrial Revolution started here.

In 1977, Queen Elizabeth II granted us city status as part of the Silver Jubilee celebrations.

And we are by no means living in the past: Derby's nightlife is amongst the most vibrant with many diverse clubs and pubs, as well as CAMRA Real Ale Festivals

THE BATTLE OF DERBY

Modern Derby is not the city that Bonnie Prince Charlie reached in 1745: our troops assembled in a car park.

I remember reading about the first *Planet of the Apes* film. Apparently, Charlton Heston noticed that the actors dressed as apes sat at separate tables from the 'humans' during breaks in filming. What's more, those dressed as Chimpanzees kept themselves from the Orangutans, and neither would have anything to do with the Gorillas. All four species segregated – a racism of latex masks.

At Derby, however, our tartan-clad Jacobites rubbed shoulders with our red-coated Government troops, and each borrowed gear off the other. We only separated for the actual battles. Oh, and for the drill. We Jacobites didn't do anything as OCD as 'forward march' and 'about turn'.

As more dribs and drabs arrived, everyone had a new excuse to start the welcomes, how-are-yous and greetings all over again. There were old friends, or they felt as such even after the briefest of introductions, and it was great meeting again or for the first time. Being dressed alike was a great leveller. We were all, at least, the same monkeys.

"I've not seen Mandy," I said.

"She'll be about," said Ross. "And yer mates are all here."

"Yes."

"Och, there's me and Liam to keep yer company."

"We're like the Three Musketeers," said Liam. "Athos, Porthos and the other one."

"Aramis," I said.

"That's it. One for all..."

Ross and I joined in: "...and all for one!"

"The Three Musketeers is a hundred years before the Jacobites," I said.

"Historians!" said Ross. "No sense of fun. She'll be here."

The van carrying the musicians pulled up. They unloaded with a variety of wails, screeches and thumps as various instruments rebelled against their unpacking. There was a confab about the choice of music, and then, starting with a few half-hearted drumbeats, the bagpipes squealed into wheezing banshee-like wailing. It set off a car alarm to much hilarity and applause.

"Och, will you no hear that?" said Ross wincing. "They be murdering those pipes."

"Here," said Liam, handing Ross a flask. "Have some Dutch courage."

Ross took a quick swig, and then a second more appreciative dram.

"Single Malt... from Holland, you say?"

It's an annual event, so the vast majority knew what to do. At some point, after surreptitious glances at hidden watches or phones, a consensus arrived and the various units began to form up.

Ross, Liam and I looked around to discover that a queue had appeared behind us: we were the irregulars. Other stragglers found sections whose uniforms best matched their own and gradually a snake weaved between the cars, ready to pounce upon the unsuspecting world. The hand-pulled carts, full of Living History displays and miscellaneous kit, took up their position at the rear organised by Kate and Reka.

The band fell silent at the front.

I caught Rabbie as he moved down the line to cajoling people into place and confiscating mobile phones. I pushed my watch higher up my shirt sleeve.

"Rabbie, have you seen Mandy?"

"Mandy..." Rabbie thought for a moment: "Is she on duty somewhere?"

"She's got a weekend off."

"Right, so she's... Jacobite or Redcoat?" he said, standing on his toes to look over the cars.

"I'm not sure. I think she's part of the crowd."

"Then she'll be on the route."

"Yes, of course."

"Anything the matter?"

"Everything's fine, Rabbie."

Rabbie moved on, repeating his usual jokey persuasion at intervals.

"What did Rabbie want?" Ross asked.

"He's not seen her," I said.

"What? Och, yer no fretting about yer woman still?"

"I'm not fretting," I said. "For goodness sake, will you all stop going on about it!"

The marching drums demanded attention, the snares sounding for two bars while the pipers held their bagpipes by the chanters. On cue, the pipers punched their bags to breathe life into the drones and it was like a huge engine revving up. The Pipe Major signalled and the band moved off, and, after a few false starts as always, the combined army followed and emerged into Wilmot Street to surprise the Saturday shoppers.

It was a left turn onto Osmaston Road and eventually, the route led us to the pedestrianised shopping area of St. Peter's Street. Yellow-attired, hi-viz police were there on crowd control, but they weren't needed. Most people paused to watch the entertainment, tucking themselves behind the metal barriers to create orderly sides along the parade route. There were families, shoppers, and tourists, a spectacle for everyone. The police waved too, exchanged pleasantries with their colleagues who shepherded us along and marched in better time than our Jacobite rabble, but with less parade ground precision than our Redcoats.

We passed the old Heritage Centre. The black powder used to be issued from the building in the morning, but not being part of the explosions brigade, I wasn't sure where it was stored now the Centre was closed. I remember meeting Richard, the proprietor, years ago now, and listening to him enthuse about all the Jacobite events. It's what drew me into the re-enacting scene in the first place. Back then, he felt he was flying in the face of apathy, trying to put this historic celebration on the map. The famous statue of Bonnie Prince Charlie, the parade's destination, had been Richard's great triumph.

St. Peter's Street became the Cornmarket, these old names decked out in the council's colours, standard shops like any street in any city.

There were more cheers from the crowd as our army, escorted by uniformed police, passed by. It was wonderful: I scanned the crowd, seeing the happy faces, babies in buggies, kiddies holding balloons, and people raising their mobiles to take pictures.

Where was she?

The Cornmarket eventually opened out on our right as it ran alongside the Market Place. Spectators thronged both sides still, filling the large open paved area, and some appeared to be floating in the air above a waterfall. In the middle of Market Place, there's a sculpture, large enough for several people to stand on top and designed to allow them to do so. The curved platform, topped in greenish metal, surrounds a pool into which a curved waterfall cascades. There's even a path leading behind the waterfall, so you can hide behind a curtain of water like a hero in a jungle adventure film. It's a water feature that would make any gardening programme proud.

"Guy, Guy!"

There was a commotion on top of the waterfall, people shifting to allow a blue coat to squeeze between them.

I broke ranks rushing forward. I knew who it was.

"Oi!" Rabbie shouted after me. "Deserter."

I found a gap in the metal barriers, pushed through the crowd and reached the sculpture.

"Mandy!"

She looked down, her blonde hair streaming in the breeze. She was wearing it loose, which was unusual, and she looked beautiful.

"Guy, Guy," she shouted back: "where for art thou, Guy?"

It's not 'where for' it's 'wherefore', I thought, but then she wasn't asking why I was called 'Guy'.

"How do I get up there?" I said.

Mandy pointed: "Go round and... I'll come down."

She disappeared, squeezing back into the multitude. I made my way around the structure. Somehow she'd taken the same direction, clockwise, and so we ended up facing each other, actually looking through the waterfall, its cascade of artificial rain adding to the sounds of the crowd.

"Come here," I said.

"No way."

I shrugged, then stepped through the curtain of water. A brief shock of a cold shower and I emerged, my white shirt plastered to my body. I shook my head, spilling water in a line across her coat.

"Oh, no, no, no," said Mandy as she backed away.

I hugged her, feeling her body protect me from the now biting wind. We kissed: without her stab vest her body felt pliant and shapely beneath my embrace, her hips supple and unencumbered with kit, the water falling powerfully behind us, the pipes' lament reaching a crescendo, the–

"Get in there, my son!" Ross yelled.

There were cheers, jeers and much shouting from the assembled Jacobites, from the spectators on all sides and from the balcony above.

I smiled, turning red, and then I kissed her again running my hand through her hair.

It was romantic, it really was.

Strange how later events change things, drain the colour from happy memories until the picture is black bordered with dashed hopes. But hell, I was heroic, a Colin Firth emerging from the water, clutching my woman to my, admittedly damp, but manly chest, so why shouldn't I remember it with pleasure, with pride even? No, I have not even that. The Rise *and Fall* of the Roman Empire is inherent in its title.

But I was happy that day, gloriously so, and I want to see it again without these ivy-tinted glasses. We look back on events, we historians more than most, and see them with 20-20 hindsight, but are we wrong?

They may have been and gone, now consigned to The Past, but those days were The Present once. Chamberlain clutching the Munich 'peace in our time' Agreement from Herr Hitler generated optimism. That optimism wasn't false optimism, it was true optimism. Fear of the Cold War wasn't groundless, it was genuine dread. It was only later that it changed, the true became false, the real became groundless, my happiness became this hopelessness.

I felt joy on that day. As I think back, I feel despair, but they are separate, pushed apart by 200 miles and two weeks. I don't want to feel this way when I think back to Derby.

I need to feel hope. I need... but I'm a drowning man clutching at straws. I'm living that cliché, but Mandy's flowing strands of blonde are even more ephemeral. I see myself again in Market Place by the waterfall, but I'm holding onto nothing. It's a nightmare now, full of running, and running, and running over tarmac towards a line of troops with guns.

Her taste was still on my lips when she took my arm and we slipped into the crowd that followed the parade as it progressed along Iron Gate towards Cathedral Green.

This time, because I was in uniform and she wasn't, she let me hold her hand.

"Hurrah for the Prince!" Rabbie yelled.

"Hurrah!!!"

The parade stopped, clustered in a semi-circle around the front of 41 Iron Gate, the George Pub, and, by the time Mandy and I joined at the back, they'd already banged on the door.

"We need billets for nine thousand men!" Rabbie demanded theatrically.

The George is a fair sized pub, but it's more like 90 standing than 9,000 sleeping. There were quite a few little nuggets of history from the Jacobite occupation of Derby, including the demand for accommodation, and our very own Kate, normally in charge of the Living History displays, arrived to re-enact this episode. Members of the public looked over the heads of the assembled Jacobites to see.

"Excuse me, fine Sir," Kate said as the crowd parted to give her space.

"Aye," said Rabbie.

"I *crave* an audience with The Pretender," she said, twisting her voice around the word 'crave'.

"Pretender!" shouted Rabbie in reply.

There was a sharp intake of breath around the Jacobites: "Ooohh."

"Yes, fine Sir."

"He is no pretender," said Rabbie. "Take her away and let her never be seen again."

A few Jacobites, briefed earlier, dragged our Kate off down the street, and then, after a brusque 'it's that way' from their prisoner, they dragged her towards the shortcut to Cathedral Square. I suspect Kate needed an extra ten minutes or so to prepare the living history tents. The hand pulled carts had already snuck off. We took the wider route via Full Street, passing in front of the Industrial Museum in a big curve to Cathedral Square.

Once there in the open, the armies, Rebel and Government alike, gathered in sections around the full-size, bronze statue that dominates the park: Bonnie Prince Charlie sitting astride his horse high atop a stone plinth. From the back, I saw Richard, the only one near the statue wearing a modern suit, step forward to address the throng:

"This statue," he announced, "the only one to Prince Charles Edward Stuart in the world, commemorates the furthest point he reached during the Jacobite Rebellion of 1745. It was here, in Derby, that Bonnie Prince Charlie turned back towards Scotland. The statue faces north to signify his return to Scotland, but we can see him looking over his shoulder towards London, perhaps thinking of what might have been."

Now it had been mentioned, a few tourists pointed aloft at Bonnie Prince Charlie forever glancing forlornly over his shoulder at what might have been. He was looking sideways really, as he turned his horse back towards Scotland on a path that led to his defeat at Culloden. He was quite the dandy, having been brought up in exile in Rome. He'd have been out of place amongst our Jacobites and even more so within his own army back in 1745.

With ceremony, a descendant of the Prince's family laid a commemorative wreath.

Our army split up. Redcoats went to one side of the grassed area and I joined the Jacobites on the other. Ross, Liam and I, the Three Musketeers, formed up in the left flank.

"For Bonnie Prince Charlie!" shouted Rabbie.

"Aye!"

"Get 'em!"

"Down with the Government!"

"For Bonnie Prince Charlie," Rabbie repeated, louder and more insistent.

"For Bonnie Prince Charlie!"

"Ready... and—"

"Charge!"

And we were off.

Rabbie's "wait for it" was lost in the cacophony and then obliterated by the opening volley from the Redcoats. We shouted, we screamed, we yelled and we died again: for Scotland, for Bonnie Prince Charlie, for freedom! All amidst applause, black powder bangs and merriment. I loved it, whooping and hollering, shouting and screaming louder than anyone.

"Told you she'd be here," said Ross between charges.

Cannons: *boom!* Smoke everywhere – fantastic!

I raised my claymore, waved it dangerously above my head, and rallied the troops to follow me. There were shouts of "Guy! Guy!" and we charged again.

It was bloody wonderful.

The Battle of Derby, 1745, never took place and never would have taken place. If Bonnie Prince Charlie and his Jacobite Rebellion had continued his march on London, he'd have crossed the River Trent at Swarkestone, just a few miles south of Derby. He'd have been intercepted by those loyal to the crown further down the country. The Battle of Milton Keynes perhaps?

As it was, while the Jacobites dithered in the Midlands, London was being evacuated and a boat readied to take King George II back to Hanover. The country was theirs for the taking, but a Government spy informed the Jacobites that the King's son, the Duke of Cumberland, was about to arrive with a large army.

Bonnie Prince Charlie wanted to press on, but Lord George Murray and the Highlanders argued for retreat and their side won the debate. The Jacobites turned back, so we, the Bonnie Prince Charlie Society, were celebrating something that never happened, wouldn't have happened anyway, and had ultimately failed.

The irony is not lost on me now.

When our show was over, we moved back to The George, a pub that had actually been used to billet troops during the conflict. Or perhaps the billeting had just been organised from there. Either way, it was appropriate. Maybe back then, they'd all had a buffet laid on for them too: hot soup and bullet rolls, as well as a supply of pints from the bar. It's amazing how many bread rolls you can squirrel away in a properly worn plaid. The whole top half above the waist that comes up from the 'kilt' over the shoulder is basically a giant pocket.

"Are you all for a pint?" said Rabbie as we went through the door.

"Aye," said Ross, "we're all for a pint."

"A pint for all," I said.

"And all for a pint," Liam added.

"You three," said Rabbie, shaking his head as if we, Ross, Liam and I, had been a comedy trio for years. It was hard to believe that we'd only known Liam for a couple of months and this was his first Derby.

Inside the dark, traditional lounge, Redcoat jostled with Jacobite, Scots bought the English drinks from the descendants of thieves transported to the colonies, and men fetched and carried for women; Christian talked to agnostic and atheist alike, Muslim said "just a lemonade" to those who had put Jedi down on the census form, and Protestants were friends with Catholics.

The Battle of the Boyne took place in Ireland in 1690, fifty-five years before any battles south of Derby might have occurred. The Battle of Culloden, which had been an acrimonious scrap by any standards, followed by butchery and more clearances, was closer to our time. And yet, here we were, celebrating it.

So why then did Ireland plunge into sectarian violence because of an event lost in deeper mists, when this other, more recent battle was cause for drinking and playfulness?

"Dorrington is really making a difference," Mandy was saying.

"Och, he's a Sassenach politician, ye canna believe anything they say."

"His reforms will—"

"It's the way forward, but..." Everyone joined in: "What if a particular community doesn't want to work with us?"

"Oh, for goodness sake!" Mandy was genuinely angry, a real surprise, but she simmered down with a double gin and tonic.

"We should have got you into a wench's skirt," I said.

"Would I look good in a bonnet?" said Mandy, touching her head as if putting one on.

"It's called a mob-cap."

"You'd have just wanted to get into my skirt."

"I'm wearing a skirt," I said. "Do you want to get into it?"

"It depends on what are you're wearing under it."

"It's a kilt," said Ross.

"It's a plaid," I said.

"Plaid, kilt, what's the difference? No! Don't tell me," Mandy backed away in mock horror.

I chased her for the two short steps the crush allowed and leant close to whisper.

"Football shorts."

"Oh, how disappointing," she said.

"What's this?" Rabbie asked, jostling through the crowd to join us.

Throughout the pub, you just couldn't move, but then, the pressure having built up, the various clumps mixed when someone forced their way to the bar, the buffet or the toilets. This had the effect of tugging people away from one conversation and bringing them into another, after which everything would stick again until the pan of sticky oatmeal was churned once more by an invisible spurtle, which I believe is the correct implement for stirring porridge. It was football shorts here, muskets of the 18th century there, computing next to us, and some mad drinking game by the bar with politics and religion confined to the corners.

"Mandy wanted to know what I was wearing under my plaid – football shorts, Man United."

"Not me," said Ross. "I let it all hang loose. Hello ladies, and what are you wearing?"

"A skirt," said Kate.

"But are you wearing anything under your skirt?" Ross asked.

"You're a saucy one," she said.

"Well?"

"Yes, I am."

"Och, what a shame."

"It's a lacy thong."

It was Mandy's turn to whisper in my ear: "Mine's black and you can see it later."

"We were promised machines, you know?" said Liam and he pushed his wire-framed spectacles back into place. He looked surprised; the writhing of the crowd had brought him into a different group, but he carried on regardless. "They'd do all the work, and we'd live off the profits. We'd spend our time on other pursuits, like re-enactments... when did... you're a historian."

"Yes, I am," I said.

Liam put his hand on my arm: "When did surplus labour become a liability?"

"Sorry?"

"Mankind discovered agriculture, which meant you didn't need the whole population hunting and gathering just to feed everyone, so you had surplus people."

"Yes, they–"

"Became scribes and metal workers and strippers."

Reka was appalled: "Strippers!"

"Er... entertainers, you know, and..."

"Police," said Mandy, abruptly called back to the conversation.

She was looking at the shelf of knick-knacks with an innocent air, spoiled slightly by the reddening of her cheeks. She blushes easily, the curse of a fair skin. How had Mandy managed to get her hand up the back of my plaid without bending down? Her hand was resting on my right cheek. Why are women so interested in men's bottoms?

"Yes, police, another occupation created by civilisation."

"You're talking about Egypt," I said, trying to concentrate but failing. "However, the fertile crescent was–"

"So, why is unemployment a problem... surely that's surplus labour suitable for other pursuits?"

"If you conscript them into pyramid building."

"And other erections," Mandy added.

45

"Yes, yes... no," said Liam, swaying about dramatically as he gestured.

I saw Ross through a gap. He looked like he was trying to chat up Kate with a bread roll.

"So unemployment ought to be a blessing – surplus population that can be turned towards something productive."

"You could conscript them into the army," I said. "Wars have always been a mechanism for reducing the excess population."

"You cynic," Mandy said and she removed her hand in protest.

"Och, whose round?" Ross asked.

"One, two, three... paper," I said. My flat hand touched Ross's two fingers.

"Scissors cuts paper," said Ross.

"But I've just bought Mandy a gin–"

"Yes," said Mandy, "Another gin and tonic."

"Best out of..." I started, but then I realised the danger and went straight to the bar. I knew that in a packed environment like this, a round could become unmanageable very rapidly: three pints and a gin and tonic was a lucky escape. I ordered surprisingly quickly considering there was an army besieging the bar, but they were all leaning rather than queuing. I passed the first two pints overhead with a "Ross" and then a "Liam" instruction. The drinks bobbed up like boats on a sea of people. I got mine topped up when the head settled and took a sip before weaving through the throng back to the conversation.

"History isn't about battles, it's about women," said Kate. "We're just taught about the Battle of Hastings, 1066, and the Battle of Britain, 1940, and the Battle of Waterloo... er..."

"1815," I said.

"Guy," Kate said. "Is that mine?"

"Sorry," I replied and handed Mandy her gin and tonic.

"So, it's all dates and battles," Kate continued, "but really historical development has always been the struggle of women: agriculture is all about what you can cook; the industrial revolution is the story of women in factories; the twentieth century is defined by woman getting the vote–"

"Because of the First World War," I said.

"Women in the police force," Mandy suggested.

"Women in the police force," Kate agreed. "And the War on Terror, the Taliban and the Islamic State is all about the education of girls in Africa and Asia."

"The treatment of women is appalling," Reka added.

"I see what you mean," said Mandy. "'Cos you can measure developments in the police force in different periods defined by the highest rank held by a woman: Women Police Constables, then... ooh, no women at all before that, then WPCs, Sergeants, the first Inspector, first Chief Inspector... it wasn't until 1973 that the Women's force was integrated into the proper police."

"Proper police?" said Kate.

"The main... well, yes, proper police rather than some sub-branch seen as second-class. There's still a way to go. The Police Federation still has a women's branch."

I gave up on that one and let the sudden flurry of human whirlpools carry me away, as another contingent of round buyers held their prizes aloft and pushed through the mire.

"Yes, yes, yes," said Mandy excitedly in the distance as she, Kate and Reka agreed. I arrived between Rabbie and Liam, squished up again into a tidy space.

"Rabbie," I said, "all ready for tomorrow?"

"Yes, yes, yes," Liam said with an odd energy, and then, "Why, what have you heard?"

"Nothing," I said, "I was just making conversation."

"No, no, no," said Liam.

"Och, yes."

"No, no, no," Liam repeated. "Or yes, that's what I mean."

"Och, do ye no ken–"

"Yes, yes, Ken?"

"Och, no."

"Yes, yes?"

"No."

Liam held up his hand so assertively that the conversation stopped, and its sudden hush infected the group either side. The crowd looked at the source of the spreading silence and saw Liam standing like an orator erect on a podium.

"Ah," said Liam – the pub waited with bated breath – and then he sneezed explosively.

There was a roar and applause.

I hadn't followed any of that, I'd missed something: "What's the matter?" I asked Liam.

"Banker's disease," he said. "I'm fine."

Mandy pushed against me: "Guy, let's call a cab," she whispered.

It was nippy outside. We'd planned to get a bus, any green and beige double-decker, No. 60, 61, 68A, 68B, 70 from Morledge, but it's funny how a cab becomes more and more attractive, and the expense less and less worrying, as an evening wears on. I can't remember where we hailed the cab. It was bracing, wide and spacious after the packed pub, and the night air livened me up as it shrivelled other parts of my anatomy. You don't wear a lot as a Jacobite. In the back of the cab, Mandy felt up the front of my plaid as we sped away on the fifteen-minute journey from Derby City Centre to Chellaston.

Mandy had parked her car by the hotel, checked in and caught a bus into town, so once we got there, we unloaded our overnight bags before making ourselves comfortable. The rest of my stuff was still in Ross's van.

I had a shower – the smell of re-enactment kit is a particular kind of musk – and Mandy joined me. She was clingy, but I just thought she was into it, and, even though it was a bit rubbish after too much to drink, we nevertheless had a sort of fumbling fun, squeaking around on the iron bedstead.

She said my name a lot: "Guy", "Guy", "Guy!" – insistent as if she was trying to prove something to herself.

Afterwards, we fell asleep entwined.

At about three in the morning, I awoke. My bladder forced me to the en-suite. The sudden white light was particularly painful and I drank some water to head off a hangover. As I stood there, leaning against the bathroom sink, I looked blearily at my reflection in that small, white-tiled room. It reminds me of this prison, a hazy past to a sharp present.

The similarity is striking. It's not simply the small, white rectangular room, but the feeling of being trapped. Back then, I stole back into bed. Mandy moaned and rolled over, her hand flopping over onto my chest. I remember moving her arm so it crossed my ribcage more comfortably.

Sometimes you don't realise what you've got.

It was quiet, countryside quiet, as opposed to this deep silence of the bowels of the earth.

Jacobites March Again

On Sunday, the Jacobites are back again in Chellaston for their march to Swarkestone.

"It's a day out for the whole family," says Rabbie MacLeod, 31, the Chair of the Bonnie Prince Charlie Society.

Come and see the historical displays at the Crewe & Harpur, Swarkestone.

ALL DAY
Re-enactments at Noon and 2pm.

Refreshments
Bring the whole family.

Bonnie Prince Charlie, Chellaston

Admission: Free.
Time: March starts at 11am

THE CHELLASTON CAMPAIGN

I always eat too much at breakfast when I stay anywhere. I've paid for it, I think, and it's a throwback to my undergraduate days. Free food! I'm still a student, after all, just one rung above undergraduate with less money and more overdraft. Also, there was lots of orange juice for the hangover. Buffets are the worst temptation, and would I like some extra toast. *Would I like some extra toast? Of course, I'd like some extra toast – if you insist.* And I still had rolls from last night's buffet for lunch.

We stayed at the Lawns Hotel in Chellaston; a big place with functions rooms for conferences. I waited for Mandy to get ready and we went down together. The bar was set for breakfast: grapefruit juice, full English with black pudding, and a pot of English Breakfast with toast in a rack and little jars of marmalade. Heaven.

Did we want a newspaper with our breakfast? Nah, and who wants to read all this nonsense about John Trudie's backbench faction in the Commons, the bloody UKIP coalition or Murdoch's press misquoting the lefties, for goodness sake? If only the BBC wasn't so weak, but then George Osborne's financial advisor had been put on the board, surely sabotage from within. Westminster's just—

"We need to talk," said Mandy.

"We've plenty of time," I said. "The Jacobites don't assemble until ten. It's only down the High Street and along Swarkestone Road, maybe ten minutes."

"We need to talk."

"Oh."

"We need to talk about our future, you know, where we're going and everything."

"Yes?"

"I'm ambitious, you know that, and I could go far in the police service."

"Yes."

"Things are changing now and this is my opportunity. The Met—"

"London!"

"I can't just stand still, can I? Surely you can see that, Guy?"

"But..."

"And you have to move forward too. You need a career."

"Yes."

"I don't want to wait another five years. I can't turn this chance down."

"Yes, but, Mand!"

"Well, what do you think?"

"Maybe..."

I sprinkled some salt on my fried egg, but my enthusiasm had waned. It was going to be a long time until ten if Mandy wanted to harp on about her hobby-horse.

Technically, I suppose, there were more opportunities for her particular career, but if you looked at our situation as a bundle of choices, Edinburgh had a lot more to offer. Not just the Grassmarket pubs, but we had roots there. I dunked a piece of sausage, spilling the yolk.

"...you could apply," I said, "and we could talk about it, if and when."

"Guy!"

She's got big eyes when you look at them, a deep blue with very blonde lashes, topped by a smooth, almost unblemished forehead. There was a tiny scar in the shape of a star, barely visible near her left temple that she got when she was young. She told me when she stayed over in my flat in Edinburgh that first time. We'd explored each other's still unfamiliar bodies, asking so few questions and telling each other so much.

"Guy?"

"Yes?"

"I got the special transfer."

"You did?"

"Yes."

"You didn't say."

"How do you think I got the time off?" she said as if it was obvious. "They gave me a few days before I have to go down."

"Go down! A few days! I thought you'd got your shifts changed and claimed back some of that overtime. You're always doing too much overtime."

"Guy—"

"You mean you've accepted?"

"Yes."

"We were going to talk about it!"

"We are."

"Yes, but before the fact."

"They wanted a decision and you kept putting it off." She touched her forehead, frowning. "Look, I don't want this to be an argument, but, also, I don't want to end up in some backwater—"

"Edinburgh is not—"

"The Metropolitan Police is where it's happening at the moment," she leant forward, enthused by her topic, resting her elbows on the white tablecloth and using her fingers as if she was throwing the words at me. "They're five years ahead of anywhere else. Sure, Scotland has some interesting laws and practices, but I've done that. I need to move on and progress. Timothy Dorrington is—"

"Who?"

"Timothy Dorrington – the Home Secretary."

"Oh."

"Guy!"

"Timothy Dorrie..."

"Dorrington."

I tried a joke: "Anything after 1939 is... hmm." It didn't work.

"He's making history."

"I think in a historical perspective—"

"The Home Secretary controls the Met directly, that's why they're fast-tracking these changes there. He's reducing all the stupid paperwork, and really getting to grips with community policing. He's bringing us back from May's police state agenda. It's the way forward."

"Sounds wonderful, but what if a particular—"

"You could finish your thesis in London."

"How the hell could I afford the rent in London?"

"I'll get London weighting."

"My supervisor is here."

"There's email. You never see Professor Chedi anyway."

"Of course I do! And our friends are in Edinburgh."

"We'll make new friends," she said. "Half your re-enactor mates live in London."

"Yes, but—"

Did we want tea or coffee?

I asked for a pot of tea and a spot of milk; Mandy had a coffee, black. While the waiter fussed, Mandy looked out of the window, but even with the bright morning sun on her face, you could practically see the clouds gathering over her head and the rain welling in her eyes.

I finished my breakfast, drank my tea – when it arrived – and sat in silence.

"You never do anything, Guy," Mandy said, finally.

"What's this," I waved my knife over the tablecloth, "if it isn't doing something?"

"This isn't doing something; it's recreating something that's been and gone. Look, Guy, you write about what other people have done in the past, you pretend you live in the past, you... oh Guy, you never do anything yourself, anything that's now."

"That's unfair," I said. "I'm a historian."

"And I'm a police officer."

"We have plans."

"Yes, Guy, we have plans, but you never start them and you never see anything through."

"I do."

"Playing soldiers is not finishing your thesis and looking in an estate agent's window is not getting a flat together."

"We're waiting for Fiona–"

"Fiona's got her decree nisi, decree absolute and got engaged to Phil months ago."

"Why didn't you tell me this yesterday?"

"Because I wanted us to have a good time."

"But–"

"I'm going to London." She stood and dropped her napkin onto the table: breakfast, this talk, everything, was over. "You can join me, or... you can play your stupid games with your stupid friends."

"That's unfair."

"You're living in the past."

And Mandy left.

I sat and finished my breakfast: the toast was cold.

You're living in the past, she had said, *you never do anything.*

But I did do something and look what happened.

We passed briefly on the hotel stairs, but there were others around and we said nothing to each other. It took me two minutes to brush my teeth and stuff all my belongings into my overnight bag.

I checked that the room was empty: I'd forgotten nothing and lost everything.

The pub in Chellaston, where we'd arranged to meet, was only five minutes' walk away down the High Street, but I wished it was further. I didn't think I could face dozens of happy friends, but I didn't really have any choice, did I? My only transport home – God, that was going to be awkward – was Ross's van.

I paused, looking back, and wondered if perhaps I could make up with Mandy. But then, if we made up, I'd miss the start of the day's activities.

Wait, she was more important than a single day's events.

I hurried back, but no, her car had gone.

I could have called her mobile, but she was very strict about observing the 'no mobiles in cars' rule. I put mine in my case in the van anyway as Rabbie would have confiscated it. Even if I borrowed one and called, she wouldn't pick a voice mail until she got to Edinburgh and switched her phone on. She wouldn't be able to pop back and collect me. The day would have gone anyway.

But she wasn't driving back to Scotland: she was going to London – shit!

Oh, bollocks to it, I thought.

The bar of the appropriately named Bonnie Prince was full of re-enactors. There was laughter and smiling faces, beer being drunk already.

Rabbie was showing everyone how to fold a proper plaid and spectators gathered as the Scot fiddled with a tartan blanket laid out on the pub floor. As he crawled about on the carpet, carefully pleating it, he explained that the kilt was actually a Victorian invention and had pleats at the back as a nod to a true plaid. Beneath Rabbie's long white shirt, his football shorts were visible to all – so much for the myth of the devils-in-skirts. He lay down on the origami blanket, fumbled for the thick leather belt (he needed help to find one end) and once this was done up, he stood. To finish off, he hoisted the loose upper half over his left shoulder, tying the end with a leather cord and attaching it to his belt. He held his arms wide in a 'ta-da' and gained a ripple of applause.

The demonstration over, the newcomers to the garment were helped on with their picnic blankets. I'd put mine on in the B&B's bedroom. It's a lot easier folding it neatly on the bed and flopping backwards onto the mattress than it is lying down on some dodgy pub carpet.

But, I mean, what is the point of it all?

For fuck's sake, these were grown-ups rolling around on the floor to wrap some woollen blanket around themselves in order to go out and play soldiers. People died in wars. A ball from a musket was a painful way to go, slowly bleeding to death with no chance of antibiotics or hygienic surgery back then. Living in the past, for goodness sake, what was she talking about?

Rabbie reached under his plaid and pulled down his shorts to cheers and shouts.

Ross tapped me on the shoulder: "A pint?"

"I'm all for a pint," I said. "Rabbie's gone commando. You still wearing your underpants?"

"Damn right," said Ross. "I've got thermals."

Rabbie stood on a chair: "Quiet!" he yelled, only for everyone to ignore him. "Quiet!"

Ross is a teacher: "Och, ken yer no be QUIET!"

"Thank you, Ross," said Rabbie. "OK, come on lads, let's finish our drinks... yes, sorry! And lasses, yes, so everyone finish your drinks and assemble outside. Reka is collecting your mobile phones, so hand them in before going out. There's a battle to be fought, Government troops to be routed and a celebration at the Crewe & Harpur."

"Hurrah!" Ross yelled.

"HURRAH!" the army responded, and then it downed its various pints and bustled outside.

I dumped my bag in the van, my ears still ringing from Ross's bellowing, and my eyes stinging for some reason. I didn't want to go and I certainly didn't want to pretend to be happy, but, somehow, my body was on autopilot and I shuffled into line, laughed and joked, and somehow even smiled, although my face felt like it was made of rubber.

"Scotland forever!"

"Down with the Government!"

"For Bonnie Prince Charlie!"

Aye, I thought, for Bonnie Prince Charlie, so I too joined in the hurrahs.

There was one slight hiccup when someone realised that our police escort were still chatting away over a pot of tea.

Someone nipped back and there were hoots of derision as the local constabulary legged it up to us. Our boys in blue were dressed in black and hi-viz yellow, more like wasps than bluebottles, but let's not go into that.

I mean, honestly, what was wrong with being a local police officer? This was community policing after all. These fine chaps were interacting with society, keeping us safe from lunatic drivers and they were taking part, marching with us. That, surely, was what it was all about? It was the way forward.

The arranged route took us along the A514, over a big looping roundabout with slip roads where the A50 crossed, and then on to Swarkestone. We passed a small milestone, a bright white object on the edge of a grass area in front of a line of two-up, two-downs.

10
ASHBY
Chellaston
Swarkestone 1½ miles
Derby 4 miles

"Och, not far now!"
But it was far, a full 130 miles and more to London.

" Wonderful, but full of **"**
strange people

The Crewe & Harpur, Swarkestone

⊙⊙⊙⊙○

MyReview72 ▼ 3
contributions
South of England
Trip type: Couples

We thoroughly enjoyed our stay in this wonderful 17th century coach house, lovely food both for dinner in the evening and our breakfast in the morning. The staff were friendly and understanding. Parking was straight forward. Very convenient for the Peak District.
The evening was noisy, rowdy even, as the bar was full of people dressed as Scotsmen from history, but we were assured by the friendly staff that this was only once a year. There was a festival of sorts going on outside on the lawn.

Luckily they had all left by the next day.

Liked – accommodation, food, service.
Disliked – rowdy crowd on the Sunday evening.

My ratings for this hotel
⊙⊙⊙⊙○ Value
⊙⊙⊙⊙○ Rooms
⊙⊙⊙○○ Location

Visit was for Holiday
Travelled with Spouse / significant other
Would you recommend this hotel to a friend? Yes
Was this review helpful? Yes.

THE SWARKESTONE STRATAGEM

Swarkestone Bridge is wide enough for two cars to pass and that's it, but it looks big. Built in the 13th century, it's a massive brick construction that slams across the River Trent. It marks the most southerly point reached by the Jacobite uprising of 1745 and it was the strategic river crossing they needed to take, the last geographical barrier on the way south to a great victory in London.

There's no documentary evidence that Bonnie Prince Charlie himself made it the six miles from Derby, before turning his horse north with a last, forlorn look back over his shoulder, but his advance guard did. It was our objective too, although we were only going as far as the pub's beer garden at the foot of the north end, rather than taking the bridge itself. We weren't unopposed either: we had Government forces to defeat.

Our army marched in formation from Chellaston with skirmishers going ahead to exchange musket fire with the opposition's contingent from the Black Powder Brigade. The occasional muffled *phutts* sounded in the fields on either side.

Ross and I weren't part of the group with muskets, but then the Three Musketeers used rapiers. We tucked ourselves into the main group, surrounded by our police escort and those hardy spectators who followed along.

"Where's Liam?" I asked.

"Och, joined the Redcoats, the Sassenach."

"Ha! Splitter."

"They were short of numbers."

"Turncoat."

"And they get to drink for longer in the Crewe & Harpur."

"Clever sod."

A musket fired in the distance and a smudge of white smoke took flight over the hedgerow.

After all these years, I've never actually been with the Redcoats – I've always been a rebel – so I've never known what they do. I know that the firearms group go out to meet our contingent for mock combat, but I suppose the rest of them were all having a swift bevvy or two in the Crewe & Harpur's lounge.

As we approached Swarkestone, more musket shots sounded out across the fields. Some Jacobites split off and ran forward for the series of set-piece skirmishes. It gave our countryside ramble an exciting edge.

The road itself turned left to the bridge, but we went straight on before skirting around the small village to approach the pub from the opposite end. This rather put paid to our stated objective of securing the crossing.

The Crewe & Harpur Pub is tucked against the River Trent, overlooking the famous bridge. Tourists wandered amongst the tents in the beer garden to look at the displays of 18th Century life before Kate, Reka and her contingent shooed them all to one side.

The police watched from a distance as they were rather out of place in their stab vests, yellow hi-viz and name badges: Spencer, Jones, Singh, Williams...

After a few shots fired, the Redcoats came out of the pub and lined up beneath the Union Flag at one edge of the grass area, while we Jacobites took up our side beneath St. Andrew's cross.

There was a five-minute lull in hostilities and both sides used the opportunity to nip inside for the loo.

"It was here..." Reka was saying to the crowd.

Again, it struck me as bizarre that we celebrated the Jacobites taking the bridge at Swarkestone on the north side. Surely, taking the bridge means that the furthest south Bonnie Prince Charlie's army reached was the other side, the southern end. One of them must have walked over it, out of curiosity if nothing else. The number of times we'd reached this point, year after year, and I'd never actually set foot on the bridge itself.

"For Bonnie Prince Charlie!"

"For Bonnie Prince Charlie!!!"

It was sudden, shaking me out of my reverie.

"-arlie," I mumbled.

I wasn't really ready and, more out of instinct than anything else, I ran towards the muskets. The space didn't allow for a proper charge, twenty paces at most, and before we were up to speed we were amongst our enemy. Talk about point blank range and overacting in slow motion, but the spectators put down their drinks to applaud.

There was only one charge and very little falling over dead. The Black Powder Brigade started explaining their firearms to anyone interested, the womenfolk started serving mead and traditional ancient delicacies, including Ye Olde Cheese Burger, and more than one rebel snuck off for a quick pint.

I joined them, but when ordering a bitter, I panicked: I thought I'd left my money in my trousers before I remembered that my football shorts had a pocket. I'd transferred a few notes there yesterday, but it gave me the idea that I ought to buy a proper sporran.

In the beer garden supping my pint, I saw a stall selling leather goods, including sporrans, but if I bought one, I realised, I wouldn't have any notes left to put inside it.

It was a lovely day outside, but all something of a blur, my mind constantly dwelling on the situation with Mandy. I'd disconnected. I was someone viewing events rather than being part of them. I was a historian.

When the sun sank into an oil painting of a sky, highlighting the clouds dramatically, everyone filtered into the pub itself. Twilight, it's called 'The Magic Hour'. I dawdled to look at the stone bridge, it always surprised me how solidly its five arches are constructed and how it thrusts over the Trent. It looked like it meant something. A sign?

"Come on, Guy," said Ross. I turned round – there was only Ross and Liam left, just the three of us.

"What's with Guy?" Liam whispered to Ross, although I heard the question well enough.

"Girlfriend trouble," said Ross quietly.

A waist-high pile of rock concreted together with a round top stood in the grass to one side. There was a metal plate set into one side with an inscription:–

THIS CAIRN MARKS THE
FARTHEST POINT SOUTH REACHED
BY THE JACOBITE ARMY OF
PRINCE CHARLES EDWARD STUART
ON 4 DECEMBER 1745

–

Erected by the
Charles Edward Stuart Society
& Marston's Brewery
on the 250th anniversary

Did the two stone structures, the cairn and the bridge, symbolise the two alternatives: stop now or move on?

"What can you do?" said Ross.

I shook my head: "One for all."

"And all for a pint," they said and laughed.

Despite myself, I smiled, and we walked quietly away from the bridge, across the little road and into the pub, my two friends falling into a marching step as we did so.

Rabbie was holding court when we walked in: "There was this Englishman, Irishman and Scotsman, who walked into the bar.... and here they are!"

"What about the Welsh?" Kate asked.

"Never mind that," said Rabbie. "An Englishman, an Irishman and a Scotsman walk into a bar."

"You've done that."

"No, no, an Englishman–"

"I thought you were talking about Guy, Liam and Ross."

"No, no, this is an actual joke," Rabbie insisted: "So, there was this Englishman–"

"This Englishman?" I asked.

"Yes."

"Was he a Northerner or a Southerner?"

"Doesn't matter."

"Doesn't matter!" I turned to the assembled drinkers for support and received a general agreement. "I think it does."

"He was a Southerner," said Rabbie. "Right, so they walk into a bar–"

"Home Counties or London?" I asked. A smile went around the group. We all knew this game.

"London. So–"

"What about Cornwall?" Kate asked.

"Cockney or–" I started, but Rabbie didn't even let me finish.

"Cockney."

"East End or West End?"

"East End, West End's not cockney. Look, it doesn't matter!"

"All right, all right." I held my hands up in mock surrender and leant back in my seat.

Ross returned with the drinks, so I had to lean forward again to pick up my pint and knock the sticky beermat off the bottom. I didn't speak, I didn't need to. I'd passed the baton and I could see the others were ready to run with it.

"So they go into a bar," said Rabbie, "and—"

"Lowlander or Highlander?" Ross said, taking his turn at the baiting.

"What?" said Rabbie.

"The Scotsman – Lowlands or Highlands?"

"Does it matter?"

"Or an Islander," I chipped in.

"Yes," said Ross. "He could be an Islander."

"It doesn't matter," said Rabbie, pointedly. "So, they are in this pub—"

"Of course, it does," Ross objected. "Completely different tipple each. It's the water, you see, it gives each one a distinctive taste—"

"He was a Highlander," said Rabbie. "So, this Englishman—"

"This Irishman," Liam began, "was he—"

Rabbie turned on him: "Northern, Belfast, Shankill Road, even numbered house!"

"OK," said Liam, he paused for effect: "Gay or straight?"

"What?" Rabbie was losing it now.

"The Irishman," said Liam.

"Stop taking the piss! You're all being incredibly childish."

"Am not!" said Liam, but Rabbie said nothing – he'd fallen for that one before.

"What's the point of being an adult if you can't be childish once in a while," I said.

"Good point," Ross agreed. "Who said that, Oscar Wilde?"

"Doctor Who."

"Classic or reboot?" Kate asked.

"Classic."

"Pertwee or Baker?"

"Baker."

"Tom or Colin?"

Rabbie was incensed: "Shut up! Shut up! You bloody Redcoats."

"Ooooohhhh," Kate started, but there was only a half-hearted attempt to carry it on.

"Would that be a Protestant or a Catholic Redcoat?" said Liam.

"I think all the Redcoats were Protestant," said Frank; I think it was Frank.

"God," said Liam. "I'm in the wrong uniform."

"No, you aren't," I said. "They weren't all Protestant."

"No?"

"No," I said. "That was the point. The Jacobite Rebellion wasn't Scotland versus England. I think there were more Highlanders on the 'English' side, and there was a Manchester Regiment on the 'Scottish' side. Hence my shorts."

I showed everyone my football kit to hoots and whistles.

"And there were lots of foreigners on both sides," Reka added.

"This Manchester Regiment," Kate asked. "Were they Man City or Man United?"

"Redcoats, Man United, they weren't granted city status until the industrial revolution, 1850 something," I said before continuing: "And the Jacobite Uprising wasn't Protestants versus Catholics either. It was Stuarts versus Hanoverians – simple as that."

"Stuarts?" Liam asked.

"Bonnie Prince Charlie was Charles Edward Stuart and King George II was from Hanover."

"And now Redcoat and Jacobite sit and share a drink together," said Liam. He raised his glass: "Cheers!"

"Cheers!" everyone replied.

"That's the point, isn't it?" said Liam. "We're celebrating a great battle, but look, Redcoats and Jacobites all sitting around the same table."

"An Englishman–" said Rabbie.

"Wish they'd celebrate the Battle of the Boyne in the same way back home," said Liam. "Bloody stupid! All those Orangemen parading along Catholic streets with drums and bowler hats. Incredible racket. Goes on and on for miles. So many police too."

I drank my beer – it was good, malty with a burnt taste – and let the conversation wash over me.

"These Orangemen," Kate asked, "tangerine or satsuma?"

"Aye, you're right," Ross said. "I mean we share a pint with anyone whether they are Protestant, Catholic, Gay, Straight, Black, Pink, Hindu, Muslim–"

"Would that be Protestant-Muslim or Catholic-Muslim you'd be sharing your pint with?" Liam asked.

"Och, what are you talking about?"

"You joke, but that sort of thing used to make a big difference on the Shankill Road and in Bandit Country."

"There's no such thing as a Protestant-Muslim and a Catholic-Muslim."

"You've not been to Belfast then."

"I don't think Muslims drink in pubs."

"Och, the mad fools."

"Course they do, there's lemonade and cola."

"Good point, there's always cola."

"Pepsi or Coke?"

It was one of those spiralling conversations that touched upon important issues, but shied away from anything serious. There were never any conclusions. It was bonding, wasn't it? Context, not content – people need to connect and that's the important aspect, not what's actually said. Hence all these soaps, reality shows and celebrity dancing. They give people a common subject to talk about, a topic that can be agreed upon, without forcing anyone to actually think. God forbid we should discuss something important. And then there's the weather. It's all so insignificant and stupid.

Ross touched me on the shoulder: "You all right?"

"Fine."

"Drink up, Guy. It's not that bad."

"Ross, what am I doing with my life?"

"Having fun," he said.

"But I'm not. What's it for?"

"Guy."

"I can't keep a girlfriend, I can't get a job and I can't seem to finish anything I start. I haven't done anything on my thesis for months. Mandy's right. I mean, every year we come here and then we go home again."

Here it comes, I think, *this is when it all went wrong.*

♦

"Let me out!" I shout.

I stand and bang on the cell's iron door again as I'd done when I was first locked in here. I'm losing it. I want to escape, of course, but it's more than that. I want to change it, I want to get into a time machine and go back to change it. If only I could tap myself on the other shoulder and tell myself to shut up, lose your girlfriend, have another drink and then go home. Anything, but stand on a chair and destroy everything.

I wish they'd left me my watch, then I'd know if it was already too late or whether I still have time.

"Fuck!" I say to no-one. It is too late. You can't change the past; it is all water under the bridge. Under the bridge – God! The clichés are coming back to haunt me. I was standing up then too, when I did it: when I sent everyone to their doom. And now, flooding back to drown me in it, the memory of the rest of that stupid, stupid, stupid pub conversation.

It wasn't me, it was the beer that made me do it.

♦

"What's he talking about?" Liam asked leaning towards the two of us.

"I've no idea," said Ross.

No! No, you haven't, have you? It's just my memories, because I'm locked in a cell about to die. And you? If you are still alive, Ross, then you are about to die, you stupid Scottish Sassenach from Kent. And Liam, you too, and Kate, and Rabbie and Frank and everyone else.

"We just 'go home'," I said.

"I dinna think ye heart was in it this year," said Ross. "His lass has moved to London."

"Rough," Liam agreed.

"Every year we come here and celebrate the Battle of Derby," I said. "It never happened."

"No," said – I can't remember who replied. I was on a roll ranting over the top of interruptions.

"Every year," I continued, "we get here and then, like Bonnie Prince Charlie himself, we turn back to Scotland. What's the point?"

"It's a bit of fun."

"My girlfriend's going to London and I'm actually celebrating someone not going to London."

"Och, it's a bit of laugh, isn't it?"

I stood up extending the circle of those listening, gathering in everyone for the moment, flicking my eye contact from one eager face to another.

"Why don't we ever just keep going?" I said.

"Yeah, why don't we?" said Liam.

"How many years have we been doing this? Has anyone ever gone over to the other side?"

"Well, I think–"

"We should cross the bridge."

"Cross the bridge?" said Rabbie.

"Yes," I replied, animated now, gesticulating wildly. "Actually finish something we start for a change."

"I'll drink to that," said Ross.

"Me too," said Liam.

"I'm going to do it," I said.

A question came from another table: "Do what?"

"Cross the bridge!" I announced.

"That's the spirit," said Ross.

I stood on a chair. God, I actually stood on a chair and rallied the crowd like some great general, and asked them all to follow me into the valley of death.

"I'm going to cross the bridge!" I said: everyone clapped. *And now, drumroll please, the big moment:* "Who's with me?"

They stood too, and cheered and... it was that time of the evening, we'd all had too much to drink, the alcohol rushing through the bloodstream and making all those mad connections in the brain: shut down common sense, roll on lunacy. It was the sort of pub talk that leads to traffic cones turning up in student flats. I heard excited voices bouncing back up to me.

"We're with you, Guy!"

"Yes, we're with you!"

"What are we doing?"

"Let's all cross the bridge."

"Three cheers for Guy!"

"Hip hip."

"Hurrah!"

"Hip hip."

"Hurrah!!"

"Hip hip."

"Hurrah!!!"

"Everyone," I said. "Follow me."

And they followed me.

Oh bloody hell, they all followed me.

As I clambered off my chair, Ross downed his pint with an "Och, why not?"

"To the bridge!"

"To the bridge!!!"

I was their general, I led them.

Julius Caesar sat astride his horse and gazed across a river. Not for him a forlorn look.

"Alea iacta est," said Caesar — *the die is cast* — and he crossed the Rubicon. From that single decision, the Roman Republic fell.

Prince Charles Edward Stuart reached Swarkestone and his Jacobite Rebellion secured the bridge over the River Trent — our bridge! Nothing stood between him and London. In the capital, the population panicked, packed and left. The throne was there for the taking.

"Audentior Ibo," says his family motto — *I will go more daringly* — but he turned back. From that single decision, history flowed to Culloden, defeat, Flora MacDonald and the Isle of Skye, and flight into exile.

And me?

Caesar or Stuart?

I stumbled towards the line of water and our Jacobite Rebellion came to the same moment of decision. With our rucksacks on our backs and a few wheeled suitcases trundling over the tarmac, we...

Headlights came towards us warning us to one side, but when the car passed the road was clear.

...climbed the brow of the bridge and descended into the dark night.

♦

Now I realise that it was downhill from there, literally and metaphorically, taking us inexorably towards disaster. Did I pause at the rear of the marching column, the Union Flag fluttering in the background, to look over my shoulder forlornly at the bridge?

Maybe.

If they make a film, definitely.

From this single decision, I had chosen a path that led directly to this cell. I sit here in the present and I now know the very moment the die was cast. I can't change it now. It's part of history: Caesar's memoirs, Jacobite manuscripts, twitter and blogs. When I—

The bolts in the iron door clank.

The cell door opens and in walks the Home Secretary, the Right Honourable John Trudie, MP.

PACE: The Police and Criminal Evidence Act, 1984

An Act to make further provision in relation to the powers and duties of the police, persons in police detention, criminal evidence, police discipline and complaints against the police; to provide for arrangements for obtaining the views of the community on policing and for a rank of deputy chief constable; to amend the law relating to the Police Federations and Police Forces and Police Cadets in Scotland; and for connected purposes.

31st October 1984

PRISONER OF WAR

"So," the Right Honourable Home Secretary says, clasping his hands together, "this is Guy Wilson."

John Trudie, an image conjured forth from television, stands nonchalantly as if it was the most normal thing in the world in the super HD of reality. It's bloody bizarre to see someone imbued with the magic of celebrity outside the confines of the telly or off the page of a newspaper, and so close that I could reach out to touch him.

Incongruously, this luminary carries a red balloon.

I don't say anything. He's the man behind it all, my arrest, the betrayal and all for... what?

"You're the architect of my rise to power."

He checks the cell as if inspecting the facilities: a prison getting the personal treatment, a visit from the Home Secretary, a politician who takes his job so very seriously – smile for the camera. Maybe he does care, maybe everything will be all right, maybe he's come to give me a present, but then I realise that he's only looking for somewhere to put his balloon. There's nowhere in the bare cell for the floating object, so in the end, he just lets it go. The balloon drifts to the ceiling and bobs there with its string dangling.

It's the first piece of colour I've seen in hours and it's mesmerising. I can't take my eyes off it.

Trudie's suit is grey, sharp and immaculate, dark with a pinstripe, and so pressed that it's a wonder he could carry a balloon without cutting it. If Cameron's cost up to £3,500 and May's thigh length patent leather boots over half a grand, how much did Trudie's attire put the taxpayer back?

"Nothing to say, Guy?"

"What's with the balloon?"

"I'm taking the kiddies to the park, photo opportunity. One wants to show the nation the importance of family values, it's what binds society together, and I thought it best to have an alibi."

He adjusts his silver cufflinks as he walks around, pacing the tiny area. I can smell aftershave and I'm suddenly aware of how dirty I am with the miles from Derby to London gritted into my pores.

"Why are you here?" I ask.

"I couldn't resist it," Trudie admits. "It's foolish, I know, risky even, but curiosity got the better of me. But there's no harm in talking to you, is there? It's not like I'm Trump tweeting to all and sundry."

"I guess not."

"You see, I was sitting in the House of Commons bar a week or so back—"

"A week!"

"It's a long time in politics," he smiles down at me, pleased with the quotation, before continuing. "I had a glass of single malt: Ardbeg or... one of the Islays anyway, a lovely peaty taste, when I first heard of your little expedition. Fascinating what Northerners get up to, I thought, and then, well, one puts it out of one's mind completely. I had a political career to build. You understand?"

He stares at me, expecting an answer, so I manage a confused expression that I hope will satisfy. It does.

"The House of Commons bar, the one that overlooks the Thames, has a superb view. There's no view of Big Ben's clock, of course, the angle's wrong, but there's Westminster Bridge, St. Thomas' Hospital, the London Eye. You'll be visiting the hospital later, so you'll get some idea. It represents a country I want to protect, a country in crisis, a country that's crying out for a new direction."

He chops his right hand into his left with each 'country'. I realise that he's making a speech. Next, he presents his hands, palms up, to show his sincere need for my approval.

"A new direction," I say. "It's the way forward."

"Very droll, but yes, it is the way forward, although we'll have to come up with a new slogan. Any ideas?"

"Down with the Government."

He studies me, sizing me up, and it's forensic, a look with the cold steel of an autopsy examination: "You're suggesting armed revolt?"

"Not exactly, I–"

"Good, because peace is paramount, but how can we have peace when there are guns everywhere?"

"Get rid of the guns."

"Anyone can buy a small automatic for two hundred and fifty pounds in pubs, not those near Westminster, but nonetheless pubs in London. The rise in knife crime is appalling," he says, layering on the reasonableness. I can feel his charisma, concentrated in this small space, swaying me. "We massage the figures somewhat, but I've seen the real graphs now I'm in the Cabinet and–"

"You're hiding knife crime?"

"Me? Good Lord no, massaging the figures up – up, up, up!" he says, signalling the direction with his arms with such force that the draught causes the balloon to nod in agreement. "There's nothing like fear to galvanize the electorate. Immigrants are taking our jobs, says Murdoch, so Brexit. Anyway, we point out the gangs of hoodies, hoodlums literally, mugging old ladies and photogenic young women. We put violence everywhere, on the front pages, the news and the internet, Twitter and those blogs, and the populace cries out for action. Do something, the public whine, but still, they don't want the police armed. It's insane. I was saying to Snitch... you've met Snitch?"

"I've met Snitch."

"Yes, of course, you have. He said, sure it's not like America though, is it? And I said, we'll see, we'll see." Trudie stabs a finger towards me: "We dress the police like paramilitaries, you know the bulletproof vest—"

"Stab vest."

"Stab vest, thank you, and utility belts with pepper sprays and batons and those electric stun guns."

"Tasers."

"Taser! Yes, so Star Trek, so modern, so stylish. Like our Security Force: all black and so damned ruthless looking, and yet, we don't go the whole hog and equip our Boys in Blue properly. With armed police, some thug mugs an old lady and *blam!*"

His finger, now a gun, fires – I flinch.

"He won't do it again, will he?" says Trudie, raising his gun as if to blow out the smoke, but he moves on to the next item. "We can cut the Crown Prosecution Service's costs too, which is more dividend for the shareholders. Deterrence, that's what we need. The prisons are full and the public backlash when one lets out some violent oik to re-offend is... raving hypocrisy. Ooh, save us from the bad men, but don't hurt them. One's as liberal as the next man—"

"I don't think you are."

"Not in terms of where I sit in the House, I'll grant you, but in terms of attitude, but there is a limit, a line in the sand, and when that line is crossed... you know the origin of the term crossing the line?"

"It's the line on the carpet in the House of Commons that keeps each side more than two sword-lengths apart."

"That's it: foils our foils, but not the points of our rapier wit," he says, pleased with himself. He has a sincere smile.

"Or the Roman General, who drew a circle in the sand around... someone to get him to retreat," I say and then I wonder why I'm trying to score points here. I'm losing this game, losing my grip on reality: I'm tired, it's been a long week.

"I see you have the advantages of a proper, classical education."

"Mea culpa," I say. How did I get into this conversation? I can see the corridor beyond the open door, but I just sit here discussing random topics of interest as if I'm in the History Department's Coffee Room.

"It's also a filming term when the director moves the camera over to the other side of one's eye line with the interviewer," says Trudie, motioning with his hand again.

"I didn't know that."

"One has to be media savvy these days."

"I guess."

"With an eye to history as well."

"Yes."

"You're a historian, I believe."

"I am."

"Writing a thesis on the causes of war."

"You've done your research."

"I have whole departments now – Special Branch, MI5, the police."

"I just use the internet."

"I think that's what they do," Trudie admits. "But you also engaged in a practical experiment, didn't you?"

"It wasn't for my thesis."

"This is one of those historic moments," he says, enjoying the sound of his own voice as it reverberates in this small, hard room. "Consider Richard the Lionheart's meeting with Saladin? I was told the tale when I was young. King Richard and the Moor met – they were very chivalrous to each other – and they compared weapons. King Richard's two-handed sword..."

The Home Secretary hefts an imaginary sword.

"...bent an iron bar," he says, clearly striking it in his imagination. "In response, Saladin threw a silk scarf in the air." I followed Trudie's throw, so convincing that my eyes move up to the ceiling and the red balloon, and then he flutters his hand down like a butterfly. "The blade of his scimitar was so sharp that when the silk fell on the edge, it was twain. They had a great respect for each other, the Lionheart and Saladin."

"Saladin didn't meet King Richard."

"Really?"

"It's a myth."

"Shame," he says hanging his head in disappointment. "So here we are then, more historic than Richard the Lionheart and Saladin."

"Hardly."

"How did you do it then?"

I think for a moment, remembering crossing the bridge and walking down the A514 in the middle of the night. It was amazing we weren't hit by anything as we staggered about drunk. The bridge is too narrow really, but no one will alter the five arches' 13th century magnificence. Somewhere along the way, it became obvious that we were ill prepared for this trek, and some must have turned back to collect their vehicles. I mean, who collected our van? I'm guessing the drivers hadn't been drinking and so, sober, they were able to make some sensible decisions, whereas the inebriated majority stuck to the drunken plan.

I'd made a choice, not the cairn but the bridge, but it was all very vague, a series of double images mixed in a befuddled montage. I thought about losing my girlfriend, and when the pub disappeared behind us, I started wondering what the hell I was doing.

By the time we reached Stanton by Bridge (the bridge the ancient village is 'by' being the one we'd crossed), it was gone midnight. We'd only gone a mile: one down, one hundred and twenty-nine to go.

Trudie is still waiting patiently for my answer.

"It sort of happened," I say.

"You didn't have a plan?"

"Not really."

"How very Brexit of you," Trudie says. "I can't think how anyone can function without a Master Plan. I expect that's the Eton education for you. It's the difference between you and me. There are those who let the tide of events sweep them along, people like you, and then there are people like me. People who make things happen, people who change things, people who control the world."

"Is that what you want to do?"

"What was it you said in that television interview?"

"I said a lot of things."

"You said, and I quote, 'Fate doesn't control you. We make our own history'."

"Did I say that?"

"An excellent soundbite, you should be proud."

"Are we making history?" I remember Ross, Liam and I slept in the back of the van in sleeping bags, an uncomfortable experience full of farts and snoring. It was hardly the stuff of legend.

"Of course. Everything is historic," says Trudie. "Historic speeches, historic laws, historic decisions."

"If it's all historic, then nothing means anything."

Trudie looks at me as if I'm mad. "Nonsense. My current making of history is the police force, finishing

May's marvellous work when she was Home Secretary. That has meaning. It'll be one's legacy."

"And last for a thousand years? You can hardly put what you're doing in the same league as... Robert Peel."

"I think I can," says Trudie emphatically. "Sir Robert Peel may well have founded the police, but I shall recreate the service as a modern force for the twenty-first century."

"If you say so."

"You know, it was the idea of the Prime Minister: the Duke of Wellington no less. He had a dream, apparently, according to that dolt McGivern."

"I've met him."

"Really?" Trudie looks genuinely surprised.

"Superintendent McGivern, not the Duke of Wellington."

Trudie's gaze narrows, the look of a teacher who knows something is amiss, but he can't quite put his finger on it. He's rethinking his strategy, I realise, behind a chess master's stare or a poker player's face.

"You know a lot about the police," he says.

"My girlfriend's a police officer."

"Oh yes, the redoubtable Amanda Reynolds – lovely girl, so keen, so ambitious, so destined for greatness–"

"A crown on her shoulder perhaps."

"A chip on yours? But yes, Superintendent or even higher for her, I think, in a number of years of course. She'll go to the top. I'm Home Secretary... did you know?"

"I heard."

"My responsibilities include the Metropolitan Police. I'm directly in charge. An odd quirk of organisation – the United Kingdom is full of them. I put in a good word for our WPC Reynolds and she has her well-deserved boost up the ladder – Sergeant. She earned it for what she's–"

"OK!" *For fuck's sake!*

Kind or cruel, yes or no – his eyes seem to debate the choice. Life is made of decisions: cross a bridge or don't cross a bridge, ask a question or don't ask a question, be free or be caught. It seems analogue, full of grey areas, but everything can be reduced to binary, Liam said: one, zero; true, false; alive... dead.

"She's doing her job, a job she loves."

"The Duke of Wellington had a nightmare," I say. "He saw English soldiers killing English civilians on English streets."

"Ah, McGivern... so tragic."

"The whole point was to avoid the nightmare," I say, "or have I got the wrong end of the stick?"

"Not at all."

"So Wellington asked Robert Peel to form an unarmed force to keep the peace. The important word is 'unarmed'. 'Armed police' is an oxymoron, like 'military intelligence' or 'honest politician'."

"Very clever," says Trudie. He's clearly enjoying himself. "How about 'civil war'?"

"You can't have 'armed, *unarmed* keepers of the peace'."

"We're just arguing semantics."

"No, it's important, it's the difference between democracy and dictatorship. Rule by consent rather than by force."

"People don't care about democracy. Otherwise, there'd be a larger turnout on election day. All those protest votes for Brexit, when they should have realised what their cross would actually do. One goes on these European junkets and meets those ex-communists and the conversation always turns to voter turnout. They achieve an A or an A*, whereas the United Kingdom scrapes a D or an E – it's embarrassing. Our nation just wants their consumer goods, their celebrity gossip and a chance to moan. We allow them that and they're happy."

"The opium of the people?"

"Marx! Don't bring that dead dogma into this."

"I was referring to the technique."

"The end justifies the means," says Trudie. "The job of the police is to protect the public and the government, and so long as we do that, it's not important how we do it."

"The ends justify the means! Just the sort of thing a politician like you would say."

"I believe it's a direct quote from Police Sergeant Amanda Reynolds."

The loathing burns: he must be able to see it on my face.

"Fine girl," he says, smiling the sort of smile I've ignored on election posters: this is a man you can trust, his face says, from his greying temples to his youthful, orthodontic grin. *What bollocks!* "She wanted a career, I gave her that, and she does her duty."

"As you see it."

"Circulate stories about crime and people are afraid. Publish a manifesto with a law and order platform and the electorate vote correctly. Propose a white paper about police equipment and the house passes a law. Release statistics showing armed police reduce crime and the public love us. Everyone's happy."

"You made them afraid in the first place. You're not solving problems, you're creating them and then pretending to solve them. You can fool some people all of the time, and all of the people some of the time, but you can't fool all the people all of the time."

"Nixon?"

"Lincoln."

"We don't even need to fool them now," says Trudie. "We're in the era of post-truth politics. Look at Boris and Trump. They speak nonsense and everyone laps it up. Extraordinary. People are such sheep. They follow anything."

"They don't."

"They followed you."

I'm unable to meet his eyes, so I look at the floor: "You're playing with people's lives for your own ends."

"Of course."

He sits next to me and puts his left arm around my shoulder. The human contact is both repellent and oddly comforting.

"Politics is a game," he says, "don't you see? The opposition makes a move, my party makes a move, you make a move, I make a move. The trick is to determine what one's opponent is up to and counter it."

"They choose paper, so you choose scissors."

"Exactly," he says clenching his right fist to ram home his agreement: rock.

"Only if it's a game," I say.

"Of course, it is, everyone's a player who just wants to maximise their position."

"Not everyone is out for profit."

"Of course not. One has to appreciate the whole portfolio. It's not just a question of maximising your salary. One should have a better car, a bigger apartment, a more attractive wife... and so on. It's about power. Money is only useful because it can be converted into many other things, but power, genuine influence over other people, is what counts."

I realise that Trudie chooses rock. I always start with paper, perhaps because I'm an academic, but his default reaction is to bludgeon the opposition.

But paper wraps rock.

"There have always been the haves and have-nots. Those of us who went to Eton or Harrow have been educated to lead. It's only right and proper. You're a historian, I thought you'd appreciate Victorian values. People want to be told what to do, they want to be led. Anyway, we've saddled the next generation with so much student debt that the country will soon be one big workhouse – and there are food banks, so no-one will starve – and they'll know their place."

"You're mad."

"Hardly," Trudie says. "You're only saying that because you're not one of us, even if joining the cabal does involve having a right chuckle in the evening and putting your cock in some pig."

It's obvious he's going to kill me, otherwise, why is he chatting to me like this, his arm around my shoulder telling me everything. He's going to kill me and he's going to kill others.

I tell him: "You're going to murder my friends!"

He removes his friendly arm and stands up: "There's no need to be like that. I'm not going to murder your friends, merely a policeman or two. In some ways, I'm on your side." He raises his eyebrows jokingly. "It will be proportionate and necessary. One can't make an omelette without breaking eggs."

"You can't make an egg pyramid!" I snap angrily.

"What?"

"If you, you know, break them. Your eggs. The police force, society even, history, why not? It's an edifice built up slowly over the years, layer on layer."

"That's clever. I like this sparring. Proper debating, and not like being asked what Tracy in Bognor Regis wants to know. Corbyn, remember him? He couldn't even think of his own questions. But this! Two adversaries facing each other, trading points, like tennis, thirty-love."

"I make it thirty all."

"I have an ace," he smiles. "I love this. It's... *gloating*. I can quite see why villains in Bond movies always do it. It always struck me as extremely stupid, but, you know, now one's actually done it, it's quite wonderful. The trouble with spin... sorry, let's put one's cards on the table. The trouble with 'lying' is that one has to believe it to be convincing. At least partially, and then once you've told a farage of lies, one can't see the wood for the trees. I mean, take Boris for example – clueless because of his own lies. However, this explaining everything clearly to someone else, someone connected but whose point of view must by necessity be in opposition to one's own. It makes everything so much clearer in one's mind."

"I'm so pleased to be useful," I say. "Can I escape now?"

"Droll, very droll."

I smile, though my sense of humour has run dry.

"This is truly fascinating... no, I mean it. Blofeld, Goldfinger, Doctor Evil: they never made sense before, but it's liberating to talk openly. All this secrecy is quite trying: 'one's not at liberty', 'one cannot recall'... it muddles the mind. We should sit down to have a proper conversation over a single malt. Somewhere more conducive, I think. My club has wonderfully comfortable leather chairs and such a relaxing atmosphere for making people say more than they should. Perhaps after a meal: venison, veal or pheasant, they do an excellent sirloin, with a Merlot or a claret, something for the palate. If I'm standing up, I always start making a speech, but to sit down and properly discuss the issues, and there are many, is something I would relish. I'm sure you'd have a lot to say that's insightful. You've a historical perspective and a formal, academic training that would help to put everything into context. Education makes such a difference. One admires you, one really does. Unfortunately, one's on a strict timetable and item five is having you killed. Cheerio."

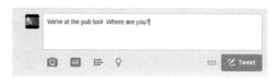

We're at the pub too! Where are you?

103 ✎ Tweet

View 107 new Tweets

Liamroberts4 @liamroberts494 · 2h
We're in the pub, where are you?

Kate Miller @katiekatiekatie · 5h
We've set off south, meet us at the pub.

40   66

THE MARCH SOUTH

Somewhere, along the way, life became worth living again. A kind of bizarre hope arose as if somehow reaching London would make everything all right. I was a knight in shining armour and at the end of my quest, my bravery proved, I would meet my one true love and it would all end happily ever after.

The poisons of hangover, exhaustion and a broken heart mixed to become a kind of ambrosia with an elixir chaser.

So the days became brighter and brighter, my pack lighter and lighter, my outlook better and better, or some such sickening nonsense. The following morning, however, was not one of those times: it was a Monday too.

Yes, it was a bright – *ow, ow, ouch!* – morning, when we emerged, bleary and in desperate need of a pee.

There were fewer people about. Deserters had abandoned our cause for sure, but looking around I thought I saw a few additions. I wasn't completely certain, and I didn't really care, because I ached. I could feel the corrugated lines of the van's steel floor across my back, a diagonally uneven awkwardness, as I went behind the bushes by the side of the road. The van was in a lay-by along with a few cars. I couldn't remember precisely how we'd got to... wherever it was. I needed a cup of tea, a hot bath and a nice warm bed: instead, we sorted the gear out between various vehicles and set off walking south.

No-one really talked about what we were doing, how we were going to do it or why.

There were moans about the early rising, complaints about the sunlight and declarations that never again would alcohol pass our lips – never, ever, ever, though I think someone mentioned a pub we could easily reach by lunchtime and that soon became our destination.

"Come on," said Ross, "let's be going."

"What time is it?" I said, checking my watch. For some reason, the big hand and the little hand made no sense: 6:47, or :48, somewhere between 'quarter to' and 'ten to', in the a.m., but the hour hand was pointing sort of straight down, which couldn't be right.

"Come on," said Ross. "We march on London."

Ross banged on my head, it seemed, but it was really the side of the van as he set off down the road.

"What's got into him?"

"He's going to walk all the way," said Liam.

"What?"

"To London. He thinks that we should walk the whole way. In shifts."

"What?"

"I don't think he's sobered up."

"He didn't drink that much, did he?"

"He had a wee dram from his flask."

"A wee dram?"

"A wee dram. Then he downed the whole flask."

"What? At..." I looked at my watch again, "...this time. What's this time called?"

"Breakfast."

"Och, ken yer no get a move on!" Ross shouted back, already fifty yards down the road.

Liam and I tried jogging to catch up, but five or six paces convinced us it was unwise. Some Rebels and Redcoats formed up behind us and started marching along. There were probably enough seats in the cars and van, but we walked. It was an unspoken agreement, possibly because no-one had the wits to object.

Just when it looked like we weren't ever going to catch up, the van passed us and stopped ahead of Ross. The passenger side window rolled down and Ross came to a halt alongside.

"Ken ye no see I'm walking," said Ross to the van.

"What?" said a voice from inside. "Don't be stupid. Get in."

"Och, I'm marching all the way. Just as Bonnie Prince Charlie would have done."

"Bonnie Prince Charlie would have used a horse."

"Get me a horse then."

Liam and I exchanged a glance when Ross shook his fist at the window. A hand showing two fingers appeared briefly in response. Anger and swearing: what was that about?

Ross set off again and the van lurched to follow and then sped off down the road.

"That's our ride, isn't it?" Liam said to me.

It was much the same as any procession, except there wasn't a police escort and we didn't look like a good advert for re-enactment.

It struck me that rather than creating a glorious march south, we were, for the first time, actually recreating the Jacobite retreat back to Scotland. I imagine that was a trudging, sorry affair full of failure and regret. Except we were heading south and, after a quick stop at a newsagent's for some munchies, our spirits rose with every step. I was still brooding over losing my girlfriend, but the others started chatting and joking and laughing. It was infectious.

Stanton-by-Bridge was soon behind us and we were Not-by-Bridge, but on that part of the map that continues on another page. This was the unknown, the exciting who-knows-what.

Liam disappeared into the bushes, and I put on an extra spurt of speed to catch Ross.

"Who's driving the van?" I said as I finally fell in next to him.

"Och, Rabbie's feet hurt, so I gave him the keys," said Ross.

"Wouldn't he have wanted to walk too?"

"Aye," said Ross, "but rock blunts scissors, so I got to march."

It was easy going.

There weren't as many people as the march yesterday, but so many people must have taken Monday off. Or been on a long summer break.

The van and various cars hopped ahead and waited for us to catch up, then we swapped roles and so most walked five miles, had a jaunt ahead and then an hour's rest while the next shift caught up.

The police passed a few times to check us out. I recognized one or two.

And there was plenty of tosh to discuss.

Liam caught up, sneezing in the clear, crisp air.

"This is great, isn't it? Isn't it?" he said, pushing his glasses back up his nose. "You can really gain a sense of history. Look at us, marching along the country lane between ancient hedges just as they did... er... Guy?"

"Over two hundred and seventy–"

"Two hundred and seventy years ago. Striding like soldiers across England on a mission, a glorious quest, the Three Musketeers with their camp followers–"

"Some very camp," said Ross.

"To... to... to do whatever is it that men have to do," he finished with a crescendo and then let out an almighty *achoo*.

"Are you getting the 'flu?" I asked.

"No, no, no," said Liam. "Just early morning... why? Has someone been saying something?"

"No."

Lunch ended up being in a small cafe, too small for us to all sit together, so we ate in shifts: the first group making progress south and the second group overtaking them with the van and cars. There were more of us too. There had been calls and texts on mobiles to other re-enactors, those who had left the Crewe & Harpur early. Kate and Reka suddenly reappeared for example.

I wasn't really part of the organisation and, in fact, I don't think anyone was. I trudged on, alternating between silent sulking over Mandy, and desperate conversation to take my mind off things.

Ross, Liam and I walked, forgoing any lifts. I think I was trying to punish myself. Or was it joining in? My mood swung wildly.

I remember Rabbie showing me our first day's progress on a map. I didn't really take it in, the thing fluttering around in the breeze like a wounded pterodactyl. We'd gone from 'here' to 'here' and that was good. If we kept on at this pace, then we'd reach 'there' and then 'there', which would be, well, real progress.

He went up and down the line showing everyone: no-one questioned the words 'first day' preferring to say "yes, that is real progress" and "real progress: it's the way forward".

By six, post meridian, we were all ready for a pint or two, for medicinal purposes only, you must understand, and merely to ease our aching feet, obviously, and, Lord above, everyone could feel their muscles. The pub was divided into small areas with large tables and everyone shuffled along a long seat to fit around. Ross bent over and struggled under the table. When at last he emerged, he sat back and let out a massive sigh.

"Pleased to be here?" Liam asked.

"Pleased to get those boots off," said Ross.

A laugh went around the table: "I wondered what that smell was," said Rabbie.

"God, yes, pongs," said Liam.

"Euuu..." said Kate.

"Should have a government health warning," I said.

There was a brief moment of calm before everyone dived beneath the table. We all tussled and tugged until we had removed our boots too. It was instantly wonderful; I've never seen so many people with the same satisfied expression around one table.

"Oh, that's good," said Kate.

I wiggled my toes, it was bliss. I could feel my feet pulsing as the blood had a chance to circulate.

"Let's just sit here," I said.

"Suits me," said Liam. He struggled under the table a second time to plug his phone charger in.

"Och, anyone getting the drinks in?" Ross looked around, no-one wanted to move.

"I can't walk," I said.

"Me neither," said Liam.

"Ye sissy Sassenachs."

We checked but the bar pumps were side on, so we all had to hazard a guess at what the pub had to offer: pints of ale all round.

I turned to Liam: "You all right?"

"Yes, fine, fine, fine," said Liam.

"You just seemed a bit down earlier."

"No, not at all."

"Honestly?"

"Honestly, fine, fine, fine. Used to sitting on my behind in front of a computer, nice to get some fresh air, see the world, walk, talk and generally, you know. I'm fine, fine, fine. I can go all night."

"All night on your own," said Reka.

Rabbie tapped me on the arm and pointed. I looked, unsure what had attracted his attention, and then I saw Ross waiting to be served.

"Is he dancing?" Rabbie asked.

Sure enough, Ross was hopping from one foot to another, each time his toe, clad in white walking socks, would circle in the air before coming down, and he was waving his tenner in the air in time. The complicated pattern started over and then, as we watched, repeated. It had nothing to do with the modern pop beat piped around the pub. Rabbie shrugged and Kate beamed with pleasure.

Ross stopped, turned and saw his audience.

We clapped and cheered.

"Ye poncy Southerners."

Ross was served and ferried the first clutch of three pints back.

"I'd say six for style, and oh, seven for interpretation," I said.

"A sexy performance," said Kate, "sure to go to the final."

"Eight," said Rabbie, "but we'll have to see what the phone vote says."

"Ha, ha," said Ross, "dozy English."

"Hey," said Liam. "I'm Irish. We appreciate proper dancing."

"I'm Hungarian," said Reka. "We don't just use our legs."

"We've something in common," Liam replied.

"No we don't."

"Drink that without moving your arms then," Ross replied, putting Liam's Guinness in front of him.

We sat in a circle around the table like King Arthur's Knights, our conversational jousts ranging over the whole kingdom of subjects. Drinks arrived in rounds and the empties vanished occasionally. We ordered food, bowls of chips to start with and then, hungry, we looked at the menu properly. It was good pub grub, nothing fancy, but just what we needed. When the waitress came round to collect our order token (a bottle with a number eight on it) and ask if everything was all right, we only needed a few more handfuls of ketchup sachets.

Thank goodness we had credit cards.

It was that maelstrom of conversation that put the world to rights, solved humanity's problems and invented a whole sub-genre of humour to boot. I remember leaning back to take a breather and noticing all these happy, earnest and spirited friends leaning forward, fingers gesticulating, and arguing the toss over everything and nothing. This, I thought, was what it was all about.

And the range of topics was extraordinary.

For example:–

"You know Rock-Paper-Scissors?" said Liam.

"Sorry?" I said.

"You know, rock blunts scissors, scissors cuts paper, paper wraps rock."

"It's definitely your round."

"I know, I know," said Liam defensively. "I wasn't going to suggest we play a decider."

"Fine, 'cos best out of seventeen is the limit."

"At Uni, we used to play this game on the computers."

"Sounds dull."

"We'd write programs to play–"

"At Uni?"

"I did Computer Science. So we had a competition, leagues and everything, to see who could write the best program."

"Surely it's just random?"

"I was getting to that part. Randomness wasn't allowed, or storage from previous games, and it was easy to test if someone cheated. All you had to do was set the program against itself: an honest program drew every single round; if it didn't, then some rule bending was involved."

"But wouldn't a random program against a random program have a random winner?"

"Yes, but never the same twice, whereas a deterministic program would always be the same."

"Got you."

"Right: so every program is fully deterministic, nothing random; so, knowing that about the competition, all your program has to do was work out its opponent's methodology. Once it had done that, it would win every time. We had a few basic programs: chose them in order, always picked rock and so on. Mine kept a long list of turns; you know, rock, paper, scissors, paper and so on, and it looked for the longest sub-list match to the current position from the previous rounds."

"The what?"

"It spots that if you go paper, then rock and win both times, then you always follow with scissors. So the program chooses rock."

"But surely next time, I'd choose paper as it beats your rock."

"Right. Hence the longest sub-list. It would see that when that combination turns up, you choose scissors, but if you lost last time then you'd choose..."

"Rock."

"Rock, right. Of course, the intervening moves would be different and so it would lose track, but with an infinite game, it would win out in the end, because eventually there'd be a repeating pattern."

"An infinite game?"

"Theoretically, except it would run out of memory long before then, and after half an hour it got really slow searching the whole dataset."

"But it would lose against a random player."

"Draw if both are random," said Liam. "Even a random computer program isn't truly random. It uses the pseudo-random number generator, which cycles, so its random moves would become predictable."

"But humans are random."

"Not even slightly. Human players were always thrashed. It might take a good hundred rounds. Random play comes out as fifty-fifty, but anything deterministic, any pattern in the human's choices, gets exploited by the machine."

"So you're saying people are predictable?"

"Yes, particularly in large quantities."

"Like the large quantities we've been drinking."

"I mean crowds, you know, mobs, they obey statistical models very accurately."

"You're saying that people are like sheep?" I asked.

"Yes, essentially," said Liam. "Or sheep are like people. Not as individuals perhaps, but en masse. The surge of football crowds, the queuing on the underground, any large group acts as a single entity. You talk about the mob doing this, not the individual members in it, but the whole as if it was a single entity."

"People don't just follow others mindlessly," I said.

"They do."

"I need the loo."

"Me too."

Wandering about the pub wearing nothing but a loose white shirt, a plaid and socks generated some looks from the other patrons. People leant over to ask and we were only too happy to explain: 'We're Jacobites'; 'We're marching on London'; 'It's not a kilt, it's a plaid'; and so on.

And they were only too happy to respond: 'What?', 'Good for you, can I join?', 'Isn't that the pattern' and so forth.

Ross leant closer. Oh, bollocks, I thought, it's that time of the evening.

"Och, I've always envied you."

"Envied me?"

"Not envied... I mean, envied. I was jealous, but not jealous. You ken? There's no word for it. I mean I'm glad for you, and I wish I was as lucky, but I don't want to ruin your... there's nothing nasty in it."

"Oh good."

"Just so long as that's straight."

"It is," I said. "What are we talking about?"

"Love."

"Love?"

"You and Mand, you're so together..."

"We've split up, I think."

"You were so good together. I mean that's good, isn't it, that you had that relationship? Better to have loved and lost, and all that pish."

"There are plenty more fish in the sea."

"No! That's not what I'm talking about. You've had a proper..." He raised his fingers to put quotes around the word: "'Relationship'."

"Yes."

"Me... *nah.*"

"You've had girlfriends. Kate?"

He did a theatrical double take to check that Kate wasn't listening. She wasn't even at the table, gone to the loo, I guess. Reka wasn't there either: they always go in pairs, don't they?

"No." Ross leant over and looked me straight in the eye, almost sobering: "I chat up the wee lassies, but I dinna get anywhere."

"Oh, right." I didn't know what to say. It was that sort of drunken conversation you have, when you realise that, no matter how much you've drunk or how many more units you knock back, you're not going to catch up with your drinking buddy, because they are far too far ahead; and so, paradoxically, you begin to sober up, your tortoise disappointment pushing your body into reverse gear as they, hare-like, get more pissed.

"Damn it, she's worth marching to London and fighting for," he said, and he banged his glass on the table slopping beer all over the polished surface and launching the beer mats as rafts. Other patrons looked over, even our fellow Jacobites, and I smiled a smile: he's a drunk, but I'm looking after him. "You ken what I mean?" he finished.

"Yes, Ross."

"I mean really ken what I mean?"

"Yes."

"Och, you're my friend."

Oh God, for goodness sake, a total cliché. I'd drunk... bollocks knew, but there were loads of empty glasses on the table yet to be collected and probably a third of them were mine, and yet I felt like I could drive, do Sudoku and take a job interview. Stone cold sober with the forthcoming prospect of a hangover in the morning. It wasn't fair, it wasn't fair, it was not fair.

"Come on Ross, let's get some water down you and get some kip in the van."

I picked him up as he nodded, but he pulled away suddenly.

"You know what I mean, though!" he said in his now broad Kentish accent as Scottish as wee Nessie models made in Korea.

"Yes, I know what you mean."

"Ye woman, she needs you."

"I need her," I said, thinking that someone to hold his other arm would be very useful.

I was stone freezing sober when we got outside. It had been a glorious day, no clouds in the sky, and now, in the middle of the night beneath the twinkling stars, it was nippy to say the least, particularly in our plaids and floppy shirts. Everything had a strange, depthless feel as if we were standing in some giant pop-up book with a cut-out pub, a cut-out van and a cut-out tree in the distance. The sky was beautiful: Edinburgh nights, like all cities, have too much orange glow. No-one takes the time to look at the moon anymore.

It felt like I was the only person in the world, apart from Ross, but he wasn't really there, and Rabbie and Kate staggering to a car, and the two policemen.

"You can't camp in a car park, Sir," said the officer. "The car park is for pub patrons only."

"We've just been patrons," I said.

"You're not drinking now, though, are you?"

"No, I suppose, technically not."

"So, you'll be moving along then, Sir."

I recognized him: "It's Spence, isn't it?"

He stepped forward and his name badge came into view, but not into focus.

"Police Constable Spencer, yes, Sir."

"I've not seen you all day."

"I have a life."

"Yes?"

"And duties other than escorting strangely dressed members of the public."

"Right, and now?"

"I'm on the night shift."

"Oh right."

I nodded: an impression of that model bird pecking into a glass. The car park, as I switched to scanning left and right, offered no inspiration.

Finally, I wondered why the hi-viz jacket looked so grey as if Spence was a time traveller, a sort of modern *Life on Mars* copper transported to *Dixon of Dock Green*'s 405-line TV. Wait, he'd explained why: he was on the night shift, so it was dark.

"Lovely night for it," I said, finally.

"Yes, it is, Sir."

"Could you give us some directions?"

"Where would you like to go, Sir?"

"Somewhere... nice."

"There's a lay-by down the way," he said, pointing south.

"We canna drive," said Ross. He wobbled as he tried to move his legs under him and toppled over.

"Some of us can't even stand," I said.

"We no need noo," said Ross. "Och, I'm pished."

"Come on, Ross," said the PC as he leant over and hoisted the Scot to his feet. "Let's get you in your vehicle."

"It's this one," I said, getting the keys out and leading the way across to our white van. "Let's put him in the back."

I opened the back door of the van and saw Liam, kneeling down and just about to snort a line of white powder. We looked at each other in a strange freeze frame, then I closed the door before anyone else saw.

"So *officer*," I said, loudly, "this is our van, *constable police officer*."

"Shit!" came Liam's muffled voice from inside.

I turned to the policeman: "It's a diesel," I continued, "twenty miles to the gallon, one previous owner and it's white."

"I can see that," said Spence. "Sir."

"Yes, and it's very spacious inside."

"I don't want to buy your van," said Spence.

"I'm no selling," said Ross.

"No, no," I said. "I wouldn't recommend it anyway, it sticks something rotten in third gear when it's cold and the CD player is—"

"Shite!" said Ross.

"...unsatisfactory."

"Keeps playing Kylie Minogue," Ross added.

"Let's get him in the back," said Spence to his colleague.

"Ye canna get the wee shiny thing out."

"Is he heavy?" the other policeman asked. His name badge began with a 'J'.

"I'm no heavy, I'm yer bruvver," said Ross. "Lucky, lucky, I should be so... all the time."

I opened the door – it was... unoccupied – *phew* – and the two coppers helped Ross into the gloriously empty, and very spacious, inside of the van. Ross crawled across and attempted to get into his sleeping bag.

"Night, night," we said and slammed shut the two doors: bang-bang, *bang!*

A moment later, Liam appeared from around the front of the van, walking nonchalantly.

"Hello," said Liam.

"Are you with this group, Sir?"

"We're the Three Musketeers," said Liam. "One for all and all for one."

"Really," said Spence. He moved away to talk to his colleague.

"You've talc on your nose," I whispered to Liam. He hadn't, but I wasn't going to let him get away with it that easily.

Liam turned away and desperately rubbed his face: "OK?" he asked.

I pointed surreptitiously at my nose: Liam looked blank and then the penny dropped. He quickly rubbed his nose again, repeating his actions when I shook my head slightly. I could have kept it up all night.

"Are you sober, Sir?" PC Spence asked me.

"I feel sober," I admitted.

"Could you put out your arms, close your eyes and touch your index fingers together, Sir."

"Well, I could, but–"

"If you'd just do as instructed, Sir."

"It is a little ridiculous, surely?"

I closed my eyes and held my arms out. It was exhilarating, like teetering on top of a tall building, and I felt myself sway in a non-existent breeze. I pointed my fingers outwards and then swung my arms forward and together, the two ends searching for each other like lost lovers... OK, I peeked, but even so, I missed completely.

"That wasn't very impressive, Sir," said PC Spence.

"No," I said, attempting to connect my fingers. Even close up, the docking manoeuvre was tricky, but, eventually, I tapped my index fingers together. "There!"

"Bill, get a thingummy!"

Bill strode over to their police car and got something from the passenger glove compartment. It was a breathalyser. He gave it to Spence, who opened the bag, took the white plastic tube out of the plastic wrapper and clicked it into the top of the device.

"Blow into this please, Sir, one continuous breath until I say stop."

"Look, this isn't necessary," I said.

"If you wouldn't mind, Sir."

I did, blowing and blooooowing and...

"All the way, keep going, keep going... and stop."

Thank goodness, it felt like I was going to pass out.

"One hundred and four," said Spence's colleague, Bill J-something, "that's three times the limit."

"Only three times?"

"Yes, so you can't drive, I'm afraid," said Spence. "Sir."

"I know. I told you it wasn't necessary. I've had loads. I knew that. I wasn't going to drive."

"What were you going to do, Sir?"

"Do?"

"How are you going to move your vehicle?"

"I was..." I trailed off as I hadn't thought that far ahead. I'd been taking things a round at a time. "How long does it take for a hundred and four to drop to..."

"Thirty-five micrograms per one hundred millilitres of breath," said PC Bill helpfully. PC 'Bill' – ha, *ha*... ha!

"Sir? Drink driving is not a laughing matter."

"Sorry. How long to drop to thirty-five micrograms per thing?"

"Give me your keys," said PC Spencer.

I looked at the keys and then at him, and back a few times: "OK," I said, finally.

We piled into the van. Spence adjusted the seat, Liam sat as far away from the policeman as he could, and I was in the middle. There was some awkwardness getting the seat belts clicked in and I tried to explain the van's bizarre quirks. You have to... but Spence started it first time and gave me an expression that somehow explained all about police driving training.

The engine purred under the bonnet in front and Ross moaned in the back as Spence pulled the van out of its parking space.

"Shall we put the flashing light on?" I suggested, and then Liam and I burst into guffaws.

"Er... hmm."

"Good point," I said, "it would be a trifle ostentatious."

The police car, driven by Bill, followed and a number of other vehicles joined our line. There was some headlight flashing as the convoy established itself.

"Where are you going?" Spence asked.

"London," I said.

"Yep, London," said Liam. "London, London, London."

We were going to London all right, fuelled by beer and good luck.

"What?" said Spence.

"Not tonight," I said. "We're walking."

"Oh good," said Spence. "Why all the vehicles then?"

"For the kit, targes, claymores, muskets and stuff."

"Oh right. You got ammunition for those muskets?"

"Dunno," I said. "I'm not in the Black Powder Brigade."

"The what?"

"The Black Powder Brigade: it's what we call the musketeers."

"Someone said you three were the Three Musketeers."

"We are," I said, "but we're the non-musket musketeers as opposed to the musket musketeers. It's a confusing term."

"And there are more of them," said Liam helpfully. "More, more, more."

"I did firearms training once," said Spence.

"Yeah?" I said.

"They gave us these German Heckler and Koch MP5s, fucking 800 rounds a minute, laser sights, the lot. Blew the crap out of the cardboard terrorists."

"Great!" said Liam.

"You still do it?"

"Absolutely not," Spence said glancing in the rear-view mirror, "it's very boring, your colleagues are all anoraks, and there's so much circuit training with the instructor shouting out questions about law, and occasionally it's terrifying with far too much opportunity to really screw up. See a shifty looking bloke, request permission, permission granted, and bang – suddenly you've been given some stupid codename and hauled before the courts. You?"

"What?"

"Ever fired one."

"*Nah*, fired a musket a few times with ball as well as powder – bloody inaccurate. You can actually see the ball zig-zagging to the target."

"You hit the target?"

"I hit one of the targets," I said, "just not sure if it was the one I was aiming at."

"And you?" said Spence, directing his question over me towards Liam.

"I'm Irish," said Liam.

"Here we are," said Spence.

The policeman indicated, and then pulled into the lay-by, bumping a rear wheel over the kerb as he misjudged the length of the van. It bounced back onto the flat with a gear grinding screech from the engine and an "Och, Fuck!" from the back.

Spence changed into first and inched us all the way along, past the emergency phone and right to the front. There were a few bursts of light as the van's mirrors reflected the headlights of the rest of the convoy as it pulled in behind us.

Only one vehicle came past, its police lights flashing.

"You aren't going to cause any trouble, are you?" Spence asked.

"Nah," I said. "Kip for me."

"No, no, no," said Liam.

"Right then, I'll be off. See you tomorrow." Spence unclicked his seatbelt, opened the van door and slipped down into the night. I saw his shadow pass in front of the red and blue light-bar.

A door slammed.

The police car wailed briefly and zoomed off.

"They've got a party to go to," said Liam. "Fun, fun, fun."

"They've got a party?!"

"Guy, Guy, Guy," Liam said taking me to one side. "What are the filth doing spying on us?"

"They're not spying on us."

"Yeah?"

"They're escorting us."

"Escorting, escorting, that's what they call it now, is it? I know all about escorts, but I don't see any tight dresses and expensive cocktails."

"What the hell were you snorting?!"

"A little pick me up."

"What?"

"You said we should break a law."

"I did not."

"On the way from Scotland."

"Not with Class-A drugs. I meant pot, marijuana, skunk and weed... not fucking cocaine!"

"I'm a banker."

"So?"

"It comes with the Beamer, the studio apartment and the lifestyle."

"Where's your flash car now?"

"I sold it."

"What for?"

"Coke."

"You're Irish, you're supposed to eat potatoes and drink hooch."

"I'm a banker."

"I can think of another word."

"The car, the apartment on the down as well, the lifestyle, all gone now."

"And the coke?"

"I've still got a few wraps left if you–"

"No, I do not!"

"Up to you."

"You'll get rid of 'em."

"I will not! Cost at least a monkey."

"My girlfriend's a police officer, our–"

"Och, ken yer no pipe down," came Ross's voice.

"Shut up, Ross," I said and turned back to Liam: "And our chauffeur was a police officer."

"They didn't see."

"By a fluke. You're out, Liam, out. We can't have drug addicts on this march. I can't... Mandy'll go mental."

"You can't chuck me out."

"Why not?"

"I need this."

"We can't have people with illegal drugs... look at all the police everywhere."

"No, I need this, this march, this rebellion, this! I lost my job and my flat and my car and I've only got three tabs. I have to get my life back on track. Everything's going arse-ways and I just need to succeed at something, you know, just to get my confidence back."

"That's it."

"Yes."

"Just that?"

"Yes," said Liam. He pushed his glasses back up his nose and his eyes appeared bigger, like some great soft kitten. "And futures to go up."

I smiled despite myself and he did too, knowing he'd won me over.

"And the rest of the crap goes."

"Couldn't I–"

I could feel the blood rising to my face and Liam saw my expression.

"I'll..." he indicated outside.

"Yes."

Liam lowered the passenger sun visor and a polyethene bag dropped into his lap. He stuffed it in his pocket of his denim jacket and left the van.

I fumed for a while, although it was out of the sheer embarrassment of it all more than anger. Seven or eight – or nine – pints and it was past midnight, and yet I felt sober and completely awake. The condensation on the windscreen smudged the red lights of the occasional passing car. A tiny trickle of water snaked down like a tear. I could feel the heat seeping out through the van's thin metal. I couldn't see Liam in either wing mirror.

What a dick, I thought.

The community way forward

by Jacqueline Fort
Political correspondent

The Home Secretary, Timothy Dorrington, has bet his own political future on the forthcoming crime figures. If he wins, the Government will have a stable future, at least until the next crisis; but, if one particular community doesn't want to work with him, then the proponents of more radical policies will see their stars rising. That community is his own backbenchers.

There was a time when Timothy Dorrington rarely answered a direct question, preferring to deliver a soundbite no matter how many times he was asked something. When pushed, he would sometimes definitively announce that he was considering alternatives. Now, he has firmly pegged his agenda to community issues: poverty, policing and, dare I say it, personalities. Not a day goes by without him pictured standing next to this ethnic minority spokesperson or that religious leader.

110

It is a policy that seems to be working. Particular communities are working together, if only to stand closer together, shoulder to shoulder, to have their group selfie taken. It is, without a doubt, a way forward, but is it the right way forward?

Fascist Times

So where does this leave his political opponents, both in his own party and in the opposition? the

> **We must work with communities to bring about social change**
>
> Timothy Dorrington, MP

Letters to *The Times* seem to be the chosen avenue. We've had Dennis Llewellyn requesting a zero tolerance policy in all marginal constituencies, John Trudie calling for the police to be properly equipped, probably with nuclear weapons, and Barking of Bournville pleading for smarter uniforms. This is what everyone wants, they say, but like the alleged quality of policewear, these are unfashionable views.

Dorrington's way forward seems steady and dependable as it slowly wins supporters. Do people, and for this read, the electorate, really want anything radical? As always some do and some don't. Despite what Llewellyn, Trudie and Barking suggest, if every marginal constituency is crammed with ruthless gun-toting fashion icons, I dare say that particular communities won't work with them either.

Crime may go down as well as up

This leads us inexorably to the forthcoming crime figures. If they are high or contain a surprise, say the mugging of old ladies by knife-wielding hoodies, then all this touchie-feelie community involvement may well take a back seat. It only takes one statistic to upset the apple cart. I think that would be a shame, and so do many others jostling to be in the frame of the next photo opportunity.

THE PROPAGANDA WAR

"Hang on, hang on," I said. "You agreed for me to appear on TV?"

It was a sunny day in the countryside. I was with the walking contingent. We weren't far from the next pub. Even though we were in the middle of nowhere, you could just hear a distant motorway din muffled by trees and hedges.

"Aye," said Ross.

"You agreed for me?"

"Aye, don't be such a wuss – it's only local TV."

"Yes, but you agreed for me?"

"Aye," Ross conceded. "No need to thank me."

As if echoing the alarms going off in my brain, a police car screeched to a halt, skidded and slewed across the country road. The two police officers jumped out and raced towards us.

"Hello there," said one.

"You lose!" said Ross.

"Excuse me, Sir."

"Och, we had a bet that you'd say, 'Hello, hello'."

"Did you now?" he said. "Are you the Jacobites?"

"Och, who else do ye~"

"Yes, we are," I said, "I'm Guy Wilson."

"Danny... and this is Tom," said PC Danny, shaking my hand.

The two policemen fell into step with the column, weirdly clean amongst the increasingly dirty tartan and red. They stood out, not just because of their yellow hi-viz, but because underneath they wore black and white. Our Jacobite look was all rustic and pastel shades.

"This is Ross and Liam," I said. "And Rabbie is... somewhere else."

"Hello," said PC Tom as he shook Ross's hand, and then he turned to Liam: "Hello."

I looked at Ross: "One out of two," I said to him.

"Half a pint each then," said Ross.

"We've spent ages finding you," said PC Danny. "Spence said you were at the Cross Keys."

"Och, did ye no ken we set off. It's ten o'clock."

"Struth, just don't tell the Super. We were supposed to be on duty at eight."

"Right."

"We're escorting your march."

"OK," I said. "What for exactly?"

"We don't know," said PC Tom. "We weren't really briefed, so we were hoping you'd tell us. We had the Op Order, but by the time we'd read the health and safety bumph, we'd forgotten the instructions. The Home Secretary wants to reduce it, keeps saying he will, but it just gets worse and worse. That's Home Secretaries for you. So, what are you up to?"

"We're just hiking," said Liam.

"Right you are, Sir," said PC Danny.

"We heard you were going south," said PC Tom.

"Yes, we are," I said.

"What route are you taking?" PC Danny this time. They were clearly taking it in turns.

"We thought, A508 and then... we're making it up as we go," I admitted.

"You're nowhere near the A508," said PC Tom.

"We aren't?"

"Och, there was a change of plan," Ross said.

"Was there?"

I looked to Liam with an exaggerated shrug: *well?*

He tilted his head in understanding and pushed his wire-framed glasses up his nose.

"Aye," said Ross. "I dinna want to tell ye yer jobs, but—"

"But?" said PC Danny.

"Shouldn't one of ye bring yon polis car?"

The whole group of us turned round and gazed back along the country road, hedgerow on one side and rolling hills on the other, and a police car parked incongruously in the middle.

"Shit!" PC Tom sprinted back.

"Matt and Bill are finishing up their paperwork," said PC Danny. "They'll be along when that's done."

"Too much red tape," I said.

"Too right."

"My... girlfriend says that."

"Really, what does she do?"

"She's a WPC."

"Oh right, well, the sooner Dorrington gets his reforms rolled out the better, the sooner he can do something about our terms and conditions. Imagine! A Home Secretary, who understandings policing."

"That's what she says."

"Well, she's right."

We walked onwards.

The English countryside, just off the main dual carriageways, is wonderful, full of hedges and patchwork fields, green and brown, with farmyards, birdsong and fine pubs.

I don't know quite when it happened. I think back and I recall feeling depressed, but I also remember a weight lifting off my shoulders. Maybe it was the fresh air and exercise. I don't think the clouds parted for the sun to shine down, a sudden spring develop in my step, my head hold itself higher or for me to whistle a merry tune, but life got better.

And as we rambled through the rural byways, some of us fell behind to enjoy the peacefulness; everything had a joy to it and I felt that nothing could disturb such serene tranquillity.

I texted Mandy: *'Mandy, how ru? Miss u, Guy'*.

"Och, here are the telly."

A woman was running towards us in trainers, but holding a pair of her high heels with what looked like a lavender quilt over her arm. She clutched a clipboard to her chest with her other hand.

"Which one of you is Guy Wilson?" she said.

"Him," said Ross.

"Er..." I hazarded.

"Heather," she said, her hand, and shoes, shooting out for the briefest of touches.

"G–"

"This way," she said, pulling me away as if I was a three-year-old. She seemed to have more arms than standard issue or a special ability to juggle more than one object: shoes, clipboard and my arm.

"Och, you'll be a star."

"Yes, give 'em hell," said Liam.

"And if you'd all go over to..." Heather checked her clipboard: "Rabbie."

Rabbie was corralling the army.

"Och, no."

"You'll be stars," I said over my shoulder as Heather dragged me over the road to meet the team.

The TV people looked designer smart, clothes that said they had money, but were casual too. The crew were easy to spot with their black waistcoats full of pockets and various toolkits clipped to their belts. The Presenter and Heather both wore huge quilted coats.

Everything had been set up to use a beautiful background of quaint country tavern complete with a rustic hanging sign and a bright, red telephone box. It looked very English even down to the eccentric-looking patrons sitting out on the veranda supping their beer and perusing gastropub menus. Goodness knows what they made of this fiasco, but they took turns to point at the sight we were making.

I became very conscious of the grime covering my body. My boots were filthy, a few days of hiking adding a layer or two, but that was to be expected. It was my shins that seemed disgusting, grey with streaked lines due to, let's be honest here, sweat. I could see the state of my legs sticking out from under my plaid, and I had a disturbing feeling that the rest of my body would be much the same. Perhaps not as Pollock-spattered with mud as my calves, but I needed a bath and my clothes needed a washing machine. I hadn't seen a mirror, or a comb, or soap, in ages. We were the Three Musketeers, the Jacobites, and we looked the part. The problem was, we probably smelt the part too.

"Yes," Rabbie was saying, "but we've come from that direction and we're going south."

"Yes, but that is a much better shot, the light, you understand," the Director explained patiently.

"Yes, it's the wrong direction."

"But our audience won't know that."

"But the sun is in the wrong direction, the light, you understand," said Rabbie, patiently.

"Is great, so if you could all go down there and start on my signal."

"But..." Rabbie shrugged and moved off to the army. He huddled up with Ross, Liam and Kate to explain.

"Dinna ye no ken it's the wrong direction," said Ross.

"Hi," said the TV man, his handshake quick and firm. He looked away as he said his name and when he turned back I managed to catch the end of his sentence: "...from Midlands Today."

I didn't recognize his face: we'd moved a local TV area. No, wait, I only knew the ones in Edinburgh, which was Reporting Scotland and we must have gone through Look North on the M6 days ago. This was Midlands Today.

It was a sign of progress.

Distantly, I heard someone say: "It's the wrong way" and then Ross's reply: "Och, will ye no get on with it."

I turned my attention back to the TV man. "Hello," I said.

"Your name?"

"Guy, Guy Wilson."

"Guy Wilson," said Heather.

"Guy Wilson," he said, carefully pronouncing a name that no-one ever gets wrong. "Sign this."

"What is it?"

"A release form."

"What's it for?"

"You can't go on television without signing it."

"What if I don't want to go on—"

"Everyone signs it."

I signed it.

"Excellent," she said, whipping the clipboard and pen away before I'd finished. "We're live in two."

"Fine," I said. "Hang on! I—"

"Shhh..." said the cameraman, somehow projecting this whisper into a command.

The wind dropped and you could hear birds chirping in the distance as everything waited, all eyes looking at the cameraman's raised hand.

Mentally, I was struggling with the expression 'we're live in two'. What exactly did that mean? Live was live and Midlands Today was seen by millions and live meant... *oh shit!*

"Don't swear," Heather hissed, under her breath. "Don't swear, don't swear, do not swear."

Don't treat me like a child, I thought.

"I never swear," said the Presenter as he shed his quilted coat like a snake. His smile came on, off, on and off again as if a switch was being thrown.

After she'd intercepted the coat on the way down, Heather began waving at Rabbie with the other.

He waved back, so she became frantic.

Rabbie's face gave an 'oh' in mock understanding and the army began marching, the wrong way for them, towards us in a manoeuvre designed to bring a seemingly endless stream of re-enactors passing behind me. (When I saw it much later on YouTube, I noted that every single one of them had waved as they'd gone past: eyes left, wave. Ross and Liam went past three times having obviously nipped round behind the camera.)

My mouth went dry.

The cameraman held up his hand: five fingers, "Five!", four fingers, "Four!", three fingers... *silence*, two fingers... and he pointed. As if his finger was a TV remote, the Presenter came to life.

"I'm here on the road to London with a rebellion. Yes, a rebellion! Re-enactors of the Jacobite era, the age of Bonnie Prince Charlie himself, are marching on London. I have with me Guy Wilson, the leader of this revolt... Guy."

"Hello," I strangled.

"So what are you doing?"

I'm doing a TV interview, I thought, but no, that won't do at all: "We're marching on London," I said.

"And may I ask why?"

"You may."

"So why?"

My mind went blank: why?

I was marching on London to see my girlfriend because our relationship was being 'tested', it was a rocky patch, or the end, or because I couldn't face an empty flat and my unfinished thesis. Sometimes you do something actively, and sometimes you're carried along by the tide of history. Or perhaps, simply because it was just something to do.

Everyone's eyes were on me, the pause stretching like a crash zoom.

My mouth opened and words came tumbling out.

"Bonnie Prince Charlie," I heard myself saying, "marched on London during the Jacobite Rebellion of 1745 and turned back at Derby. We've been re-enacting this event for many, many years, and this year we decided to make a change, to cross the bridge as it were, and march on London, just as the Jacobite Rebellion of 1745 had planned. We're not re-creating, we're creating what could have been."

"So today, you are marching on London for what reason?"

Bastard, for goodness sake, I thought, that was brilliant, err-less and um-less, and in complete grammatical sentences. The man wanted a soundbite for the evening show.

"Fate doesn't control you," I said. "We make our own history."

"Admirable," he turned back to the camera. "And, Gurpreet, you can catch them at various points along their route to see the historic displays and there's plenty of interest I can tell you."

Gurpreet, back in the studio, clearly said something to the interviewer, but she did so through his earpiece, so it was private, meant only for him and the millions of viewers at home.

The Presenter laughed: "And toss the caber."

As Gurpreet finished her comedy routine, the Presenter beamed a smile across the network and nodded.

"That's right," he said. "History."

Everyone froze, and then, an endless moment later, the cameraman said, "We're off!"

As if a Sergeant Major had yelled 'dismiss', all the film crew took out their mobile phones and began packing the gear away with their free hand.

We were left, comically not knowing what to do, as it all dematerialised.

"Is that it?" I asked.

"Yes," said the Presenter. "An absolute fuck-up."

"No swearing," Heather mouthed.

"We're off, we're f—"

"Shhh, shhh, what was wrong?" she asked, so quietly and with a glance towards the camera.

"They're going the wrong fucking way."

"Zach thought it better."

"Did he? What an arse. I'll get angry tweets."

We all watched the army, now marching back, and it looked just as picturesque as the northerly version.

"You fancy a pint?" I asked.

He thought, then: "Oh, why not? Jim, pint?"

The cameraman nodded.

Jim, Heather and famous Presenter, who told me his name again just as we were going through the pub door but I didn't catch it that time either, found a table and menu.

"Jim," said the Presenter, "you're driving the van, aren't you, and we're not insured, so perhaps best if you don't drink – health and safety. I'll have a G and T, Heather'll have the same and if you'd order us both the sausage and mash."

Jim simply went to the bar, followed by a plaintive "cider, half, and the salad," from Heather. Ross got our pints in, the tall amber castles surrounding the two tumblers and the sad looking orange juice.

"So," said Liam. "TV people, all designer labels, fast cars and gin."

"I'd say so," the Presenter replied.

"Do you have any... you know."

"No, he doesn't," I said.

"Have what?" the Presenter asked.

"Common sense," I said.

Beep beep: I fumbled for my mobile and looked at it, a text, from mandy-mob: *'g miss u2 luv m xxx'*.

Either she had a plan to see U2 in concert or things were suddenly and utterly, brilliantly wonderful.

"Where did you keep that?" Heather asked.

"I'm wearing shor—"

"Up his arse," said the famous Presenter.

"You didn't have that on during the interview?" asked Heather, horrified.

"Er... yes," I said, fiddling with my phone.

"Oh, Christ!"

"Heather, language," said the Presenter.

"What's your ringtone?" Heather asked, her hand over her mouth.

"Er... dum, dum, de-dum—"

"I Should Be So Lucky by Kylie Minogue," said Ross.

"No, it isn't!"

Heather looked pale, an expression made worse when two plates of sausage and mash arrived. The Presenter tucked in, while Heather seemed to be mentally converting the carbohydrates into a belt around her midriff. It was too much; she downed her gin and tonic.

I texted back: *'Mandy, can u claim back some overtime and we can meet. Guy'*.

"Have you told them?" Kate asked Ross.

"Told us what?" I asked.

"Nothing," said Ross.

"Tell them what you're doing over the Autumn half-term," Kate insisted.

"Half-term?" I said.

"You're a teacher?" the Presenter asked.

"Aye," said Ross.

"Teachers have it easy," said the Presenter.

"Och, we do not!"

"Twenty weeks' holiday – no, no, I know what you're going to say, but – thanks, luv, another – but you wouldn't last five minutes in news broadcasting, that's broadcasting. You deal with, what, twenty, thirty kids, tops, whereas we are responsible to two point one million members of the viewing public. We shape opinion. Two point one *million* in all demographics, including the important ones. Whereas you, what thirty kids over what, thirty-five years, tops, is– Jim, thirty times thirty-five?"

Jim's reply was instant: "One thousand and fif–"

"A thousand, a measly thousand."

Ross huffed up: "I've two classes at A-level and–"

"Two thousand then. Versus two point one million, that's... Jim?"

"A thousand times more," said Jim, again without looking up.

"Do you see? Media..." said the Presenter holding his hand high, before lowering it: "...and education. Thanks, love."

Heather put a new gin and tonic down complete with ice, lemon and an umbrella. Jim smirked.

"Och, I think you'll–"

"Och," said the Presenter, "I'm only messing with you."

Ross seethed, and pulled his arm away from Kate when she tried to calm him down.

"I'm not going to be in local news forever," the Presenter said. "My agent says that National TV, that's

London, have their eye on me. We were told from on high, all the way up to the Trust, that we weren't to report on left-wing protests, but suddenly they want this march covered. So, it'll be on the National News. That's a real break. If you want to achieve anything, you have to go to London. That's where BBC1, News 24, ITV, Sky and so on are, proper professional news rather than the local, amateur nonsense."

"I'm going for a slash," said Ross.

"What's important is your name and reputation. I've built that. And I fought a court case to keep this name, my name, my acting name. Just because some twerp in America has done a play in New York didn't give him the right to steal my name, my household name, loved in people's front rooms all through the region, the country and the world. Yes, the world. There are people in Australia, who log on in the middle of the night to watch my reports on the iPlayer."

I didn't hear the rest; he droned on as Kate nodded to me urgently. Her head tilted towards the gents.

"I... er..."

She pointed urgently, so I got up, downed the remainder of my pint and followed Ross.

The convenience wasn't as pristine as when we arrived, and I wasn't exactly happy with the idea of going in wearing just my socks. I realised that every time I reached a pub, I automatically took my boots off. As I considered going back for them, there was an almighty bang.

"Och, he's a complete wanker!"

Ross had his forehead against the mirror, which was still distorting from the head-butt. Why it didn't shatter into a thousand sharp shards, I don't know.

"Ross–"

"I'll teach him something about media and wipe that smug, supercilious grin off his twat face."

"Ross–"

"Scoop! Scotsman beats TV Presenter to a pulp."

"Ross, Ross!" I grabbed him, but slipped and the two of us came down in a complete heap on the slippery floor. He wrenched away from my grip: "You can't, you're a teacher, you'd be suspended."

Ross turned, his genuine anger directed at me: "Would he be suspended too?"

"Not the point!"

"It is."

"He'd only get more ratings," I said. "Don't give him the satisfaction."

"Och–"

"I'm right."

"He's right," said Liam standing beside the condom machine. I hadn't heard him come in, but Kate must have decided to double our forces.

"I dinna see you trying to stop me," said Ross.

"I'm holding myself in reserve," said Liam standing tall.

"Get down 'ere and help yer drunken friend like this idiot," said Ross.

Liam looked appalled.

"One for all, Liam," I said.

"It's covered in urine," said Liam, pointing half-heartedly as if the full extension of his index finger would contaminate him.

"Dinna be such a lassie."

Liam pushed his glasses back up his nose, and then carefully squatted down onto his haunches getting as low as possible without actually touching any of the tiles with anything other than the soles of his socks.

"Och, here we are sitting in piss."

"It's a low point," said Liam.

"I've got an idea," said Ross.

Beep beep: '*g got leave cu 2morrow ez to find u yr route on website luv m xxx*'.

Isn't life just the best?

Something smells in local TV

Tuesday, 24 June

The silly season started early (or is it late?), when a belated April Fool's joke surprised a local TV presenter, who remains unnamed despite shouting "Do you know who I am?" repeatedly. Allegedly, he discovered something unpleasant in his coat pocket and a mysterious liquid seeped out to stain his £1,500 designer suit.

RELATED ITEMS
- ▸ Today's top news headlines
- ▸ Jacqueline Fort's latest faux pas
- ▸ Rebellion moves further south tomorrow
- ▸ Police exercise announced for this week

According to eyewitnesses, he had been drinking during the afternoon, imbibing a large quantity of spirits, and, unfortunately, he took out his displeasure on a junior colleague by calling her a 'silly cow'. Adding insult to injury, the outside broadcast crew 'accidentally' drove off and left him stranded in the middle of the countryside.

This last incident was described by locals as 'just taking the mick', an expression based on 'taking the micturition', which literally means 'taking the....': well, you know what we mean.

"Do you know who I am?"

A BBC Spokesman declined to comment saying that the incident was subject to an internal enquiry.

Your views

Serves the overpaid, smarmy tosser right.
- jack, warwickshire

It's a terrible comment on the state of our society. Clearly, the education system is failing us and we need a return to basics. I blame the teachers.
- Tony, West London

Add your comment

ENCAMPMENTS

"So they come out, the three of them, with expressions like naughty schoolboys and each of them holding their socks like they were dead rats..."

"Yes, thank you, Kate," I said.

"All of them covered in water from head to toe," she said.

"We had a wash," said Liam.

"In the sink," said Ross.

"It was vile," said Kate.

"Funniest thing I've ever seen," I said.

"Och, Kate, you are in need of some Eddie Izzard DVDs," Ross added.

"Disgusting."

I'd had my fifteen minutes of fame, and it had attracted crowds. In every village, we had an audience, every campsite was packed and every footstep was echoed as others rallied to our cause. We stopped at one field to find our vehicles already parked in an orderly line. Beyond them, the place was packed with tents and two marquees.

Something was up: there were protestors!

A hand-made sign declared: 'Keep the gipsies out!'

"Are we gipsies?" Ross asked.

"I guess so," said Liam.

Then the clapping and cheering started: it didn't stop. Well-wishers blocked the road completely, but it wasn't until we reached the open gate to the field that we realised what was waiting for us.

Hundreds! The roar was incredible!

"For Bonnie Prince Charlie!!!"

We raised our hands to acknowledge it. There was no-one else, it was for us.

"Hip hip."

"Hurrah!"

"Hip hip."

"Hurrah!!"

"Hip hip."

"HURRAH!!!"

It was just mental.

Suddenly, people grabbed us and propelled us aloft. From my high vantage point, I could see a huge field completely packed with a folk festival in full swing. I was more concerned about desperately pushing my plaid down as we soared above in triumph.

Thankfully, they only carried us over the threshold and then brought us down to earth to shake hands and high five, and just how do you react to this sort of thing?

Clearly, we landed on another planet.

Three girls, dressed as nymphs, fluttered past casting flower petals to the wind. My expression must have had the same amazement plastered across it as Ross and Liam's.

After the day's walk, however, my first priority was relieving myself. There was a convenient hedge, but there were people on the far side, and then I saw a sight that almost made me forget my bursting bladder: a queue for three portaloos. I joined it, said "Hi" to the woman in front of me and signed three petitions before I'd shuffled to the front.

Inside, it reeked with a powerful aroma of fresh chemicals.

Strolling back, I took a wide, circular route through the community of tents, just to soak up the atmosphere. There were stalls selling fair trade goods, jewellery, woollen hats and mystic crystals. I could hear two or three different refrains competing in the air: guitar, violin and the inevitable bagpipes.

In the distance, there was a St John Ambulance and some bored-looking police. A little girl shot past me holding a red balloon, chased by an older brother and a mother's "don't go too far away".

At the van, I opened my arms in a gesture of complete incomprehension.

All the other Jacobites and Redcoats, who hadn't been enticed away, looked equally perplexed.

"Where did all this come from?" I asked.

"Och, it's..." Ross trailed off, lost for words. "Full of hippies."

"Did we order any of this?" Liam asked. "Is there a bill coming?"

"Well, I've not..." I continued, "and... er..."

They had all just turned up. I dare say that someone in authority, seeing the vast numbers traipsing towards them along the road, made sure there were police, perhaps they had contacted the St John Ambulance, but I doubt the Council, whichever one we were in, had rushed out to contact the local Incense Stick Retail Guild.

"What do we do?" I asked.

"There's a scrumpy stall," said Ross.

So, we all just went with the flow.

The drink was cloudy, strong and refreshing in a scary way. Once I got used to the shock, and the drink, I began to enjoy it. We'd started something wonderful: completely mad, but amazing; and the spontaneity made you believe that anything was possible. It was exactly how I imagined the Sixties must have been like.

"Hello, Guy."

"Hi... er...."

"Danny."

"Oh, the policeman," I said, finally recognizing the copper from the other day. He was out of uniform, wearing, of all things, a grey hoodie. "Are you undercover?"

"No, I'm off-duty."

"Or are you just saying that to throw me off the scent, because you are really closing in on some master criminals?"

"No, my shift finished."

"In that case, I'm not sure you want to go over the far side of the field."

"No, that's why I'm over here," he said. "Nothing until the shift starts tomorrow."

"Oh right," I said.

"It's only dope for smoking."

I nodded, finished my pint and said: "It's not like we're indoors, so it's not covered by the smoking ban."

"What?"

"Joke."

"Oh, right you are, Sir."

"So?"

"I thought I'd pop along and see how you were all doing, Sir."

"I thought you were off-duty."

"I am, S... oh, bollocks."

"I think you need a drink."

Apparently, Danny sold things on eBay so he could fund his astronomy hobby: he said he's just found a refractor and tripod for a third of its normal retail price, the 150 you understand, not the 120, fantastic for galaxies and good for planets too.

It became a wonderful clear night, and you could see the stars, the faint smudge of the Milky Way. Even I recognized Orion when we gazed up. He pointed others out: Pleiades or the Seven Sisters, Pisces, Cassiopeia and, turning back towards Derby, the Plough. It's all myth and legend, Danny pointed out.

Later in the evening, there was entertainment: fiddle playing, dancing in next field and stories. The songs were all about highwaymen, fiddlers and cunning foxes and by a large oak tree, a man wearing a wizard's hat held court by an open fire, storytelling: King Arthur, Jason and the Argonauts and the myths of the Sioux. The Wizard took a break to drink some mulled punch, so a thin stick of a woman took over with a tale of unrequited love.

I was entranced, not least because I didn't dare turn my head in case I caught Rabbie or Ross's eye. It really got to me, and I wasn't alone in that.

What more was there if not love and quests?

"Och, ken ye no switch that bloody thing off!"

"I was just texting Mandy."

"Rabbie'll confiscate it. Can ye no give it a rest?"

"I can't get a signal."

"Good."

The fire crackled, blackening marshmallows and sending sparks up into the clear sky. It was easy to follow them up and imagine them carrying on to become stars. The landscape had a timeless quality and it could have been any time in the past, a forgotten country, when things were simple and spiritual.

Ross was sitting staring into his cider.

"Ross," I said quietly, "what is it?"

"Och, I'm thinking of packing in the re-enactment lark."

I blinked: "What?"

"I've been thinking about it for a wee while now."

"You're not coming with us to London?"

"Och, no, I'll be finishing the march, I want to, but I think that, maybe, it'll be my swan-song."

"Why?" I said, flabbergasted, amazed, staggered – Ross of all people – I nearly spilt my scrumpy.

"Well, I've been doing something else."

"Something else?"

"Aye."

"What?"

What on earth was this all about? Ross had been a stalwart of the re-enactment crowd, a rock around which everything else revolved, the point man, the Greek hoplite who stood on the right, his shield protecting the man on his left and so turned a collection of soldiers into a unit, he was... this was strong stuff, I thought, swilling the golden liquid around in the plastic pint glass.

"Aye," said Ross, "Morris dancing."

"Morris dancing!?"

Blood rushed to Ross's cheeks: "'Tis an honourable tradition steeped in history."

"'Tis a lot of grown men jumping up and down and hitting each other with sticks."

"To the untrained eye, but there's meaning and symbolism."

"So is this."

"I was interested and Kate said they needed a Ragman–"

"Kate?"

"Och, I have a van and I'm quite used to moving stuff around."

"And Kate?"

"She said they needed someone, I've experience and a Ragman is just like our Quartermaster. We went to an Ale."

"And had a few."

"What?"

"Ales."

"Aye. They serve ales at an 'Ale'. It's a private party for Morris dancers. They're a bloke short in their set and needed a Ragman, that's all."

"And Kate suggested you?"

"Will ye no leave it alone."

"And Kate's in this too."

"Aye," he said gloomily. "I dinna ken what to say, 'cos I know this re-enacting is important to you."

"It's not a problem."

"Really? It's just that there's a team here."

Stick clattering and a jangle of bells heralded a performance as a clutch of men dressed in uniform rag waistcoats cajoled everyone to make room.

"Go on." I laughed: "So long as we can watch."

"Aye. That would be grand."

"But Morris dancing?"

"Why not?"

"Because, Ross, it's English."

"Och, I ken ye'd take the pish."

With the bonfire in the background, the Morris dancers weaved back and forth. Ross took such delight in explaining it all: there were ten in the team, four on each side, with a 'fool' weaving in and out, neither aiding nor abetting the dance, and a 'beast' moving around and frightening the children, who should have been in bed.

It was all very ancient, well before my period, the origins of the World Wars, and even the Jacobites. Indeed, Morris Men stretched back to the 15th century – arguably earlier. It tapped into something primaeval, mythical even, harking back to an age when humans had discovered fire and hunter-gatherers met other tribes to celebrate being human and alive. I knew what it was like to be on a quest, to be a hero striding over the hill and into the unknown land of the next valley: 'here be dragons'.

Perhaps fate does control us and history makes us.

I felt genuinely connected to the land and its aeons in a way that dusty books and web searches never allow. I was living it, I was part of it, I was carried aloft by it as a strand in the rich tapestry.

It could have been the cider. That was brewed in a traditional style since... but I was having trouble focusing on the sign by the stall.

"You know why this gathering is working, don't you?" Liam asked. "Why we're all connecting?"

"Because it draws us to our common cultural heritage," I said, "we're a step in the great story that starts in Africa before Homo Sapiens and goes on, into the future, when people will gather around a fake fire on Mars and–"

"No."

"No?"

"It's because there's no mobile phone connection here... see!"

I looked at his pointing finger for a moment trying to ascertain its meaning, and then, with some head swaying, I gazed across to a corner of the far field. There was, under-lit by the blueish glow of small LCD screens, a clutch of semi-human creatures, hunched over their glowing votive objects and texted away into the ether.

"Not a single Pokémon anywhere at all," Liam said.

A cry of glee snapped my attention back to the dance. Ross was swinging Kate around as if he was an industrial carousel steaming out of control and she was a bedecked and painted horse flying through the air, around and around. They glowed, reflecting the orange warmth of the fire and lit from within by exertion and enthusiasm. They were alive.

The crowd whooped and started clapping in time.

"Do you fancy a jig?" Liam asked.

"I think a jig is a dance for one person."

"Or two?"

I smiled: "Our dancing friend over there said it was one. And at such length too."

Liam raised his elbow and I threaded my hand through the opening. We spun, broke and rejoined describing a crazy figure of eight, our cider sloshing dangerously high in our plastic tankards.

Suddenly, I was away, caught in another orbit by a Redcoat, swung around and passed on like a space probe's slingshot with each close pass adding to my whirling speed. The Milky Way pitched and tossed, a celestial horizon to our voyage through time and space itself.

"Jesus," said Liam.

I paused, breathless at the edge of the happy maelstrom: "Yes?"

"My feet were in agony when we arrived," Liam started explaining, "and now I'm dancing, I can't feel them at all."

"That'll be the elixir."

"The what?"

I answered by making a drinking gesture with my hand.

"Right," said Liam. "Perhaps we should have one more, just in case."

"For medicinal purposes?"

"Of course."

"OK... one... two... three... Paper."

"Rock," said Liam.

"Paper wraps rock," I said, putting my hand around his fist and nodding to lament his loss.

"I won't be long," he said.

"I'll be..." I circled my finger and Liam went off in the wrong direction, corrected himself and then veered forth again.

I found a suitable place to sit, where the land rose sharply, bulging around the roots of an old ash tree, and faced the warmth of the bonfire. I felt strong, virile, with my muscles exercised and my heart pumping, the master of all I surveyed. I had started this, I had made all this possible and I liked that.

The fire roared and happy people clustered, the faces animated by the flickering light. Music and laughter assaulted my ears and I smelt the countryside, the grass, the heady mix of incense and marijuana.

Breathed in, breathed out: satisfied.

From the circling throng, a beautiful sight shimmied her dance towards me, skipping this way and that, closer and closer, beguiling. She wore a cotton dress, she had flowers in her hair and her lips were red. Finally, her teasing game complete, she fluttered in front of me like a butterfly.

"Hi," was all she said.

She tilted her head to one side, her eyes signalled come hither and then she smiled, a roaring gorgeous happy explosion of innocent pleasure.

"Hi," I said.

She joined me where I sat upon the grass.

"You're Guy Wilson," she said, and reached out ever so nonchalantly to put her hand on my bare thigh a crucial inch above the hem of my plaid. The hairs there stood on end, gradually rippling upwards. "Aren't you?"

Despite goodness knows how many drinks, my mouth went dry. She went misty like gauze over the lens in black-and-white movies when my breath condensed between us: no words came.

She leant forward, her hand rising up within my plaid: "I think what you are doing is so wonderful, you and the others, but especially you." She lowered her voice: "Especially you."

"And you are?" I managed.

"Yours..."

I swallowed hard.

"...if you want me..."

136

I did want her.

"We could go into the woods or a tent."

"We have a van."

"I don't mind a small bed."

"No, it's just a van, we've sleeping bags on the floor."

"I don't mind."

"I have..." I began, but Mandy wasn't here and there was no mobile phone connection. I was in a different world with different rules.

It was a magical time.

♦

Item five: get killed.

I wonder about my tick boxes.

In the cell, as I wait on Trudie's timetable, I count them off on the fingers of one hand: one, cross the bridge; two, lead a rebellion; three, lose the girl... get betrayed by love; four, get captured; and finally, five, get killed.

I could have slept with that girl, made love, experienced a little pleasure in my short life. Mandy wouldn't have known – hell, what difference would it have made? Perhaps, if I'd been led off the straight and narrow path, I wouldn't have ended up here.

I'm feeling sorry for myself, I know. My life has been fine, a privileged middle-class background, good school, University and then one glorious summer of excess before it's all cut short.

That's all I can complain about. Never mind the quality, I could say, regret the length.

Did I have a choice? Do you count to three, pull out paper only to discover that Fate has chosen scissors? Is it all astrologically written in the stars and readable with a 150 (not a 120) refractor?

"Ha!" I laugh aloud – Romeo and Juliet, star-crossed lovers. I did it at school. That was all fate and inevitability and destiny and a lot of seemingly random events that linked in a long chain from this decision to those deaths. The only difference for Mandy and I was that our route was parallel to the M1 motorway.

God, I'm living dramatic irony.

I lie back on the hard bed and stare upwards as if to see through the white ceiling to read the stars above. There's only an old lightbulb, yellow and unrevealing.

If I had known then what I know now, would I have done anything different?

Of course, stupid question – I'd have drunk up, got in the van and been driven back to Edinburgh, but it all went south. But you only have the information you have, you can only choose between the options, paper, rock or scissors, before you know what Fate will decide.

But I couldn't, even now, even knowing what I know now, I couldn't, because that would have been a betrayal. Not a betrayal of Mandy, although that too, but a betrayal of myself. It was a test to see if I was worthy. It's not winning the Holy Grail that counts, it's the test. You pass, you don't pass; I'm English, it's how you play the game that counts.

Is that something I could take from all this maudlin reminiscing: that I won despite the actual result, because I stayed true to a cause? I'm a knight, so I get a stone statue of myself to sleep upon my tomb.

But there will be hundreds of deaths on my conscience, so it's just fiddling with definitions.

♦

So, back then in the field, I said: "I'm taken," to the maiden with the promise in her eyes.

"Oh."

And the girl in the cotton dress with flowers in her hair was disappointed, her lovely expression marred by my callous refusal, a woman scorned they say, but it was only for a fleeting moment.

"That's good," she said, "I'm happy for you."

And then she was away with a skip. Her hand would feel other men and someone else would part her thighs.

"What are you smiling about?"

I turned and found Liam standing next to me holding two drinks: he passed me one, and I sipped the fermented apple. Forbidden fruit, I realised, and an image of the Garden of Eden flickered through my mind.

"That was unconditional sex," I said. "The summer of free love and..."

"And?" said Liam, two fires burning, one in each lens of his wire-framed glasses.

"And I turned her down," I said indicating with both a nod and a gesture with my plastic glass. She'd gone now, her promise passed to another.

"Good for you."

I felt pleased with myself, honourable. I had faced temptation and, like a true Knight of the Round Table, I had come through chaste and intact, I had saved myself for my lady love. Although to be honest the cider would have prevented me anyway, it was still right and moral. In fact, I had been saved from both faithlessness and embarrassing incompetence, so silver linings and all that.

Back at the parking area, the van was pitching gently like a tied up rowboat.

"I've drunk too much," I said.

"Nope, it's definitely moving," said Liam.

"I'm drunk."

"No, see the land swaying?"

"Yes."

"Not the same sway as the van."

"Oh yes."

"The swaying of the land is due to your breathing."

"Not the drink?"

"Nope, just your breathing."

"If you say so."

"And the van is going at a slightly... much faster rate."

"I wonder why," I said.

"Yes... yes... yes," said the van in a female voice.

Liam and I consulted each other's faces as if somewhere amongst the out-of-focus collection of eyes, nose and mouth there would be an explanation. Luckily, the van still had something to say.

"Oh god, yes," it said, and then, "Ross! Ross!"

Liam and I looked at each other and I raised my finger to make a point. We stared at it and then burst out laughing.

"Shhh," we both went, insisting on silence from each other, but it was impossible not to giggle foolishly like schoolboys.

"All that morality and you couldn't have done it anyway," said Liam. "The honeymoon suite's taken."

"Oh, I don't know," I said. "It's a big van."

It was, at that moment, the funniest thing we'd both ever heard.

"Holy cow!"

I stretched my arms out trying to hold onto the air to steady myself. Burning light streamed through the van's windows, searing the floor like ultraviolet laser beams searching for vampires. I was in the van – somehow – and it was the next day.

"Morning – oh shit."

How had I got in the van to sleep?

What had happened to the night?

And I was seriously unwell, I thought. I needed to stay very, very still and then perhaps, against all the odds, I might actually get away with it. All I needed to do was lie completely motionless, drink half a dozen pints of water and take a long piss: three things all at once and I'd be fine.

"Och," said a thunderous voice. "Where does the expression 'pissed as a newt' come from?"

"There was a type of Victorian mourner, who were silent," I said. My mouth tasted vile. "They were known as 'mutes' and they used to have a drink at every funeral to be polite. Hence 'as pissed as a mute'." I held up my hand to fend off a reply. "The operative word is 'silent' as in 'please don't speak' – ever."

"Here you go," said Kate as she handed Ross a plate. She looked in the back of the van where Liam and I were suffering and beamed the grin that only people who have had sex can manage.

"Thanks, love," said Ross and he tucked into his full English, dunking his sausage into his runny egg. All that grease! I felt sick.

"Jesus," said Liam. "How can you eat that and where did you get it?"

"There's a tent," Kate replied, "just follow the cooking smell."

"Great!"

Spasms of pain racked my body as Liam clambered out of the echoing metal van and then – oh god – he slammed the door.

"Does it hurt, Guy?" Kate asked.

"Yes," I said. "I just want to die."

That wasn't to happen then, though, was it?

♦

As I lie here now, I feel dead already, but I survived that morning, I survived until now and I'm not dead yet, but I will be. There were still items three and four, betrayal and capture, to come before I reach item five: being killed, and then finally I'll get to tick that box too.

But it did hurt, really hurt, and, bloody hell, the evening before must have been good.

Metropolitan POLICE: *Working together for a safer London*

Introduction

The Metropolitan police is London's biggest employer, with over 31,000 Police officers, but there's a lot more to the Met than Police officers. For more information on the diverse range of careers available within the Met, see below.

Pick your career: Police Officer

Policing is a unique job with unique demands, particularly in a city as incomparable as London. It's not easy, but it is rewarding – packed full of new and interesting experiences – and the key to making our capital city the world's safest.

More info

Rules of Engagement

Back in the days of *Dixon of Dock Green*, the police wore smart uniforms with polished buttons and shoes you could see your face in. A uniform you could trust. Today, they wear black paramilitary, pseudo-combat gear and trainers; nothing is standard, no two police next to each other the same. It's not 'uniform'. Both eras make a statement.

It all changed when television news developed exciting credits, thriller music and pop video graphics. Every disaster, every catastrophe and every calamity had to have its own animated logo. So information took second place to entertainment, usefulness was replaced by style, reporting compromised for ratings, and modern life was cranked up a gear or three. No longer was journalism about research and references; there were papers to shift, deadlines to meet, ads to sell and demographics to appease. So was born that great expression about a news story: 'Too good to check'.

If the Credit Crunch (cue giant red arrow plunging into the ground) was caused by a herd mentality of panicking idiots; then clearly alarmist headlines, with statistically dodgy facts, delivered in doom-laden tones between clanging bells was going to make things worse.

Local news is just repackaged from the agency wire, soundbites are extracted from in-depth analysis until even Osama Bin Laden's death is a tragedy.

Then came post-truth politics.

So, someone dressed to kill with weapons, no matter how non-lethal, dangling from their bat-belts isn't the type to tell you the time or give you directions. When the door is smashed in and black figures burst into your home, fear makes people stupid. "It's a fair cop" becomes swearing terror and resisting arrest. The "Have you got the correct address, officer" becomes a spur of the moment challenge to shoot-to-kill SWAT teams.

Of course, it wasn't all decent coppers and a fair society back in the days when the boys from *The Blue Lamp* stood up against the tide of a new breed of young criminal, all the more dangerous for their immaturity, as the film puts it.

There was corruption and institutionalised racism, but in stepping on the bad apples, we've lost the decency. The old look was important, and still should be, but it's been replaced with another image in a world where image is everything.

It's a question of trust. If you treat people well, then they tend to act well. If they don't play by the rules of a civilised, liberal society, then it's back to the station and out with the full weight of fascist force – fair enough.

The trick is to scale up the response, appropriate escalation, rather than firing your intercontinental nuclear missiles at the first hint of an angry look.

In America, the cops have to take out their firearms when they stop a vehicle with a broken taillight because the whole country shoots first and asks questions only later in court.

We Jacobites put on our plaid and our sporrans with our claymores strapped to our belts, and so we behave in a certain way, and we are treated in a certain way by the public. The costume makes the actor.

Therefore, the police should not look scruffier than the stylish, bling-ridden hoodies.

That's what I think.

As the right-wing ridicule the left and the benefits of the needy are cut to increase the bonuses of the greedy, then the thin blue line becomes a thick black line.

Beep beep: *'g all leave cancelled sorry luv m xxx'.*

Bloody police.

"Och, what's the matter?"

"It's Mandy," I told Ross. "We were going to meet today, but they've cancelled all leave."

"Why?"

"Give me a chance," I said, thumbing a reply: *'Mandy why? Guy'.*

"Och, it'll take ages for a rep–"

Beep beep: *'g some emergency up north luv m xxx'.*

"Go on then, why?" he asked again as I read the text off the screen.

"Dunno, some emergency up north."

Ross glanced behind us: "We're south... wonder what it is?"

I tried ringing but there was no answer, so I sent her another text: *'Mandy, ring me if you can. Guy'.*

We walked in silence for a while, the steady rhythm of marching now second nature. We were travelling along a wide pavement made from a patchwork of tarmacs as if giant slugs had left trails to lay the gas and electricity.

"Ye canna meet her today anyway," said Ross.

"Why not?"

"'Cos you have to complete your quest, face impossible odds, and then, when you get to London, only then win the wee lassie."

"I'd rather meet her today, book a hotel room, have a hot bath and then–"

"I ken ye would."

"And then, when I'd woken up, have sex."

"Och, it's–"

"Anyway, you can talk, Mister Van Shaker–"

"OK, OK. Will ye no settle for a pint," said Ross. "There's a pub in yon village."

"Sure," I replied. "I could do with something to make up for–"

My phone rang: it was mandy-mob.

I answered: "Hello."

"Guy, are you all right?"

Her voice was tinny, distorted and wonderful; I put my finger in my other ear to hear better.

"I'm fine," I said. "Lovely to hear you. Are you all right?"

"Where are you?"

"Heading south," I said. "And you?"

"I'm not sure, north somewhere."

"What?"

"North somewhere. Why are you heading south?"

"I'm coming to London, I'm coming to you."

"You're coming to London!"

"You said I never do anything, well, now I'm doing something."

"That's insane."

There was a laugh in her voice. She wasn't completely heartless then. No, of course not, she was torn between me and career, and logically I could complete my thesis anywhere. I might even be able to claim a few things, London research libraries, museums and so forth. You know, it actually made some sort of sense. Except all my notes were in Edinburgh, but I could sort something out. Or did it mean that I'd decided to be one of those students who never finish their thesis?

"We've crossed in the night," I said.

"Yes."

146

"You should see this," I said looking round at the red, tartan and tie-dye. "It's great. There are so many people. I've no idea where they've all come from."

"I'd love to," she said, *"but I can't. All leave was cancelled."*

"It's a bloody shame. Honestly, you'd love this. It's great. I wanted to see you."

"Well, perhaps soon."

"Why was your leave cancelled?"

"We're... it's nothing. Dorrington, the Home Secretary had to do something after getting a pasting in the Commons."

"Oh, political?"

"It might not come to anything," she said, but, even over the bad connection, I could hear a catch in her voice. She was ringing because she wanted to hear my voice – something was wrong – and I wanted to do more than just cradle a plastic object. I held the phone closer.

"Can you talk?" I asked.

"Yeah, sure. There are others, but they won't mind."

"You can talk dirty if you want, Mand," said a gruff voice in her background.

"Where are you?" I asked.

"We're in a police van, you know, the big mini-bus ones with the metal grill over the front and the roo bars."

"I don't think they are for kangaroos," I said.

"I know."

There was a silence.

"You be careful," I said.

"I'll be fine," she said. *"There are loads of us."*

"I worry that's all."

"Don't be silly, we're all trained for this – OK, OK, one minute – Look, whatever it is, it'll be kicking off any moment. Just, Guy please, tell me what are you doing?"

"Me?" I said.

"Yes, tell me what you are doing."

Knowing it wasn't the content that was important and that she just wanted to hear my voice, I said: "Well, I'm in charge."

"In charge of what?"

In front of me, people were skipping along, the sun was shining and the birds were singing. It was a beautiful summer's day, the sort that you can only get in England in a quaint village with its old church, traditional Post Office and its red telephone box guarding the cricket ground. It seemed that everything was right with the world.

"It's the re-enactors. We're just in a sort of procession, you know. We crossed the bridge at Swarkestone, instead of going back to Scotland. It's fun though and we've loads of extra people, hippies Ross calls them, with violins and drums and storytelling in the evening and cider and scrumpy and..."

I was rambling, but it didn't matter.

"That sounds fun," she said. *"Wish I was there."*

"I wish you were here."

There were other sounds in the background turned up loud by Mandy's silence.

"What's the matter?" I asked. I knew Mandy well enough to know she was really worried and I needed to know.

"We're..." her voice lowered. I instinctively pushed my finger further into my left ear and the phone harder against my right, *"...here for a riot."*

"Riot?"

"Yes, some trouble, political," she said. *"They bussed us all up here, no idea where, as back-up. It's all very rushed, no helicopters yet or negotiators. We weren't going to be deployed. No-one's said, but they are getting out the riot shields and... there are ambulances on standby. That's not a good sign. It's going to be rough."*

"Mandy?"

I didn't know what to say. Here I was idling my summer away on some glorious joy ride and my girlfriend was facing who knows what. I'd not seen the news or read a paper for days. I should be by her side, I thought. I mean, I know I'm not trained and I'd be a complete liability, but I genuinely wanted to be there: duty, love, I don't know.

"Mandy, I... there's something I want to tell you, ask you... it's–"

"*We're going!*"

I could hear the resonant banging of boots against metal, a kind of mad claustrophobic percussion of drummers trapped inside a steel can, and then running on tarmac. There were shouts, garbled over the phone, but intense, clipped and military. A short steady barrage of crashes, louder and then–

"*Guy. I. Bye.*"

"Mandy... Mandy... Mandy."

The phone was quiet: call length 4:53.

Jesus!

Jacobites and Redcoats laughed and smiled, happy to be part of these festivities that wound through the cobbled streets.

Whereas my girlfriend was... *oh god.*

There was a little girl, five or six, standing underneath a big oak tree, the dappled light playing across her face as the wind moved the branches. She waved and smiled, shyly, gripping her mother's hand and holding a red balloon.

"This is unreal."

"What's unreal," said Liam.

"It was Mandy, on the phone, and..."

"And?"

We reached the corner, my feet leaden beneath me. I was leading, or following, the procession on auto-pilot. I could feel my brain shutting down. Shock! Was this shock? I felt an icy sensation prickling along my arms and, despite the hot weather, I felt cold.

"Come on, Guy," Liam was saying, "round this bend there's bound to be a good old English pub with real ale and pie and chips. You can tell me all about it."

We rounded the corner and collided with the front of the procession.

They'd stopped, suddenly.

Now what, I wondered, as we lurched to a halt in front of a line of riot police, five deep, dressed in black paramilitary uniforms and all holding round transparent shields. I remember realising that the birds weren't singing.

"Oh feck," said Liam, summing it up for us all.

I was still holding my phone.

"I think I'm in charge of the riot," I said into it, finishing a conversation that had already ended.

♦

I know that people are going to die in a riot. I know it for a fact, but there's nothing I can do. I'm in a cell, remember, and soon, before long, they'll come and take me somewhere and I'll be dead. A final loose end tugged and teased, and then finally cut off.

♦

For a long while, there was a strange Mexican standoff: an ordered troop of riot police facing an unruly, disordered mob of marchers. In between, there was a wide expanse of no man's land and at either end, the combatants squared up. Our side inched forward by the pressure of new arrivals as they turned the corner oblivious, squashed against those trying to stay still, the whole mangled mess forcing our front forward, inch by inch.

The police stood firm, a solid black wall erected across the leafy by-road.

150

Ting!

A bell sounded and a woman, a pensioner, emerged from a tea shop. She fussed with her bags, ambled to the pedestrian lights and pressed the button. She waited, we all waited: there was no traffic, blocked one way by our carnival and in the other direction by ranks of police, blockades and armoured vehicles. Presently, the lights changed: amber, red and then the crossing man appeared with an incessant beeping. Mesmerised, both sides watched as the old woman crossed, so slowly that the green man was flashing by the time she reached the other side, and then she ambled towards us only to disappear into the Post Office.

The spell was broken. Grim faces turned back towards each other.

"THIS IS AN ILLEGAL ASSEMBLY!"

The statement came from some unseen policeman with a loud hailer hidden behind the line.

A shoal of whispers rippled through our numbers: "Illegal?", "What?", "Stop pushing".

PC Spencer, tucked into our ranks, tried pushing to the front of our lines: "Illegal... what's going on?" He and PC Danny could make no progress through the scrum. I remembered that Culloden had had English troops on both sides.

"DISPERSE NOW!"

Crowds have a life, mobs move as if they are creatures, the whole more than the sum of its individuals. Ours shuffled at the front, turning itself inside out as some people retreated, and others, driven by curiosity or who knows what, went forward. The colours were bizarre, the different waves of movement coded by their outfits: white moved back, tartan moved forward, and one clutch of red huddled. I tried to decode it, my thoughts grasping irrelevances because I couldn't quite believe what was going on. The camp followers, women who dressed in white blouses and long skirts, moved back. The lads of the Jacobite cause moved forward and the Redcoats were–

Fuck!

There's a sudden moment when you 'get it' like a joke that takes a while.

"Rabbie, Rabbie... for God's sake no!" I yelled, pushing against the tide, my desperation propelling me through the treacle of bodies. I was alone, a single man in a multitude trying to stop a catastrophe. I know it's not a true metaphor, but I was the lone lemming with his paw in the air saying, 'Excuse me, but'.

I could see the Redcoats slipping between the Jacobites. A red edge formed faster than I could believe.

I heard Rabbie's clipped delivery: "Present!"

The Redcoats raised their muskets.

The word "shit" was uttered from at least three different places on the police line.

"Wait for it," Rabbie said. For goodness sake, this is ridiculous: the police meant business. This wasn't a re-enactment: this was history in the making. I struggled forward, but the tide of bodies was against me.

"Stop, stop, stop," I shouted, but it came out as a single, squeezed syllable of shrieking.

Rabbie raised his arm, brought it down: "Fire!"

Slow motion, I swear it, everything went into slow motion. The hammers leaping forward, the flints striking the frizzen plates, the spark (and that's all it takes) touching the priming powder, the flaring in the flash pan, the barrel jerking against the soldiers' shoulders and the smoky discharge exploding forwards.

Boom!!!

Everything rushed to real time again.

The smoke began to clear.

The Redcoats started laughing.

A word floated clearly across no man's land: "Blanks!", but the police clearly did not see the funny side.

"One!" came an order from somewhere, a policeman with white epaulettes.

The police line stepped forward, their batons crashing against their shields, and I was struck at how ancient the scene appeared. Except the shields and clubs were up against unloaded muskets. How many thousands of times had humans performed this bloody ritual? But our weapons were all pretend, the edges of our swords deliberately blunt; everything we did was pretend, none of it was real. I tried to push it all aside, to make it stop, to fix everything and suddenly—

I shouted: "Stop, stop—"

The front of our lines tried backing away, and my pushing forward built up such a pressure that I popped out like a cork from a bottle. My momentum carried me another five or six paces and I stopped metaphorically, and literally, between the two sides.

It was very quiet standing alone in no man's land.

"Er..." I felt a bit silly to be honest.

"For Christ's sake, do something," Liam cried out.

I took a few more steps and measured up to the opposing line. It was amazing how little I could see of their faces through their riot helmets. They could be machines for all I knew, for there was nothing human: no eyes, no mouth, nothing.

I took a deep breath and raised my finger as if to make an academic point.

In ancient times, a hero would step forth and face a champion from the opposing army in single combat. It was something to pass the time before the eventual massacre, I suppose. History is a list of battles, just places and dates: Culloden, 1746; Hastings, 1066; Nowheresville, 11:23.

"Er... is..." I coughed, my throat was dry.

God, I fancied a drink and there in front of me was the pub, a Red Lion sign hanging down invitingly. It was one of those wonderful old-fashioned places that would have oak beams in the ceiling, horse brasses on the walls and strangely named ales on tap. The seats would be leather, comfortable, and a log fire would burn in the hearth. There it was, sanctuary, a mere twenty paces away, but protected by a million riot police.

I tried again: "Er..."

"WHAT?" squawked the loudspeaker, a Dalek voice for the Terminators.

"Is Mandy there?"

"Pardon?" No idea which copper spoke.

"Is WPC Amanda Reynolds there?"

Finally, the faceless machines reacted, each turning to the other and some strange Chinese whispers began:–

"Who?"

"Amanda Reynolds, he said."

"Mandy."

"Mandy?"

"Mandy Reynolds."

"She's not here."

"Mandy?"

"She was with us."

"With who?"

"Are you Mandy?"

"No."

"Where is she?"

"Who are you then?"

"Here, she is."

"Go on, Mand."

"Mand."

"Go on."

The mass of faceless robots suddenly ejected one of its number. Perhaps it was Mandy, perhaps it was their champion ready for single combat, but it was an 'it' for

154

it was impossible to tell whether the figure was male or female beneath all that body armour. It came forward and took off its helmet. She looked gorgeous, a flawless face. She looked like the statue of a Greek goddess, where the sculptor had perfected the face but left the body roughly hewn in bulky outline.

"Mandy. Hi."

"Guy, for God's sake, I'm on duty!" she hissed.

We walked towards each other, closing the narrow gap, and I raised my arm to put it around her shoulder to guide her to somewhere more private. It was ludicrous, we were surrounded on all sides, but even so, we took a few steps away from the centre.

"Er... how are you?"

"I'm fine," said Mandy. "And you?"

"Not bad."

I could hear the leaves rustling in the trees, the breathing of expectation from the two sides, and I was aware of just how surreal it all was. This must have been what that football match on Christmas Day during the First World War, when the two sides climbed out of their trenches and had a kick-about for fun, had been like. If only all wars could be sorted by a footie match. Perhaps I should've suggested it? I'm sure someone would have something we could use, plaids and stab vests for goalposts. I was wearing Manchester United shorts.

Mandy was staring at me: "Guy.... Guy... what are you doing?"

"I'm... oh, well..."

"This is a riot. You shouldn't be here. You could get hurt."

"Yes, well, so could you."

"I'm wearing body armour."

"Yes, of course, sorry."

"What are you doing?" she insisted.

"Oh, well, I'm sort of leading a riot... and you?"

"I'm preventing a riot."

"Yes, of course. Er... silly question, but why?"

"Keeping the peace... my job!"

"Sorry."

"Please don't mess this up, Guy. It's still early days and I want to make a good impression. The Chief will be watching." She looked behind her at the black-clad anonymous mass. "And the Sarge."

"I won't keep you," I said. "I just wanted to ask you something."

"OK."

"And then we can get back to... er... whatever."

"Yes."

"It's just... will you... you know..."

Ross shouted from behind me: "Guy, for fuck's sake, ken yer no do it properly."

I looked to the Jacobite side and recognized faces urging me on.

OK, I thought, OK.

I stepped back and dropped to one knee: "Mandy, will you marry me?"

If I'd imagined hearing the rustling breeze in the trees before, I definitely heard it now along with an intake of breath all around. Mandy went pale, her jaw didn't exactly drop, but her mouth opened and stayed open, and her hand, hidden in a thick protective glove hovered in front of her expression. Everything stopped as if someone had pressed 'pause' and gone to the kitchen to make a cup of tea. It couldn't last, the strain of waiting began to tell on both sides and there was a sudden flurry of phrases.

"Mand, make 'im beg," is the one I remember, followed by another "Quiet!"

Mandy closed her mouth, her head jerked slightly: was that a nod or a shake?

"Ga," she managed, the power of speech having left her.

"Mandy, will you–"

"Yes."

"Yes?"

"Yes, I will."

Everything roared, the Jacobites, the riot police, the blood pumping past my own ears. Mandy bent over and kissed me, a cool, sensual experience that focused me in the present. This was a moment I want to remember, to savour, and I knew it at the time. Nothing could beat that kiss, and then she moved away and smiled, topping every experience I'd ever had in my life.

And then all the buggers on both sides rushed forward to congratulate us with slaps on the back and friendly punches to the shoulder. They bloody hurt. I managed to stagger to my feet before the buffeting had subsided. People started congratulating each other. Grown men gave each other tearful hugs. It was just bonkers. I held on to Mandy for dear life, assuming she was somewhere under all that padded protection gear.

"This calls for a drink," said Liam nearby.

"We're on duty," said... possibly Spence.

"Och, can ye no make an exception."

"Well, the riot's over, so I guess, why not? You paying?"

"Now, see here, I'm a poor peasant rising up against the man, whereas you've taken the King's shilling."

"Pint of bitter do you?"

"Aye."

Mandy and I pushed our way through the crowds and found a park bench under a massive oak tree. Various Jacobites took time out from walking to the pub to give me the thumbs up or some lewd gesture.

"Are you serious?" said Mandy.

"Yes."

"But what about Edinburgh?"

"I'm going to London," I said, indicating the marchers, who were filing haphazardly into the pub opposite. "To be with you. I want us to be together. I really want us to get engaged."

"But your thesis? Your supervisor?"

"Details, hurdles to overcome, who cares? I love you."

"I love you."

We hugged again, my hands just reaching around her armoured torso, and then, despite that uniform, we walked hand-in-hand to the pub.

When we went inside, the applause was amazing: we bowed, we waved, we turned bright red.

"A drink for the happy couple!" said Rabbie, but he was unheard.

"Be quiet!" Liam yelled.

"What'll ye be wanting?" Ross asked.

"Pint of... oh, Black Sheep and..." I looked at Mandy.

"Lemonade."

"Lemonade?"

"I'm on duty."

"But we should celebrate."

"With lime then."

I smiled, she was funny, gorgeous and mine. "Mandy, I—"

"Reynolds?" It was a deep voice behind my left shoulder. I didn't know him, but I saw Mandy jump in recognition.

"Sir!"

I didn't know his rank, but he was the only policeman I'd seen who wasn't in riot gear. Instead, he was in a traditional, smart uniform with a variety of symbols stitched onto his shoulder epaulettes. I took a shuffled step backwards separating myself from my snapped-to-attention fiancée.

"At ease, Reynolds."

"Sir!"

Drilling to perfection, Mandy changed posture, but even 'at ease' she was standing rigidly, her bottom clenched in a distracting way.

"May I say, remarkable," the officer said. No, they were all police officers; Mandy was a police officer, so I guess he was an Inspector, or a Superintendent, or a Mega-overlord. "I'm very pleased."

"Sir, thank you, Sir!"

"Less than a week with the Met, and already you've defused a very dangerous situation."

"Sir!"

"Clever thinking – just the initiative we're looking for in the modern police force."

"Sir, thank you, Sir."

"An imaginative solution," he said. "I'm not sure we want our women police constables using their feminine wiles on unsuspecting troublemakers – if I'm allowed to say that – especially when said WPCs are in uniform."

"Sir, the job of the police is to protect the public," she said, "and so long as we do that, it's not important how we do it, Sir. The end surely justifies the means."

"Perhaps."

"The public are safe, Sir."

"Yes, they are. As I said, inspired. Well done."

"Sir, thank you, Sir!"

He turned to me: "And you would be?"

Mandy answered: "Sir, Guy Wilson, Sir."

"Superintendent McGivern," he said. He shook my hand. "Do you know anything of history, Wilson?"

"A little," I said.

"See that!" he pointed over towards Ross and Kate, or the table with all the condiments on, or the ladies, or... and finally I saw a painting.

"Battle of Waterloo," I said.

"That's the ticket."

He looked for a moment across the crowd to gaze upon a particularly bloody picture of the Battle of Waterloo. It was faded, brown with age and probably ancient cigarette smoke from a bygone era, but the horses cascading down upon red-coated soldiers were easily recognizable.

"The defeat of Napoleon," I said, wondering where this was going.

"Quite," said McGivern. "English soldiers firing in ranks on the enemy. Imagine that, Reynolds."

"Sir?" said Mandy.

"The Duke of Wellington's great victory over the French. Reynolds, Wellington was Prime Minister, you know."

"I didn't know, Sir."

"1828 and 1834," I said. "I think, until Robert Peel took over."

"You are informed... the Iron Duke had a nightmare: English soldiers firing on English civilians on English streets."

"I understand."

"So, the Duke of Wellington asked Robert Peel to form an unarmed force to police the peace," the Superintendent said. "It was Sir Robert Peel, who invented the police, the 'Bobbies' and the 'Peelers'."

"You couldn't really call 'em 'Wellies', could you?" I said.

"Quite," he said. "And now this John Trudie wants to arm the police. It's a contradiction in terms: armed *unarmed* keepers of the peace. I mean, it'll be like America soon."

As if on cue, a wailing police siren screamed past outside.

McGivern reacted to it: "Yes," he said. "More like America every day. Whatever happened to *Dixon of Dock Green*, 'evening all', 'it's a fair cop' and those ringing bells on panda cars? Eh, Reynolds?"

160

"Sir, before my time, Sir," said Mandy.

"Before mine too," McGivern admitted. "Reynolds, I think we need someone with your talents in the Home Secretary's office. I'll assign you. Congratulations."

"Sir, thank you, Sir."

"You see, Reynolds, I need someone with some imagination to keep an eye on the Right Honourable gentleman."

"I see, Sir."

"Between you and me, Dorrington's a bit of a fool. How can we do our reports, if he removes all the paperwork? I mean PACE was—"

"Pace?" I asked.

"The Police and Criminal Evidence Act, 1984," said Mandy.

"Yes, PACE, a good act, clear lines of what we can, and can't, do. Snetterton. Snetterton!" McGivern lowered his voice: "I'm cursed with some Home Office civil service lackey. I swear he's watching me. Anyway, Reynolds, report to my office first thing tomorrow."

"Sir!"

"That'll be all, Reynolds."

"Sir! Yes. Sir!" Mandy saluted.

"Oh, and Reynolds, congratulations on your engagement."

"Sir, thank you, Sir!"

"Have a drink on me," he said, handing over a twenty to the barmaid.

"I'll have a lemonade, Sir."

"Gin and tonic suit?" he said. "Keep the change."

"I'm—"

"You're celebrating a job well done, a special assignment and an engagement. We can bend the rules, Reynolds, if we get the job done."

Mandy's posture hunched, and I realised that she was crossing her fingers behind her back. She was nodding. I'd seen this movement before and never knew what it meant. Perhaps she thought it doesn't count, drinking on duty, if your fingers are crossed. Oh hell, we were engaged, and we'd stopped a riot – mitigating circumstances surely?

"But bend them only so far, Reynolds."

"Yes, Sir."

Superintendent McGivern strode away, the police parting quicker than the rebel contingent, but they let him through readily enough. As soon as he was out of sight, Mandy knocked her drink back.

"I'll have another please," she said to me.

"Aren't you on duty," I teased.

"We can bend the rules, if we get the job done."

"OK," I said. "Another gin and tonic here, please."

"We will get the job done?" Mandy asked me.

"Yes, of course."

"With a ring and everything?"

"If there's a jeweller's in the village, we'll buy one now."

She threw her arms around me, barely getting "I love you" out before kissing me. I kissed her back, I held her as if forever.

♦

It's heavy, the small box: I get it out, turning the tiny object over in my hand. It's red with a fake leather finish. I lift the lid, which requires a little force before the hinge snaps open. There a gap like a dash that used to hold the most beautiful ring ever, gold, with a tiny cluster of diamonds. It's empty now – gone. I see drops of water splashing onto the tiles and I realise I'm crying. It's just water coming out of my face, it means nothing.

♦

There wasn't a jeweller's in the village.

I bought a round: I stood at the bar waiting. As I did, I alternately looked at myself in the mirror behind the optics and then down at my feet. My face looked flushed and young, and my boots dirty. Other faces caught my eye, each in their own conversations all animated and talking ten to the dozen. Other feet too caught my attention when I noticed that they were an even mix of walking boots, often with bare shins above them, and black trainers of various pedigrees. Some of the latter didn't even have black laces; they were yellow instead.

Now that they were out of their issued riot kit, the police uniforms were a strange mix, all unique in a way that the civilians with their fashion-conscious look aren't. Even the Redcoats were more regulation and some of them were from the wrong period (it's the buttons, always a giveaway).

Carrying the pints, I found our corner empty, but Mandy was waving from the door. It was a balmy afternoon and gradually everyone had gravitated outside to sip our pints by the wooden furniture in the beer garden. When I'd handed out the drinks, I realised that the entertainment was about to start.

Rabbie stood on a bench, wobbled to a "woah" from the crowd before righting himself to hold his hands aloft for attention.

"Everyone! Everyone!" he yelled.

"Will ye no be quiet for the man!" Ross said and he clapped.

People joined in, Mandy and I as well, and then Rabbie got the hush he wanted.

"We have come many miles," he said to a chorus of 'too many'. "And we have many miles to go."

Hoots of derision.

"We will overcome them all. Bonnie Prince Charlie may have turned back at Derby, but we haven't. We've gone on, we've grown in numbers, we've become a force to be reckoned with. We'll prove that Bonnie Prince Charlie could have reached London, because we will reach London, and King George will quake with fear. We will oust King George! Down with King George!"

"Off with his head," came a reply.

"Down with the Government," another shouted.

"About time!" came a third.

"Long live the Jacobites!" said Rabbie raising his arms aloft to lead a call and response.

"Hurrah!"

"Long live the Redcoats!"

"Hurrah!!"

"Long live the Revolution!"

"HURRAH!!!"

The Black Powder Brigade presented and fired a volley into the air, a fifteen-gun salute all at once. Everyone went mad, screaming and yelling, and generally having a good time: all of us. It didn't matter whether you were dressed in red, tartan, tie-dye or riot police black – we were intermingled.

We all drank to that whether we were on-duty or off-duty or without duty.

Long live the Revolution!

Bill and Amber Reynolds
request the pleasure of

on the occasion of the marriage of their daughter

Amanda Chlöe
to
Guy Wilson

St. Chad's, Conky Whallop on Saturday 17th August at 2pm

165

INTELLIGENCE

The front desk of the police station is grey, a scratchy grey, as are the walls, but the desk sergeant's uniform is a darker grey. The policeman himself is grey too, old and wrinkled and instantly trustworthy, with his pointed helmet perfectly set on the crown of his head, its star shining brightly. His kindly eyes are full of that particular wisdom that comes with long experience.

"Evening all," begins Jack Warner, and we feel safe. "You know, crime doesn't pay. Let's consider the case of Guy Wilson. A pleasant sort of chap, who studied history until he fell in with a bad lot: revolutionaries, insurgents and terrorists. You know the type. Now, most of the crime we deal with here in Dock Green is of a simple sort. The young tearaways scrumping for apples, for example, who just need a sharp clip round the ear to bring them back to the straight and narrow. They don't mean any harm and generally turn out all right in the end. But there's another sort, a growing swell of young criminals, hoodlums, who are trained in the army, not in the British Army as part of National Service mind, but in other armies: the Taliban, Al-Qaeda, Daesh or the Bonnie Prince Charlie Society. All these re-enactment groups want to do is drag us back to

166

medieval times, and let me tell you, there's nothing bonnie about them. They're a sorry sort – no respect, no discipline, no moral fibre. They're made up of the kind of man who would shoot a humble copper in a cinema doorway, blow up a rucksack on the underground or march on London wearing Guy Fawkes' masks. They belong to a movement called terrorism. Yes, 'terrorism', it's an ugly word and it's an ugly crime, and the only way to deal with it is to take the culprits behind the chemical sheds and have them shot. Think of it as a kindness. They all want to be martyrs."

He gives a little salute and smiles, and you know that everything is all right, that the thin grey line, which we know is true blue on a colour TV, will protect us, we'll all be safe in our beds tonight and house prices will go up. Unless you happen to be a terrorist, or anyone who falls into the growing category of terrorist, or someone mistaken for a terrorist, or someone with a shifty look, or someone ethnically diverse – and then, you know, you'll get what's coming to you.

Bang!

"Rise and shine, sonny boy."

Fuck, I'm asleep.

I try to open my eyes and pull myself up, but I'm hopelessly lagging behind events. Strong hands grip my lapels and haul me vertical. It's all I can do to get my feet under me.

"Where am I?" I ask. I'm in the cell.

"Never you mind," says a voice: it's Vaughn, the one built like a gorilla. "We're going on a little trip, a shooting party if you like. I'll fire off a few rounds and then... oh, overcome with remorse, you shoot yourself."

"What?"

"I think the term is 'Patsy'."

"No-one's going to buy that. The evidence will be–"

"I think our forensic team won't have any problems interpreting the evidence. Knowing Mister Trudie, he's probably got 'em to write the report already. Likes his graphs, does our Mister Trudie—"

"That's—"

"Used to be proper paper maps, perhaps a model of the target's location, but now it's bloody PowerPoint."

"That's—"

"History is written by the winners," he says pushing me onto the floor. "I'd have thought you'd have known that."

He really jerks my arm back and expertly snaps on handcuffs.

"Other arm."

"What?"

He yanks my left arm backwards and fumbles the other side on. My arm is twisted, my wrist bones dislocating as the angle forces it to turn in the steel oval. It's never going to rotate: "Please, the—"

I'm on my feet again with such force that my arms straighten and I retch with the shock from my wrist. We leave the room before I even start to recover and outside it's a reeling agoraphobia.

The corridor is long with framed notice boards at intervals, though all that remains of any posters are faded rectangles of space and blue-tac stains. Vaughn keeps his hand on my shoulders, forcing my eyesight down, and I see his black boots: he has yellow shoelaces, an orangey colour – ochre.

"What?"

"Sorry," I say, "I didn't say any—"

"Not you – quiet!"

I'm quiet.

Craning up, I see Vaughn nod and realise that someone is talking to him via an earpiece. He's wearing a green camouflage combat jacket over a black stab vest, a strange mix of mercenary and paramilitary police.

"OK," he says, finally.

He turns round, hauling me with him, and takes a single step back towards the cell.

"Ah, to hell with it," he says to himself before turning his attention in my direction. "I've a little treat for you. They don't have these rooms nowadays, damn shame. I used to love these places when you could switch the tape recorders off. Now it's all continuous video. Takes the fun out. Bloody PACE."

Pace of what, I think – progress?

We start along the way we were going, but after ten feet or so, we stop. Vaughn opens a door and pushes me in. It's pitch black and I stumble into something. There's a clatter of wood and metal along with a sharp pain in my hip.

"Wait here," he says.

The door is already closing, the rectangle of harsh light narrows and is gone, and it's closed when I look back. The lock when it engages sounds big, solid and dependable.

"Fuck!"

It's dark and frightening, and I catch a wish for the white cell. As my eyes adjust, I can see a white edge under the door and a keyhole. I realise that I'm still bent over, my back aching, so I straighten up. My breathing is quick, loud, and I make an effort to deepen it. It works, after a fashion.

On my left is a red light, the tiniest of dots and it's fascinating.

I take a tentative step towards it careful not to trip over anything, but even so, my shin bangs against a hard object. Tapping it with my toe, I work out that it's a chair, probably what I knocked over when I was pushed in. I shift it to one side and approach the light.

Stunned!

I've walked straight into a sheet of glass.

I put my forehead onto it and let the cool surface soothe; it gave me a bruise, so it can bloody well ease the headache. I can just about see an outline of my face reflected, a mist growing and fading on the surface as I breathe.

It's like a mirror, and the red dot has a few echoes as the light bounces around inside the thick glass, which means the red dot... yes, there it is. Shifting back and forth gives me some idea of its distance. It's about seven feet, I take seven tiny, careful steps and my thigh touches the edge of a table before I reach it.

Leaning over, I can see a tape recorder, still whirring. It's a 'record' light. How odd.

Vaughn got a message over his earpiece. The plan has been changed, so I've been locked in here. There has to be a way to use this to my advantage. I look round again, but all I can see is the tiniest of orange dots floating in front of my eyes.

"Shit!"

I'm blind.

The light is camera-flash dazzling; my feet are awash with huge orange phantoms as I look down and away. I blink, desperately, and I can't rub my eyes because my hands are cuffed behind me.

There's another room beyond the glass.

The light came on: it's one of those interrogation rooms and I'm on the observing side.

Someone's talking: "...it's a difficult decision, one understands, but this job requires sacrifices. It's an honour, a duty and a responsibility."

I recognize the voice. It's fucking Trudie and... oh God. It's... it's...

I can't take this in.

"We can talk in here?" Trudie says.

"Yes," says Vaughn, his voice ethereal. I see him now standing just outside the door; he looks straight into the dark half I'm in, just to my right. I turn, but I don't see anything that could be attracting his attention, and then I realise that he can't see me. He's just letting me know that he knows I'm watching.

He grins, showing his teeth, enjoying the jest.

"That will be all, Vaughn," says Trudie.

"Sir," says Vaughn as he closes the door, leaving the MP and... Mandy, it's Mandy... Mandy – only a dozen feet away. She's dressed smartly in her uniform, hands behind her back with her shoulders, complete with brand new sergeant stripes in gleaming silver, straight.

They think they are alone.

I check my half of the double room now my eyes have adjusted: chair lying prone, door, bits of paper on the floor, table with the tape recorder on it, cream coloured speakers on the wall at either corner, cream coloured phone stuck on the wall, light switch, a volume control, damp patch in the ceiling tiles, grey stone textured lino, discoloured skirting board, crappy walls.

"I have friends," she says as clear as a bell, but dislocated as her voice is coming from either side of the room.

"Yes, of course," says Trudie.

I yell for all I'm worth: "Bitch! *BITCH!!!*"

She looks at me, *thank God, thank you, God*, and then with a small frown across her brow, she turns back to Trudie. She smiles, not a happy smile, but an acknowledgement directed towards that smartly dressed political piece of shit.

Double-glazing, soundproofed beyond belief.

"They've been misled by infiltrators," she says, her voice calm and collected. It's coming from the speakers. "It's an appalling shame, but... it's just..."

"One wouldn't be human if one didn't care. That's why one does it. Why we do it. That's what separates us from them."

"Thank you. We must be resolute, Sir."

"Good girl."

He touches her gently, tucking back a loose wisp of blonde hair and there's a tender expression on his face as he does so. She lets him, her hands stay behind her back and she nods, for a moment caressing his hand with her cheek, before they step away from each other. Mandy isn't 'at ease' or 'attention', she's just standing there with that vile monster. She flicks an errant lock of blonde hair behind her ear with her left hand: she's not wearing her engagement ring.

"Do you have his things?" Trudie says.

"BOLLOCKS!" I head-butt the glass and end up dazed on the floor.

Mandy holds up a transparent plastic bag. She must have been holding it behind her back. It's an evidence bag with scribbles on a label that's too far away to read. Inside though, I can see a mobile phone, orange notes that are tenners, loose change, a watch, keys and... it's mine. All my stuff sealed in a tamper-proof bag.

"You better dispose of those," Trudie says.

"Sir, surely he would have them on him," Mandy says, "particularly his phone."

Yes, yes, I need my phone.

"Why do you say that?" Trudie asks.

"It has to be believable and no-one is ever without their phone, Sir."

"Bollocks," I say again – to myself. *"Bitch!"*

"Good point," says Trudie. "Make sure you give Vaughn the bag with those instructions."

"Yes, Sir."

Trudie looks at his watch: "You'll make Inspector before the week is out."

"Thank you, Sir."

"Time to go."

"Let's break some eggs," she says.

The other door opens, there are sounds of them leaving – the lights go out – and suddenly I'm in a deep, dark pit of a place.

♦

We snogged.

Outside, in the sunlight, after we were engaged.

I didn't care: everyone watched, so what. All those police vying with each other to come up with the most suggestive and outrageous jibe possible. When we'd finished and Mandy turned her scarlet face away from me to board the hired transport, I smiled.

OK, I grinned like an idiot, happy to see all those pulled faces, obscene gestures and '*way-hay*'s from the windows of the coach.

A copper ran along the side of the vehicle and banged the side twice with his hand, the traditional 'go-go', and the vehicle indicated, paused for a gap in the traffic and then pulled away. I waved and a hundred butch blokes waved back and blew me kisses. Mandy sat quietly with a little knowing expression.

Back at the pub, I met Snitch for the first time, although it didn't register at the time. I don't remember much to be honest. I must have seen lots of friends, listened to them all saying 'congratulations', accepted drinks, Scotch amongst them, and I didn't look at the Battle of Waterloo picture again, didn't see its ranks of soldiers bearing down in a volley of gunfire.

"So," said Liam, "we're to tie you to a lamppost naked."

"Och, all very embarrassing."

"Let's not then," I said. "We don't want to frighten the natives."

"Och, no, horrible sight it would be too."

"And pointless."

"And degrading," said Liam.

"We'll have to do something," I said, sipping through the frothy head of another pint. "And not just drinking in a pub."

"Not just drinking, but some drinking," said Liam.

"I study history, there's tradition to uphold."

Ross finished his pint: "I ken just the thing, a wee video."

"A video?" I said, worried.

"One of those wee shiny things."

"DVD," said Liam.

"Guy," said Ross. He was serious with that teacher's look of absolute certainty.

"Yes?"

"You are a lucky man."

"I know."

I did know.

♦

What do I think now? I sink to my knees and topple over, feeling utterly defeated, and yet before I realise, I'm struggling to get my hands below my fat arse.

"Ah!"

The cuffs feel cold against the back of my knees. I push down my legs, the metal catching on my socks and then on the top of my boots. It just won't go past the heel. I squash my stomach against my thighs, feeling the hard cube of the jewellery box in my sporran until even the hungry sensation goes away, but it doesn't help. Reaching out with my fingers I can actually feel the soles of my boots, first... almost to the second joint.

I purse my lips and breathe out, a slow exhalation deflating my lungs, tugging my diaphragm up and giving my insides more room. Red flecks appear in my vision, tiny explosions; these must be the actual stars you see when you're passing out. If I get stuck now I won't be able to inhale.

Push!

Can't shout, no air.

Something gives.

Done!

At the very last nanosecond.

My lungs ache as the air rushes back in, stinging as the oxygen penetrates. Sitting up, I lean against the wall below the one-way mirror and look at the red dot, watching it blur in and out of focus. That's the table, to my right is the door and I can see its white line where it reaches the floor. I know where everything is. I stand, walk carefully to the wall, suddenly remembering that now my hands are in front I can feel forward.

Once at the wall, I feel around for the light switch. There... *click*.

A gloomy red light comes on barely illuminating the room, the very photons seem sluggish and reluctant, but it's enough.

I snatch the phone off its hook and put the old style receiver to my ear: there's a dial tone! But only four buttons on the dial, panel... dial, why's it called a dial when it's a panel. Never mind. OK, who ya gonna call: A, B, C or D?

What could they be?

Perhaps I could call reception and say, please come and lock me up again? Or a direct line to Trudie's office to remind him that his underlings haven't killed me yet? Or dial-a-pizza? Or... or... what do I want: the press, an outside line, International Rescue?

I press 'A' and hear a ringing noise coming from my right. Through the one-way mirror, I see a phone on a side table happily purring away, a red light flashing. I hang up. It stops.

'B', rings, and rings, and rings, and–

"Vaughn."

Slam!

I breathe like a woman in labour, short panting gasps. He might figure it out. This is an abandoned police station or something, so there might not be that many people here. How many wrong numbers do you expect in a place when there are only four buttons on a phone?

Button 'C' clicks in and stays there, stuck in and wonky, so, clearly, that's not an option.

OK, this is it: 'D'.

It rings, and rings, and rings, and just carries on ringing out. I've no idea how long to leave it; each '*burr-burr, burr-burr*' seems like an alarm or a countdown.

Eventually, I hang-up.

I'm sweating. I'm also exhausted. I couldn't sleep in the white cell when I had nothing to do. Now I have options and I can't seem to keep my eyes open. Perhaps I should just sit in the corner and rest for five minutes. There might be a dream waiting to be lived, where everything is all right and there's Ross and Liam, laughing and smiling, and behind them, it's Mandy, not the Mandy of today, but the Mandy of the past, the one who was true. She smiled, broad and unselfconscious, her eyes sparkled and she held her hand in front of me: her fingers crossed. She showed me this sign and nodded. Yes, yes, she seemed to be saying, my fingers are crossed.

I start, jerking oddly and bumping the phone. The receiver rattles on its hook and makes a tinkling sound. I'd dozed off, actually disappeared to the Land of Nod while standing up.

Options:-

Plan A: pick up the chair, hide behind the door and clobber Vaughn when he comes back. He'd beat the crap out of me, let's be honest, but I'm going to die, so why not make the attempt. Surely I could do some damage with a pre-emptive strike?

Plan B: find something to pick the lock on the cuffs and then the lock in the door, and then run away. This a good plan, I like this plan. However, searching the room for some paperclip or nail, I begin to feel disillusioned that Fate isn't lending a helping hand. Someone has swept the room and cleaned this sewer of a building of every atom of detritus. I mean I've no idea how to pick locks – true, but I'd like to try.

Plan C: just give up.

Plan D: I could press button 'D' again and wait for an answer. Sod it, I could press 'B', ring Vaughn and ask him to get a move on, I'm tired of living.

Err... err... click.

Across the room, I see the tape recorder's red light go out.

It's so surreal.

I go over and look at it. The cassette's no longer rotating. It's a C90. God, you can buy them as joke covers for your phone.

C90 – so someone pressed 'play-and-record' 45 minutes ago. How long have I been here? Surely no more than ten, maybe fifteen, minutes. No-one would record nothing for forty-five minutes.

I press 'rewind'. The device comes to life, whizzing the little wheels around and spooling the tape back. I wait and then press 'stop'. OK, I press 'play'.

"...we must be resolute... good girl..." it begins and then, suddenly, loudly, "BOLLOCKS!"

"Too right," I say aloud.

I listen on as Mandy explains about the phone, my phone, as if I was bothered about my mobile. She's going now to give Vaughn the bag.

"Let's break some eggs," she says at the end.

There's the sound of the door closing and I press 'stop'.

I press 'rewind' again and, this time, leave it whirring, the tape whizzes back into the past.

The past.

Grassroots rebellion
Jacqueline Fort | 09:23 BST

A political march, the New Jacobite Rebellion, is approaching London, figuratively, metaphorically and literally. For too long, our political masters have doled out soundbites, petty arguments and conflicting points of view, so it should come as no surprise when the people rise up to do something about it. That it comes as a historical re-enactment, full of tartan skirts and knobbly knees, is the shocker. Perhaps Britain is saying that modern politics is not for them: bring back the good old days.

People like Rabbie MacLeod and Guy Wilson are a new breed, taking the arguments to the country lanes of this fair land and into the virtual streets of the blogosphere. Not for them the tired techniques of politicians, but the new wave of internet rebellion. With their muskets and their claymores, their dress is colourful, their language is colourful and their idealism is colourful. They don't represent the blue, red or purple of the main parties, or even the green and yellows of the minorities, but a kilt of many different shades. People have flocked to their march bringing their own particular causes, campaigns and crusades.

With the Prime Minister's Office desperately trying to show that the government isn't completely out of touch, rumours of an imminent cabinet reshuffle are not helping confidence. The FTSE is down by 120 points and the PM has scored the lowest rating in the polls since the local elections.

The ruling party's hopes rest on the shoulder of the Home Secretary, Timothy Dorrington, MP: how will he deal with this growing situation?

Commentators, including myself, wonder if his laissez-faire approach is wise. After all, a particular community marching on London has decided not to work with the Home Secretary. Every day, the march gets closer and everything is up for grabs.

John Trudie, MP, and others have called for action, decisive and unequivocal, and it is a test of his policing policy. You've only got to read his recent white paper on armed response to understand this. Dorrington must be tough and, more importantly, he must be seen to be tough, and to do so he must shift his position from the left of the party. If not, then the right wing will have the Home Secretary by his musket balls.

Permalink | Comments (17)

INSURGENCY

At some point, we passed the half-way mark.

I don't mean literally; though, of course, we did that too. Rabbie must have had that milestone marked on his map: 130 miles divided by 2 must have been somewhere. What I mean is half-way psychologically. What had started as a drunken dare facing an impossible uphill struggle, became a movement inexorably rolling downhill towards its destination.

Put simply: there were fewer miles in front of us than behind us, and we knew it. It was easier to go on than to return. The race between blisters and muscles had been won, so our jumps forward didn't just increase in mileage; they became reliable.

'If' became 'when', and 'when' became 'Thursday'.

We began to *Audentior Ibo*.

"What's that?" Liam asked, doing a double pace to match the march of Ross and myself. We finally had a proper pavement by the road.

"Och, you've asked a historian," said Ross.

"I will go more daringly," I said. "It was Bonnie Prince Charlie's motto."

"Sort of 'To Boldly Go'?"

"To Boldly Go... I will go more daringly... yes, you're right."

"But it dinna split the infinitive," said Ross.

"Doesn't matter," I said.

"Och, will ye no hear the Englishman talk pish about his own language."

"Shakespeare split the infinitive."

"Ye canna change the rules of grammar."

"These rules were invented by the upper classes," I said, "so they could look down on the uneducated."

"Och, ye have to teach grammar properly, it's because of Latin. It's one of Gove's curriculum changes before Brexit wrecked his career."

"That's the excuse, but only because you can't physically put an adverb into a conjugated verb in Latin. 'Praecessi' is one word."

Liam spoke up even though he was fiddling with his smartphone: "So Bonnie Prince Charlie's motto could be: I'll daringly go more?"

"Och, put that wee thing away," Ross said. "Rabbie'll go insane if he sees it. What are you doing anyway?"

"I'm checking it out on a translation site," Liam said, holding up his stupidly expensive mobile phone. "'To go', 'to boldly go' and 'to go boldly' all translate differently. They come out as 'Pray-ee- Pray-ee–"

"Here," I said, taking it off him. I was holding it longways, so it switched to landscape confusing me for a moment. "Praecessi. Ut audacter vado. Praecessi audacter."

"What happens if you put those back through the system?"

I tried clicking, but couldn't see what to press. I gave it to Liam, and presently he handed it back.

"To go," I said. "When Audaciter go. To go audaciter."

"Och, who's Audaciter?"

"I dunno," I said. "But 'Go Audaciter go!'"

And we did: fifteen miles a day, on average, made 130 miles divide into 10 days, a week and a half. So, the maths isn't quite right because the Cross Keys had been a nice pub and an afternoon slipped away there, and the Festival of the Field lost us an early morning start and there was also the Stag Party – which was a farce all of its own.

That was something of a detour, and weird to leave the country lanes to enter suburbia, but Liam knew this bloke, who owned a house, which Liam could use on weekends if it was free. Or so the story went originally.

It was always vacant, Liam said, as the client had to spend at least another nine months abroad for tax reasons, and the client had told Liam where the key was hidden and, more importantly, the access number to the alarm.

So, Ross, Rabbie, Liam and I bumped off down a few B-roads in the van, which was all right, Ross informed us, as others were walking the short side of the triangle, and we could re-join the actual marching by lunchtime tomorrow in a 17th century pub, no less.

"What if he changes his mind?" Rabbie asked.

"A weekend in this country before the new fiscal year would cost him ten million at least," Liam said. "For ten million, he could hire an entire five-star hotel somewhere sunny. The man had a fit when he lost a mere three-quarters of a million, so he'd freak out completely at the very thought of losing ten million."

"Och, but it's sunny here and he could stay in his house for nought."

Liam said we didn't understand modern tax avoidance strategies. He was right, we didn't.

The house was big, but not as enormous as some in this village, though it still had a long gravel drive that ended in a circle around an ornamental pond that was framed, when you approached, by the classical Greek columns of its porch.

Although we had the use of the house, there were a few areas Liam decided were off-limits: the west wing, the east wing, the third floor, the garage with its collection of sports cars and a few other rooms. But we could go to the 'Den' and this had everything we could possibly want: beers in the fridge, a pool table and a stupendously massive television screen.

"Sub-woofers, Dolby 5.1," said Liam pointing to various corners of the room. "And popcorn. Perfect to watch this film."

"What is it?" I asked.

Ross stepped proudly forward: "Och, only the definitive Bonnie Prince Charlie film."

"*Chasing the Deer*?" I said.

"Aye. And you know why?"

"We're Jacobites."

"Och, no, this is a Stag Party. Chasing the deer, geddit?"

"Oh..." That was appalling, I thought.

"What's *Chasing the Deer*?" Liam asked.

"It's a film about the Battle of Culloden," I said.

"Independent film," said Ross.

"It was funded by the people. Film-making democracy in action," I said. "A few hundred people put up the money, a thousand quid, and they all got to appear as extras."

"Rabbie knows one, don't you Rabbie?"

"What?" said Rabbie. "I was one."

"Well, it's appropriately titled," said Liam, "but does it have any naked women in it?"

"It's got Brian Blessed in it," said Rabbie.

"That's not the same. After work, we used to go to this lap dancing club."

"I'm not convinced we should watch a film about the Jacobites losing," I said. "Surely it has the wrong karma."

"Och, we'll have a few beers first."

"I was joking."

"Aye, we'll still have a few beers first."

"I'll get 'em," said Liam, and off he went to the fridge.

"Should we be drinking his beer?" I asked.

"He owes me."

"Yes, but—"

"He owes me. We drink as much beer as we want."

It was a strange house to me. I was used to student digs. I wasn't intimidated by the surroundings as such; the 'Den' was like a brand new student union room complete with a pool table, but I realised that this wasn't the sort of place that I would ever live in. Money would be an issue, certainly; historians don't make much unless they become media personalities and my recent foray into television hadn't been a startling breakthough.

There was more to it, though. Mandy was a career person, her house, our home, would be functional, a place to recuperate before the next shift, and I was someone who frittered their time away. This upmarket playpen just wasn't us.

I wondered what was. If we were going to London, we'd only be able to afford a part share in a shoebox, whereas this rich man had so much money he couldn't use his luxurious country retreat.

Ross decided we'd shoot some pool.

I mean sure, I could get used to having a pool table, and perhaps the swimming pool, but the ornamental pool in the driveway was an embarrassing pool-too-far. If I won the lottery, it wouldn't even cross my mind to buy such an ostentatious statement and if someone suggested it, I'd have just laughed.

However, rich people seem to have these ludicrously over-the-top items – perhaps more money than sense is a statement about proportionality: more money, less sense. Being forced into a nine-month exile for tax reasons didn't sound like freedom to me. It should be 'go anywhere', not 'have to go somewhere else'. A holiday abroad is different from an exile aboard.

"Standard rules," said Ross.

"What are those?" Liam asked.

"Ye ken."

"Seriously, at the end, when it's just the black – is it nominate and stick, or nominate each shot."

"Och, I dinna ken that. We'll ken when we get there."

"Look, it's important to decide now to avoid arguments later."

"Not when ye breaking."

"But at some point, rules are necessary."

"Ye all a bunch of rule ninnies."

"Winner stays on?" I asked.

♦

Winner stays on, I think now, and the winner writes the history and the rules. I wonder if it is that writing of the rules that makes the winners. Lawyers decide how the law is interpreted and, surprise-surprise, we always seem to need more lawyers. What was that credit crunch fiasco: English counties suing the state-owned Royal Bank of Scotland for their money back – council tax money used for the prosecution and income tax going on the defence – folly of Brexian proportions. The winners are the lawyers, the losers are everyone else.

And the politicians bleating 'it's legal' whenever they're caught in some scam: well, of course it's legal, they pass the laws. Expenses fraud for them is embarrassing, expenses fraud for everyone else is prison.

Fighting evil when the enemy dress in Nazi uniforms with skulls on their caps is straightforward, but fighting an insidious inch-by-inch squeeze on your rights isn't. Especially when the law changes sound so convincing, so reasonable and so necessary.

After all, we don't want terrorism here, do we?

I could do with my rights read out, my phone call and my lawyer. The broken button, 'C', represents my rights quite accurately. PACE, of course! Vaughn had meant that the days were better before the Police and Criminal Evidence Act in – what year did Mandy say? – 1984.

Now there's a significant date: did George Orwell predict this police state and get the start date right?

Wait a moment!

Criminal Evidence.

I get up off the floor and take the cassette out of the recorder. It's a Boots own brand, they can't have sold cassettes for decades. I'm tapping it gently against my left hand as I think about it: this is evidence. If I could just get this to someone: the press, someone with access to the internet, a police force somewhere other than the Home Secretary's playground... but how?

I can't hide it in the villain's secret base. If I keep it, they might search me, but then again I might get an opportunity to pass it on later. Or I'll die and some pathologist will find it.

That might work. If they re-equip me from the evidence bag, then some policeman would go through my things and sum up the contents of my existence: £35.34 in tenners and loose change, credit card (maxed), keys, mobile, shirt, plaid (bet they write 'kilt'), football shorts (Man U.), underwear, socks (used), boots (worn), engagement ring box (empty) and this C90 cassette. It would all go back in a transparent bag and into a box marked 'Guy Wilson Evidence'.

Would someone be curious and requisition an old-fashioned cassette player and play it? But who? One of Trudie's lackeys or one of the many good apples in the tainted barrel? I need someone with black shoelaces.

My final words might even be written down somewhere for posterity: "Bitch. Bitch. Bollocks! Bollocks" – alliterative, if not literate.

It's worth a try. What choice is there? If they found it, what else could they do? In for a penny in for a pound, hung for a deer as for an apple. My brain is rambling. I'm tired. I want to lean back, rest my head on the wall and sleep, but my thoughts go back to the Den and the Stag Party.

As if that's going to help? Why am I drawn to what happened in the past? How does knowing how I got here help me get out of here? Or am I simply trapped by everything that has happened.

History is bunk.

No, history may save me, or save my reputation, or something... I must hide the evidence, but where?

Here it is again, the past playing out unbidden in my memory. I'm not going to escape it.

♦

"Beers," said Liam, handing out bottles of Bud.

"I want to make a toast," said Rabbie.

"Och, Rabbie, dinna spoil–"

"It's Guy's Stag Party."

"Aye."

"Guy," said Rabbie, raising his bottle.

"Yes," I said.

"To Guy, lucky sod."

"To Guy, lucky sod," they chorus.

"Guy, we've a wee thing for you," said Ross. He handed over a badly wrapped package, a lumpy pink item, although luckily that was the champagne motif paper.

"Thanks," I said. I felt genuinely moved, this was great. I plonked my beer down on the pool table's wooden edge, and ripped the wrapping off. It was black leather with silver fittings: a sporran.

"Thanks! This is... perfect."

"Och, go on, put it on."

I tried, but needed Rabbie's expertise to fit it onto my belt properly. It dangled in front of me, feeling heavy and unusual.

"There ye go," he said. "Ye may be a Sassenach Highlander, but at least ye now look the part."

"I've always wanted one of these," I said.

"Och, we know."

"How?"

"We saw you looking at the stalls back at Swarkestone."

♦

Sporran!

Of course.

I can tuck the cassette tape into my sporran, although it's tricky to open the fastening with the handcuffs on. I must get these off. There. I slip the cassette in and close it up, and then tap the sporran to check the evidence is secure. It took ages to get used to the bulky thing banging against my bollocks.

The cuffs shine, stainless steel, and have elegant curves now I look at them closely. The keyhole is like a deep dark well with a central pinnacle, an ornamental steel cairn standing in a black pool – the Stag Party again.

No, come on, come on, concentrate. They have a simple key, I think, so any bent paperclip or nail ought to do the trick.

God, I'm hopeless, I think I remember Rabbie telling me so. We were dancing. I smile at the memory despite it being disjointed and distant like a film fast-forwarded. We danced around and around while the world turned and corruption gathered. It's a force of darkness I feel now is the encroaching fatigue lowering my eyelids. I want to sleep, curl up in the darkness. Mandy's slipped away into that darkness.

I'm laughing: Mandy went over to the dark side of the 'force'.

I stand, must keep moving, must march south, must... find a paperclip or a pin. I check my plaid, but I know there isn't one there. I remember Ross explaining back at the Stag Party.

♦

"'Course, the Sassenachs banned our traditional dress after Culloden," said Ross as he gathered the pool balls dropping them into the wooden triangle. "And they kicked us out of Scotland."

"You were kicked out by sheep," I said.

"Och!"

"What's this?" Liam asked.

"The Highland clearances, crofters replaced by sheep farming. 1792 was known as the Year of the Sheep."

"Och!"

"It's what you Highlanders call it, even if you are from Kent. The crofters, small holding farmers, were 'improved' away for sheep farming."

"By English butchers," said Ross.

"They did not," I said. "The clearances were started by Scots–"

"Rich landowning Scots."

"Rich landowning Scots to gain control of the land. It was an inevitable movement towards larger farming practices and it happened all over Britain... and the world for that matter."

"Kick 'em out, the poncey upper class... and every other Englishman," said Ross without any real fire.

"How many times have we had this argument?" Rabbie asked.

"Each year or over time?" I said.

"Och, we should kick out all the immigrants that arrived after, say, 1065."

"You can't mean that," said Liam, new to this discussion.

"I think," I said, because I'd heard it all before, "he wants that date, because he'd inherit most of... Wessex, is it?"

"Aye."

"He said 1065, so everyone after, and including, the Normans."

"Right," said Liam.

"Aye," said Ross. "Keep out the French."

"I'll drink to that."

"Down with the French!" we chorused.

"Didn't the French help the Jacobites?" Liam asked.

"Aye, they did."

"But you're a Jacobite."

"Aye, so I am."

"Did you hear about those dickhead BNP fascists?" said Liam.

"What?" Rabbie asked.

"They created this poster, '*The Battle For Britain*' they called it, and put a Spitfire on it, a huge photo in sepia of the plane in flight. Fantastic sight. They used this for their anti-immigration policy – it was when all those Poles were coming over – but, get this, the picture was from a squadron that was made up of Polish fighter pilots."

"303 Squadron," I said.

"How can you remember that?" said Rabbie.

"It's the same as the .303 rifle."

"Och, how come you know everything, but are complete pants at pub quizzes?"

"They ask questions about pop music and sport."

"Och, 'pop music', ye do live in the past."

"But these Polish fighter pilots," said Liam. "I mean, come on, proof or what that this country needs its immigrants. We needed 'em for our finest hour and we need 'em now."

"The bloody Poles coming over here to protect our women and children," I said.

"Och, the fascists say they dinna need Poles until their toilet backs up," said Ross.

"And the Irish to dig the canals, you mean?" said Rabbie to Liam.

Liam paused to think about this, unsure whether to object.

"Navvies, Navigators, in the 19th century," I said. "Essential for the Industrial Revolution. It's a good thing."

"Yes," said Liam. "Yes, it is."

"It's what made Britain great," I said to snorts of derision from the others.

"And they don't want us immigrants now," said Liam, "since that the canals are finished and the banks are all crap."

"The canal banks are being renovated," said Rabbie.

"Not those banks, the financial banks."

"You'd get your job back if we kicked out all the other bankers," said Rabbie.

"Nah, Irish and proud, I'd be the first to go."

"After the Irish, who?" I asked. "The Asians, the Afro-Caribbeans, the Jews, the Huguenots, the Normans, the Angles, the Saxons, the Jutes, the Vikings, and, for Fuck's sake, there's an Oz bar on Candlemaker's Row, let's get rid of the Aussies. Where do you draw the line?"

"1065," Ross said. "I did say."

"How about the moment that Britain became an island when the land bridge across the Channel flooded?" Liam suggested. "Get rid of the Picts, I say."

"Europe for the Neanderthals," I added. "Pangaea for the dinosaurs. Gondwanaland back to the Trilobites."

"Or we could just get on," Ross said. "Are we going to play pool or what?"

"Sorry," I said.

"So," said Liam, "do we nominate and stick?"

It's life really: romance, dating and so forth. You nominate and stick. That's what getting engaged and having a Stag Party was all about. I'd chosen (so you can make fun of me over this) to stick. I suppose being single is nominating for each pocket. Or not potting anything.

Did I really want happily ever after, the No.8 ball and chain, with Mandy?

"We nominate and stick," I said.

"Och aye," said Ross passing me a cue. "You break."

I did very well at first, all the old tricks from my undergraduate days coming back, but then I started taking it seriously, thinking about each shot first, and so it all went to pieces.

I took aim, feeling the cue slide easily over the valley between my thumb and forefinger: *clunk... clack... clatter.*

"Good shot."

I moved round the table to the far side. Hmm, the ricochet off the white hadn't been kind. I could have gone for the ten into the corner or the twelve into the side. There were a lot of easier shots for the Spots. There was the five nicely lined up with the corner pocket, for example, and the three into the middle easily, whereas the eleven was snookered by the five – hopeless.

I could try a safety: *clunk...*

"Bollocks."

"Och, fortune favours the brave."

Bop, bop, bop: five, three, two, lined up on the black. I might as well have handed my cue on to Liam and let Ross thrash him instead.

"I was good at this," I said. "It's lack of practice."

"Aye," said Ross, who didn't even look up from the table to reply, "but you went and got yourself a girlfriend."

"A bachelor is a man who chases women until one catches him," said Liam.

Ross laughed and miscued the white; it managed to hit the black but only nudged it towards the hole. It hovered over oblivion, but didn't go down.

I got the eleven in and snagged the fifteen.

"Glad you chose to nominate and stick," said Ross as he sank the black. I still had three balls on the table.

At about 9:30pm, it was time for the film. We sat on the sofa, while Ross loaded the 'wee shiny disc' and Liam fiddled with all the settings – 16:9, Dolby, subtitles off, sub-woofers on, bass speaker active, lights down, shields up, warp factor six, Mr Sulu. It took him so long that we all had time to nip to the loo and claim another beer before the film.

We started: "Pa, pa, pa-pa, pa, pa, pa-pa.... *pah!*"

The popcorn was moreish, it's the salt, and then we drank more.

We were some way into the film before Rabbie piped up: "This is me, this is me!"

He tapped us all on the arm to gain our attention, even though the film already had it.

"Where? Where?" said Liam.

"Look... top... that tree... and... to the right... me!"

We all applauded: "Rabbie, Rabbie, Rabbie!"

The film finished, we had a few more beers and Liam was nowhere to be seen. I went looking for the loo and I saw a light in the hall. I followed the trail of 'on' lights, up the curved staircase and along the balcony landing, a corridor and another landing. The place was like a hotel.

♦

Where the hell is Liam now, I think. He got away, didn't he? It wasn't like Ross and me. He's with the Rebellion. I'm part of the plan to kill them, so they're still all right.

♦

At the Stag Party, I found Liam in a small office space, scrabbling around on the floor as he searched through a cupboard.

"What are you doing?" I asked.

Comically, Liam started and thwacked his head.

"Well?"

"Nothing," said Liam as he emerged. He blinked a few times before pushing his glasses back up his nose.

"You're looking for cocaine."

"I am not."

"You are."

"Just a line or two to steady my nerves."

"Liam!"

"I can't find his stash."

"Perhaps he took it with him."

"Through customs? I doubt it."

"It's not yours and you shouldn't take it anyway."

"The bastard owes me," said Liam. "I sorted out his system when he screwed up the short selling screens, nearly lost one point two."

"What?"

"I kept the bank's computer systems going, administration, very important, passwords and all that, very important, what with millions of dollars and millions of euros, very important."

He was agitated now, and I was finding it tricky to focus, so he took me completely by surprise when he bolted past. Down the corridor, he went, with me in

194

pursuit. I was still holding a bottle of Becks, which I'd taken to the loo, for goodness' sake. The stairs came up suddenly too, and I transferred the drink to my other hand, so I could use the wide, polished oak bannister.

"Look at this place," Liam said. He was standing in the hallway waving his arms about as he turned, his baseball boots squeaking on the marble. "It reeks of money. The money I made for the bastard."

Ross and Rabbie settled down on the first couple of steps of the wide staircase. I sat a few rows behind them as if joining an audience on raked seating for a theatre show.

"I made this man fifteen million over three years," said Liam, "and saved him a fortune when it all went tits up, and he hangs me out to dry. 'We have to make cutbacks', he said, 'we have to let you go' – *bastard!* Cutbacks didn't include his bonus. All that taxpayers' money bailing us out just went towards his Christmas card and a cheque for two million. All straight to fuck knows where via Panama. He's on that leaked list with David Cameron. Or has everyone forgotten that now?"

"Liam..."

"And the stupid, arrogant banker forgets he's given me a key to this place."

"You mean you don't have permission?" said Rabbie.

"Och, we're breaking and entering."

"We're not breaking!" said Liam. "We're just entering."

"It's illegal!" I said. "I'm marrying a policewoman."

"He won't call the police," said Liam.

"He'll call the police once he sees his house has been burgled. Our fingerprints are all over the place," I said putting down a bottle of Becks and almost seeing the incriminating greasy marks.

"He won't call the police. He won't want sniffer dogs within a million miles of here."

"But–"

"You said, one illegal thing!"

"He's right," said Ross. "Yer not wrapped around her little finger yet."

"Excuse me," said Liam. "I was..."

"Ranting?" I said.

"Ranting!"

"Och, go on," said Ross.

Liam did: he told us how everyone arrived at the office at 6am, worked until 8pm with a half hour lunch taken at your desk before you went out drinking with everyone from the office. Over shots, the boss would decide who got what portfolio and female employees didn't like going to lap dancing clubs, so it was a de facto gentleman's club. Your bonus depended on being in the in-crowd, so that was that. You drank until two in the morning, you were pissed when assigned your task, and hung-over as you massaged the figures and packaged the debt into ever more attractive parcels to sell on. The whole money-making machine was based upon cranking the handle, selling riskier and riskier products and everyone was happy, just so long as no-one sobered up.

Then some sub-prime debt-ridden loser in the States made ends meet by defaulting on his repayments. You could probably work out who it was: Hank Jackson at number 2050, Hicksville, Arizona.

The Queen of Spades had been sliced and diced, and everyone had a piece. And those left holding the Old Maid found it a pristine cardboard box and a security guard to escort them from the building – 75k a year to nothing faster than the express elevator could go down.

"I met a tramp living rough," Liam explained. "You know, some squalid refugee – he had nothing – and I thought, lucky man!"

"Lucky?" I said.

"Yes," said Liam, "I have a £650,000 mortgage on a property worth a dismal £375,000. That's £275,000 negative equity. Plus credit cards, loans on cars, boats and a sixteenth of a racehorse and I'm looking at half a million down. Some of my colleagues are out to the tune of seven figures and needed to borrow money in the queue to the bankruptcy court to pay the fee required to be legally destitute."

"Och, ye canna mean ye have to fork out to admit yer stony broke?"

"Absolutely."

"Och no."

"So, dosser, don't you dare ask me for loose change," Liam screamed at an imaginary down-and-out begging in the street, "you're well off. Look at those coppers in your rescued Costa coffee cup, that's financial solvency. You're in the black, while I'm down here in the red. What's that quote?"

"What quote?" I asked.

"You know, annual income twenty pounds, annual expenditure nineteen pounds, nineteen shillings and six – result, happiness. Annual income seventy grand with an annual bonus of thirty-five grand, annual expenditure a hundred and five grand, five credit cards and all those direct debits and sixpence – result, a wonderful, wonderful, blissfully stupid fourteen months and then bailiffs. Fecking misery."

"Micawber in Charles Dickens," I said.

"God, Guy, you know everything, what are you, a walking Wikipedia?"

"I studied history."

"What? All of it?"

"Up to 1939, yes."

"I've lived through a historic time," said Liam. "I remember all the screens going red, sell-sell-sell everyone was going. The prices just kept going down, it gave you a sick feeling here." Liam pointed to his throat. "There's this rush you get when you make a million, it's a high, like coke, you know."

"Not really," I admitted.

"It's a high, a buzz, your feet don't touch the ground, but it wasn't like that, it was the reverse, like coming off something cold turkey. I felt heavy and my peripheral vision closed down. All you could see were the numbers going red, the background going red, everything out of focus and red. Fecking red everywhere. And Gaz and I, he came round to my desk, and we went to Dolman's—"

"Dolman's?" Rabbie asked.

"Preston Dolman owns this place," Liam said waving his hand to encompass the pool table, cinema-sized TV screen and everything expensive that lay within these walls. "You know, Brookes, Dolman and Thomas... Brookes, Dol—"

"Och, aye." Ross made a face at Rabbie: for goodness' sake let him finish.

"Anyway," Liam continued, "we got to Dolman's portfolio and sold. I mean really sold. Click, click, click over all the stocks and shares. Get it into gold, oil, anything that wasn't futures related. And avoid the UK and the EU, which is just toxic since Brexit and Trump's one-sided trade deal. So, I'll admit some of it wasn't the best choice, but a delay of a second was costing thousands. It was dropping faster than the spreadsheet could update. There was screaming in the office, proper screaming and people from the fifth floor running about with bits of paper. It was like they were waving flags or something. If the building hadn't got that modern air conditioning, they'd have opened the windows and thrown themselves out. Anyway, so Dolman's stuff is safe, shored, and he's like lost one point seven five, I don't know, a lot, but nothing like some of our clients. Particularly those we'd sold our stuff to... I mean, some went bankrupt. By the time

Mick had had a quick snog with that girl from accounts in Costa, his client lost eight million. That's an expensive kiss. So, OK, so the next week, Wednesday, we get called in and they had these cardboard boxes already assembled for your stuff. And, I think Gaz was first, and he said, look – to Dolman – we saved you a fortune, but Dolman says he lost one point seven five, or whatever it was, and I mean, shit, he could have kept us on, made a case to the brokers, our actual employers, but no, one point seven five, bottom line. It's money, you see, that's more important than people. I did know that, but it's easy to forget when you're on the money's side. But when you're not... and suddenly you're deleting all the crap off the PC, while the security guard watches you, then pens and pencils into your cardboard box, but 'oh no, sonny Jim'. Lost millions, but you can't take a couple of biros with you. Elliot, from the other side of the office, just chucked his box down. Keep it, he said, keep it all. 'Cos that's what it was, I mean, nothing. A picture, an empty lunch box, and that potted plant that died as soon as it got to my flat. I mean, I didn't know Zara watered it, did I? And I nearly gave the whole lot away 'cos I didn't want to carry it around when we got to the pub. Three years at that place and it didn't even fill a cardboard box."

Liam finished, head bowed, his empty hands holding a non-existent cardboard box, all the air from his lungs spent. His unfocused eyes seemed to scan the lost contents to do a quick mental stock check.

"It was all pointless," he said.

"Tough break," said Ross.

Liam was shouting: "What's the secret?"

"What's this?" Rabbie asked.

"The magic word, the secret," Liam yelled, clearly ranting at the world in general. "The password to happiness?"

"What's he on about?" Rabbie said looking up at me.

I shrugged, getting up to go back to the Den, but Liam was in full flow: "You should choose a password that alternates across the keyboard: you know, left, right, left, right, left, like... 'England'. I want to stay in England, I don't want the Brexit racists to kick me out."

"It's the beer," I said, waving my Becks to underline the point.

"'Beer', no good," said Liam. "Double E."

Ross appeared behind Rabbie. I put my beer down and sat down again on the plush carpet a couple of steps up.

"And your name for that matter," said Liam. "I'm Liam, '*Lee*-am', useless because the first two letters are... right hand; Ross, starts well, but there's that double 'S'. Rabbie... hopeless. Guy... nope..."

We suddenly realised that we all had our hands out as if we were holding them up for inspection, our fingers wriggling as our nerves remembered where the keys were, a sort of weird Rock-Paper-Scissors game to divide the touch typists from the two finger stabbers.

A thought struck me: "Ah, 'Mandy': right, left, right, left, right." It was a marching word.

Of course, it would be a ridiculous password: girlfriend, mother's maiden name, pet's name, would all be obvious, and the University's systems insisted on an alphanumeric password with capitals and special characters.

"You know," I said, "the one at the Uni—"

"I need some air!" said Liam and he left, suddenly gone through the front door.

The three of us remaining, Ross, Rabbie and I, dropped our hands to our sides. I picked up the bottle and took another slug.

"Should we go after him?" said Rabbie.

"One for all?" Ross said.

"All for one?" I said.

It was cold outside.

Liam was standing on the gravel driveway crying, his massive shadow thrown across the ornamental pool when the security lights snapped on. It was as if he'd stepped from the theatre onto a film set, his woe magnified. The rest of us were just a trio of embarrassed spectators.

"Ross?" said Rabbie.

"Guy?" said Ross.

I took a few steps forward: "Liam, what can we do?"

"All this?" said Liam, waving his arm to encompass the whole driveway, ornamental fountain and house. "Look at all this. It's a fecking abomination... mock Tudor with Greek columns, only built six years ago. Fecking ridiculous. And this!" Liam pointed at the fountain and then strode forward, stepped over the low wall and sloshed across to the ornament as if somehow we wouldn't know what he was referring to unless his index finger was actually touching it. "It's a mermaid."

It was: I hadn't realised.

"Liam," I said. "Let's go inside."

"This is what I wanted," yelled Liam.

"Do ye no ken it's a wee bit nippy," said Ross.

"No!" Liam stamped his foot like a child, splashing the water in the fountain. It was a moment balanced finely between pathos and mirth. "I wanted all this: a flash car, a country villa, a holiday home by the coast, an apartment and a string of women, girls and more girls, and... and..."

Liam was laughing, laughing for us at himself and at the ridiculousness of it all.

"Fine Stag Party this is," Rabbie said.

"Och, man in a pond, what more could you want," said Ross.

"I've found myself," said Liam.

"Really?" I said.

"Yes," he said, sloshing across to us such that a wave overflowed the wall onto the flagstones around it.

"It wasn't me, the banking lark. My apartment was so up-to-date, modern, designer, but cold. It wasn't a home. The pictures on the walls still had thee photos the frames came with, which I bought online. The fridge never had a vegetable in it. Whole weeks would go by when I wouldn't even sleep in the bed, I'd fall asleep at my computer working the stock market... or playing an online adventure game and then wake up stiff and virtually dead."

"Och, I've often felt like death in the morning."

"No, I mean virtually dead, dead in the virtual game – killed by another player or eaten by a monster."

"Bloody hell," I said, but only because I thought I ought to say something.

"Every day it would be the same. Get up, clean teeth, make a quarter of a million for the shareholders, eat expensive food, go home, have a beer, fight monsters, fall asleep, discover I was dead: day after day, week after week, marked only by the cleaning lady replacing one set of perfectly clean black satin sheets with another identical set."

Good grief, I thought: "Black satin–"

"Ye had a maid!" said Ross.

"Cleaning lady! Hungarian."

"I wouldn't say no to a Hungarian. Reka's–"

"She was eighty!"

"Oh hell," I said and I went forward, stepped into the freezing water and patted Liam on the shoulders. "All for one."

"Aye." Ross was next to me suddenly and we hugged, the Three Musketeers. We did a little paddling dance. If we stuck together, it seemed like we could achieve anything.

"You're all mad," said Rabbie.

The three of us looked at him and cracked up.

"Och, we're pished," said Ross.

"Yep, we're pissed," I agreed.

"Pissed as mutes," said Liam.

We looked at each other, nodding: we were all agreed.

"There's the porn film," said Rabbie, pointing back into the dry warm palace.

"Porn film?" I said.

"Aye, pish, though," said Ross.

Acting as spokesman, I turned to Rabbie: "Nah, we're fine," I said.

As one, the three of us went back to the dancing, slosh-slosh, quickly developing quite an intricate series of steps.

"You're hopeless," said Rabbie. "You are. You'll catch your deaths. Think about it?"

He went in.

We danced on.

I remember the three of us lying on the grass looking at the sky pointing out Pleiades, Orion, the Wombat and Heather behind the Bike Sheds. Later, we were inside, safely walking each other to our respective rooms, two of us saying goodnight to the third, which clearly couldn't have worked for all three of us, but it's how I remember it.

Then I was alone in the unfamiliar guest room.

I did think about it, while I had a hot shower in the en-suite. Every room, even the Den, had an en-suite. The bathroom probably had an en-suite. The hot water was ecstasy after so long hiking, and then paddling in the cold water. I finally lay down on the unfamiliar bed with its pristine sheets – bliss. I was so tired, and so relaxed, and yet I couldn't sleep.

I wanted her, I did, but I wanted to keep my options open – didn't all blokes? – just in case. In case of what though? This was the infamous 'fear of commitment' that women complain about. Life is a journey, I thought, and other such clichés, much like our Jacobite march. You've a general direction perhaps, a starting point, and you know intellectually that at some point it'll end, but as for the actual route, no-one knows that.

There should be a satnav for life: turn into a student for the next three years; write a thesis for the next five years; in six months, at your wedding, turn up; in your advancing years, bear right.

Ha, but how to get it to work?

You'd have to know the postcode of your destination: B4 2L8.

My final destination was SW1A 0AA, though I didn't know it then.

Could do worse, I thought, and then berated myself for such an appalling thought. She's a woman, a human being, and not something going cheap on eBay: not 'she looks good, make an offer'.

A car went past.

Across the ceiling, its headlights made a searchlight sweep through the crack in the curtains. I thought of the sea despite being in the middle of the country. I was queasy with the alcohol and the room swaying as it did.

Whoosh went the car, clear, like a wave breaking on the shore. The silence here was different in quality to Edinburgh. Your mind filters out the traffic and the late-night revellers coming home and calls it silent. I guess those living in the country can't hear the birds and the rustling trees.

Do you think that's the problem with the world nowadays: we've lost our direction? Civilisation used to build great cathedrals – no, hear me out, it's not about the religion, it's about the planning. They used to plan things that they'd never see in their lifetimes. It's Liverpool Cathedral, isn't it, that took seven generations to build? I saw it on a documentary once.

Today it's all 'five-year plan' and 'a week is a long time in politics'.

God, remember the EU referendum? A day was a long time in politics back then.

People need hope.

But it's tax credit cuts, benefit cuts and budget cuts. Public assets like the NHS, prison service, police, Post Office and the BBC are sold off for others to profit. We're told to live within our means as our means are taken away by liars. And they laugh and laugh during the Chancellor's budget speech as they do so.

These same right honourable men who say you can live on £53 a week take home £134,565 topped up with expense claims worth fourteen times a job seeker's allowance and they max out their official credit card on £38 breakfasts.

It struck me then, lying in bed and feeling distinctly woozy, that I'd given people hope.

That moment back in the Crew & Harpur pub, when I'd stood on the chair and suggested we cross the bridge, had changed many things, and for the better. They'd gained a direction or so it seemed back then: Ross and Liam had found themselves, and I had given myself away.

So why not?

Why shouldn't my life have a new day: PM to AM, 'Pre-Mandy' to Guy 'And Mandy'.

People need hope.

The party's over

by Jacqueline Fort

Political correspondent

When John Trudie, MP, stood in the House of Commons yesterday, the party faithful held their breath. He was armed with all the facts and figures. Somewhere in the Home Office, there's a leak straight to Trudie.

So the House was given a catalogue of knife and gun crimes: muggings with knives and guns, assaults with knives and guns, and resisting arrests with knives and guns. Trudie used these figures to beat down all attempts to interrupt. It was remorseless.

Rebellion

After fifteen minutes, the rebellion from the North was mentioned: either a) peaceful and nothing to worry about; in which case why did the Home Secretary deploy all the Metropolitan Police reserve in an area outside his jurisdiction, or b) they are a serious and growing problem, one which Dorrington's boys-in-blue entirely failed to stop.

As John Trudie, MP, pointed out, 'the Home Secretary can't even stop a simple armed rebellion marching on London.'

History in the making

With the words of Guy Wilson, 27, the leader of the armed rebellion, Trudie took great delight in baiting the

> **We make our own history.**
>
> Guy Wilson

Home Secretary: 'We make our own history.' As we all know, history has its winners and, as the Home Secretary Timothy Dorrington may soon discover, its losers. The Prime Minister has the thorny problem of deciding who are friends, and who are enemies, and whether to keep them distant or close.

Destinations

The march is now only a few days away from London, and despite numerous pundits and many predictions, no-one seems to know what will happen. More importantly, the whole of the PM's Front Bench, don't know what to do about it. It seems like the entire Government's Law and Order Policy is unravelling before our eyes. A week is a long time in politics and we'll have to see what happens when the march reaches London.

INSURRECTION

There's a paperclip on the floor, partially trapped under the skirting board. It's thick and big and it looks perfect. Plonking my head against the wall, I stare down at the wonderful spiral almost in tears. It's the first lucky break for a long, long time.

Picking it up, I open it out and fiddle it around to the handcuff lock. Probing about randomly doesn't do the trick and I shuffle over to the light to get a better look. It doesn't help.

I've seen Mandy's cuffs, played with them, even suggested kinky games with them and the key isn't that complicated. I just need a sharp right-angle bend about half a centimetre, but the wire won't budge. I try my teeth, but that hurts.

The gap under the door is too large, but the side by the hinge is about right. I put the right length in between the door and the frame, and bend. The door dents and the angle is shy of 90°, but I finish it off by pushing the end against the wall.

Back in the light, I feel around inside the lock, but I might as well be in the dark for all the good it does.

Oh, this is useless.

Come on!

I try again, probing systematically until I'm nudging up against the tumbler. I try another angle and it gives... slightly... falls back. Carefully, I try the action again and find the right spot.

It moves and the cuff releases.

I pause; I don't want to jam it or botch it... or ratchet the thing tighter... *ah*, I need another hand as I have to keep the tension on the paperclip. Reaching with my mouth doesn't work as I can't bend my elbow far enough.

I go over to the table and carefully put one of the metal teeth against the corner: it eases, moves and opens.

My face is screwed up with concentration.

I slip my wrist out and stretch.

God, it's good. I rub my freed left hand with my right, the handcuffs clattering like some mad bracelet. There's a red mark.

A couple of seconds fiddling with the other one convinces me that it'll take longer. My left hand isn't as good at manipulating the paperclip and I think I was lucky the first time. Doesn't luck come in threes, and I only need to...

I could escape!

The thought crosses my mind as I move to the door. I kneel down, still idly fiddling with the cuffs, but now my attention is on the door's keyhole.

Could I pick this lock?

I try the handle. It's big and round and turns, but all it does is disengage the opening mechanism. There's a keyhole for a big, old-fashioned key. There's light beyond it and once I stop seeing my own eyelashes, I can focus on the far wall of the corridor outside. I try to see into the lock itself. There must be a similar tumbler to the handcuffs, no doubt bulkier and more complicated, so I try the paperclip, but it's clearly inadequate for this job. I need a bent nail or a wire coat-hanger.

I stand up and notice for the first time that there's a spy hole at eye level. I squint and the corridor leaps forwards, huge and tantalisingly close. The hole is to look out to check who wants to enter this secret room.

OK, I can't get out.

There's no nail and picking the door lock with the paperclip won't work. Smashing it down isn't an option either as the door's wood looks solid enough to splinter any chair, even without taking the metal reinforcing into account.

I sit down on the floor and lean against the wall while I fiddle with the handcuffs, more out of something to do than anything else, and finally the right cuff releases. My wrist needs rubbing and I flex my fingers, out and fist, out and fist: paper and rock. I make a scissors shape, oddly fascinated, and then paper again. If 'rock' is brute force, then 'paper', academic thought, wraps 'rock'. I must be able to pit my brain against Vaughn's brawn.

There must be a way out, surely?

Perhaps I could pretend to have escaped?

They did that in Colditz. I remember the black and white film. Yes, the guards would count the prisoners, realise one was missing and the hue-and-cry would spread across the country. Once it had died down, then a real escape wouldn't attract any attention. I could simply drop the handcuffs by the door, leave the paperclip mangled in the door lock, and perhaps they'd assume I'd managed to pick the lock. They'd search the police station, the country, occupied France, but not this room, then... the door would be locked, though.

I could probably force the bent wire of the paperclip through so that it stuck out the other side, so pretending to have locked the door again. I'd need to hide in this empty room, though, and one glance would be enough, even in this rubbish light.

There's a table with the tape recorder, a broken chair, an OK chair, big window, boring walls and nothing remotely like a cupboard or a wardrobe. What did they do in Prisoner of War films? Dig tunnels. The floor is hard, lino on concrete probably. What else? Didn't John Mills dress up as a Nazi and stroll out? I could wear yellow shoelaces.

I have no shoelaces in my boots. They'd taken them to stop me committing suicide; strange that, stopping me from killing myself when they actually want to kill me.

What am I thinking? I'm dressed as a Jacobite, they're going to see the plaid and my knees long before they look at any shoelaces. I'm not going to fly out... they built a plane in Colditz to escape, glide off the roof and... it was constructed in the attic. The ceiling here is polystyrene tiles. They're stained with tobacco smoke from the days of indoor smoking.

I can't reach it standing, I try the chair, but even then it's out of reach. Carefully, I put the good chair onto the table with the tape recorder. It fits, just, with a few centimetres clearance all round. Raising my boot up to the table makes it apparent that clambering up is going to be dangerous. The broken chair on its side makes a wobbling step and I'm on the table holding the good chair. It's moved, but, although it's tricky, I manage to shift the chair back into place while teetering on the edge.

Up and... jeez, that was close. The chair twisted and one leg is very close to disaster, but I'm up. I almost daren't move in case the house of cards comes tumbling down.

The ceiling tile is easy to reach, I lift it and it is a false ceiling. There's space above, so I slide the panel to one side resting it on the top of the ceiling. I push my

211

head up and wait until my eyes become accustomed to the dark. It smells musty and damp. There's mould somewhere.

It's a half-metre gap, maybe a touch more, to the true ceiling and it stretches over the whole room. Rods at intervals hold the frame, and thus the polystyrene tiles, up. There are pipes across the space, one white one with peeling paint goes right overhead. The gap might be high enough. I could clamber up, hide.

They'd see the chair on the table.

So? Kick it off, no problem.

Could I reach a pipe and would it take my weight? Only one way to find out. I take hold, but I realise that my hands will simply slip off. And where am I going for that matter, I'll need somewhere that'll support me lying down. The fake ceiling won't.

There's a thick pipe that goes laterally. It must continue, passing through the wall and above the interview room on the other side of the one-way glass. The brickwork is faulty and the gap around the pipe is far bigger than it needs to be. I could crawl across perhaps, pull out a few bricks – the one on the left has nearly fallen out already – and then squeeze through. I'd probably fall straight through the polystyrene tiles on the other side and down into an ignominious heap, but I'd be in the other room.

♦

I awoke the day after the Stag Party with the vilest taste ever in my mouth, impossible to ignore. I'd hoped for a lie-in, a chance to recover not only from last night's party, but also from the walking. My body needed a few extra hours to repair itself, but it wasn't to be. Eventually, giving up any hope of sleep, I pulled myself out of bed.

My watch said '12:30' – struth, a morning lost and no benefit from the lie-in.

The Den was empty. I found the kitchen. The others were there and the kettle had boiled. The place reeked of fried food.

Rabbie was cooking bacon, which just seemed revolting at this time in the morning... afternoon, and everyone griped about the smell, but even so, we wolfed it down when it arrived: fried bacon, fried eggs, fried bread, orange juice by the gallon and a mug of tea.

"Others have walked it, so we can meet them at the pub," said Liam.

"Och, we're supposed to walk it all," Ross complained, "and do yer no ken I've given up pubs on account of my head."

Liam insisted that we tidy up, wash up, make the beds, hide the dirty laundry and so on, so we all traipsed around the huge house being useless. Finally, Liam's quality control threshold dropped enough for us to declare the job done, and off we went to the van.

"Are you sure you're not still over the limit?" I asked Ross.

"I barely had a wee dram or two."

"Of whiskey after the beer?"

"Aye."

"Did you have any hair of the dog?"

"Och, no," he said, before turning to the others accusingly: "It had all gone."

The van kicked itself forward, almost stalled and then scrunched around the water feature and off down the gravel drive, finding every crater and mound on the way to the B-road. No-one threw up, which was a miracle, and things settled down once we'd reached an A-road.

Liam navigated and we arrived at the 'och, absolutely not' pub. It was the one on from the meeting place; Liam had done it deliberately, crafty sod, but we all appreciated avoiding a walk. We found a quaint teashop with scones, cream and jam. Ross moaned that it was cheating, but he leant against the wall and actually fell asleep. To be fair, he'd done the driving.

We were having seconds, cucumber sandwiches cut into triangles, when the first of the Tartan Army strolled past the window. I started to get up, but Liam pulled me back.

"Let 'em gather and finish your sarnies," he said.

I didn't need any more persuading.

It gave me a chance to watch the rebellion gather as if I was one of the middle-class, middle-aged, curtain-twitchers who complained about the rowdy oiks. Beneath the frilly nets and through the scrollwork of the window design, I saw this phenomenon assembling on the small triangular green by a war memorial.

One day off had given me enough distance to see it objectively and I was shocked at the size of it. When we were inside the mass, we didn't notice the ones and twos, half-dozens, and finally, coach parties joining. Looking at it from the outside, we all commented on how big the movement had grown, and after that, we had to comment again as the gathering didn't show any signs of petering out.

"They're going round the back in a circle," said Liam, motioning above his head in a big circle, "like on the TV."

It might have then, but it didn't need to now.

We had a quick game of Rock-Paper-Scissors, and Rabbie's scissors to my paper meant it was his turn to move the van. He took his coat off the back of the chair and nipped out while the rest of us ordered dessert.

Finally, a sticky bun each later, we emerged and strolled over to the crowd. Once we were recognized, we were greeted with cheers and gentle, friendly jibes: the Three Musketeers – skivers!

We bowed and were magnanimous in accepting both applause and ridicule.

"One for all," said Liam.

"And all for one," Ross and I said.

Rabbie was talking to the police.

♦

Key jangling in the lock!

Another!

Fuck!

I'm still looking into the ceiling space!

Instinctively, I leap off the chair, catch it, and totter it back onto the table. Before any plan is assimilated, I cross the room and barely make it to the wall before the door swings open. I hold my breath.

The door bumps against my boot on opening and by chance, the spy hole is just in front of my nose. I flex slightly to see through. A pie slice of light is laid out like a red carpet across the room, turned up at the corners and magnified because of the fisheye lens in the spy hole.

Vaughn stands distorted and impossibly close, staring at the table, the chair, the black hole of an exit in the ceiling. The handcuffs lie on the floor, half-in and half-out of the light.

"Shit!" he says.

He steps into the room.

I think to put my finger lightly on the door handle to stop it from closing. It wouldn't do to be just standing there against the wall when he turns round. I daren't check, there's not enough space to tilt my head down.

Vaughn struggles to clamber up the table, sees the chair shifting and almost tumbles over backwards. He tries again, but it's clear he isn't going to be able to do it. In fact, I've no idea now how I managed it. The whole arrangement is that rickety and dangerous.

"Fuck!" he says.

He kicks the table and the tape recorder scoots dangerously close to the edge. He might look inside it and immediately know the evidence is in my sporran. It's an irrational thought, but I feel a hollow emptiness in the pit of my stomach.

The man rages silently, his fists clenched, in a strange little jig like a clockwork boxer winding himself up for a bout. Suddenly, I can't see him, but I can hear the broken chair being kicked, and then silence.

Where is he? Where is he? Where is he?

Mustn't look. Mustn't look. Mustn't look.

To my left, I hear the phone receiver being lifted. I turn my head and I can see through the crack between door and jam: Vaughn presses 'B'. He'll see me – he looks round, straight at me, Christ!

Then he looks back at the phone.

I'm standing in the dark, he can't see through the crack; it's like an arrow slit in a castle, wide inside to allow a range of directions to fire the arrow, but narrow outside to prevent an arrow from entering.

"Come on," Vaughn says under his breath. God, he's a big man, now I get a chance to scrutinise him properly. Plan A: hitting him with the chair would not have worked.

I think back: 'B' was the button Vaughn answered when I tried it.

"Come on," he says again. "Come on."

There's clearly no answer: Vaughn himself is not there, so I wonder who else he's trying to contact.

"Fuck!"

Vaughn storms out; the handle zipped from beneath my finger as he pulls the door to behind him. I hear a couple of stamping footsteps and then he's gone.

He's left the red light on.

I stand with my back hard against the wall unable to move. It's as if the triangular hiding place is still there, and my breathing feels ragged and unpractised before an out-breath like a sigh conjures itself forth. I lean forward, my hands on my bare knees, and gasp.

OK, I think, I've got the door unlocked.

No turning back now, I'm escaping.

♦

"I'm afraid you'll have to turn back, Sir," said a policeman.

"What's going on?" I said, genially.

It was a beautiful, bright sunlit day. The Jacobites were accessorized with sunglasses. The air was still, so the dappled pattern from a big oak tree gave the green a pattern of tiny shapes until the wind gusted and the old tree shook itself like a Great Dane with a stick in its teeth after clambering from a boating lake.

"We've crossed a line," said Rabbie.

"What's happened?"

"No, I mean, we've crossed a line, we're in another county and... what was it again?"

"You don't have the council's permission to proceed, Sir."

"Surely, we've freedom of assembly?" I said.

"Yes, Sir, but not to march."

"There's freedom to march," I added.

"Ah, Sir," he said, apologetically, "only if you've registered the route."

"So we can stay here, but not leave?"

"Yes, Sir."

"That's a shame because we've come such a long way."

"Be that as it may, Sir, but you don't have the permissions."

"So..?"

"We have to enforce the by-law."

"Could we perhaps just go, in ones and two, down the road to the... er..."

"King's Head," said Rabbie.

"King's Head, yes, it's just a mile or two."

"That wouldn't really be in the spirit of things, would it, Sir?"

"It's just assembling in a different place."

"But there's a route between the two places that you haven't registered, Sir."

"Right," I said. I looked down in chagrin at my boots. My toe caps were scrapped and damaged. I think they were still wet from the paddling pool the night before. The policeman wore black trainers, dirty too from all the beat duty.

Another set of footwear appeared near me, black and polished, yellow shoelaces, and I looked up to their owner.

"I think we should let them go through," said this new policeman, his dress uniform smart and ironed.

"Sir, I think—"

The smart one showed something to the first copper, an ID snapped open-and-closed like a flashgun popping. "On you go!" he added.

"Thank you," I said. I nodded to him. He was smart, and when my nod took my eye-line down, I saw his shoelaces again – it rang a bell.

A 'hurrah' echoed down the Jacobite line and the whole procession lurched into gear. We moved on and I saw the new policeman join some colleagues up ahead. They were standing, watchful, by an unmarked car. As we marched past, I looked at their laces: red to his yellow. It struck me as odd, perhaps they'd bulk-bought as a collective. Hitler had ordered black shirts to imitate Mussolini's fascists, and when the wrong colour arrived, the Nazis formed the 'brownshirts'.

Quite soon, we traipsed downhill and picked up speed, a pub not far away apparently, and I'd have put it out of my mind, but it nagged. Hang on, I thought, I've seen this before when—

"You showed them, didn't you?" said a voice.

"I did," I said. "Er..."

218

"Snetterton."

"Hi," I said, "I'm Guy."

"Snitty," he said, shaking my hand. "You don't want to let the filth curtail your rights, do you?"

"Rights are important," I replied for want of something to say.

Snetterton was dressed in a long, dark brown leather coat like he was a civilian of our period rather than a Jacobite or Redcoat, or one of the many other groups. They'd all adopted tartan or red as our ad hoc uniform. Snetterton did a shuffle every few paces to catch up as he was walking sideways watching my expression. His shoelaces were yellow, which was hardly a re-enacting colour.

Hang on, I thought, most of the march consisted of other groups now.

"We should *fight* for them," he said. He seemed to twist his diction around the word 'fight'. "Fight," he said again.

"Yes," I said.

"Stop the filth eroding our rights."

"Yes."

That night, the floor of the van, after the overly comfy bed I'd forsaken in the morning, seemed very hard.

Superintendent killed in police car crash

Police today named Superintendent Alfred McGivern as the senior police officer killed in Monday's fatal road accident involving several cars on the M25 near junction 21 and the M1.

Luckily, nobody else was killed, although several people were injured and had to be taken to St. Thomas' Hospital. The M25 clockwise was closed for three hours after the incident.

The Metropolitan Police have appealed for witnesses. A spokeswoman said: 'We would particularly like to talk to a heavily-built, dark-haired white male seen wandering from the scene of the incident.'

Superintendent McGivern was widely regarded as a fine officer, although he came under criticism for his zero tolerance approach to abuses within the police force itself and for his insistence upon correct procedure.

His funeral will be next week. No flowers, but donations to the Police Benevolent Fund would be gratefully received.

220

THE COST OF WAR

I open the door of the Observation Room very gingerly and look forward, then left and right in a move I've rehearsed mentally, and immediately pop my head back.

No-one.

OK, right is back towards the cells and I don't want to go that way, and left is towards Vaughn and Trudie, and I don't want to go that way either.

I step out.

It feels utterly open and exposed in the corridor, which stretches in both directions, pale cream walls lit by stark strip lights. I'm completely visible from both ends.

I can't stay here; I have to move.

Left it is.

Do I try doors as I go along? When I've done this for real in computer games... no, this is real, but does all that simulated training actually apply? Should I try every door as I go past? Should I save my position at every turn? Should I test the walls for secret passages as I go?

I need a weapon: a magic sword or an unfeasibly huge machine gun. Or a phased plasma pulse-laser in the forty-watt range.

I try a door: it's a broom cupboard with a few mops and a bucket on wheels. It smells stale. I could hide here, wait until it's all over and then, when the hue-and-cry has died down, sneak out.

But I can't do that: I owe it to my friends to avenge their deaths.

I could get forty winks, maybe.

Sit down, get some rest and think: that's a good plan. I'm so tired that I can't think straight. That's why I keep thinking about what happened. Yes, this is definitely the right thing to do. A fresh mind would make for a fresh approach.

My friends are still alive. I could save them.

Who am I fooling? What can I do?

I can try.

As these thoughts cross my mind, I close the door and venture further into the warren.

At the far end, I gaze at the security camera perched high on the wall. If someone is on duty at the other end of the CCTV, then I'm already caught. If I'd hidden in the broom cupboard, they could have checked the recording easily enough and found me.

I could have broken the mop and used the handle as a spear. It works in the movies. I don't turn back at this thought. My feet move with a will of their own, despite my brain's rambling. I'm reminded of those long days marching south when the blisters and exhaustion set in. You thought, I can't go on, I can't, I can't... and yet your feet just went one in front of the other. It's like that now, one soft pad after another, along the parquet floor.

My boots flap – I need some shoelaces.

The next corridor is wider and full of junk: double-parked office chairs and old desks, filing cabinets out of a museum, a broken hat stand, a collection of waste paper baskets. It's all '70s stuff, I think; it's not my period. On one desk, there's an ashtray complete with cigarette butts, which dates the site. It's like a collection of archaeological finds by a dig: this type of flint axe, that pottery fragment and these cigarettes make this layer pre-2007. They must have been emptying this building and, when they'd moved all this into the corridor, they must have realised it was all just tat.

There's water damage, everything smells of damp, and the floor is sticky and grasping. I touch a fancy chair, an old-fashioned work of art made of teak with red leather upholstery ripped to shreds. It rotates easily before it catches and creaks loudly.

Near the next intersection, I hear voices.

I stop, the soles of my boots squeaking against the polished surface as I hit the pedestrian brakes.

They're coming closer.

At the last moment, I throw myself to the ground and scurry beneath a desk. Something stabs my back, a metal bracket that's come loose or something. For a moment, I have this visceral memory of hiding under my bed when I was seven or eight.

Ninety-nine, one hundred, ready or not, here I come.

I see a collection of shoes scoot past: boots with yellow – she'd said 'ochre' – laces, smart black shoes with red laces, and a pair I recognize.

"...and find the little shit before Trudie finds out."

"I'm not responsible for security," says Snitch. "I'm intelligence."

He's talking to Vaughn.

"Don't screw with me," says Vaughn as they reach the corner. "Intelligence my arse, you're just..."

Someone stops at the corner, pausing, turning, taking a half-step closer. I can hear the glutinous floor glueing the leather to the ground, giving in tiny snaps sticky of sound, as the person approaches: *schlop-schlop*.

"Did you let him wander off?" says a female voice.

A bearing creaks.

The leather chair!

♦

It was a Sunday, a day off from the march.

Mandy wanted to go shopping and there was a High Street en route. I can't remember how many shops we visited, because it was all a blur. She was trained in unarmed combat, local club kickboxing champion and all-round tough cookie, and she wanted to do the whole girlie bit, try this on with those shoes with that matching accessory and this bag.

"Don't wander off," she said, more than once. "I have to keep looking for you."

So, I was dragged along, uncomplaining for the most part, for my opinion. I mean, come on, it's '*phwoar*' or not '*phwoar*', isn't it? It's really hard to give an opinion of yet another delightful entree of haute couture, when it's the blonde, blue-eyed, fresh-faced, slim and fit body you are interested in, rather than something on sale that comes in size 12 to 16. When you rip the wrapping off a present, you don't give your opinions on the paper's colour, form and pattern, do you?

After a while, I became the baggage train.

"Ah, does diddums want a beer?"

"Yes."

"What do you think?"

"Well..."

"Well, what?"

"Isn't it a bit similar to that red trouser suit thing you've already got?"

"This is the red trouser suit thing I've already got."

"Is it?"

"I've been wearing it all day."

Oh shit: "You've been trying things on."

"What," she said pointedly, "do you think of the shoes?"

They were black, flat, sensible ladies' smart shoes with double knotted shoelaces. Mandy had already re-laced them, so that they went straight across, neat yellow lines, rather than in some cack-handed, shoe-shop criss-crossed arrangement. This meant that she had already decided. Straight across meant that the laces could be easily cut from a wounded foot: basic army training, you dork, she'd said, and you say you're in re-enactment – honestly.

"Very functional," I said. "They don't really go with the outfit, though."

"They're for work."

Outside, a gang of hoodies surrounded us, good-naturedly, although in a way that felt it could go nasty.

"Transvestite poofter!" was the gist of one phrase.

"She wears the trousers and forces you to wear a dress," was another.

"Look," I began, "let's–"

"WPC Reynolds!" Mandy said, showing them her warrant card. They scattered, weaving in and out of the crowd. Long after they'd disappeared, their wake had been visible in the distant shoppers recovering from near collisions.

"Are you allowed to do that?" I asked.

"Bend a few rules, gets things done."

I chuckled, it was funny then.

There were a few jewellers just off the High Street and we picked one Mandy knew all about. She'd checked on the internet, I realised. Why hadn't I?

Well, I'd been on the march – still was – and they didn't have the internet in the 18th century.

How much do you spend, I wondered?

I'm a poor postgraduate student, so my finances aren't great. My bank balance had been taking a hammering from all the rounds we'd been buying each other on the march. I prepared for the worst, girding my loins, but it went the other way. I was shocked at how cheap some of them were. This was for life and I wanted quality for my fiancée, I thought, not some cheap tat.

Also, I felt she shouldn't know the price, but how do you – *cough* – say, er, this display cabinet I think, dearest. There were single diamonds, clusters, birthstones, or in Mandy's case bloodstone as her birthday had been a few months back in March, and gold, white gold, platinum, and so on. At least there weren't designer labels... oh, there were.

"Oooh!"

The choice was made – instinctive and final.

Fairly quickly, we had three rings: engagement and a wedding ring each, those being plain bands of gold, which Mandy popped in her bag for safe keeping. The only box I kept was the engagement ring's. I went to put the ring on her finger in the shop, but she snatched her hand away.

"Not here," Mandy said, "somewhere romantic."

Top of Arthur's Seat with the view of Edinburgh below as the sun comes up, or Derby while stepping through the waterfall, or in front of massed police in riot gear... Bonnie Prince Charlie married Clementina Walkinshaw, who he'd met on the 1745 Jacobite Uprising, and I wondered where he proposed to her – probably in France.

We found a statue in the corner of the park, secluded enough by some trees, and beneath some 19th century industrial benefactor, I got down on one knee again, my other acting as a side table to lean on. Mandy stood above me, straight and expectant, with her hands clasped together in front of her in a demure, old-fashioned pose.

I did the full looking at her from toe to brow, slowly panning my gaze from her sensible black shoes with their yellow shoelaces, up past her ankles, up the long red trouser of her legs, the tightness around her hips and her slender waist, nice breasts and clear, healthy face framed by blonde hair. She looked down with her blue eyes, expectantly.

"Mandy... Amanda, will you marry me?" I asked.

"Why?"

"Why?"

"Yes, why do you want to marry me?"

A few people had stopped in their perambulations to watch. I felt a pressure to think of something quickly.

"Because I love you," I said.

"Do you really, Guy?"

"Yes, look, I'm marching to London to be with you," I said. "Isn't that proof?"

"It's certainly a demonstration," she said, "but, I believe, without permission."

"You want me to ask your father or the local county council?"

"Why?"

"I want to be with you."

"OK. So..."

"So?"

"Ask."

"Will you marry me?"

"Yes."

I took out the tiny box from my sporran, flipped it open and eased the ring onto her offered left hand. It went onto her third finger easily. I remember the ring box shut with a loud clunk. I put it back into my sporran as we walked across the park towards the others.

Mandy had bought a few things for a picnic. We settled on the corner of a tartan blanket, which looked suspiciously like someone's plaid, although I couldn't see who was wearing only shorts... or nothing.

Everyone had hot broth, crusty bread and thick slices of meat; whereas, upon opening the package, I discovered Mandy and I had opted for Japanese: sushi, soba noodles, botamochi and chimaki, I think, with disposable chopsticks. She had a bottle of saké and some plastic glasses. It all generated a few glances of surprise.

"I like this," Mandy said, flickering my sporran up and down.

"I know you do."

"I mean the purse."

"Sporran," I said. "The lads bought it for me on my Stag do."

"You've had a Stag Party already?"

"Yes."

"We've only been engaged..." she checked her watch: "Ten minutes and you've had a Stag do!? It's supposed to be before your wedding."

"It was before my wedding."

"Just before!"

"You want me to get married with my head shaved and my eyebrows dyed?"

She laughed: "I wouldn't mind, but I suspect my Aunt would disapprove. Hang on, you had your Stag Party before I had the ring."

I took a mouthful of sushi. It was cold and slightly slimy in its seaweed wrapping, and a very pleasant change from steak and chips. I like pub food, but it had become monotonous and–

"Did you have strippers?" Mandy accused. This was an interrogation.

"No!"

"What did you do then?"

"We had a few beers, played some pool and watched a film."

"Porn?"

"*Chasing the Deer.*"

"That? Whatever for?"

"'Cos we wanted to."

"Likely story."

"Should I have a lawyer present?"

Mandy sat back, her hand coming up to wave away my comment: "I'm just asking."

"Is this the beginning of the change? Jealousy perhaps?"

"No." Mandy leaned away, pouted rather childishly, and then repeated: "No."

Ross and Liam arrived at that moment carrying beers. There was something of a hunt to find a bottle opener, but then we were all knocking back Bishop's Finger.

"I don't like drinking out of a bottle," I said.

"Och, next you'll be complaining it's too warm."

"No, just real ale shouldn't be drunk out of the bottle."

"Here," said Mandy, taking my bottle. She sloshed it into a plastic glass. The head was extraordinary.

"It had saké in it!"

"What are you complaining about now?"

"I prefer my beer in a proper tall glass."

"Is this what it's going to be like from now on?" she asked. "Endless complaints as well as the history lectures?"

"Och, listen to the old married couple, will ye?" said Ross.

"No," I said to both of them.

Mandy leant over and showed off her ring.

"Och, you've got a ring," said Ross.

"It's lovely," said Liam.

"Yes," said Mandy, beaming, as she showed it to them. "Wait until I show Kate and Reka."

They made appreciative noises, even though I knew they weren't that interested in jewellery.

"It's nice," said Snetterton. It was Snetterton. Did he have a first name? I hadn't realised he was sitting on the edge of the group.

"Thank you," said Mandy.

"Fine shoes too," said Snetterton.

"Thank you," said Mandy. "So are yours,"

Mandy was looking down and I followed her gaze. I saw her shoes, tucked to one side as she'd folded her legs back to sit, the grass and then Snetterton's boots, but I couldn't see what had warranted her comment. It struck me as odd, because his boots were scratched and unpolished like everyone else's on the march. They'd obviously taken a hammering because his shoelaces were new, and the colour was wrong.

"He's got yellow shoelaces," I pointed out.

"Ochre," said Mandy.

Ross and Liam stood and brushed off the few loose snags of grass and twigs.

"We're off to the pub before we start south again."

"There are drinks here," said Mandy.

"Och aye, but I need a piss."

They went off across the park, followed by Snetterton, and as they went a few others joined them, a tartan-and-red army gathering strength, disappearing amongst the brightly coloured, hot and cooked civilians.

Mandy stood: "You going too?"

"I've a date in London."

"Who with?"

"My fiancée," I said, and I licked my fingers of the last of the soy sauce, got up, held her in my arms and we kissed. It was the end of a glorious summer day. "I'll see you in London."

She gave me a last peck on the lips: "I'll see you in London."

♦

I'm in London now.

Oh God, please don't let her see me!

Her shoes, with their ochre laces, squidge on the lino, coming closer.

"Ah-ha," comes out with the smallest of breaths.

Report #378 – Shift 1, Zulu-03
Officers: ███████, ███████ and ███████.

06:00   Took over surveillance of
        vehicle BTR from Zulu-07.
09:17   Movement observed within vehicle
        BTR.
09:58   Target GW left vehicle BTR and
        entered shop.
10:12   Target GW returned to vehicle
        BTR with bottles of water.
10:25   Target RT and Target GW exit
        vehicle BTR and enter the King's
        Arms.
10:32   Target RT and Target GW reappear
        and are observed talking to
        Agent ███████████.
10:46   Target RT and Target GW re-enter
        vehicle BTR.
10:48   Target LR leaves vehicle BTR for
        the King's Arms.
10:53   Target LR returns to vehicle BTR
        at 10:53am.
10:55   Target GW leaves vehicle BTR and
        joins march joining Target RM.
10:56   Vehicle BTR drives off South.
11:23   Vehicle BTR stops at petrol
        station. PC ██████ enters to
        observe as they purchase snacks.
11:42   March reaches petrol station.
        Target GW talks to Target RT.
        Target RT joins march, Target GW
        travels in vehicle BTR.
11:45   Vehicle BTR continues South.
11:58   Car Zulu-05 takes over
        surveillance, en route.

Report ends.

SHOCK AND AWE

Vaughn's angry voice: "Come on!"

The desk creaks, its old chipboard and cracked veneer complaining. Feet in sensible shoes bang against the drawers. She's sitting on the table.

Vaughn's stride brings him right up to my hiding place. I can see his workman boots, steel toe caps ready to kick someone's head in – mine.

"We're not going to find the shit by sitting around."

"I suppose not."

"When I find him, I'll break every–"

"Proportionate and necessary," Mandy says. Trudie said that right before the breaking eggs cliché.

Vaughn snorts: "You going to read him his rights! Just do the job and don't arse about with due process."

"He's no use as a means to an end if you've broken him."

"You're a cold one," Vaughn says, "I like that. When this is over, do you fancy–"

"My face is here. If you don't mind."

"Suit yourself, your loss," says Vaughn, and he steps back, suspicious perhaps.

"I'm up here," says Mandy.

Vaughn straightens: "Let's be clear here about who's in charge."

"Of course," Mandy says, sweetly. "It's Mister Trudie, MP – the Home Secretary."

Vaughn coughs and turns.

I see his feet, legs and then all of him as he walks back along the corridor. If he turns now, he'll be able to see under the desk.

Mandy's legs appear, landing a few inches from my face.

"I said, come on," Vaughn shouts.

Hesitation... and then Mandy moves away. I turn my head away, better to obscure myself from any backwards glance, but mostly because I don't want to look.

My palms are attached to the floor by the sticky adhesion. I pull myself away and squirm round to look along the corridor. I'm still under the desk. I don't want to move. I think if I hadn't been so dehydrated, I'd have wet myself. I'm amazed at the ability of the human mind and body to feel fear; you'd think your capacity would diminish. Mine hasn't. I can't get used to it – it just goes on and on. Fight or flight: there can't be that much hormone left for the stress to squeeze out of my adrenal gland.

They say the Truth is the first casualty of war. Aeschylus, the Greek playwright, was the first to note that, two thousand five hundred years of war destroying Truth. He was the father of tragedy, and it is a tragedy that we historians can never be sure of what really happened, never know the truth.

Why is it that warmongers require justification?

Hitler, mad and ambitious, plotted with the Russians to invade and divide Poland up in an act that spawned the Second World War. But even the Fuhrer couldn't simply invade, so he had the SS pretend to be Poles and attack a German Radio station. Hitler wanted to save the Aryan race, but he had to fake being the victim. Why did he need to justify a war that the Nazis already felt was just? Trudie wants to... can I compare the Second World War, the deaths of 70 million people, with that of some poxy rioters?

I need a plan.

Crawling around on the scummy floor in random corridors just isn't going to cut it.

But what's the point?

Even if I get out of here, I can't go to the police. Supposing my luck changed and I handed myself over to a good apple, they'd just shunt me up the chain of command to the authorities and top of the heap is the Home Secretary. I'd be back here before I knew it.

If not the police, then... the press.

Murdoch is the pocket that the right-wing snuggles inside. 'When I go into Downing Street they do what I say;' Rupert Murdoch said, 'when I go to Brussels they take no notice.'

It's suddenly obvious: trial by television, contempt of court and stories too good to check. Splash it everywhere, television, newspapers, Facebook, Twitter, Pinterest, a page on Wikipedia – throw so much muck that some of it has to stick – and get it to go viral. Under the glare of flashbulbs and cameras, Trudie couldn't cover it all up, surely?

Which one though? The ones I'd met were a couple of regional zones up north... sod it, just go through the doors of Broadcasting House and ask to see the head of BBC News.

I wriggle out from under the desk and make my way down the corridor in the opposite direction from Vaughn and the other goons. With a final destination in mind, my mental satnav seemed to have found its satellites – 'calculating route', here we go.

I'm learning.

♦

Ross lectured on learning.

"Learn and churn!" he'd said.

My panic has made me lose my thread, but then a lot of what happened was confusing. Events seem riffle-shuffled in my memory. I do remember that the days after I'd given Mandy the ring were a blurred montage of walking, pubs and trying to sleep in the van. It was almost impossible to remember which part of which conversation happened where.

"As opposed to..." I'd said.

"Proper teaching," said Ross. "The thing that gets me is that I sound so old. I catch myself saying things that start with 'the youth of today...' Every generation does that, I know—"

"Plato complained that things were never like this in his day," I said. "Of course, the youth of today don't study their Plato."

"Aye, but things are different now."

Ross held up his palm to me: 'Stop'.

I stopped and the Jacobite rebellion separated into two streams and flowed around us. We'd be at the back if this took long, I thought.

"This is a doorbell," he said.

"Right," I said.

"Och, go on, press it."

"What?"

"My hand, it's a doorbell, press it. It's not a trick."

"OK." I pressed his hand: "Ding dong."

"You used your forefinger," said Ross.

"Well, duh."

"Students use their thumbs."

"Sorry?"

"It's the PlayStation, computer games and texting they do. The default finger is now the thumb. This is for a whole generation," Ross said, playing an imaginary video game with his thumbs. "Even walking around, they're always playing catch a Pokémon."

I considered my forefinger, and then tried the doorbell with my thumb – it felt awkward.

"That's weird," I said.

"It's all push button and it affects exams. I had a student who did a question and she wrote: 'ye dinna use chlorides'. OK?"

"OK."

"The answer was 'chlorides', so I gave her zero."

"Because she got it wrong."

"Aye, but she argued back, kept on saying she should have got a mark, because she checked the mark scheme."

"They're allowed the mark scheme?"

"Standard practice," he said as if it wasn't a question. "The mark scheme said you got a mark for using the word 'chlorides'. Her answer, 'ye dinna use chlorides', did use the word 'chlorides', so she insisted – and she wouldn't let it drop – that she was entitled to a mark. No amount of persuasion would shift her view. You see, for her, the word 'chlorides' was a button to push, a doorbell to open up the next level, gain the mark, pass and gain get a place at University to do medicine. They don't want to understand the subject, they want the password. It's all magic now: *examus passiosum*."

Ross waved his hands as if conjuring.

"We have to make our targets, increase our value-added," he continued, "so, we take shortcuts to get 'em through the exam and thus shunt the problem up to the poor sod at the next level. It'll be getting to Universities soon."

"Already there," I said.

"Aye?"

"We're having to run remedial classes in English and other departments have to cover basic maths."

"Och, I've just realised. It's reached teaching."

"Really?"

"Aye, the latest NQTs are shite. We had a temporary teacher in, you know, supply teacher to cover a maternity leave, and she said, och, I can't teach Edexcel, I teach AQA–"

"AQA?"

"It's the board, A-levels are examined by AQA, Edexcel or the Welsh one. Anyway, she only knew the AQA syllabus... I mean, they're all Chemistry. It's not like molecules know what board is running the practical. The boards themselves are getting easier and easier. It's competition, basic economics. If your board lowers its standards, more students get better grades, therefore more students apply to take their exams via your board. The other boards have to follow suit otherwise market forces will put them out of business."

"Is that why it's all multiple choice?"

"Aye. They've a 25% chance of getting it right by guessing. Untrained monkeys can get a D at least."

We walked on and I mulled this over. Was life just a series of multiple choices? Not sure what to do: phone a friend. I'd not heard from Mandy in a while. I remember reaching into my sporran for my mobile.

Ask the audience, fifty-fifty, phone a friend, take a wild guess – choice of four buttons, A, B, C or D.

♦

That's what I need, a phone, and not one with A, B, C or D, but the digits 0-9.

Having slid out from under the desk, I tiptoe down the corridor. There's an intersection: this place is huge, and every route looks the same... shit, I've gone round in a circle. I think. I've four choices, bloody A to D again. Maybe that was the trick, go back to the Observation Room. It at least has the appeal of being unexpected.

Could I really pull off something genuinely unexpected?

These thugs had chased people their whole careers and I'd done it a few times, but only in a computer game. With my thumbs.

The only battles I've done all started with a discussion with the 'enemy' about our rules of engagement or a surprise attack into Kamchatka, and ended with a friendly pint with the 'enemy'.

Computer games had websites devoted to hints and tips, even cheats. What I wouldn't give for a secret code that teleports me to safety.

The options really boil down to the right one or the wrong one.

◆

"Every choice is binary," said Liam. We'd stopped at a pub, of course.

"Och, no it isn't," said Ross. "What if it's multiple choice with four options, A, B, C or D?"

"It can still be reduced to a Turing Machine."

"What about the beers at the bar, Bishop's Finger, Abbots Ale and Summer Lightning and..." said Ross craning his neck to see, "...Pedigree? See: four choices."

"Or paper, rock, scissors," I said. "That's three."

"Aye."

"No, look, you can choose Bishop's Finger or one of the others. You see, binary."

"Och, much easier to choose between the four."

"Yes, but computers can–"

"Och, computers."

"But the principle is that you can reduce it–"

"Och–"

"Ross," I said, "let him finish."

"Thank you. You can reduce it to a binary decision."

"Paper or one of the others, then rock or scissors," I said, "two choices."

"Two branches, yes."

"So?" said Ross.

"So," said Liam, "any ethical problem can be reduced to a right or wrong."

There's always a right or a wrong, Liam said, and much later, when we were in a pub, I forget which. It might have been one earlier. These memories are all a blurry montage for some reason.

"That's not right," he said.

"What's not right?" I asked.

"Her," Liam pointed. "Look!"

Everyone's eyes followed this girl as she strolled to the bar. She was slim, thin you could say, and her jeans were impossibly low over her hips. "She's had her bum crack surgically lowered."

"Fashions today," said Kate.

"Och, you should see the students," said Ross. "I mean, ye try to be understanding. It's fashion. But for goodness sake, you can see their underpants and knickers. Trousers right down around the tops of their thighs, they canna walk. When we were at school, we'd laugh at someone whose underpants showed. And as for the girls, we'd beg for a flash of knicker, but now, all on show – takes the fun out of it."

"You like seeing knickers, do you?" Kate asked.

Later, on the road again, Ross and I fell into step again, and Ross returned to his topic of conversation.

"They've no idea," he said. "We had a fire at school, a proper one, 'cos something in the labs caught fire."

"Dangerous chemicals?" said Liam.

"Och no, dishwasher caught fire."

"Dishwasher!"

"I dinna ken, I was outside," said Ross. "Anyway, two students turn up, texting most likely, and walked straight past the fire engines with their flashing lights. Dinna bat an eyelid. Then they walk under the hazard tape that had been stretched across and go to the front door. Only, when they tried the handle and found the school locked did it cross their minds to wonder. 'Oi, Mister Templeton, Sir, the school's locked'."

"What did you say?"

"Nothing, I just pointed. 'Oh', they go, 'ooh look, fire engines'."

"Never?"

"Straight. They've no curiosity, they just don't see things. No wonder so many get killed crossing the roads. It's spam, that's what it is."

"Spam?"

"Aye, email spam."

Ross must have seen my perplexed expression.

"When we were bairns, there weren't a million TV channels and YouTube, Instagram and all that pish–"

"You sound like my parents – 'we had to go to libraries'."

"Aye, so to satisfy our curiosity we had to go out and search for stuff. Actually buy a box set that came in a box."

"OK."

"Not always the right stuff, I suppose, but nonetheless it was education."

"Fair enough."

"Now, the skill isn't how to find things, use the library and so on. The current coping strategy is to push information away. Otherwise, it swamps your inbox and you spend your life clicking this and that, and deleting two hundred emails a day – right?"

"Right."

"So, I come to teach them something, benzene rings or whatever, and their first reaction is to push it away: not bored, or ignoring it, but actively rejecting anything that pops up. The powers-that-be want everything to be exciting, all flashing lights, bells and whistles, and that makes lessons more and more like it was planned by a five-year-old with Attention Deficit Disorder. Bloody Gove wanted to recreate the education of his independent public school youth, but thought it was Newton's Laws of Thermodynamics and not Kelvin's. Newtons and Kelvins, the clue's in the name. Morgan and now Rudd are just as bad. And May. This grammar school utopia of theirs doesn't address the modern world of phones and websites. No good going on about heat moving from one system to another, when the students just push it away. To them, it's spam."

"I see what you're saying."

"Aye, when was the last..." Ross petered off. He stopped and I looked back at him. A few stragglers overtook us. I waited, I wasn't in any hurry. "This is the first time this year, since September... no, the first time in years, that I've had time to think. No marking to do, lesson plans, no OFSTED looming. Just one foot in front of the other, thinking."

I smiled.

"Guy, thanks, really."

"My pleasure."

We walked a little further, our moseying failing to close the gap between us and the others. It was a sunny day with a light breeze. Beyond the hedge, the land dropped away, a rolling patchwork... such a cliché, but this was the English countryside at its best. Fields reshaped by the centuries, divided by walls and hedges, with farmhouses and only the occasional pylon, windmill or phone mast. It was summer, the days were lighter and longer, the beer was lighter and hoppier, and girls' skirts were lighter and shorter.

We reached the pub.

Other Jacobites were already leaving, mostly the followers in their tartan tam-o'-shanters, going on to the next. We held the door open for them. It looked like standing room only. I went to go in, but Ross was just standing there holding the door.

"He hit him," said Ross.

"Pardon?"

"Clive, my colleague, hit him. The little git pushed and pushed and pushed, and Clive told him off over and over and over, until, well, there was nothing left. No support from the senior management team. We should be a school, not a business. Clive was suspended and then told to consider opportunities in other careers. The Union did fuck all. The kid, the lousy piece of shite, is still in school, he wasn't expelled or anything – given a detention he dinna turn up to. No investigation because we don't want an expulsion on our records for the next OFSTED. Fucking outrageous."

"That doesn't sound fair."

"The kids saw that, saw it, saw the behaviour, saw the result, saw the complete lack of punishment. Now try and maintain discipline. It's gone to pot completely. Bring back the cane, I say."

We were inside now: Rabbie made a motion with his hand and I held up my hand making a paper sign, a pint for Ross and myself.

"Do you, honestly?"

"Och, no, but... corporal punishment was bad. They banned it before my time, but my Dad was slippered when he was a wee lad, but I don't hold with this 'it didn't do me any harm' pish. It was right to take it away, but it wasn't replaced with anything. I mean suspending a kid for playing truant, it's like giving criminals money to stop them stealing – insane."

"I think I read in the paper that they did that."

"Och no!"

"I think so."

"They all know their rights, you know – God, they all know their rights and God help anyone who doesn't give the buggers 'respect', but responsibility, studying, anything socially acceptable – fuck no. GCSE in Rights, A* every time. Chemistry, they dinna ken what a chemical is, U for the lot. I went into teaching to teach, not to be a fucking parole officer, but the wankers have more rights than the adults."

"Really?"

"Aye, they're that stupid," said Ross. "Not all, some, the troublemakers. The only time you see any change in the cocky bastards is during the exams. You walk up and down, invigilating, and see the looks of panic on their darling little faces. They're all pissing themselves in their pants, and then, only then, when they catch your eye, do they realise what you were trying to do. All that teaching crap was for their benefit, but then it's too late. And here's the computer game playing generation for you: they fail and then say, och, it's all right, I'll do a resit next year, but then do they revise for that exam? Och, no. Just try again, wiggle their little fingers for another attempt at life. They're children."

"Maybe it'll give them a chance to grow up."

"Aye, maybe, but Universities are gonna be full of mature students, not like we had. You ken those who'd taken a year out and done something."

"Yes, they always seemed more together," I said, remembering a few examples from my first year.

We found some empty seats, a plush red bench arrangement with an oak table.

"We're gonna have Universities full of old people who have spent their lives endlessly attempting each school level."

"Take your exams, press 'save'."

Ross started laughing, a deep irrepressible outpouring of mirth.

"I canna do it, Guy," he said. "I just canna face going back next term to waste another academic year trying to turn around these thankless gits."

Ross put his head in his hands and seemed to sink into the chair, his surrender somehow affecting the spring of the upholstery. I'd never seen him like this:

down and yet manically up. It was clear that his resolve had gone and it was all simply crushing him.

"Ross, I..." My hand hovered of its own volition just above his shoulders, unsure whether to comfort him or not. "I had no idea, mate. Why not do something else?"

"I canna do anything else."

"There are lots of things, surely."

"If ye canna do, teach."

"If you can't teach, teach teachers."

"You have to work at things," said Ross, "but they just want everything to drop into their laps."

Liam arrived, plonking three pints down in front of us. I thought Rabbie was buying the drinks.

"I should have finished my thesis," he said. That struck home. Mine was lying idle in the hard drive, accumulating age but not wisdom. "Och, why not?"

"Doctor Ross Templeton?" I said. I held up the bitter. "Cheers."

"Cheers," said Liam.

"Sláinte."

We faced each other, the Three Musketeers. This trek was revealing more and more: a watershed. It wasn't finding the grail that was important, it was the search. I realised it at that moment. I'm English, after all, and it's how you play the game that counts. It's all cricket: runs, catches, bowls; they aren't important in themselves, it's whether you are a gentleman. After all, whatever you do in life, sooner or later, you end up walking to the pavilion. What you leave behind, other than runs for wickets, is a reputation.

The means, not the end.

"You three! We're outside," Rabbie shouted across. "Your beer's getting... cold!"

We finished the pints Liam had bought and then the three of us, Ross, Liam and I, went to join Rabbie outside. A whole group were out in the beer garden sitting on a bench table combination. Rabbie had bought us a couple of pints and they did look flat. They tasted fine, though.

There had been a celebration amongst the Jacobites. Ross and I missed it, and Liam didn't think to mention it as we sat outside and supped our ales. The only cloud on the horizon seemed to be the cigarette smoke from the clump of social rejects chatting amiably together in a small shelter by the pub's entrance.

"Excellent news," said Rabbie, as he scooted out to the van. "Brilliant really," he said when he returned.

Ross and I exchanged a look and ordered a couple of bowls of chips. Ross accidentally covered some in mayonnaise. Liam ate those, reminiscing about Stag Parties in Brussels. I bought another round (scissors beats paper).

"Mayonnaise on chips?" I said when I came back with a tray full of drinks.

"The right thing to do," said Liam.

"Bollocks."

"The Belgians invented fish and chips."

"Och no, battered fish was invented in the Netherlands, chips over here."

"And they put mayonnaise on their fries," Liam dunked another chip to make the point, "the British innovation was ketchup, that's all."

"You're winding me up."

"Have you not seen Pulp Fiction?"

"Yes."

"That scene, you know, they talk about it."

Ross levelled both index fingers in our direction, a two-gun cowboy trying to take us both out with his argument: "Look, fried potato, chips, was started in Scotland and spread south, just as fried fish shops spread north from the Sassenach lands of Kent and Sussex." Ross brought his hands together! "Where they met, the British chippie was born."

"That would be..." Liam asked.

"Derby," I said.

"Aye, thereabouts."

"So the Jacobite Rebellion was fried potato shop owners trying to keep fried fish shop owners out of their territory," said Liam.

"Doubt it," I said.

"Och, why?"

"Well," I began, "the Jacobite Rebellion was 1745 and potatoes didn't come from the Americas until... Dickens mentions chips in A Tale of the Two Cities, which is Victorian."

"1536," said Liam. "Potato introduced to Europe."

"Och, you and yer pub quiz cheating gadget. See what I mean, Guys – all thumbs."

Liam, head down, ignored him: "1860, the first fish 'n' chip shop was in Oldham. Is there a plug out here, I'm getting low on charge?"

I drifted off, letting my attention wander around the pub. The beer, it was a guest ale, was good: dark for once, a rarity on this trip, but it was summer after all.

My taste buds prefer malt ales, those rich tasting winter brews, whereas summer was always the lighter, hoppier beers more akin to lager. People wanted their thirsts quenched in the midge-ridden, boiling hot, tanned-and-lotion covered beer gardens. No-one wanted to hide in the dark, secluded interiors on such a lovely day. I'd rather it was winter. Then you'd be free of the burning sun and the cigarette smoke wafting around.

I'm not really a man for all seasons, more a man in the wrong time. There I was wearing a costume years old and based on something a few centuries past, pining for beer brewed half a year ago, and studying events a century old. And talking about the good old days with Ross and how the next generation are worse, just as

Plato had bemoaned the youth of his day. Or was it Plato's dad complaining about Plato?

I did live in the past.

A cold breeze blew up, so we went inside.

The very names of the beers, Old Hooky, Bombardier, London Pride and Spitfire, harked back to a bygone age, each crafted at a brewery that boasted its heritage. We were even in the oldest establishment in Hertfordshire, Cambridgeshire or Essex, or wherever the hell we were by that stage.

"Aye, so what were you doing when the world changed?" Ross said.

"Nothing, I was eating chips," said Liam.

"With mayonnaise."

"Why not," said Liam. "I was once sophisticated and cosmopolitan and–"

"A wanker."

"True, but a rich and successful wanker."

The pub was open plan, but tasteful in that ramshackle, but fascinating, rag-and-bone shop with the occasional intrusive flashing games machine. One-armed bandits were the olde-worlde equivalent of blaring sirens on a horse and cart rushing through a pea-souper in a Sherlock Holmes movie. I wonder whose job it was to collect all these brass watering cans, stringless violins and drinking pots. There were books on the shelf next to me, red or black leather with gold inlay, but when I tried to take one down I discovered that they were all glued together in one big brick.

Over by the bar, Rabbie was talking earnestly to Kate, Reka and that Snetterton bloke. Rabbie took out his map, unfolding the battered sheet to indicate something. I realised that I'd only been seeing our route in the SatNav's 4-by-3 screen each time it was my turn to ride in the van, and even that wasn't switched on every time.

"Funny about Dorrington," said Liam, eventually.

"What about him?" I asked.

"Been kicked out as Home Secretary."

"Really," I said, my tone reeking with disinterest.

"He failed to stop a rebellion and got the shuffle," said Liam, so nonchalantly Ross and I nearly missed it.

"What rebellion?" I asked.

"Ours, ye ninny," said Ross.

"PM's only gone and given the job to that John Trudie," Liam said.

"What the porter like?" I wondered aloud.

"Och, only one way to find out."

So we sipped the porter. I'd had a Belgian beer earlier. That's a lager really. We'd paused at a string of continental cafés and that was the price we'd been paying. The countryside was disappearing as the villages became towns and the gaps were squeezed away by development.

We were letting the world go by.

London beckoned.

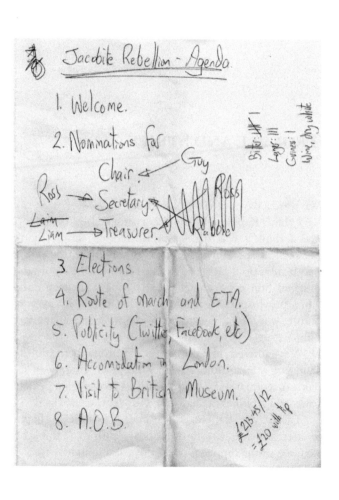

Jacobite Rebellion - Agenda.

1. Welcome.

2. Nominations for
   Chair. → Guy
   Ross → Secretary → ~~Ross~~
   ~~Liam~~
   Liam → Treasurer. → ~~Rabble~~

   Bitter: IIII I
   Lager: III
   Guiness: I
   Wine, dry white

3. Elections.

4. Route of march and ETA.

5. Publicity (Twitter, Facebook, etc)

6. Accomodation in London.

7. Visit to British Museum.

8. A.O.B.

£21.5 + 5/12
= £20 with tip

TROUBLE AND STRIFE

We were a day away from London.

I think Rabbie was the most shocked by the report and I think I was the least affected. I simply didn't believe it. According to a witness statement, the police had beaten up a protester, kicked him on the floor, and dragged him off somewhere. It took a while for the Chinese whispers to reach us. The march, by its very nature, was a thin, ragged column bottlenecking at every pub.

We gathered in another beer garden beneath the shade of a table umbrella and the green canopy of an oak. A woman went from group to group selling single roses and a bloke was hawking Guy Fawkes masks.

There was Rabbie, Ross and Kate, Reka, Liam, Snetterton, Zoë (Crystal Methods), Clifford (I think he was one of the hippies), two Andys and myself.

"A protester's been beaten up by the police," said Snetterton.

"Really?" I asked. "Do we know this as a fact?"

"Do you need documentary evidence from two sources?" said Snetterton.

"Yes."

"He got his head kicked in," said Snetterton.

"That's terrible," Kate said. "What did he do?"

"Nothing, just minding his own business – that's the filth for you."

"There must have been something to trigger it," I said, remembering all sorts of conversations with Mandy about rules of engagement, just cause and so on. She'd always been ambitious, reading and studying to get ahead. People have a need to get what's on their mind off their chest, as it were, and so I heard about police procedures over romantic meals, during television adverts and when she couldn't sleep.

"They just do it, they're thugs," said Snetterton. "They keep lowering the criteria to join the police, so what do you expect."

"I thought it was just the height requirement they lowered," I said.

"And their qualifications," said Snetterton.

"Standards are dropping everywhere," said Rabbie. "I blame the teachers."

"Och, aye, students today have no respect and they go out with a couple of scraped A-levels and no understanding."

"My girlfriend– I mean, my fiancée, she's in the police and–"

"Och, we don't mean Mandy."

"Look," said Kate, "let's not argue about this, we need to decide what to do."

"Aye."

"This protestor... what was the protest?" I asked.

"Och, it's us, ye wee ninny," said Ross.

"Us!"

I was amazed: the police had escorted us; we'd been on first name terms with Danny, Tom, Bill and Spence. Well, technically not on first name terms with Spence, but I'd shared a few rounds of cider with him at the folk festival. We'd talked about astronomy. They were mates, regulars, until the march had moved into another constabulary's patch. For goodness sake, I was engaged to a police officer. I'd been the partner at various pub outings and joined C-Shift's Quiz Team, including that time all the questions had been about history and we trounced the competition. The look of glee on Desk Sergeant Milton's face had been an absolute picture. We knocked 'em back that night. Off-duty police pour the lager in without it touching the sides.

"This is bollocks," I said.

"It isn't," said Snetterton.

"It's got to be some other protest," I insisted. "This... look, it's peaceful."

"Och, we're marching on London with guns."

"Guns! You can't call these ancient flintlock pea-shooters guns!"

"Och, I'm winding you up."

"We don't make history, we're re-enactors," I said. "Someone else makes the history, we just keep it alive."

"You said 'Fate doesn't control you, we make our own history'," said Snetterton.

"Did I? When?"

"In that television interview."

"Yes, but..."

Kate came back with a round of drinks and asked what was up. I hadn't noticed her nip away.

"Köszönöm," said Reka, taking her drink. "Have you heard about the protestor?"

"No," Kate said.

So, the whole story was repeated for her benefit.

"Maybe it was another group," Kate suggested.

"Aye," said Ross. "There were a lot of others at that wee folk festival."

"They're part of our group now," Reka added.

"I saw a lot of tables, you know, trestles, with leaflets," said Liam.

"What were they?" I asked.

"I don't know, I didn't go over."

"Why not?" asked Kate.

"Er... cider tent."

"Me too," said Kate.

"Anyone?" I asked.

They all shook their heads.

"Did you all go straight to the cider tent?" I said.

"Yes."

"Yep."

"Yes."

"Aye."

"I was running my stall, you know, sacred stones," said Zoë, piping up suddenly.

"Och aye."

"There were the anti-frackers and..."

We supped our ales: Old Speckled Hen, I think.

"We need to form a committee," said Rabbie.

"Och no."

"This your idea?" I asked.

"It's Snetterton's," Rabbie said.

"I heard someone suggest it," said Snetterton. "If we have a structure, then we can define who's in this rebellion and who isn't. Then we can weed out the troublemakers."

"Aye, and we'll have meetings and meetings and it'll cut into drinking time."

"We could drink during meetings," I said, "like now."

"Och."

Rabbie turned to me: "You fancy being in it?"

"Me?" I said, surprised.

"Yes, you."

"Do I have to?"

"Yes."

"Oh... OK," I said.

"Table's free!" said Zoë. She jumped up and everyone followed. A huge round table had just been vacated by a family group. We claimed it, and ferried the dirty plates and cutlery to our old, smaller table.

So, we ended up sitting around the big round table with a hole in the centre for an umbrella, and, much like the Knights of Arthur's Court, we debated: starters or just main, separate drinks or bottle of wine, red or white, drinks while we decide or not, and so on.

We had a vote between starters and main course, and after some argument, I was the Chairman, Ross was Secretary and Liam, on account of his financial experience, was voted in as Treasurer.

"Not a single woman on the committee," Kate complained. "Outrageous."

"At least we're not taking the minutes," said Reka.

♦

My progress through the police station is slow, I move from shadow to shadow, doorway to doorway. My calves feel tense and my stomach muscles ache. I realise that I've been sucking in my stomach, as if being an inch thinner will mean I won't be seen.

Something shines in the distance, and as I approach, a series of strange shapes form, weird splotches of white, pink and tartan. There are two burnished steel doors and my distorted reflection lurches upon them.

It's a lift. At the side is a single button: 'up'.

I came down in a lift, I remember now.

I notice that I use my index finger to press the call button.

A few moments later, an engine starts in the bowels of the building.

De-dum.

My heart is pounding in shock. It was just the doors, distorting outwards as the air pressure changed in the lift shaft. Whatever resource, gumption or courage you use in dangerous circumstances is finite. I've used all mine and I'm drawing on the emergency tank. I get another shock when the lift clatters into position and the doors open.

It's a metal lift.

I get in and look for the control panel next to a vandalised phone. It's by the side of the door, which closes with steel finality sealing me inside. One button is lit: "B", so the choices are: "G", "1", "2" and "3". It's multiple-choice again and phone a friend's still not an option. The exit has to be on the ground along with a reception area, guardhouse, Vaughn and a million heavies. The upper floors in a police station will be offices. I want to get to "G", but going straight out the front is madness. I could go to "1" and find a fire escape.

The lift jolts and moves up.

Someone's pressed a call button.

They are watching the lift display, humming a tune, as I am being delivered straight back into their custody. The metal cell shudders as it rises.

Which floor am I going to?

Do I press "G"?

The lift comes to a halt. I throw myself against the corner away from the controls as the doors judder open.

No-one gets in, but I hear voices.

"One's moved into Marsham Street now–"

"Eh?"

Bloody hell, I recognise both of them.

"The Home Office," says Trudie, "wonderful building, and one can tell when one has one of the three desks – shame it's not in Downing Street, though. One doesn't have the ear of the PM quite the way that the Chancellor and the Foreign Office does. Or that useless Brexit committee the bloody difficult woman housed next door."

"I'm sure it has its advantages," says Snitch.

"Building a safe, just and tolerant society."

"Eh?"

"It's the Home Office motto," says Trudie.

The metal plate around the buttons reflects their colours like an impressionist painting. There's Trudie's dark suit and Snitch's pastel and tartan colours smeared on the burnished surface.

"Right."

"Dorrington was so 'safe', 'just' and 'tolerant', but the civil servants much prefer someone like myself, an empire builder, and they are champing at the bit to reclaim criminal justice, the prisons and probation, broadcasting and sport. Culture and Media can keep Sport in my opinion, but one quite fancies broadcasting. Imagine controlling what the News says about one or about other politicians. Fiona Wright has no idea the gold mine she's sitting on over at Culture, Media and Sport – silly cow."

I can sort of see Trudie turn towards Snitch.

"She'll have to go," says Trudie.

I lean across and quickly stab '3' – nothing happens.

"You can't make an omelette without breaking eggs," says Snitch.

"If that's the best you can do, I'll stick with my speech writer."

As I'm reaching across to try again, the lift doors close.

"Shit!" I hear from Snitch, "the lift's going–"

Please, please, please, let the lift motors engage before either of them press the 'call' button. I'm still praying as the cabin starts to ascend.

I feel sick as the metal box clatters its way up three storeys. The lift disgorges me on the third floor and I almost tumble out. I'm in a corridor, almost identical to the ones in the basement, except it's lit by natural light. It feels like I'm outside as I've been in the depths for so long, but I'm not.

The window opposite is high and made of small squares in a metal grill.

On tip-toe, I can see a derelict dockyard outside. I think they are docks, and all that expensive real estate that would make waterfront properties full of penthouse apartments, somewhere Liam's tax exiled friend would love to own and never live in for financial reasons. I didn't think these views still existed in London – is it industrial or Dickensian? I'm in the middle of nowhere. Those loading cranes stand like Martian war machines in the distance, I think. I can't be that far from the Thames, but all the riverside has been developed, surely. I must be outside London... east maybe. The car journey here was long, or at least felt long, but it was all stop-and-start and lacked the zooming constancy of a motorway.

My God, I can see people below.

The street below is bustling: businessmen going about their business, shoppers going about their shopping, passers-by passing by.

A yell, half-strangled, a gurgling mess jerks from my throat as one part of me wants to attract attention and another unconscious mental process stops me from doing something that stupid. Somewhere, not far away, there are men hunting me. I could smash the glass, stick my head out and perhaps yell for all I'm worth.

What with?

The corridor is empty, both ways, but I see a red fire extinguisher attached to the wall. I go along and get as far as touching the handle when I see the table and chair tucked around the corner. The Formica is covered in bits of paper: flyers, information sheets, junk, but there's a pen too. A plan forms. The window has that lattice of metal wire reinforcing that would make it impossible to break anyway.

Leafing through the flyers, I gather a handful that are mostly blank... no, wait! There's a whole batch only printed on one side. I drag the chair down the corridor. I was right. High up, there's an open window, a section that's tilted inwards. I can write a note and chuck it outside.

But the pen won't write!

Scribbling desperately, while resting the paper on my thigh, only produces red lines across my skin as if the flyer is some stupid red, carbon copy sheet. Of course, my leg deforms under the ballpoint. I'll have to drag the table all the way down the corridor. No, I could write the note on the table and bring it back. I'd have to risk being visible down both this and the other corridor. What am I thinking? I kneel down and use the floor, a few spirals and the ink starts to flow.

"Help!"

OK, I have to add more than that. I'm trapped in a disused police station and they are about to kill me, cause a riot and... there's not enough space on the A5 for an essay. Get the police isn't going to work either, as Vaughn and Co have ID badges: 'Oh yes, madam, we've been having trouble with one of the prisoners, schizophrenic case, very sad... he has delusions, but he is getting the right treatment, you can be sure, madam'. Or: 'Come this way, sir, and please hold still while I shoot you'. I'm suddenly an eight-year-old having written 'Nana, thank you for my new mp3 player' and then wondering what to write that'll fill the rest of the page. I suppose I could have written "Help!" in bigger letters.

"I'm Guy Wilson. Illegally held by Home Secretary. Inform Press. Please. Hurry," I write, and then I sign it: "Guy Wilson."

After positioning the chair under the open window, I stand on it. The page flutters urgently even before I've got it to the open frame. This is hopeless, it'll just fly away and land who knows where to become just another piece of litter hidden in plain sight amongst all the detritus of the city.

I have to put it round a brick or something. A bottle smashing would attract attention. I might hit someone. That might actually help. The ambulance crew would read it, wouldn't they? They'd tell the police. But that might help too. With lots of uniforms running about, the good apples will outnumber the bad apples. I won't be believed, but then I don't have to be. They just have to get suspicious enough to investigate and the whole tangle will unravel.

I don't want to injure anyone.

Bollocks to that.

Tie it to the fucking fire extinguisher, let it off and throw the squirting weight as far as possible.

Would it go through?

The window swings open and stops on the edge of a metal guide, but that's loose. A couple of knocks and it would swing up easily.

Back at the corner, I take the fire extinguisher off its hook with a yank that causes the metal bracket to come away and clang onto the floor. Throw the fire extinguisher out to attract attention, I think, people look up, then chuck the note tied to the metal bracket! But with what? Sod all on the table, and there's a drawer. I open it, almost too quickly and nearly pitch the contents onto the floor.

There are paperclips, pens, and a great collection of odd-sized rubber bands all in a plastic tray. I dump the contents on the table and take the drawer, the plastic tray, a handful of rubber bands, and some pens.

It's all tricky, so I stop and load the stationery into the plastic tray.

With a nice thick, red whiteboard marker, I copy the note three times. One goes on the metal bracket, another on the plastic tray and finally the third on the table's drawer itself. That won't go through the window. Sod it! I prop it up against the wall at 45°, kick it with my boots and it breaks. The third note rubber bands to a length of wood.

OK – here goes.

Standing on the chair, I use the heavy fire extinguisher to hit the metal frame and bend the edge enough to let it open fully. The window drops down on its hinge.

I read the fire extinguisher instructions:

Hold upright, pull pin.
Stand back eight feet. Aim at the base of fire.
Squeeze lever. Sweep side to side.

If you hit the button does it go off and keep squirting or do you need to keep the pressure on?

It's not really upright, but I need to fire through the window. I pull the pin. Eight feet – ha! I shove the small length of hose through the window and squeeze. Water fires out, the nozzle whips back and forth spraying the air and soaking the outside of the window. It stops when I let go.

It'll be a bugger to get through, but I glance down and see people looking up. One man is wiping his jacket. I leap down and grab my missiles.

The extinguisher slips out of my grip and clangs heavily on the floor. I slide on the lino, I seem to have got water everywhere, even inside. I must hurry, get the messages out before they walk away. The chair skips and hops when I jump up.

Which should I throw first?

Something that'll attract attention and get people to move out of the way: plastic, then metal and finally the length of wood. I can only hold the first two, one in each hand.

The fucker won't go through the gap!

It crumples, bits splinter off and then it's through, my hand briefly feels the breeze outside. I throw it, the object spins away and down out of sight. I swap the metal bracket to my right hand and then out it goes.

I think, maybe it's more hope than anything else, but I hear the clang as it hits the pavement below. I drop down and grab the length of wood – I see ochre shoelaces, Vaughn, the deep black eye of his gun pointing at me.

"Writing little messages, are we?" he says, cocking the weapon.

I glance down and see the flyer trapped forlornly on the timber.

"The pen is mightier than the sword," I hazard, thinking a joke might defuse the situation. I don't really think that. The thought comes after the words have bubbled forth. My hand grips around the length of wood, trying to form a fist around this club. He has his weapon and I have mine, but although he holds it casually enough, there's no contest. I let go and the wood clonks to the floor discarded like driftwood amongst the puddles left by the fire extinguisher.

I stand up straight; I had a good run... over now.

"The pen is mightier – ha! You academics with your words, I'd like to see words beat this, a Heckler and Koch VP9, 'volkspistole', the people's pistol – fucking 'A' or what?"

"Interesting name."

"Heckler and Koch, why?" Vaughn seems genuinely interested.

"Well, it's you and me, isn't it?"

"Eh?"

What am I doing? "Someone who uses words is a kind of 'heckler'."

"Oh right, you're a heckler."

"And someone who needs a gun is a cock."

I'm sure I see the whites of his eyes all around his iris before his face muscles tense.

He hits me!

I have an image of the gun and then the force throws me across the corridor. It proves that the butt was stronger than the jaw. It doesn't hurt, incredibly, but soon there's a stinging, burning sensation up the side of my face. He's talking, but I'm busy blinking, trying to see straight with my vision blurring as my eyes fill up.

"Ugh."

There's a speck of blood, a splatter so vivid on the lino, scarlet drips spread in the water on the floor. He pulls me to my feet.

"Not so clever now, are we?"

I try to reply, but my mouth is wet inside.

"All your fancy degrees, masters and doctorates, ivory tower bollocks, won't help you. Special forces training, me. Discipline, teamwork, being part of something – that's what counts. Come on, patsy, you've a date."

He shakes me, and slips.

We both go down in a tumble, separating. His gun clatters away. For a moment, I think about going after it. Our eyes meet.

It's just a moment, but then I'm up running away down the corridor.

Vaughn yells, "Fuck!" and fires – *crack!*

"No, no!" It's a female voice, distant in every way: Mandy. For a fleeting moment, I think she's going to save me, but then she says: "Trudie wants him alive."

I run.

There's a door at the far end.

"Obey orders!" Mandy again. I don't look back.

The brick arch above the door explodes, raining plaster and debris in front of me. Blinded I grab the door handle, yank it open and go through. It's dark beyond, I pull the door to, just as a bright hole opens up in the wood panel. It casts a searchlight that flickers as I hear Vaughn pounding down the corridor. I see him, like I did through the spy hole earlier, for a few moments before my questing hands find a bolt. I slide it home.

Vaughn hits the door. It bounces on its hinges. That bolt isn't going to hold at all.

I turn and run, blindly, crashing over boxes and dislodging shelves. It's just a room... no, there's another door. I pull the handle, fucker's locked... then I find the bolt. I open it. Another black corridor, no there's light further down. I shut the door behind me. I run. Straight into something. Further on. Another corner.

It's a bloody maze, endless corridors with the Minotaur's hot breath on my neck.

There must be a way out!

I throw myself forward, my hands out flailing around as my legs work to keep myself from falling and propel me forward. There's an automatic door. It bumps awkwardly as it opens. I go through. I've lost my bearings. Am I going back the way I've come?

Someone moves ahead, a shadow. It's a woman, no, wait! He's a Jacobite wearing a kilt. I'm saved, reinforcements at last, but of course not. There's something wrong and I know it, somehow, unconsciously, some ancient survival instinct coming to the fore. I step into a doorway to one side and the darkness there hides me. The figure comes forward, attracted by the sound of the door opening.

It's Snitch, of course, the piece of shite. Maybe I could take one of them with me. He's not that big and I have the element of surprise.

He walks past, reaches the door which opens again. He pauses and turns around.

Does he know I'm here? Somehow sense that he's being watched? Do the hairs on the back of his head stand on end?

He steps back with a puzzled expression, and the door bumps open again.

A shock of realisation forms on his face.

A red mark appears on his shirt and then, so quickly, a spreading stain of blood soaks everything. His hands come up and grasp his chest as his knees crumple, and his body falls. He pitches forward, jerks a couple of times and then he's still.

Eventually, the infrared detector decides there's no-one there. The doors close, but bump and catch on his legs, so they open again.

Five seconds later, it happens again.

And then again.

I can't move.

Someone has died.

Someone has really died because of all this.

Died right in front of me.

I have a memory of an explosive thunder, a sound boom reverberating around the hard concrete walls, but I didn't hear the gunshot in real time.

The door opens and Vaughn stands over his victim, his squat heavy handgun in repose.

"Shit," he says. "I've shot Snitch."

I hear Trudie's voice reply: "That's inconvenient."

"Fuck it! I saw a figure and fired."

"Don't be so trigger happy! We need Wilson alive."

"I thought you wanted to kill him."

"Yes, but not here."

"Well, I haven't, so that's all right then."

"Couldn't you have set it to stun or something?"

"Handguns only kill."

"A Taser has stun."

"Poof's weapon."

"Move the body."

Vaughn seems to think for a moment: "Right," he says. "You take the legs."

"I can't get blood on this suit."

"Too high and mighty to do your own dirty work?"

"I'm going to a photo opportunity," says Trudie. "One can't get blood on a Savile Row, it shows."

"We need to find Wilson."

"Here."

From where I stand, hidden in the alcove of the doorway, I can't see what they're doing... I stay still.

"But I've got yellow shoelaces," says Vaughn.

"Ochre."

"Ochre then. It means I'm in charge, so I shouldn't have to move bodies."

"Get a red shirt then," says Trudie.

"What!"

"An underling – didn't you ever watch it? It was on the BBC."

"What was?"

"Snitch wanted different levels: yellow for command, red for security, blue for intelligence and so on... all very Star Trek."

"I've not seen any blue laces," said Vaughn.

"They don't go with the suit," says Trudie. "We stuck with ochre, bought a job lot. It makes it all very exciting, one supposes, but one drew the line at changing the radio protocols: F.A.B., Spectrum is Red, Thunderbirds Are Go – all very amateurish."

"What?"

"It's Gerry Anderson. Thunderbirds? Captain Scarlet? It was on the commercial channel, Mother wouldn't let me watch it. I mean, we're making history today and one doesn't want posterity to think us childish."

"I suppose."

"Guy Wilson knows all about history," says Trudie. "Don't you, Guy?"

I don't move.

"Penny for your thoughts, Guy?" Trudie says. "No. Nothing for the record: if you don't have a penny, a ha'penny will do. If you don't have a ha'penny, then God bless you."

Trudie takes a step sideways, clearly moving into view. He's holding black shoelaces in his hand.

Vaughn follows his gaze: "Fuck!" he says.

"Nothing to say?" Trudie asks.

I swallow before speaking: "Would you write it down?"

"And add it to one's history," Trudie shakes his head as if genuinely sorry. "No, that wouldn't be wise, would it?"

He hands me the shoelaces. Dumbly, I take them.

"Black," I say.

"You've heard of the other Guy, Guy Fawkes?" Trudie asks.

"You mean bonfire night?" I say.

"I see you are pleased to remember, remember the Fifth of November," Trudie says, almost pondering. "I wonder if that's the origin of the expression 'Fall Guy'?"

I don't answer.

"That was a conspiracy in a much simpler time. He was hanged, drawn and quartered, head stuck on a pike – such imaginative deterrents in those days."

"It was barbaric."

"Yes, but he did try and blow up Parliament. We can't have that, can we? Vaughn?"

"No, sir," says Vaughn.

"It's a long way away, isn't it?" says Trudie.

"What?" says Vaughn.

"Guy Fawkes Night, the Fifth of November. Do you think perhaps that today will be celebrated? With fireworks and Tartan costumes. A different Guy on top? Another face on all those ridiculous masks?"

"Your version of the police wouldn't allow it," I say.

"One does have the power to stop such things," says Trudie smiling. "The power of life and... phone tapping, now there's a wheeze."

266

"You'll get found out."

"How?"

"Freedom of Information."

"That's genuinely funny, Guy, wonderful," he leans closer, his grin evaporating: "Anti-Terrorism Act trumps Freedom of Information."

"I won't bow down to you," I say.

"Of course not," says Trudie. "Put your shoelaces on."

I kneel down and begin lacing my boots

Vaughn laughs.

"Who usually moves bodies?" Trudie asks.

"Snitch," says Vaughn.

I glance across at Snitch's corpse: his eyes look vacantly back at me. When I've finished the right boot and switch to the left, taking my time. While I'm doing it, Trudie drones on.

"The devil is always in the detail," he says. "They'd ask: why wasn't he wearing shoelaces."

I finish, double knotting the ends before standing.

"One was so pleased when you and Amanda stopped that riot," Trudie says. "It kept your rebellion going and made Dorrington look a fool. He dipped so deeply into the Home Office budget. The Treasury were furious. What are County Councils for, if it's not to pay for things? So, he had to spend more time with his family and we all shuffled round the cabinet table. I wasn't the only one to get a promotion. Your girlfriend, Sergeant Reynolds now, so well deserved for her quick thinking."

I say nothing.

"The winners write the history, you know that, so no-one will know your point of view. One wonders who will write the history book of all this. We lack our Herodotus, Bede, Wood or Schama. There'll be no Wilson, of course, in the venerable list. Of course, one will do an autobiography, but this episode won't make it into the appropriate chapter – pity. I'll use that excellent ghostwriter who does the rounds. Employed by MI5, you know, for all the cross-checking with the cabinet notes. He knows everything. A useful man to have in one's employ."

"You won't get away with this," I say. "People have a right to peaceful protest."

"Peaceful?" Trudie looks genuinely perplexed. "Oh no, it's not going to be peaceful."

"But why?"

"The people need protecting."

"From you?"

"From each other."

"And that justifies murder," I say, sarcasm in my voice.

"Breaking eggs and all that," says Trudie.

"You hypocritical bastard."

"Oh Guy, that hurts – one's a person too."

"The end doesn't justify the means."

"Would you sacrifice yourself to save your girlfriend?"

"Yes."

"Even now?"

"...yes."

"But suicide is wrong, isn't it?" He looks at me, I say nothing. "Isn't it?"

I nod.

"So, it's a means that justifies an end. One wants to make Britain great again. I went into politics to make a difference and achieved nothing by following the rules. They're made to be broken. One means well, one has a virtuous soul, one knows that, so one's actions are always for a greater good. I have a moral compass that points in the right direction even if the route isn't always straightforward."

"The road to hell is paved with good intentions."

"The road to utopia has a few potholes, I'll admit."
He leans forward until I can smell his aftershave.
"Look, you'd sacrifice yourself to save everyone, surely?
And you'd feel the hero for doing so. I'm just doing the
difficult part for you."

"What do you mean?"

"You're going for a fall, Guy."

Trudie nods to Vaughn, who grabs me and
manhandles me towards the lift. He walks down the
centre of the corridor and, at arm's length, I'm bounced
along the wall. There's no fight left in me. We reach
the lift, he presses the button and we descend.

Trudie stays behind.

By the time we reach the lower floor, Vaughn has
turned the rough handling into assault. I'm thrown out
of the lift, tumble and Vaughn follows. The door closes
behind and the lift ascends.

Vaughn kicks me.

And again.

"Stop it!"

It's Mandy, her voice crisp and loud. Thank god.

"'Cos he's your boy–"

"Trudie wants him alive! You idiot."

I spit slightly, blood spattering the small patch of
floor that I can see. Mandy's shoes loom large, smart
and black with their ochre shoelaces.

"Make sure he has these on him," she says. I crane
my neck round to look up. Mandy passes a plastic bag
containing my belongings over.

"Mandy! Mandy!" I yell, Vaughn holds me back
and forces me down.

"He'll need this," I hear Mandy say.

"His phone... why?" says Vaughn.

"Trudie says–"

"Trudie says – I doubt it."

Mandy raises her voice: "Yes, Trudie says–"

The lift clatters and opens: it's Trudie himself.

"Trudie says what?" says Trudie.

"She says you said to give him his phone," says Vaughn, still leaning on top of me. "Likely story."

"One did say that," says Trudie.

"Whatever for?" Vaughn demands.

"Because if he's found without his phone, then... it won't be believable," says Mandy. "No-one is ever without a phone."

"She has a good point," says Trudie. "The devil is in the detail, I think you said."

"Yes, I did," Mandy says. "And leave it on, just to be completely convincing. It's charged and—"

"He might call for help," says Vaughn.

"Then don't let him make a call," says Mandy.

"Here," says Trudie. He takes the phone off Mandy and bends over, checking my clothes.

"So, I get my phone call," I say.

Trudie realises the obvious: "He's got no pockets."

"Put it in his bum bag," Vaughn says.

"Sporran," says Mandy.

Trudie fumbles with the catch and then shoves the phone in, pushing it in next to the incriminating tape cassette.

"What's this?" Trudie says as he yanks something out of the sporran. He's holding the ring box. He opens it. "Ah, how sweet, you kept the box."

Mandy takes a few steps back. Her boots squeak as she turns on her toe and she marches off. She doesn't look back, not once.

It's over, it's all over.

"Here you go," says Trudie. He puts it back. "It'll give the tabloids a suitable motive. So sad."

I see Mandy down the end of the corridor. She's turned away, her hands smartly held behind her with her fingers knotted and twisted into claws.

Trudie goes over to her.

"Mister Trudie," she says to him.

"John please," says Trudie. He puts his arm around her and leads her away into an office. They disappear through the glass door. I see Mandy's police uniform reflected in the glass cases beyond, the ghost of three stripes hovering amongst the spines of the books, a male face mockingly masked with concern before it smiles broadly.

There's a line that once crossed means you can't trust them again. A stranger, well, you can give them the benefit of the doubt, of course, but once you've been let down by someone, then they are likely to do it again and again. Fool me once, shame on you; fool me twice, shame on me.

Maybe she meant well, maybe she was taken in by Trudie's charm and persuasion, but you have to judge your actions against some criteria, an ethical framework that has some error checking.

I've the measure of Trudie. He's a game player: paper, rock, scissors; anything for an advantage. Vaughn can only beat me up and kill me. But Mandy's really guilty. She must know, deep down, that she's killed her fiancé; stood by, followed orders, while everything turned to shit.

Vaughn takes me away. I'm already dead inside.

She betrayed me, she betrayed everyone.

Dorrington's gone - cabinet reshuffle

▸ **Working with other communities**

▸ **Home Secretary John Trudie's rise and rise and rise**

Biography page 8

The PM's rushed cabinet reshuffle shows a marked move towards the right and a move to generate distance from the laughing stock that is Tim Dorrington, the ex-Home Secretary.

Not only does the particular community of Dorrington's own party not want to deal with him, no community does.

❝ I won't demand, I won't request, I won't even ask. I'm begging: give me the right tools for the right job. **❞**

John Trudie, MP

Does this usher in a new age of politics? Possibly, but it certainly sends a message that protest marchers can make a real difference. Surely, People Power or Jacobite Power is the new force and politicians need to take note.

What can the new Home Secretary do, that the old one didn't?

More on 2, 3, 4

Twittering down the country lanes
We know so much about the Rebellion because a thousand tweets an hour stream out of the march.

More on page 3

Backbench revolt due, say pundits
No-one likes an iron fist holding them down, and many backbenchers fear that the new Home Secretary will usher in a stronger whip.

Everything will be three-line from now on.

More on page 5

We make our own history
More on people who have made a difference.

Article page 7

A CALM BEFORE THE STORMING

Mandy saved us, Mandy saved everyone.

She texted the police plans to me: there was a huge mass of riot police waiting to intercept us just inside London's border. Trudie was in charge and we didn't think we'd get off lightly like last time. After all, I was engaged, so the proposing trick wouldn't work again. Her text ended: *g meet @ waterloo station under clock 12 noon sat sorry luv mandy.*

"Och, we take another route," said Ross.

"They'll cover them all," said Liam.

"We've got to do something," said Rabbie. "The police attacked this newspaper seller... what was his name?"

Snitty replied: "Ian–"

"Yeah," Rabbie continued, "he had his hands in his pockets and was just hit with a baton and pushed to the ground. That's a bloke just going home from work. Imagine what they did to the real protesters. Now imagine what they'll do to rebels."

"And that woman they beat up," said Kate.

"She was a Fractivist," Reka added.

"That stuff isn't on the news."

"Aye," Ross agreed. "You never hear about that on the news, do ye?"

"So what do we do? Listen, there are only so many routes," said Rabbie, waving his hand over the map. "We have to choose one... or do we just give up."

"We take them all," I said.

"Yes, but they'll realise."

"Not..." I said, a plan beginning to form, "...if we arrive at the police lines and..."

"And what?"

"...do something."

It wasn't that well-formed a plan, obviously. The trick is to out-think your opponents. They'd have a procedure (wish I'd listened more when Mandy went on about these things). It was a game of chess. We move our pieces down the board; they've created a defence here.

"It's not chess," I said.

"Pardon?" Liam asked.

"Getting into London, it's not chess."

"I have no idea what you are talking about."

"If we're a rebellion, then marching on London is like a war. It's a game."

"A war game?"

"Yes, so what tactic do we use?"

"What did Bonnie Prince Charlie do?" Liam asked.

That was a thought: "He didn't get this far. He turned back at Derby."

"I meant, what would he have done?"

"Do you know, I've no idea," I said and I stepped to one side to mull it over.

"Och, while our master tactician does his thing, let's get a move on," said Ross.

We started marching in our usual shambolic way. As we moved away from the vehicles, it was like a signal shivering through the crowd. Soon, the army was on the move. There were cheers, both from contingents

274

starting to move off and from the small gatherings that stood on both pavements to wish us well. It was a heady rush to walk between so many well-wishers and be the focus of so much applause.

Oh, we were very English about it: 'It's fine, please don't'; but we began to need the fix, enjoy the thrill and believe, under the influence of so much hope and beer, that we could do anything. After all, a single man standing in Tiananmen Square stopped tanks.

"What game do we play?" Liam asked, catching up. Both of us were falling behind Ross, who was on point.

"Mornington Crescent," I said.

"How does that–"

"What are you doing!?" Ross yelled loudly. "You!"

Ross stormed across the road.

A Ford Fiesta slalomed as it braked, avoided Ross and then shot off with some angry revving. Ross ignored it, striding with large steps that only someone in a plaid can do.

"Aye you!"

Ross's hand shot up to grab the youth and then hesitated above the hood. The lounging group hanging about outside the shop pulled their limbs together and lolloped in Ross's direction. It was as if the whole scene had escalation tattooed on its forehead.

The kid, teenager I suppose, flinched away from this huge, hairy giant of a Scot, but now his peer group was assembling, he stood upright, cocky in the face of thunder.

"Pick up that chewing gum!"

"Not mine, innit."

"I saw you."

"Yeah, so?"

"Pick it up!"

"Make me."

"Aye, I'll bloody make you all right."

"Yeah, you and whose army?"

It was an ironically stupid thing to say. I was crossing the road, Liam was coming back to see what was going on, Rabbie was leading some redcoats out of the shop itself.

We had an army – literally.

The girls in the group hitched up their jeans and melted backwards into the shadows. The yobs noticed their retreat and taunted their girlie craven attitude, but when they saw the situation, they began to back off too, strutting like peacocks in an effort to appear tough.

"Pick up the f... chewing gum!"

Ross was losing it, I knew that. I was first there, but hesitated too when I reached the invisible bubble that marked this confrontation as somehow private. Go in, and it could escalate or see sense, stand back and it could kick off or calm down.

"Or what, get the pigs on me?"

"Aye, you idle child."

"I'm no child."

"You're as childish and selfish as a three-year-old."

"Fuck you!"

I was nudged aside from behind and a figure in black and white strode past: "Everything all right, Sirs?" said the policeman.

"Yeah," said the youth.

"He dropped chewing gum."

"Did he now, Sir?"

The copper was standing straight on to Ross, ignoring the kid.

Ross turned to the policeman: "Littering is against the law!" Ross said.

"Yes, Sir," said the policeman evenly, "if you'd like to step aside, Sir."

"He touched me, he did," said the kid, "I've got rights, he fucking touched me."

"No, he didn't... Sir."

The slow, deliberate turn of his head somehow conveyed the officer's utter contempt and turned the word 'Sir' into an insult. He'd gripped his belt, easing the weight off all the kit, and suggesting that this wasn't a confrontation that would need batons, tasers or pepper spray.

The kid backed off. His gang were nowhere to be seen.

"Fuck you!" The kid turned and ran.

"Are you all right, Sir?"

"He littered, the little twerp dropped it there."

I'd stepped forward: "He's fine, officer. Hot day. Long walk ahead. We're all tired."

"Guy, he–"

"OK," I said, finishing the discussion.

We walked on, Ross, Liam and I, without talking. I waited until I was sure Ross had simmered down, and then I counted fifty more paces before I nodded to Liam. He looked back with a 'what' expression and I signalled with my hand to get him to talk. The penny dropped.

"This is the future," Liam said, getting out his fancy phone and waving that under my nose.

"It's an iPhone," I said, letting my voice reverb with sarcasm.

"No, the app, look at the app."

He swizzled the black object in front of me. There was the picture of a spirit level and as he moved the bubble of air moved too, swaying back and forth. Liam stopped shaking it and let it come to the horizontal.

The bubble came to rest in the central marks.

"OK," I said.

"This looks like a level made from a tube with a bubble of air in the water."

"I can see that."

Ross was becoming interested despite himself. You could tell by the way his stride changed. It would just take a little more.

"It's imitating a previous form," said Liam. "Soon no-one will know what a real spirit level was... like the icon for saving a document."

"Eh?"

"What's the icon for saving a document... in Word?"

"It's a blue square like... it's a floppy disk," I said.

"Right!" said Liam. "When was the last time you saw a floppy disk?"

"Last month, I helped Professor Chedi move offices. He had a whole box of them."

"Apart from some old bloke who keeps souvenirs, when was–"

"No, no," I interrupted, "I take your point. We don't have anything in the department that can read the old, actual floppy ones... the blue, hard variety, the diskettes... no, wait, my new computer doesn't even have those disk drives."

"But the symbol remains."

"It's a lot of pish," said Ross, moving closer.

Liam and I exchanged a glance.

"Here's another," said Liam and he showed me the screen.

"I can't see..."

"Exactly, it's showing the image that the camera sees," he said.

The image on the screen included a large, fuzzy pink shape. I pointed and Liam shifted his grip so his finger wasn't over the camera lens. Now I could see the pavement, a bit of grass, the odd weed and the white marks of dropped chewing gum.

"So?" I said.

"It's so you can see where you are going while texting."

"You're kidding."

"There have been a lot of text-related injuries."

I started laughing.

"Seriously," Liam said. "They've padded some lamp posts in Brick Lane."

"What?"

"Cushions, so that when you walk into the lamp post, you don't injure yourself. And traffic lights... pedestrian lights in the kerb in a city in Germany."

I did try for a moment to stop laughing, but that just made it worse. I lost it completely; Ross came over to find out what the joke was about and by the time he reached me I was in tears and quite incapable of explaining.

"Cushions," I managed, pointing at Liam's iPhone.

Ross leant over to see, so Liam handed him the gadget. It broke the ice, thank god.

"They don't respect anything," Ross said.

"They dis you?" I said.

"Ha!" said Ross.

You 'dis' me, as in 'disrespect' me is a common phrase. The Youth, with a capital 'Y', want respect, I dare say some are disrespected, but respect is something that is earned and that needs time and effort. It's not something instant. There's no push-button solution. However, we don't teach respect anymore, or if we do it's some nebulous politically correct version. Our elected elders and betters, who milk the expenses system for all they can, hardly set an example that's worthy of respect. So the Youth learn all about respect in the playgrounds, just as a previous generation learnt about sex in the playground. And bullying.

Of course, their lessons are riddled with misunderstandings, untruths and plain invention. So, a kid, thinking he has been dissed, decides he must knife someone, anyone, that innocent passer-by, in order to regain his 'respect'.

"I dinna agree with the Head about chewing gum," said Ross. "It was one of this new regime changes. I mean, sure the replacement carpets cost nearly sixty grand. Sixty grand for carpets!"

"Really?"

"Aye, but I took the point, and we all agreed to ban chewing gum. You look under the tables and there's loads of these little deposits, soft and covered in spittle when ye reach under and... the hard, rock-like.... every desk and chair... and we banned it, had fines for charity, but they just kept bringing it in, every day, this white stuff and you're talking to the inconsiderate gits in the corridor and their mouths are just moving all the time. Chomp, chomp, chomp, building up saliva with every sentence fragment, 'cos they don't talk in complete sentences. They whine, everything's just too much like hard work. It's all like this, like, and like that, like, innit, and they never look anything up or do any work! Do your coursework, do your coursework, every lesson, three times a week and twenty weeks later, bugger all! Then their parents complain that their darlings aren't making progress, that they pay their taxes that go into your salary, so that their princes and princesses don't have to think, but will somehow magically pass their exams. These cretinous examples of some sub-species of stupid, retarded morons and they will not put their phones away!"

"Have you finished?" I asked.

"Aye, I've finished," Ross said. "I've seen the future generation and they're hopeless."

"Ross?"

In the pub that evening, Ross didn't say much: instead, he sat nursing his pint.

"What's the plan for tomorrow?" Rabbie asked.

"Someone told the police our route," I said.

"Och no," said Ross, "the polis ken?"

"Bet you?"

"Aye, pint?"

"Pint!"

We shook hands.

"OK," I said, leaning forward. Everyone did the same, conspiratorially. "We're already within the tube system – yes?"

"Yes," said Rabbie.

"We still have to march," said Liam.

"True, but not all of us. Most of us can catch a tube, lose ourselves in the population, hide within the nearly eight million people."

"They'll know," said Liam. "More surveillance cameras in this country than anywhere else."

"Och, and there's the anti-terror laws," said Ross.

"They don't apply to us," I said. "We're not terrorists."

"Och," said Ross. "The Regulation of Investigatory Powers Act–"

"Freedoms Act is worse," Liam added.

"Aye, a licence to do anything. It used to be just the polis and security services, but they extended it to other organisations including local authorities and thus education."

I tried to get things back on track: "OK, I think–"

"Aye, over seven hundred times."

"Seven hundred!" said Liam.

"Nearer eight," said Ross. "Aye, and used for catching people faking sick leave, illegal use of disabled parking badges or putting out the bins on the wrong day."

I remembered then reading that anti-terror laws had been used over a thousand times by councils to combat such appalling crimes as littering, dog fouling and over-charging with hardly any of these resulting in an actual conviction. Oh, and nicking Christmas lights off a tree and dropping chewing gum (Ross might like that one though) is counted as terrorism.

"OK, I think someone needs to keep the police busy, somehow," I said. "Give them something to follow."

"Och, who would ye get to be so daft."

The conversation moved on to other things. We talked such drivel in the pub, all so irrelevant now, but I wish I could remember it all. It was the last time we were all together. The last time we were safe.

That night, we were lying in our sleeping bags in the back of the van. Street lights shone through the corner of the roof where the rust had finally won. It had been a good summer, thank God, so we'd been spared the rain coming in.

Our camp was shambolic with vans and cars all over the place like so many dice shaken and dropped haphazardly.

The police were hopeless at parking too, used to bumping up on the kerb over the double yellow lines. One of the coppers with us had mentioned that there was a poster in his station to park sensibly and not leave the police car's doors open, but then no traffic warden is going to slip a ticket under the wipers of a marked police car.

It was strange to think that they were still with us when we knew that other police would be waiting for us. The long arm of the right hand of the law not knowing what the long arm of the left hand was doing.

"Liam!" I whispered and gave him a tap. "Settle down."

All those arguments about ID cards and CCTV ushering in a police state are nonsense.

The Taliban and the Khmer Rouge were two of the worst regimes of the 20th century. Both states lived in the technological dark ages, yet managed to kill, torture and subjugate millions.

George Orwell's 1984 image of dictatorship wasn't TVs that can look back at you. If you want a picture of the future, he wrote, imagine a boot stamping on a human face – forever.

It's not the gadgets, it's the attitude.

Our civil liberties are in our laws and our behaviour, not our appliances: freedom of speech, the right to a fair trial, voting – none of these are real objects, things that can be held in the hand. They are ideas, powerful and, if we don't defend them, ephemeral. The evil subjugate people using whatever tools are their disposal and it's up to us to protect our rights with everything they can muster.

Every generation has to do this.

History teaches us that the 'war to end all wars' doesn't. It's a continual struggle.

We're all in this together, as David Cameron said, but, you know, that does rather depend on coming together and working in the national interest rather than for your offshore account's compound interest.

Because, you see, ideas are not bulletproof.

People should not be afraid of their government, but neither should the government be afraid of the people.

Liam was still shaking.

"For God's sake, Liam."

No, it wasn't from the cold, it was more serious. I turned over, but I couldn't see him as I'd been staring at the lights.

"Liam, Liam," I said.

"I'm... I'm OK, just... OK."

Ross woke up: "What's going on?"

"It's Liam."

"Aye, what!"

"He's got the jitters."

"Och, we need a doctor."

"We don't. He took something."

"It's not working."

"He was snorting coke."

"What?"

"Cocaine," I explained, "you know."

"No."

"Me neither."

"Is this normal?"

"How would I know?"

"Should we get the polis?"

"What?"

"They'll know first aid."

"If you like, but he might have hidden his stash in the van."

"In the van... och, no, no, no!"

Ross and I leant over Liam.

"Liam?"

"Liam?"

"It's OK," Liam said. "I'm good, cold turkey, that's all. Means I'm coming off the fecking stuff. It's good."

"Really?" I asked.

"Honest."

None of us got much sleep.

Mornington Crescent

A game played since 1978 on Radio 4's *I'm Sorry I Haven't A Clue*. Players take it in turn to name various stations on the London Underground and the winner is the first person to reach Mornington Crescent. Full rules are included in N.F. Stovold's *Mornington Crescent: Rules and Origins*. There are variants.

THE WALLS AROUND THE CITY

"Let's face the music."

We got back into the old van and, a lurch or two later, Ross pulled out into the traffic flow and we made our way south again. Liam, apparently recovered from the previous night, navigated while I examined the London Underground map. It was going to be tricky to pull this off, I realised, as we had to be in a very specific place at a very specific time – that, and the fact that we were making it up as we went along.

"It's appeasement," said Ross. "You ken, you want a quiet life, everyone does, the school does and the Head in particular. So any troublemaker gets the 'oh, please be good, what can we get you to make you be good.' So, we are encouraging them, and any others who see how it works. The diligent students get nothing, the troublemakers get the carrot when we should use the stick, and we never use the stick. What's the incentive for the good students, eh? They see troublemakers getting all the resources and they get nothing, squeezed every time there's a budget review."

"Well, stand up for yourself?" said Liam.

"How?"

"You–"

"Look! It's me against 750 children and the whole education system from the fiddling politicians down! We won't just have to answer to OFSTED and the DfE, it'll be bloody academy shareholders next."

"Ross, Ross," I said putting my hand on his shoulder. "Liam meant you should stand up at school, not stand up against him."

Ross's looked angry: "Aye," he said, finally.

"You're going through a bad patch, that's all," I said.

"Och, yer right, I need to get my confidence back."

"Right here," said Liam.

"Och, we're not going into the Congestion charging zone, are we?" Ross asked.

"No, that's way down," said Liam.

"You know," I said, having checked scribbled biro line on my map, "they're effectively defending the Congestion Charge Zone."

"Och, the polis stopping a Scotsman from paying a bill."

"It's a topsy-turvy world."

Ross slowed the van to a halt, parking just before the double yellow lines that orbited the street corner. He didn't have to say why; we all saw it in the windows of the houses facing us on the street to the left. There was no reflection to be seen as such, just a pulsing of blue and red lights. Quite clearly, there were a hell of a lot of police cars waiting for us.

Dorothy followed the yellow brick road with the Scarecrow, the Tin Man and the Cowardly Lion. I wondered which of us was which. What was it they wanted: a brain, a heart and courage?

So, Three Musketeers, one for all and all for one, needed what? I was being led by my heart, drawn to London by love and the promise of sex; Liam, because he had found the courage to actually do something and Ross because intellectually..., no, Liam had found his common sense on the road, and Ross had found the courage to tell his friends that he didn't want to re-enact anymore and I had lost my heart. I was the tin man.

One thing I did know: we weren't in Kansas anymore.

"Guess you were right, Guy," said Ross, "someone did tell the polis our route."

"I'll collect my pint later," I said, and then, thinking aloud: "If nothing happens here, then they'll come looking for us."

"What do we do?" Liam asked.

"Rush 'em," Ross suggested.

"One for all?"

Ross and I finished the sentiment slightly out of phase: "And all for one."

"The Three Musketeers going out in a blaze of glory," I said.

"Butch Cassidy and the Sundance Kid?" said Ross. "Only there were only two of them."

"There was Katharine Ross."

"Och, I bags Katherine Ross."

I thought about the three of us performing a highland charge across the open field of fire that was this sleepy suburban street. We'd yell: 'For Bonnie Prince Charlie!' And screaming, with our polished, but blunt, claymores flashing in the noon sun, we'd charge, Light Brigade style, into the opposing lines, and into history.

My metaphors were all over the place: we shouldn't be someone else. We make our own history.

"I don't think they'll put a memorial cairn in the middle of the street," I said.

"Och, it'd be a good speed bump."

"Jesus," said Liam, sitting back in the chair. I realised that we'd all been sitting forward, concentrating.

I relaxed too.

"OK," I said. "If we don't appear here, then they'll work it out, so we have to appear."

"No shit Sherlock," said Ross.

"A diversion."

"We could pop round and tell 'em we called it off," said Liam. "Give 'em the old gift of the gab, spin a yarn, tell a tall tale."

I turned to Liam just as he pushed his glasses back up his nose, and did my best 'what' expression.

He sort of gulped a little, like a goldfish: "I was just saying, like, or we could just tell 'em to feck off."

"He's right," said Ross. "Give 'em something to think about. You two, in the back and keep out of sight."

I didn't like the sound of this: "Ross–"

"Och, don't worry."

We followed Ross's pointing, and squeezed between the seats into the back.

"I've faced down five hundred screaming kids in the playground," Ross said. "This'll be a walk in the park."

Ross started the engine and pootled round the corner.

"Jesus," said Liam.

"Keep down," said Ross.

We did, but even between the seats, we could see the mass of police, a black line but it was the light that was amazing. The red and blue rippled across the top as the hazard lights on all the vehicles came in and out of phase, sometimes like Christmas tree lights and sometimes like a pulsing supernova. They were parked right across the road, and it looked like they were two or even three deep. Along the line, there were flashes of brilliance as the sunlight caught their riot shields like paparazzi clicking away.

They'd been issued with the Long Shields, transparent, polycarbonate protection from foot to above the head. I remember Mandy telling me that

289

those were the ones that prompted crowds to throw things. If they swapped to the smaller, round shields, then everyone would stop throwing stones. Riot by consent.

The police in London charge for 'security' and one march said they didn't need any, not even a private security firm at £1,000 an hour. It was a march that started peacefully enough, but then *didn't* descend into violence with the police needing to step in to safeguard the public. No vandalism, no injuries, no trouble... clearly someone didn't want that here, they wanted the TV footage to show an angry mob.

The van came to a halt.

Ross sat for a while, probably contemplating what he was going to do and the scale of the obstacle. In the police line, heads turned towards this white van that had parked and then just sat there.

"They are going to know there's someone in the van," said Liam.

Nothing continued to happen for what seemed like a geological age.

"Right," Ross said at last, "not a word, stay where you are and be off with you when you get the chance."

"There are so many of them," I said. "They've riot gear and... guns probably."

"Och, they're just boys with their toys," said Ross. "I'll just show 'em who's boss. Can't be worse than a playground full of oiks."

"If you say so," I said.

"Good luck," said Liam.

I heard a loud *CLICK*, like a gun cocking, as Ross undid his seat belt. He opened the driver's side, got out and then there was the most thunderous *BANG* as he slammed the door shut.

The dark interior felt so unsafe, but I reasoned it would make us invisible to anyone in the sunlight outside. The police presence, now I had a chance to peek, included a barricade thrown across the road while above and behind red and blue lights flashed atop armoured vans.

They were ready for a war.

There was a sudden snap that rippled along the police lines – all their attention was focused on a single, tartan-clad individual, who walked towards them along the white, dashed line in the centre of the road. I was reminded of a western, the lone gunslinger striding down the street towards the sheriff and his hired posse, as the townspeople closed their shutters and hid.

Yes, his feet were wide apart, his hand twitched where his holster would have been slung around his plaid, and he stopped a good hundred yards short, squaring off as if waiting for them to draw first.

"THIS IS AN ILLEGAL GATHERING, PLEASE DISPERSE."

"Good God," said Liam in response to the loud hailer request. "I have to video this."

"Shhh..."

Ross, now a good twenty metres ahead, looked very alone, surrounded as he was by acres of empty tarmac.

"TURN BACK NOW OR WE WILL USE WATER CANNON."

"What?" said Ross. He was much quieter, but there was no other sound, so even hidden in the van, we heard him distinctly. Liam held his phone up, I could see the action on the screen and through the gap in the seats.

"TURN BACK OR WE WILL BE FORCED TO USE BATON ROUNDS."

"I can hear you," said Ross. It seemed a foolish thing to point out, the loudhailer was deafening. It was surreal to have Ross chatting to a distant, unseen Police Inspector.

"TURN BACK. YOU HAVE BEEN WARNED."

"Och, it's only me, you ken."

"YOU ARE UNDER ARREST."

"What for?"

"ILLEGAL GATHERING."

"There's only me."

"THIS IS AN ILLEGAL GATHERING."

"How can it be an illegal gathering, when there's only me?"

"PARDON?"

"I said, how can it be an illegal gathering when there's only me?"

"I DON'T KNOW."

"And you don't need to yell with that wee thingummyjig."

"DON'T TELL ME WHAT TO DO."

"Sorry."

"WHERE ARE THE OTHERS?"

"There's only me."

"WHAT?! YOU FIND... YES, YOU FIND OUT WHAT'S GOING ON... I DON'T KNOW, GO AND ASK HIM. YES, YOU, YOU STUP—"

After an abrupt whistling feedback, a policeman broke ranks and doubled over to Ross, his running looking faintly comical.

Liam and I hunkered down behind the front seats, Liam's hand stuck up like a periscope.

"What's going on?" the copper asked Ross.

"Hello, I'm Ross," said Ross. He held out his hand to the policeman, who looked at it doubtfully. Perhaps this wasn't the 'hut-hut, go-go, bash-bash' that the morning's briefing had led him to expect.

Hesitantly, he reached out and shook Ross's hand: "I'm PC Meadows."

"I'm *Ross*."

"Er... Felix."

"Hi."

"Hello."

There was a 'now what' moment that stretched on.

Ross, how he controlled his nerves I don't know, adopted a nonchalant, I've got all the time in the world, stance. Perhaps, I thought, he could just face-off the police for the few hours we needed for all our supporters to sneak along the rail system. I mean, could it be that easy?

"There are supposed to be thousands of you," said Felix.

The policeman cast about as if searching for the very thousands of rioters hidden somewhere on the empty road. Perhaps they were hiding behind the red postbox or secreted in the rusting yellow skip... or in that white van.

Liam and I ducked again. I hoped the light from his screen didn't illuminate us.

Ross copied the copper, searching about for a clue as well. For a moment, the officer seemed to look me straight in the eye before turning his attention to a red Fiesta. He shrugged as if to say, 'nope, I give up, where have you hidden thousands of rioters'.

"There's only me." Ross folded his arms, his body language confident and triumphant, and, as he appeared to gain height, the policeman became more bent and dejected.

"We can only arrest you if you are in groups of six or more."

"Oh dear."

"Public Order Act, so you can't come through one at a time."

"Why not?"

"It's... cheating."

"Och, do yer no ken that–"

"Sorry?"

"Do you not know that we decided to call it a day?"

"No."

"Och aye... oh yes, and we thought it best if I popped along, helpful like, to let the polis know."

"Oh."

"So, anyway, we decided to call it a day."

"Thanks."

"So you can all take the day off too."

"Oh... very kind."

"My pleasure, just doing my civic duty."

Liam stopped recording, and turned to me: "He's going to get away with it."

"Bloody pointless diversion if he does."

"It's not going to plan," said Liam.

"I don't think it's going to the police plan either," I said as I saw the policeman look back to his lines, arms wide.

"ARREST HIM."

"Oh, we're up," said Liam and he raised his phone again.

"On what charge?" said the policeman.

"ILLEGAL ASSEMBLY."

"Fucking five short," the policeman said under his breath, but quite audibly, before he shouted in reply: "There's only him."

"THEN ARREST HIM."

"On what charge?"

"JAYWALKING."

"What?"

"HE'S STANDING IN THE MIDDLE OF THE ROAD."

The policeman turned back to Ross: "Er... you're nicked. If you don't mind."

"Jaywalking's an American offence."

"Is it? I didn't think I recognized it."

"Och well."

The policeman indicated towards the police lines with a very polite gesture as if he was opening a door for someone. Ross nodded and they both walked side-by-side away from us.

"CUFF HIM."

"What?" said the officer.

"CUFF HIM... HE'S A DANGEROUS RIOTER."

"But–"

"HE MIGHT COMMIT AFFRAY."

"Och," said Ross, holding out his wrists. "I'm a dangerous rioter."

The policeman dropped his handcuffs twice in his fumble to restrain the big Scot. Ross for his part waited patiently.

Finally, the two wandered off towards the police lines, which opened like a Venus Flytrap and Ross was swallowed up. The black lines reformed, the ripples vanishing like they do on dark water, and soon it was as if nothing had happened.

Liam stopped recording and sat back in the van: "Now what?"

"OK," I said. "We're in a van."

We were in a van, parked in the street and in full view of the entire Metropolitan police force, the Territorial Support Group, the Commissioner's Reserve and all, as the 24-hour mobilisation plan was in effect.

Technically, we could open the back door and sneak out that way, hidden from the constabulary's many eyes, but the blind spot, with the police line being so wide, would only be a tiny triangle behind the van, enough to open the doors and huddle. I saw movement, a twitch of lacy curtain, another and then another repeating down the semi-detached houses.

"We're stuffed," said Liam.

"Not necessarily," I said.

"Not necessarily what?"

"Well, they've arrested the rioters... rioter, so logically, the next thing they'd do would be to–"

"STAND DOWN, STAND DOWN... WHAT? YES, MILK AND TWO SUGARS."

Liam and I had to struggle not to laugh too noisily as the loud hailer squealed and was silent.

The police line broke into small clusters of conversation.

"OK," I said.

We both held the rear door and opened it together, four hands to stop it making any noise, before we slipped out onto the road. Rather comically, we couldn't shut it quietly, pushing and shoving the last centimetre didn't work, so we slammed it.

It was loud.

A peek around the van revealed that no-one had noticed. No doubt, they were all too busy with their milk and two sugars.

With exaggerated strides, we managed to walk slowly and nonchalantly for all of five steps, before we legged it. We didn't stop when we got round the corner, but kept going, keeping pace, and eventually letting our delight burst forth from our grins.

"I've got a stitch," said Liam, coming to a halt. He bent over holding his side. I stopped and took the opportunity to check behind us.

The street was remarkably ordinary.

"No-one's following us," I said.

"No."

"It doesn't feel right leaving a man behind."

"What do you think they'll do with Ross?" Liam asked.

"Well, what can they do? They'll take him down to the station and after a while, dunno, a couple of hours maybe, they'll have to charge him, but with what?"

"Yeah, that makes sense. Never come to court. Unless they've privatised the judiciary and they're more on message about locking up political prisoners."

What was he talking about, I thought: "Political prisoners?"

"Yeah, this is political, isn't it?"

"Is it?"

"Well... yes."

"Let's get to the tube."

Liam nodded.

We ran, half jogged to the Underground station, one of those above ground, and we had a twenty-minute wait. We sat on the bench, hunched over occasionally, and eventually, we got our breath back.

As the cliché says, nothing could go wrong now.

The train arrived just as my mobile beeped: '*remember meet me at waterloo 12 m xxx sorry*'.

We'd pulled away before I could finish my reply, and the carriage plunged into the darkness, rattling as it did so, and I dropped off the network.

"Too late," I said, showing Liam my phone.

"Never mind," he said. "Oh feck, I recorded Ross with my phone vertical."

"Does it matter?"

"Wrong aspect ratio. I look like a fecking amateur."

"You're not in it."

"As a cameraman."

Stations arrived in a painful blur of posters rushing by too quickly to focus on. We re-watched Ross's big moment on Liam's smartphone, sharing an earphone each.

As we went deeper and deeper, I felt a growing unease. It seemed we were trapped now, somehow railroaded, literally and metaphorically, to a certain course of action.

For the first time, I wondered what we were actually going to do once we reached our destination. Up until then, it had been a journey, one foot in front of the other, but now, as the little dots were ticked off on the coloured line, we were approaching a destination.

National Demonstration

ANTI-GOVERNMENT PROTEST

Thousands will march to say:

Protect our Civil Liberties

No to War

National Demonstration

ANTI-GOVERNMENT PROTEST

Join the Jacobites

Join the Revolution

This Saturday, Waterloo Station

National Demonstration

TUNNELS BENEATH THE RIVER

I remember getting neck strain looking at the picture of the tube line. Every so often, we'd reach a station and the dark windows would become a strobing blur of passing posters before the train stopped.

The carriage was full of rebels.

"You'd have thought London Underground would have had a group discount," said Liam.

"I think we're under the Thames," I said.

"You could be right."

"Crossing another river."

"Hardly crossing it." Liam shuffled round in the seat to face me. "What's the matter, Guy?"

"We crossed the Rubicon," I said, thoughtfully.

"We crossed the Trent."

"That's not what I meant."

He seemed fragile, his thin wire-frame glasses and his wiry thin frame. We all looked tired and haggard. It wasn't like an army going forward, but more like one in retreat stumbling towards some Culloden field.

"Don't you think it's all got a bit out of hand since Swarkestone Bridge?" I asked.

"It's just a bit of fun."

"I just think, Westminster Bridge is a bridge too far."

"You're a weird one, Guy," said Liam. "Always in your own head, thinking."

"You can talk," I said. "You're always fidgeting."

"I am not."

"Yes, you are."

"I hate London," he said. "I've not been in one of these sausage machines in ages."

"Really?"

"I worked here, well... down aways." Liam waved towards the left side of the train. "Canary Wharf. But then, you know, credit crunch and suddenly we were laid off. The IRA bombs the place and the Irish are treated like scum, and then, just as things seem to get settled, the bloody sub-prime shite hits the fan. And then all the bonuses and pay rises and Paradise Papers. I'm hated 'cos I'm a banker."

"Was a banker."

"Yeah. Was."

"Were you really treated like shit after the bombing, because you're Irish?"

"By some... nah, people liked having the day off mostly."

"I can't imagine you in corporate finance."

"I can show you!"

Liam turned and grabbed my arm, excited, like a kid wanting to open a new toy. He pulled me up.

"I'm not sure–"

"It's not far, we're on the right line, couple more stops – we've plenty of time."

"I have an appointment."

"Plenty of time for a pint too."

"OK."

There were a hell of a lot of escalators and passageways at the next tube station. Liam strode off unerringly like Theseus in the labyrinth, but I lost my sense of direction as if a kitten had played with the ball of string.

Eventually, we emerged into the light, fought through the crowds around three corners, and suddenly everything was quiet. We'd stepped off the usual thoroughfares and into another realm of tall, quiet buildings, losing the noise of traffic and the bustle of people trying to navigate this high walled maze. The tarmac of the pavements and road was salted with squidges of discarded chewing gum.

Liam stopped; looked up, pushed his glasses up along his nose, and stared with his mouth open slightly.

I looked up too, following Liam's gaze. It was an anonymous tower block, neither offices nor apartments, but somewhere in between.

"Here," said Liam.

"Yes?" I said cautiously, not knowing what to expect. We weren't anywhere near Canary Wharf, that was on the East Side – even I, who lived in Scotland, knew that. This was nowhere, a road with an ancient name but nothing else of note.

"I lived there," he said and pointed.

I looked again: "Oh yes," I said, although I'd only narrowed it down to the general area, say three floors by five windows across.

"It wasn't a home!"

"No."

"It was an investment opportunity."

"Right."

"My life was dictated by a fecking spreadsheet with coloured backgrounds and fancy fonts. God, I'd have calculated the return on my friends and girlfriends, if I could have been arsed to invent the codes. Bloke in the office – Danny Something – did it. Can't have worked though, 'cos I can't remember his name. Or perhaps I had a low rating."

"That doesn't—"

"What was the point? I was a robot controlled by software. My personal spreadsheet, the office expert system, the boss's scheduling software – they told me what to do and I did it – and then, when it all went tits-up, some executive in the parent company's parent company entered the figures into his spreadsheet and it automatically issued all of us with emails to see Francine in HR. She was nice, but hassled."

He was right: this didn't strike me as a place to live. There was no green, except in the 'to let' signs. It was all concrete and glass as far as the eye could see made from different Lego sets with more Meccano-like cranes putting up more – someone was enjoying a boom – but they were just storage boxes.

The only sign that people actually lived here were the ones with 'residents only permit' emblazoned on them.

Liam shook my hand: "Thank you."

"For what?"

"Giving my life meaning."

"I beg your pardon?"

"This march, I've done something, finally, actually done something."

"We walked to London."

"Yes, I realise that as my number one achievement, it doesn't rank highly and it makes me pathetic, but it made me feel alive and it's spurred me to do... more."

"More drunken challenges?"

Liam laughed.

"No time like the present," he said, putting his arm round my shoulder to lead me down the street. "I know a trendy wine bar."

"I'd rather find a pub."

"I know one of those too. Hang on."

Liam turned and theatrically made V-signs with both hands at the hideous tower block.

"We're Jacobites," I said.

"And?"

"Let's show our arses."

He laughed.

302

So we turned and lifted our plaids to waggle our Manchester United shorts and whatever team Liam's were, at his ex-apartment, old parking space and an existence he didn't want anymore.

What are those phases: denial, anger, pleading and acceptance? He hadn't talked about his redundancy when I met him, he'd lost his temper at the Stag Party, and he'd certainly done some pleading, so maybe this was acceptance.

I wondered if his old colleagues would recognise him. His face had changed with his beard growth and he was wearing quite outlandish clothes. I'd never seen him in a suit, but I imagine it would have been sharp, expensive and fashionable. His glasses and his accent were the same, maybe, but his conversation was less hurried, lacked that cocaine fizz of repetition. He was no longer a city man.

The pub had London Pride.

"I don't want to be too drunk," I said.

"Bet you don't."

"Clear head, clear mind."

"Clear glass, clear... er... up."

I laughed. The glass wasn't clear, though, as the head had left tide marks at intervals down the sides.

"Time for another?" Liam asked.

I looked at my blank wrist.

Liam checked his phone: "It takes thirty minutes from here, straight along, change at Green Park and it's the Jubilee line."

"A half," I said.

"Two pints it is then," said Liam, getting up.

◆

Tick, tick, tick... time's running out.

Before a charge, even though it's pretend, you feel nervous, all that tension building as flight-or-fight pumps adrenaline into the blood.

"For Bonnie Prince Charlie!" – charge!

Suddenly, everything is the present, a roar of noise and immediacy. There's no time to think.

An officer gets picked on, insulted, again and again, and bottles up their frustration, and then, for nothing, they react, without thought, and a legitimate protester or an innocent civilian gets thumped. It makes the headlines and we wring our hands in anguish. There are calls for enquiries, more enquiries, trial-by-media...

Give 'em guns and that reaction is fatal. Brazilians jumping ticket barriers and *bang!*

The whole struggle between law-and-order and anarchy-and-chaos escalates. Protesters start carrying weapons, newspaper vendors are issued with coshes. Soon, it becomes commonplace, like the streets of America, and it happens every month, every week, every day. Shootings on the hour.

I know the plan.

The Rebellion will be trapped, kettled, then an officer dies. They'll fight back, and in the cauldron, there'll be more casualties. We'll get even, they'll get even; if not straight away, then at another protest or another family day out.

So the cycle will start, and go round and round.

Tick, tick, tick went the clock in Waterloo station.

♦

Two fresh pints of London Pride joined our empties. I moved them to recover the beermats and slipped these under the new drinks as Liam settled himself. The beer tasted good sipped through the fresh froth.

"Guy?"

"Sorry?"

"Do you think Ross'll be all right?" Liam asked

"I hope so," I said after a moment's thought. "He's not committed a crime, has he?"

"They'll think of something."

"What? Like affray? Resisting arrest? Illegal gathering? Jaywalking?"

Liam laughed: "Rebellion, revolt, blowing up parliament."

I laughed too and I tried to imagine Ross at a police station, but I couldn't. *God, I hope he didn't end up where I did.*

"Look," said Liam, "he's been arrested by the police, he's not been chucked in the back of a black van, has he?"

"Black van?"

"You know, when people get 'disappeared'."

"Oh right." I shook my head. "No, that doesn't happen in this country. He'll have such a tale to tell in the bar tonight."

"Yes, I know he will... och aye, I ken he will."

I laughed again.

"When's your girlfriend due?"

"She's not pregnant."

"I meant–"

"Twelve."

"I'll go and find Rabbie and the others."

"You sure?"

Liam looked at me as if I was mad. He pushed his wire glasses back up his nose before shaking his head.

"Guy," Liam said, patting me on the shoulder. "I don't want to be a gooseberry."

That made me smile.

"It's going to be an amazing day tomorrow," he said.

"Yes, it is."

We finished our pints.

Back on the street, Liam gave me directions before we parted.

I had to go north.

For the first time on the journey, it felt like the wrong direction.

"I'd personally like to see the Human Rights Act go because I think we have had some problems with it."

Theresa May, October 2011

"For too long, we have been a passively tolerant society, saying to our citizens: as long as you obey the law, we will leave you alone."

David Cameron, May 2015

"British values are the best in the world: freedom of speech, democracy, a fair trial, tolerance and so forth. These must be protected and we will protect them – whatever the cost."

John Trudie, January 2018

POLICE ACTION

Vaughn pulls my jacket up and over my head like I'm a prisoner who doesn't want to be photographed. At one point, as he hustles me through the maze, I hear the automatic door open, and, as we go through, the carpet squelches underfoot. Looking down I see I'm leaving damp and dark footprints, but after a few steps that fades. It's not something I want to think about.

When we get to the lift, he shoves me against the far wall. We go down, descending to the ground, and then he drags me along until we reach a big, empty space. I can hear the echoes and the floor is a pale concrete stained with oil.

There's a sudden wrench as Vaughn whips my jacket away.

"Stay here," he says. He looks at me. Somehow, I'm not registering his expression.

Satisfied, the big man moves away to talk to the others. They aren't real, just shadows, and they give him an attaché case.

The large space is a loading bay, dark, sullied with a yellow light from inadequate bulbs hidden amongst the dirty metal girders. Pigeons obviously roost in the roof space. The shutter is up and the outside world is bathed in daylight so bright that it bleaches away all colour. There's a white van parked beyond, merely an outline, as if partially invisible.

Used to the darkness, I squint and have to look away. The bright, shiny world is not for me now; I'm in a dark place.

Things are moving, time is running out.

I'm shivering: I don't think it's actually cold, but I can't stop this trembling.

I remember the last time I saw the light.

♦

I got off the tube train and walked through the tunnels of the station to make my way to the surface. I seem to have been underground and in white tiled rooms since then. The tunnels went round and round, the escalators up and up, and all the time it seemed brighter and brighter.

I stood under the clock, I remember, at Waterloo Station, watching the strangely animated commuters as they rushed by. I was amused by all this concern for schedules, timetables and deadlines. The long march had changed my perception of time. Putting my watch away was a symptom of this. Originally, I took the anachronistic object off to look more period – wrist-watches didn't arrive until the 20th century – and later it became a symptom of a slower pace.

I examined every figure that flickered past, trying to turn them into Mandy. I didn't know what she'd be wearing. To start with I focused on those with blonde hair, then any woman because she might be wearing a scarf, or perhaps anyone with smart black shoes. After a while, I saw the shoes rather than the people.

The Duke of Wellington, before suggesting establishing a police force to Sir Robert Peel, defeated Napoleon at Waterloo. This huge monument to the Victorian Industrial Revolution was named after that.

The main concourse, white and sterile, sweeps round. I'd found the clock, its four black faces on each side of a cube, easily enough. Waiting under it meant I had to keep shifting to find out the time. My watch and phone were in my sporran, but I didn't even think of checking those.

There was one entrance there, and another way over there, and various logical arguments convinced me that she'd come from there, or over there, or... for all my careful observation and theories, she didn't arrive, she was just suddenly there.

"Guy!"

We faced each other: "Mandy, I–"

"You have to und–"

There are a few moments in your life when something completely unfamiliar happens and for some reason, you know exactly what it is. It's beyond your experience, but you're already pre-programmed for it.

"Guy Wilson?"

"Yes," I said to the man who asked. Another reporter perhaps, or... he had yellow shoelaces. There were others too, behind me, and suddenly I felt afraid.

You see a picture of two faces, it's two faces – Mandy and me – and then, suddenly, you see the fragile, breakable shape of a vase.

She had yellow shoelaces.

Fight or flight?

But they'd hemmed me in, I couldn't raise my arms and embarrassment, of all things, prevented me from shouting out.

The police came from different directions, six of them, I imagine one for each possible exit, running efficiently through the crowd. An old lady dropped her shopping: apples and oranges rolling foolishly across the white floor. I didn't look. I kept staring at Mandy. There was someone standing next to her, but I didn't see him.

"Guy," she said, "we can't have civil disorder, not at a time like this, not when there's terrorism."

"Mandy, I–"

The first running policeman hit me full on, rugby style and I was a punch bag thrown to one side. There were two on top of me before I hit the ground, and another landed a moment later, fouling attempts to get the handcuffs on me. I could see the white floor, tiling again, and boots stomping towards me. There were yellow shoelaces, there were black shoelaces, and another pair I recognized, the single pair of women's sensible black shoes, and the colour of the shoelaces: yell–

No, she'd said 'ochre'.

This was it then, the prelude.

Tomorrow, when everyone arrived for the demonstration, the police would pick us off en masse, or one by one, brutally. Waterloo: Wellington's victory would be Wellington's nightmare – English soldiers firing on English civilians on English streets.

I floated through the air as they manhandled me away.

OK, so I'd been arrested like Ross, but even if I was charged, the case would never hold up in court. I mean come on, we'd not broken any laws. Citizens of this country have the right to free assembly, free transit, free speech, free... dom.

Why do I keep trying to cling to thinking about my rights? It's pathetic! Ross said everyone whines about their rights. But then I am pathetic. I've lost my fiancée, the Mandy I knew, when she became that person who stood by. It's something I don't think I want to get over.

"Everything's under control," a copper said in such a reasonable voice, his hands held up, placating the passers-by. They carried on passing by, gawping or looking away. "Please go about your business."

"My name Guy Wilson, Guy Wilson. Someone! Tell the press! Tell the press, Guy Wilson, tell–"

One of them, the big gorilla I discovered later was Vaughn, waved a warning at those raising their phones to film us.

Outside, they shoved me along the pavement and out of a police cordon of blue and white tape fluttering in the breeze.

Snitty, still in his re-enactment gear, waited.

"We'll take it from here," said Vaughn. He flashed something, a warrant card perhaps, and the policeman flinched.

"Sir," the copper said. He saluted and quickly made himself scarce.

I looked at Snetterton, trying to understand. There he was, dressed as a Jacobite, one of us, and yet... he's dead now, but then he was alive.

"Snitty, they got you too," I said.

Snitty just laughed: "He thinks I'm one of them."

He and Vaughn dragged me further down the road, out of the police cordon, to an unmarked car parked on the double yellow lines and the kerb.

Vaughn went round the front and wrenched the parking ticket off the windscreen: "At least the dick hasn't clamped us," he said. He examined the polyethene wrapped object, complete with 'do not ignore' in big letters as if it was something he'd found on his shoe, and then he tossed it aside.

When you discard one law, you discard them all.

I just thought: he's littering, which almost made me laugh. The wind whipped the ticket along the street, and it seemed to dance along as it went.

"In you go," said Vaughn.

"My girlfriend–"

"Yes, meet me at Waterloo, 12, M, kiss, kiss, kiss, sorry."

Snitty bundled me into the back of the silver Ford Focus, his hand pushing my head down to avoid banging it against the doorframe. The other man, Vaughn, was already getting into the driver's seat. I was squeezed between Snitty and some other thug, bent over in the backseat and pushed down, my lungs compressed.

I found it difficult to breathe. Even so, I managed to say something. "Er..." I said, trying to hold up my cuffed wrists. "Seatbelt?"

Vaughn looked at me as if I was mad.

The car jerked forward and bumped awkwardly as it dropped off the pavement. There was a single blaring of a siren and we were in the traffic flow. I couldn't understand it, and then I remembered that there are unmarked cars with flashing lights hidden in their radiator grills.

I struggled to sit up and managed to see the blue lights flashing reflected in the shop windows. It was strange to see all the cars suddenly slow down, steer to the gutter and generally behave themselves. Those drivers who looked in their rear mirrors notified us with red brake lights, others sped away until it was obvious that there was a police vehicle approaching. The cars going at the speed limit looked very slow.

"Get out of the way!" Vaughn yelled. The siren wailed suddenly, a brief banshee-like burst of sonic pummelling, the wavefront almost visible as it pushed cars out of the way to create an exhibition of bad parking.

Vaughn slammed his foot down. The car bucked and complained before racing forward, slaloming around the corners recklessly. He looked like he was enjoying throwing the car around.

Snitty pushed me down into the seat well, so I saw nothing more.

"Bloody woman!" said Vaughn.

This guy is insane, I thought.

"Sunday driver!" It was Friday.

"Why can't we have proper sirens in these black vans," Vaughn said with glorious observation. It's a silver car, you cretin, I thought, and then... oh shit, 'black van'.

♦

It's Saturday now – today.

"Put the bag on his head," says Vaughn.

"What?" A hessian bag looms. "Please–"

I spit inside the bag to clear the straw taste from my mouth as the thing is pulled over me. Some big rugby type swats my cuffed hands as I try and get the thing off.

"Come quietly."

It's no warning at all, because I'm already being pulled along. The bag obscures my vision, but I can see light flickering through the hessian weave in a kaleidoscope pattern.

My shin connects with the tailgate of the van – this 'black van' is an actual van, but painted white – and the heavy hands on my jacket pull me vertically. I must look like a sack of potatoes. I'm being treated like a sack of potatoes. I struggle up to my knees, but he pushes me to the floor and I connect with a cymbal of sound. I haven't managed to get my feet under me. I suppose that saved me from banging my head on the ceiling.

"Stay there!"

I'm not going to move.

The acceleration, when it comes, is extraordinary. I hear the tyres spin as they try to grip the road, and then we come to an abrupt halt almost at once. He'd put his foot down and then had to brake savagely for the London traffic. The van turns, edging onto a major road. Through the hard floor, I feel every jerk forward, every skid to stop, every lane change and every expletive aimed at some moron, idiot, bloody woman or Sunday driver. Vaughn, I realise, doesn't have a large repertoire when it comes to commenting on other people's driving. He didn't when he was driving the silver car: he doesn't now he's driving a van.

It seems as if I've spent my whole life crashing against the metal floor, like some tortured fly bashing into a window. It merges into the previous journey in the car as if I've spent no time at all in the deconsecrated police station.

But I don't want this journey to end.

♦

That other drive in the car was only yesterday (or was it this morning or a century ago?) and it did stop.

I heard and felt the front doors slam.

The gorilla, Vaughn, though I didn't know his name then, grabbed my ankle, dragged me up and bodily out of the car and yanked me vertical.

"Put the bag over his head," Snitty said.

"Eh?" said the other. "What's that, Snitch?"

They called Snitty 'Snitch', I realised. They knew him. He was one of them. 'Snitch'; apt, if nothing else.

"He's supposed to have been wearing it on the journey."

"He was in the unmarked," said Vaughn. "He'd have been seen."

"Well, put it on him now," Snitty... no, Snitch insisted.

"What's the point?"

"So that he won't see anything that.... oh, all right, I'll do it. Where is it?"

"In the car," said Vaughn.

"Where in the car?"

"In the boot."

Snitch opened the boot and rummaged about. The boot was full of plastic boxes, the fold-out variety, each filled with the same unsorted mix of paraphernalia. Perhaps once it had been organised, but Snitch was just moving things randomly from box to box until he found what he was looking for. It was a hessian sack and–

"Hang on," I said, "I have–"

But clearly, I didn't.

It was rough, like having sandpaper pulled down my face and it smelt of oil and bad breath, which meant it had been used before. I struggled, but what could I do? Evidently, I wasn't the first to go this way.

Suddenly, I was being marched along, through a door and then, maybe, a corridor. The echoes sounded like... I couldn't tell.

We reached a lift, not the hotel lobby variety but something industrial and functional, and we went down. I felt it in my stomach, a moment of falling and sickness. If there was a display going G... B1... B2, I couldn't see it. The corridor at the bottom sounded more antiseptic, like a hospital, because our boots squeaked as we walked along. When my minder shoved me through a doorway and pulled the hessian sack off, I saw why.

It was a cell, tiled with white squares on every surface, except for the blank ceiling and a raised concrete platform. It took me a while to realise that the slab was a bed, devoid as it was of any pillows, quilts or tiny foil wrapped chocolates.

I looked at the man standing alone in the doorway. The other minder must have left us at some point.

He spoke: "Welcome to... I can't say," he said with a shrug before he started to leave.

"Oi, oi!"

"What?"

"Cuffs, cuffs."

The man looked at me, the slightest flicker of compassion before he came over, wrenched me around and undid the handcuffs. I saw the key briefly, a simple, almost blank looking piece of metal.

"Do I get a phone call?"

"Get your phone out."

I did.

He took it off me.

"That's mine," I said.

"No signal down here."

"Then can I–"

"Shoelaces!"

"Sorry."

"Take off your shoelaces. We don't want you doing anything stupid."

I sat on the concrete bed and undid my shoelaces. I tried to do it quickly. I didn't want to hold him up, but I simply couldn't get my fingers to work.

"Here!" he said, as he bent down and expertly whipped them out of my boots. I felt eternally grateful, pleased by this act of kindness. "Belt!"

"Thank you... I'm sorry."

"Your belt."

"Oh, yes, sorry."

I started on the buckle and thought better of it.

"I can't, the plaid will fall apart."

"What?"

"The plaid–"

"Your kilt?"

"Yes."

"Forget it then."

I did the buckle up once more.

"Aren't you going to read me my rights?" I asked.

"Your rights?" said Snitch, who had stayed by the doorway, leaning against the frame. He and Vaughn glanced at each other as they contemplated this novelty.

"You've been arrested under anti-terrorism legislation," said Vaughn. "When they wrote that, I don't think the word 'rights' was even in the spell-checker."

"Do I get a lawyer?"

Vaughn snorted.

"I have rights," I said.

"You always know your rights, don't you? You practically quote the legislation as if you understand all that legalese, but mention a law they've broken, oh no, never heard of that, have you? It's all, I didn't know, I didn't see the sign, I climbed the fence by accident. Ignorance is the best defence."

"Knowledge is power," said Snitch.

"And the fucking psychologists," Vaughn continued. "Ooh, voices told him to do it, don't arrest him, arrest the voices. All these psychologists and psychiatrists and... they're all women with glasses, tight skirts and tight arses. Bloody evaluate this and evaluate that when we should be beating two shades of shit out of them for a confession. They're a danger to society whether they're sane or mad, so what does it matter. Lock 'em up, chuck away the key, that's what I say."

"You've no right!"

"Emergency Powers Act," said Vaughn.

"When was that activated?" Snitch asked.

"I don't think it was stood down from last time," said Vaughn.

"I didn't think we bothered with that," said Snitch.

"Of course, we do," said Vaughn, apparently genuinely offended. "This is all legal. We're protecting democracy, law and order – we're the good guys for Christ's sake."

"Under law, I–" I tried.

"I'll see your law and raise you," said Vaughn. "Anti-terrorism trumps everything."

"How long will I be here?"

"Not long," said Snitch.

"We can hold you for 42 days," said Vaughn, "although Trudie's bound to get that extended."

"Extended?" I said, realising how long 42 days was. "That's monstrous."

"Blair wanted 90 days," said Snitch.

"You need at least 60 odd," Vaughn added, "'cos often we bung 'em in a cell and forget which one."

"Paperwork," said Snitch. "You need a few end-of-the-month double checks, particularly if you've forgotten to inform a lawyer or whatever."

"Right, let's see," Vaughn said, taking out a transparent polyethene bag. "Watch, twenty-five in notes, and ten thirty... one, two, three, four in change, mobile phone, keys and an engagement ring box... empty. How sweet!"

"Bastard," I managed.

"Here," he said. "Keep it for sentimental value."

He threw it to me and I caught it.

It meant... oh god. I put it back in my sporran.

"I want to make a formal complaint," I said.

"Fuck no," said Vaughn, "think of the paperwork."

"What's my crime? What's the charge?"

"Treason, terrorism," said Snitch. "You crossed a line."

"I crossed a bridge!" I said.

"You burnt your bridge," said Snitch, and laughed at his joke. The only one who did.

They turned – *squeak* – and walked out. The door closed and then, with dreadful finality, the lock engaged. I heard a slight jingle-jingle of keys as the pounding boots faded, echoed in the corridor outside, and then I was truly alone.

I looked around the cell. There was nothing in it.

I had no shoelaces; there wasn't anywhere to hang myself from anyway, but I was dead, and I knew it.

They've thrown away the rulebook, and once that happens, what's to stop them going the whole way.

In fact, they had... *and have now,* no choice. They are so steeped in blood that it's easier to go on than to go back, or some rationalisation worthy of Macbeth.

We have rules about knives and forks. If you worry about etiquette – the wrong knife for the fish, red wine with chicken, an upside down fork and so on – then you are less likely to commit murder. It's a long escalation to parking in a disabled bay, keeping your seat when a pregnant woman stands or dropping chewing gum. It's only one step in a society where the only rule is 'thou shalt not kill'.

Rules for the sake of rules are for the sake of rules.

So, reading my rights, a lawyer and a phone call denied... what's to stop them doing anything they want like torture and murder?

Nothing.

I sat, and felt despair.

It's hard to know how long I waited locked in that white room. I had no watch and time lost all meaning.

Vaughn brought a sandwich at one point, throwing it in when he opened the door. It landed on the concrete platform that was supposedly a bed. BLT, the label said. He offered me a plastic bottle of coke too.

"Eat your food," he said.

"What's this, a hearty breakfast for the condemned man?"

"It's a late lunch."

I carefully opened the triangular cardboard container and ate the bacon, lettuce and tomato on granary slowly. After a couple of mouthfuls, I put the sandwich down on the cardboard and opened the coke. It fizzed and I waited before taking the cap off fully. The coke tasted wonderful.

When I finished the first sandwich, I noticed that there was an offer sticker attached.

"Doesn't this come with a snack?" I asked.

Vaughn grimaced, but he did reach into his pocket and chuck a packet of crisps across to me: salt and vinegar.

When I'd finished, he took the rubbish away, and I was on my own. Mid-afternoon, assuming his comment about a late lunch had been correct, slipped away and I suppose tiffin, afternoon tea and dinner zoomed past without a morsel being offered.

I tried to sleep but I couldn't. Fear held me and every bump and knock, every door slam and every footfall, seemed to herald the end. Was it night? Morning? Next week?

"Let me out!" I'd shouted.

♦

I'm in the van now being taken to die. Please, I want to be back in the cell.

♦

It felt like days and the blink of an eye at the same time. I had plenty of time to think, sure; aeons to go over and over what had happened. I tried so hard to understand how this all started and I'm still doing it.

It was almost a relief when, to my absolute amazement, the Home Secretary, John Trudie, MP, came in carrying a red balloon.

"So," he said, "this is the Architect of my rise to power."

"What's with the balloon?" I asked as if that was important.

He was going on a photo opportunity, an alibi, for my murder. We traded jibes, talked about historical figures: Sir Robert Peel, the Duke of Wellington and Marx. Trudie obviously fancied himself as Richard the Lionheart to my Saladin. He saw himself as a man making history. He just seemed like some preening lunatic, identifying with Bond villains because, like him, they can gloat. It was surreal, scoring academic points with this murdering psychopath.

"You can't have 'armed, *unarmed* keepers of the peace," I said.

I won, match point, but he had an ace up his sleeve: Vaughn and his heavies. He was going to kill me, I worked that out otherwise why would he have told me everything. Kill me and kill others.

"Proportionate and necessary," he said. "You can't make an omelette without breaking eggs."

"You can't make an egg pyramid if you break your eggs," I replied calmly.

I wouldn't mind that being attributed to me in the history books, but no-one would record it.

Certainly, Trudie wouldn't.

I knew that the coming events weren't history just yet, but they were going to be. The Rebellion was weaving its way out of Waterloo station and gathering beneath the gaze of the London Eye.

Later on, Vaughn took me out and locked me in an Observation Room. I saw Mandy, beautiful, ambitious Mandy, who'd betrayed us all, plotting with Trudie.

'We must be resolute' and 'good girl' and... *bitch, bitch!*

Then I escaped, and I came so close, inches away from freedom, and now I'm in the back of a van.

I'll see all my friends one last time before the shooting, the violence, the 'proportionate and necessary' response, and then it'll all be over. I'll die. A witness to history is no witness if they cannot tell their story. You have to survive, build your egg pyramid, in order to be a historian.

"It's the winners who write the history," Trudie had said. "I thought you understood that."

BREAKING NEWS: inster Bridge...   Jacobite March reaches
Westminster Bridge... Jacobite March reaches Westminster Bri

THE WAR ON WESTMINSTER

The van pulls up and stops.

"Any pissing about," Vaughn says, "and you die here and now."

He has a black case slung over his shoulder.

But dying here and now would be better, I think, surely, because then I could stop them. I'd be a martyr, a hero, one of the Three Musketeers fallen in glorious battle, but somehow the blood in my veins is too thin. He takes me through the back entrance, I think. There's a coat thrown over me; he isn't allowing me much room and I'm handcuffed, but I can see my boots and the lino, occasionally a wall through a slit in the brown leather. He nods to others. I can't decide if they are with him or simply ordinary people, but is now a good time to–

It's a hospital.

Really surreal, but this is a hospital, two-tone, beige painted over a pastel green with hard lino floors. It's got that smell too. We've come through a service entrance, sure, with trolleys of linen parked along the side, that's a fire extinguisher, there's medical... what's the word? We reach a small cupboard at the end, it's dark, the strip light above has failed and... no, Vaughn presses a button and I realise that it's a lift.

Now?

As he waits, he turns and nods down the corridor. I look and a shadow shifts, moving away. There were others in the corridor waiting, keeping people away perhaps; yes, that must be it and—

The lift arrives and Vaughn pushes me in. His body, and the hard case hanging over his shoulder, trap me for a moment in the doorway. I catch a glimpse of a metal interior before Vaughn shoves me against the far wall.

Now?

The lift door is about to close.

Now?

Yes, now, fuck it!

I explode, throwing everything into a single, backwards kick – surprise!

I feel something tense under my sole and then it gives, his leg and he stumbles. The case bangs hard against the metal wall, defending, as I shove my leg down and strike out with the other.

I'm cuffed, but I can kick.

Got to keep the blows going.

Again.

I kick again, whirl round using my shoulder to bounce off the wall and bring my knee up, followed by a headbutt that impacts against the cushion of his shoulder.

I move for the closing doorway.

If I can just get through with him behind, I can run. Not the way I came, another way, any other way.

The door's closing, I make it, I'm going through and—

I'm not.

The air is like treacle, the jacket pulls me back. I turn, I've no choice, and Vaughn is still standing.

He taps me on the side of my torso, a slow, casual looking blow, and my legs disappear.

I hit the ground in a tangled mess and – *Christ!*

My lungs scream for air, my mouth gaping, but the air doesn't come in. My diaphragm isn't working. Push, push, against the floor, pull, get some air, push – snot and spit burst from my nose and mouth before wonderful, blessed air, with all the filthy odours and muck from the floor, floods inwards spilling its oxygen into my suffocated blood.

"I wondered when you'd try that," he says.

I hit him, how many times?

He hit me once.

The door closes.

The lift goes up.

Suddenly I'm on my back, being slapped in the face.

"Wakey, wakey, rise and shine."

I must have passed out.

Vaughn pulls me to my feet and leads me outside. There's gravel on the floor and at first I think we're on someone's driveway, but we're not. It's the roof.

"Come on!" says Vaughn. I'm not aware I knelt down until he yanks me up again.

A street zooms into view below. I'm looking down over the world, the busy, busy world and then Vaughn drops me and I can't see over the parapet anymore. He goes to look over, checking with a professional eye, while I can hear sobbing. Someone is weeping. I look round to see who it could be.

Oh, no, wait, it's me.

Vaughn finds a place near the edge. He pushes me to the floor before unlocking a cuff. I squirm about, trying to flail, but it's hopeless.

The roof is covered in gravel with a metal barrier around the edge. There are aerials and air conditioning fans, but it's mostly a wide flat area. It's littered with cigarette butts. Clearly, those working in the higher storeys of the hospital find it easier to sneak up here than go outside to a designated area.

Vaughn fastens me to a railing near the edge.

The view over London, once I've struggled to a sitting position, is stupendous.

Vaughn clicks the solid clasps and opens the case. I almost laugh. It's so typically a sniper's rifle case, complete with depressions in the foam for the various components of black steel. He takes out the stock, taps it and then clicks it into place on the butt. The barrel is next.

"No-one's going to believe I've used a sniper rifle," I say.

Vaughn grunts.

"I've never fired a rifle in my life."

"What about those muskets?"

"I'm not in the black powder brigade."

"Doesn't matter. We've video of you lot firing muskets, we'll show that."

"Not of me."

"No-one'll check."

"They will."

Vaughn grins: "This is the era of fake news, no-one'll check."

Brass shells catching the light in a black metal magazine.

I look away, feeling sick.

In the distance, the London Eye slowly turns, there's St. Paul's and opposite, dominating the view, are the Houses of Parliament. Big Ben showing twenty to twelve. Happy day-trippers and excited tourists jostle along as if they have all the time in the world. Red balloons bob along at head height, markers for the children walking with their parents, eating ice cream, laughing and pointing.

When I look back at Vaughn, he's screwing on a silencer to the now complete rifle.

"I can't have anyone hearing where the shot comes from," he says in explanation. "I need time to escape."

"Don't do this," I say.

He lies down on the roof, right leg bent up to support himself in a practised, familiar posture. He aims.

"Who shall we choose?"

"What?"

He looks at me: "I have to check the scope is calibrated correctly."

"No! No, no... please."

"Let's see..." He points the rifle, tracking left and right, and pauses briefly to fix on one person, then another. "How about that old lady, no-one will miss her... or the Paki, or..."

"No!"

I look down too, but can't make out any particular person in the confusion of the crowd. Everything's blurred as the individuals scurry hither and thither, oblivious to their observers.

"Ah yes, a tricky target... that little girl."

Somehow, I make out a little girl, dressed in an oversized red duffle coat, holding a balloon. She's still, a pivot around which the mad, unsuspecting world jostles and rushes. She smiles, laughs at something, as innocent a face as it is possible to imagine – sweet Jesus!

"No!!!"

I make a grab for Vaughn. Stupid, but I have to do something. I'm nowhere near reaching him when the handcuff yanks me back, straining the joints in my wrist.

Vaughn laughs, I see his fillings, and he grabs me, twisting my head around to look through the telescopic sight.

"You want to look, go on, look..."

A black circle, cross-haired careering wildly about the river – I see pedestrians on Westminster Bridge as if they were two feet away. I bounce against the roof again and Vaughn resumes his firing position.

"Where is she... ah, there, see the red balloon?"

I do, impossibly, manage to see where he's aiming. "Please, please don't," I whine.

"She looks so sweet, so pretty, so easy... nice head-shot, follow the target, ready to squeeze the trigger... it takes only the slightest caress... hold my breath and..."

Phut!

That's all it does. The tiniest noise, not even a breath, and over by the river the girl's balloon disappears. The string stays vertical for a moment, comically, as if it obeys the physics of cartoons, and then it drops. The girl looks at it in bemusement before a dreadful understanding.

Her mother bends down: *there, there, never mind.*

"You fuck!" I say.

"Would you prefer I shot her?"

"You piece of piss."

Vaughn ignores me, checking the sight and making a microscopic adjustment.

I lean back and close my eyes for a moment. It would be so easy to give up and fall asleep listening to the life pulsing all around me. London is peaceful out of the crowds and there is a breeze, gentle and fresh. It's a nice day. I open my eyes. High in the pure blue, cloud-scudded sky, the vapour trails of two aircraft have intersected to create a giant white cross. St. Andrew, the patron saint of Scotland, was martyred on a saltire. I remember seeing that 'X' in the sky at Culloden.

I look at Vaughn as he fumbles in his pocket for something. What can I say? What can I do? The man takes out a smartphone, a fancy one. I've a mobile in my pocket with battery life and credit. I could fish it out, one-handed, but he'd spot that.

Vaughn thumbs his touchscreen.

Suddenly, there's noise, tinny, but clear, and the screen comes to life. I crane my neck to see, full of dread and curiosity. It's the BBC News 24 channel.

"...this is the showdown between the Rebellion and the Government, here in the heart of London, as hundreds of Jacobites stream from Waterloo station towards the London Eye and the Houses of Parliament..."

I see faces briefly, people waving madly as they shuffle past.

"...what will the new Home Secretary, John Trudie, do? He says, and we heard him earlier in our exclusive interview, that he'll do what he can to protect the home of democracy, but his hands are tied."

The image cuts to show a man sitting at a desk.

"Jacqueline, what does he mean by that?"

"You wanna see," says Vaughn, shoving the black rectangle into my face.

The screen shows a woman, standing in a white blouse and holding a black microphone in front of her. Her background is the same panorama I can see, but twisted. The London Eye and the Houses of Parliament loom high above her, whereas here we're looking sideways at them. I can see a few clusters of people where she must be... behind that statue perhaps.

"He's referring, of course," the woman called Jacqueline is saying, *"to his armed response white paper and his speech begging for the right tools for the right job."*

A group of tartan-clad yobs shout and gesture behind her. I see a couple of Redcoats amongst them. Is that...? They laugh and move on before I can be sure. Everyone still thinks this'll be a grand day out.

"Do you think," says the presenter from his safe studio, *"that those tools will be needed today?"*

"I can't say that I do, Alistair. The crowd is unruly, certainly, but boisterous and friendly. There are plenty of police on Westminster Bridge, unarmed police I should say, and once this Jacobite army has reached them, it'll all be over."

"And that's all?" Alistair asks.

"I'm sure — a lot of shouting, a lot of chanting, and a lot of raised voices. These people will have their voices heard."

"I'm sure they will," says Alistair. *"Well, thank you Jacqueline, and enjoy the festivities."*

"I can't see her," says Vaughn. He's squinting down the sight again, "but there's the camera crew."

I try, although I'm too far away from the edge to look down at that angle.

Vaughn laughs: "I can see your friends," he says.

I'm barely able to spot anything of Queens Walk below. No, there's nothing except... no... wait... there's a reddish mix to the crowd and the flow seems to change.

"For Bonnie Prince Charlie!" It's as clear as a bell, a recognizable Edinburgh twang floating up from miles and miles away.

"Rabbie! Rabbie! Rab–" I don't even see the punch coming.

"One more sound and you'll be unconscious... and it would be a shame to miss the show."

I sit still, blood in my mouth and my teeth feel loose.

Below, the cry is answered: "For Bonnie Prince Charlie!"

"For Bonnie Prince Charlie."

The reply is huge, a muffled roar as the phrase ripples along the crowd.

"We're going live to Westminster now," says the black mobile phone and Liam suddenly appears on the screen.

"Do you consider yourselves to be traitors?" says an unseen, tinny voice.

And then Liam speaks: *"Since when was supporting the current Prince of Wales treason?"*

He pushes his spectacles up his nose and grins. He can see the funny side, the turning of expectations, but it's not a joke. Some copper, with a wife and two kids, who's been on the force for three years and always wanted to be a policeman ever since he was seven, is about to need a funeral cortège and a memorial service.

"...is Guy Wilson. We haven't been able to obtain an interview with the reclusive leader of this rebellion, but we hope to bring you one soon. Back to you in the studio."

God, she's pretty and wearing a tartan... no, a Burberry scarf. The man in the studio is looking sombre in a dark suit and behind him, there's a huge picture of police on one side and Jacobites on the other. The screen changes and a series of pictures riffle across, too small to see on this smartphone, and then there's a graphic showing a route down England. With a jolt, I realise that we've rated our own animated logo.

"You want to watch this?" Vaughn asks. "I don't need it."

He passes it to me and I take it.

On the screen, people keep mouthing like goldfish; there are shots of crowds, police, and studio graphics, and then we have the sport. David Beckham is kicking a ball around a field in training and then in a match. He's being re-signed or resigned, I don't know, and there's Posh being photographed. No, it's a retrospective, I think.

"You won't get away with this," I say.

"You want to bet."

"Shouldn't there be police marksmen on the roof?"

"I'm a police marksman on the roof," he replies. "Trudie sent the others away."

I remember Trudie coming into the cell, so many hours ago that it seems like it belongs to another lifetime.

You expect Death to wear a black cloak with a cowl, carry a huge scythe in skeletal hands and stare at you with magically piercing eyes set in the dark recesses of his skull. You don't expect him to be wearing a sharp suit and carrying a balloon, but that was what the Home Secretary, the Right Honourable John Trudie, MP was wearing when he arrived. I didn't expect Death to be quite that chatty either.

"Item five is having you killed," he'd said. "Cheerio."

It was very near now, not long – shooting an innocent policeman must be Item Four.

"One understands, but this job requires sacrifices," Trudie had said to Mandy. 'One' – honestly, pretentious git – he even used that cliché about breaking eggs. I don't see him making any sacrifices.

My phone beeps.

I practically have a heart attack.

Vaughn too is startled: the first time I've seen him unsure, but he settles quickly once he realises the source of the jolly tune.

"That still on?" he asks.

"I guess so," I say.

"Well?"

I get the phone out, awkwardly because one hand is securely cuffed to the rail. I thumb the buttons and there's a text.

"It's a text," I say.

"And?"

I scroll: *'Guy, where are you? This is great. Liam.'*

"Well?"

"It's from Liam wanting to know where I am."

There are a lot of texts in the queue: Ross, Ross, Rabbie, Kate, Ross, Mum, top-up offer, Ross and finally the one from Liam I've just read out. What button can I press, that'll... I look up.

Vaughn is watching me like a hawk. His eyes seem to know what I'm thinking.

"Show me," he says.

I hold the phone up so he can see.

"I should reply otherwise he'll get suspicious," I say.

"You guys probably have secret codes," he says.

"My last text would be my famous last words."

"Back in your pocket with it."

I put the phone away: it's on, it might ring at any moment, but I can't call International Rescue.

I'm going to become some monster, who shot an innocent police officer, sparked a riot and ushered in the police state. Thank God we have our boys in blue equipped with peacemakers; otherwise, those Guys, those Fawkes and Wilsons, would bring anarchy to our streets.

But would I be remembered at all? Would I be a character in someone's thesis? Would I be burnt in effigy?

"Here we go," says Vaughn. He cocks the sniper rifle, a small metal noise of finality, so much more clinical and ruthless compared to black powder muskets. He isn't a soldier, he's a technician; this isn't glory, this is murder.

He pulls the butt into his shoulder and squints down the scope.

"Let's break some eggs," she'd said.

Public group   Joined ▾   ➤ Share   ✓ Notifications   ⋯

Discussion   Members   Events   Photos   Files   Search this group   Q

Air Supremacy

King of the Hill: take the high ground!

The first Gulf War was the first Space Battle. You can't get higher than that. Saddam Hussein fired Scuds at Saudi Arabia and Israel in the hope that he'd bring about World War III. These Russian missiles were ballistic, practically left the atmosphere and re-entered. The Americans used satellite technology, their spies-in-the-sky orbiting around the globe, gazing down on our every move.

The satellites were higher than the missiles.

In the Battle of Britain, the Spitfires were told to gain height and then it was every man for himself.

Napoleon took the hill at Austerlitz.

They all won.

Bonnie Prince Charlie's Jacobite charge at Culloden was over the marshy ground and uphill.

He lost.

From the rooftop, the whole scene unfolds beneath me. To the East, south of the Thames, the Jacobite army ambles and strolls, jokes and jostles, as they weave through the tourists towards the slowly turning wheel of the London Eye. To the north, across Westminster Bridge, the black formations of riot police stand their ground, a line not to be crossed, and, to the west, somewhere, tucked away, are Trudie's storm troopers.

In the middle is the killing zone, the bridge itself, and perched high above is Vaughn.

Bop, bop, a couple of police down and everyone will over-react, or maybe, considering the proximity of the seat of democracy and a few casualties, it will count as a 'proportionate and necessary' force. Trudie's goon squad will trap the rebels in a vice and dog will eat dog as they beat the crap out of those tarred as cop killers.

It's called 'kettling'; corralling the demonstration into a smaller and smaller area, denying the rioters (and innocent bystanders, like the little girl without her balloon) food, water and toilet facilities. At the G20 summit in 2009, the tired protesters gained their freedom only if they gave their name and address to be added to their photographs. Legally the police can't insist on this, but those who didn't agree went back into the kettle. It was called Operation Glencoe, perhaps to commemorate the infamous Scottish massacre.

No, they don't call it 'kettling' anymore: it's a 'containment area', so that's all right then.

Or perhaps Trudie will just cut to the chase and have English troops firing on English civilians on English streets.

"We must protect our democracy," Trudie will say and who could possibly object? "We live in appalling times and action must be taken," he'll say at the hero police officers' funeral on Wednesday with thousands in attendance.

And, after two minutes' silence, the police will be packing arms and, according to history, I will have been the person who fired the first shot. I'll join the ranks of Lee Harvey Oswald and John Wilkes Booth... no, I'll be in the ranks of Gavrilo Princip, the student who assassinated Archduke Franz Ferdinand on 28th June 1914 and precipitated the Great War.

Oh God, can I really compare this with the First World War? These are my friends.

Yes, history repeats: the only thing we learn from history is that we never learn from history.

Bang! Everyone will start killing each other, and finally, overcome with remorse, I'll arrive at the front doors of the hospital by jumping off the roof with my place in history assured. Here, the tour guides will say, is the very spot where he landed.

The door to the roof opens...

Do something – shout, scream, something, anything!

But the word 'police' appears, written in white on black, and my heart sinks as I see the ochre laces. The copper, a sergeant according to the stripes on the shoulder epaulettes, approaches with stealth... slowly, deliberately, inching the red door wider, and... it's a policewoman, blinking in the light.

It's Mandy. She can't see anything, momentarily dazzled by the sunlight. I look between her and Vaughn, his fat arse stuck in the air as he hunches over the rifle, concentrating on the view through the telescopic sight.

She's come to watch the killing, the moment in history, but wait! She holds up her hand to me.

I remember: when she was in that interview room with Trudie and her hands were behind her back, and when she talked to Superintendent McGivern about drinking on duty, she'd had her hands behind her back, and I know that posture. She had her fingers crossed. So... the realisation is startling, my whole treatise is wrong and all my assumptions fall like dominoes in the light of this new evidence.

I've got to warn her, help her, do something, make a difference.

Mandy works her way across, toe-step by toe-step. Expertly, without needing to look, she draws her truncheon; it goes on and on, comically like in a cartoon. It's one of those long, extendable nightsticks, an ASP. My brain seems to bring up this irrelevant information as I struggle to understand what's happening. Who cares what it is, just get in there and hit him with it.

Her sole squeaks.

New shoes.

I was with her when she bought them.

Vaughn pauses. His head tilts and then he looks at me. I snatch a glance at Mandy, but she's vanished.

"What?" says Vaughn. Instinctively, he knows something's up, I can tell by his tone, but he doesn't know what. I must look guilty.

"I didn't say anything," I say. My voice cracks with uncertainty, and Vaughn's eyes narrow suspiciously.

I didn't dare look, but in the corner of my eye, Mandy's shadow trickles over the roof. Vaughn is looking at me, and so long as he keeps looking at me, he won't see Mandy.

"So," I say conversationally, "any hobbies?"

"What?"

"You know, apart from shooting, obviously, with that sniper rifle and the handgun in your left coat pocket, and the martial arts, I suppose, although tricky with that limp in your left leg."

"What?"

Mandy is nearly on Vaughn.

My mobile phone chirps happily demanding attention. I get it out and shrug apologetically.

"I know that's supposed to be on, but could we have it on silent," Vaughn says.

"Yes, of course," I say. "Let's see..."

"Get on with–" but he looks up and sees.

I throw my mobile, underarm and harmlessly, but Vaughn instinctively swats the irritation away.

Ping!

My attention follows it, drawn by the small spinning object as it sails into space chirping as it goes. It drops below the edge of the roof like a toy thrown from a pram. I think about buying a new one; the thought actually crosses my mind that I'll have to re-enter all the names and numbers again, assuming anyone in my address book survives.

A black shape moves across the sky: a raven from the Tower of London, a vengeful angel, a spitfire diving out of the sun.

Mandy floats in the air.

My perception stutters into single frame images of the unfolding combat.

Vaughn pulls the sniper rifle round. It's an unwieldy weapon at close quarters. I think he's not going to manage it, but he fires off a shot: *phut!*

The clutch of plaid tied at my shoulder explodes in red and green tufts. He's shot me! No, just the plaid was hit, but the bastard shot me!

Mandy crashes onto Vaughn, a missile of black stab jacket and nightstick, and the two clatter over each other across the roof. The rifle skitters one way; the baton dances the other.

They roll over and over, then separate. Mandy's left hand comes forward, a trained move, but Vaughn knows these methods and has dirty tricks besides. He blocks, pushes, shoves, and punches, his two fists outnumbering Mandy's hand as she reaches into her utility belt. In contrast to the chaos of the boxing, her right-hand works expertly.

She pulls out the pepper spray, levels the non-lethal weapon and discharges just as Vaughn's blow connects. The liquid spatters over the floor and then across the air as Mandy spins and falls.

The droplets fizz in the air, a mist like spreading mustard gas, and I throw my free hand up to ward off the vapour coming my way. I feel my hand go wet, cooling and pleasant, before it stings like hell.

Can I look up?

The stuff is still falling around me like mist, the sunlight playing rainbows through the halo.

I'm shoved and pushed suddenly from behind as two bodies roll across me.

I look, my eyes streaming, but I have to look.

I can't rub my eyes – Christ, it's all over me! – what do I do?

I rub them on my shirt, up and down, side to side, and then wring them through the rough material of my plaid. I wipe my eyes, *ahhhhhh*, but blinking I can see, just about, *blink-blink*.

I see the worst.

Mandy kicks Vaughn towards the edge of the roof, but he twists around and pushes her down. She hits the ground awkwardly and he lunges, his hands clasping around her exposed throat. She flails under his weight, but already I see she's fading – he's bigger, he's stronger, he's deadlier.

I punch at him, straining to pull the pipe from the wall, my wrist from handcuff, my arm from its socket, but it's only the air I strike. Vaughn is just centimetres from my outstretched fist.

My girlfriend is being strangled to death and there's nothing I can do. I swivel round. Yes, my feet will reach. I kick as hard as I can.

Vaughn grunts with the tiny impacts, rocks over and then disappears, both of them falling over the edge like dolls.

"Oh fuck!"

I stand as best I can, crouched over by the short chain, and crane over the edge.

For a split second, a freeze frame, I can see the two of them, locked in combat, tumbling into the nothingness.

Mandy catches hold of a pipe, something, I don't know. Vaughn's lower down. A metallic screech and a retort of concrete dust fires out as bolts fail.

I stand, pulling myself up as far as the cuffs allow, but I can only just see.

Mandy is holding on, still on the edge, but she isn't safe. She's leaning out far too far.

"Take my hand," Mandy shouts. "Take my hand."

She reaches out with her hand.

"No," I say, reaching as far as I can, but the short chain means I'm a metre away – miles and miles.

She gets her hand over the parapet and pulls herself up: hand, wrist, elbow, arm, chest and then she's safe on top.

Vaughn, bastard to the end, stretches too, grabbing at her, trying to pull her over and take her with him.

At the last moment, Mandy's right-hand reaches for her handcuffs and in a single motion flips them open, clicks them around Vaughn's wrist, then she attaches the other cuff to a metal railing. Mandy lets go, Vaughn drops, held aloft in a sudden arm-wrenching jerk with a teeth-clenched, hard-man shriek – and then he dangles helplessly, his wrist broken.

Mandy stumbles back, falling over herself as she does so.

"Mandy, Mandy," I say and realise that I'm talking.

Mandy stands, angry and hurt, but alive.

She walks back to the edge of the hospital roof with the Thames behind her and St. Paul's in the distance. Her blonde hair streams out to one side as she stands on the edge of the precipice.

Carefully, she adjusts her uniform, tucking her blouse into her combat trousers and straightening her stab jacket.

"Bitch," Vaughn shouts, "Bitch, fucking bitch."

Finally, she looks him in the eye.

"You!" – She steadies herself – "...are under arrest! You have the right to remain silent, but it may harm your defence if you do not mention, when questioned, something which you later rely on in court. Anything you do say may be given in evidence."

Mandy turns back to me.

We make eye contact properly, at some level for the first time ever, and a big smile breaks out on her face. Her split lip starts bleeding.

There's a roar of noise from below, even at this height above the bridge. It's a simmering angry sound like the noise I imagine the ground makes before a volcanic eruption.

Stupidly, I try to get up. The handcuff rattles as I shake my hand, which jogs Mandy out of her reverie. She's startled, almost not knowing where she is, but given a directive, she fishes out her key and bends over to unlock the handcuff attached to the metal pipe. We're close as she bends over, her hair whipping around in the breeze, and–

"You're wearing yellow shoelaces," I say, accusingly.

"Yes."

"You helped them! You fucking helped them!"

"Of course."

"What?"

"Superintendent McGivern gave me the job of keeping an eye on them."

"You were..."

"Undercover," she says.

"Yes."

"You knew that."

"Yes... of course."

The picture of the vase is two faces looking into each other's eyes.

She glances over her shoulder, her attention drawn to what was distracting her mentally. Indistinct cries

342

and shouts, angrier in tone drift up from the distant mob.

"Guy, they're going to kill each other!"

"What?"

"Guy, they're–"

I stand, shaking my hand to refuse her assistance and hobble unsteadily to the edge. Giddying, far below, a maelstrom of colours approaching a black cloud, a thick line strung the far side of the bridge like a huge storm brewing on the horizon.

"Get me up!" Vaughn shouts, but I'm above him.

I'm on higher ground.

History records the battles: 1066, 1746, 1940... but never the awful calm beforehand when everything reaches the tipping point before it topples and all comes crashing down. They say Nero fiddled as Rome burnt, Bush listened to a children's story as planes crashed into New York, I'm standing on top of a fucking hospital roof just before–

It's almost as if Mandy considers this for a moment before unlatching the handcuff from my wrist. My right hand moves instinctively over to rub the sore area.

Mandy's face is already blooming with bruises. She's distraught, helpless, and fiddles into her stab jacket to pull out a small locket on a chain. She holds it for a moment, almost praying, and then she opens it. Inside is our engagement ring. She tries, but can't put it on her finger.

"I took it off to keep it safe," she says, "and to convince Trudie we weren't involved. You know, undercover."

"Undercover in police uniform?"

"Yes."

I lean forward to help and she winces as I ease the gold over her cracked knuckles.

She smiles: "There," she says, "that's better."

"I can stop this," I say, meaning the riot below.

"Can you?"

"Yes."

I see her profile as she looks and then the small shake of her head. She thinks it's hopeless.

"I can try!"

"Good luck," she says, and she holds up her hand, fingers crossed. In that moment I again remember her standing with Trudie, her back to me, her fingers crossed, and when she was talking to him in the interview room, her hands behind her back, childishly crossing her fingers to counter the lie. I love her for it.

I kiss her, her blood wetting my lips, and then I run, I run and run and run, throwing myself down the staircase, pulling myself along with the bannister because gravity simply isn't fast enough. The corridors in the hospital are anonymous and endless, the signs complicated and confusing.

"Exit! Exit!" I shout. "Where's the exit?"

Someone in blue scrubs starts to explain, but I don't hear them. I follow the pointed finger and finally, there's the bright light of outside.

The open air is hot. People amble along, randomly. I've no idea which way to go. This isn't the way I came in. Going round and round the stairs means my mental compass is all over the place. I look up, but if Mandy is on the roof waving, she's far too far away to see. There are so many people: medical staff, visitors, patients out for a walk, passers-by; all going in all directions... no, there is a forward, a gathering, and in that direction more tartan and red and... shouting.

Once I'm off hospital property, the street is packed and I have to push and shove to make progress.

I started this, I have to end it. I'm like Frankenstein: 'It's alive!' I screamed as we crossed Swarkestone bridge, but now I'm out in the wilderness, alone in my personal Arctic wastes trying to kill the monster. Except it's packed, the noise is chaotic and there are people everywhere. I must get through – I can't, I'm English – but I have to barge to the front.

"Sorry."

A big woman in a black coat, a Sikh–

"Sorry, excuse me."

A family, pushchair, a gaggle of scantily dressed women, an office worker with a coffee, spilt suddenly.

"Sorry, sorry, sorry."

A man in a red coat, a beige something, tartan, more tartan, another Redcoat.

"Guy!" says someone, then someone else: "Guy."

They are gathering around me, hemming me in. It's impossible. I'm being buried in hellos and my message will be drowned out by my name, but then, amidst the clamour, for a moment, one small moment, I see the bridge and then, from somewhere deep inside, I find something.

"Make way!" I yell.

The crowd parts, so many people!

They are shouting: "Guy! Guy! Guy!"

I'm jostled, pushed forward, slapped on the back and propelled beyond the edge of the Rebellion. I'm in the open. The clamour subsides as I step away from the mob towards the police lines and I see down the Thames, the open water with the city crowded on either side.

I turn as I walk and everything flashes past in front of me like the view from a fairground ride: the hospital, the Jacobites and Redcoats, the tourists, the London Eye, the river, St. Paul's, offices, a statue of Boudicca, police, more police, a million, billion police, the Houses of Parliament, the balustrade of the bridge with its line of trefoil holes. It's green like the seats in the House of Commons.

Now or never.

There's a notice on the bridge: 'Bridges By-Laws'.

I bet it says you not allowed to climb on it, I think, as I clamber up onto the stone wall and grab the iron lamppost with its three huge lamps for support. The stone barrier is wide there and affords a platform. I face the mob, diagonally, the River Thames a dizzy drop behind me. I hold up my hand, and there's a hush.

I glance to my left and I can almost see the ranks of police lean forward to listen. The mass of people seeps around, filling the bus lane until there's a semi-circle of faces looking up.

"I'm English!" I shout.

A hush: the Thames laps gently and in the distance, a ship's horn sounds. I can barely hear the distant traffic snarled up behind the closed roads. A raging pulse hammers time in my ears. Elizabeth I told us of her English heart, Martin Luther King had a dream, JFK asked what you could do for your country, Collins said we should be magnanimous: hell, I open my mouth and words come tumbling out.

"I'm English! From England. My flag is the cross of St. George and the Union Jack. But that flag doesn't seem to stand for what I believe in anymore. There are all sorts of bastards who march under the Union Jack now from the bloody English Defence League and racist UKIP supporters to the God knows what. Our flag represents England, Scotland and Northern Ireland, and Wales and all the people who flocked to our shore. It's about bringing people together. We're a country that welcomes and celebrates other cultures. That's not Nazism. We had the biggest empire history ever saw, and we gave it away – OK, OK, there were bad times and things we could have perhaps done better, but we can choose what to celebrate and remember and pass on – and those we conquered and subjugated formed an old boy's club: the Commonwealth. That means something, surely? It's a sign that things weren't all bad, some things were good, and we, the British Empire, made the world a better place: Pax Britannia. And that gives us the responsibility to carry on making the world a better place. So we should be part of a United Kingdom, part of European Union, part of United Nations, and, why not, part of the United Federation of Planets. That's what it's all about. That's what this flag represents. It stands for tolerance, inclusion, getting along with each other, for democracy, freedom of speech, croquet on the lawn, cricket, losing at football, Spitfires, Winston Churchill and Stephen Fry, red telephone boxes, warm beer, cucumber sandwiches in triangles with the crusts cut off, fish 'n' chips, chicken tikka masala, Chinatown, the Year of the Lion..." – dear God, I'm rambling, and I think I called it the Union *Jack* – "...er, the festival of lights, Auld Lang Syne in Trafalgar Square, the bobby on the beat, the unarmed police officer, the Queen, organic farming and Bonnie Prince Charlie!"

There's a roar in response.

"I want to live in Great Britain, not Little England," I roar. "This is our flag and we want it back."

Or at least that's what I'd have like to have said.

And that's what I'll say were my words.

It's gone now, whipped away on the breeze and as ephemeral as anything in this age of ubiquitous phone cameras. Really it was full of 'er's, 'um's, 'ah's and 'shut-up-and-listen's, but hell – I win, so I'll get to write the history. You understand.

The cheer is amazing and then: *hip-hip, hurrah; hip-hip, hurrah, hip–*

Big Ben chimes on cue.

The pipers start up with *When the Battle's Over*.

The crowd gather me up and hoist me aloft. It's all I can do to keep my plaid down. The Union *Flag* unfurls behind me with the House of Parliament in the background and it'll all be framed perfectly tomorrow on the front of every newspaper.

New Jacobite Rebellion

From Wikipedia, the free encyclopedia

(Redirected from Jacobite Rebellion)

For other uses, see Jacobites (disambiguation)

 This article **does not** cite **any references or** sources. Please help improve this article by adding citations to reliable sources. Unverifiable material may be challenged and removed.

Contents [hide]

1 Overview
2 Aftermath
3 See also
4 External links

The **New Jacobite Rebellion** was a political movement reminiscent of the Jarrow March of 1936 and involved a group of re-enactors from the Bonnie Prince Charlie Society[1].

Led by Guy Wilson, Rabbie MacLeod and Ross Templeton, the march began in Derby and over ten days moved south towards London.

During this time the 'rebellion' grew in numbers and in political aims. Speeches by John Trudie, MP, referring to the then Home Secretary, Timothy Dorrington's inability to stop even a simple armed rebellion marching on London, led to a cabinet reshuffle and Trudie's rise to power.

Overview   [edit]

Apparently started as a drunken bet in the Crew & Harpur pub in Swarkestone as to whether the Jacobite Uprising of 1745 could have actually reached London, members of the Bonnie Prince Charlie Society set off in that direction.

348

The Rebellion was escorted by the police, although at one point an attempt was made to stop them on the orders of the then Home Secretary, Timothy Dorrington. This plan failed and so Dorrington resigned to be replaced as Home Secretary by John Trudie.

Many different political movements joined the growing numbers as the march approached London. Estimates range from 500 to 2,500, with at least 25 different groups represented.

John Trudie organized a marksman to murder members of the public and the police. This sniper was arrested after a rooftop struggle by police sergeant Amanda Reynolds[citation needed].

The main rebellion had nearly reached the Houses of Parliament by this time and faced over 2,500 police. It was stopped when their leader, Guy Wilson, made a speech on Westminster Bridge and the crowd dispersed.

Aftermath [edit]

Main article: The Fall of John Trudie

The Home Secretary, John Trudie, MP, was arrested at Stansted Airport. The Home Secretary, who was still technically in charge of the Metropolitan Police, was trying to flee with his Polish mistress, Katarzyna Wiśniewska, and £500,000 hidden famously in a tartan suitcase. His ranting demand to be obeyed became a YouTube phenomenon.

Timothy Dorrington was reinstated as Home Secretary after an emergency cabinet meeting.

See also [edit]

- Police use of firearms in the United Kingdom
- Gun politics in the United Kingdom
- The Jacqueline Fort Controversy

References [edit]

1. ^ Bonnie Prince Charles Society. Website of the re-enactment group.

External links [edit]

- Jacobite! A New History – Rabbie McLeod's blog.
- The Jacobites March Again – a BBC Panorama special
- The Causes of the First and Second World Wars – PhD Thesis by Guy Wilson

Categories: Political movements | Historical re-enactments

EXILE

Long after the real Jacobite Rebellion of 1745 and his march south turned back at Derby, Bonnie Prince Charlie did reach London.

He'd moved to France, where he married Clementina Walkinshaw, someone he'd met during the Uprising of 1745. They had a daughter. Four years after Culloden, he visited the English capital incognito.

Can you imagine it, the man who had tried to bring down the Hanoverians popping over for a coffee in one of the new drinking houses? He came to England secretly in order to convert to Protestantism, having realised that he couldn't gain the English, Scottish and Irish thrones as a Catholic. So much for it all being a Catholic versus Protestant struggle. Of course, once he was back in France he was as Catholic as anyone.

He became a drunk and died in Italy.

Strange, because we all end up in Little Italy: a pasta restaurant, a proper traditional Italian place rather than some corporate clone, in Clerkenwell. Pizza is just a small section on the card menu. The lighting is low, tall candles flicker on the tables, the ambience is relaxing and my face feels pummelled and sore. I am so glad to be here. I am so glad to be alive. I am so glad everyone is alive.

I find Rabbie and make him text everyone: the old crowd, the Jacobites and Redcoats, Hippies, anti-frackers, Guy Fawkes mask-wearing Anonymous types and the off-duty police. Basically, those of us who started this quest a million years ago and who made it all the way to the end of the adventure. My phone is in pieces at the foot of St. Thomas' Hospital.

When I walk in, I see his legs first, hairy, booted and sticking out at a relaxed angle from his plaid. He's just standing there, leaning on the bar as if nothing has happened and trying to look down the barmaid's blouse.

"Ross!"

He turns round, registers my presence and nods before turning back. He's chatting up the barmaid just as he had in the George.

"What happened to you?" I say going over.

"Och, Felix and I—"

"Felix?"

"The copper."

"Oh right."

"He dinna fancy going back to riot duty. They'd deployed Tea Pot 1—"

"Tea Pot 1?"

"Aye, from Lambeth, the catering van, a sign that's it's got a wee bit serious, so instead we went to the canteen for a fish supper. Well, I had the pie with chips."

"Did you?" I feel exasperated.

"Turns out yon Felix is a wargamer, figures and all that pish. We got chatting about Austerlitz – he's got some damn silly ideas – and I lost track of time."

"Oh, you did, did you?"

"Aye and, well, I missed all the fun."

"Missed all the fun! You stupid insane Scottish bloke from Kent."

"Och, never mind. Anything exciting happen?"

"Exciting... only got arrested and I was on this roof and–"

"Och, will ye no look at that, they've got proper Guinness on tap, not the ice cold pish."

Ross goes off followed by as much annoyance as I can muster and psychically project in his direction. It has no effect. I should be tired, exhausted beyond belief, but somehow my body is either beyond that or hyped up with adrenaline.

"So you don't want a pasta supper then?" I say.

"Spaghetti and chips? Och, sure," he says without turning round. "You want something?"

Drinking got us all into this, and in my current state, it would be a massive, massive mistake. Exhaustion, lack of food and high spirits shouldn't be mixed with alcohol.

"Yes!" I say. "A pint."

"And me!" It's Liam, smiling broadly as he comes over to embrace me. "That was a hell of a speech."

"Och, Sassenach spongers."

"Irish," says Liam.

"You heard me?" I say.

"Yes."

"Speech?" Ross asks.

"Yes, wonderful rousing stuff," says Liam, taking the first pint off the bar. "Nonsense, of course."

"Of course," I say, and I laugh.

Ross hands me a pint and I weigh the dark object in my hand. Liam hasn't supped his yet and we wait for Ross to gather his change and hold his trophy aloft. The final pint has a thick head and foam slips down the side, causing Ross to swap hands and fling the damp off his wet fingers.

We wait a moment, savouring it all.

"One for all," says Ross raising his glass and there's only one thing we can all say: "And all for one!"

We're sitting down around a table, Ross, Rabbie, Kate, Reka, Liam, Zoë, Andys galore, and great friends from the crowd I met only five minutes ago, each of us drinking our pints, when Mandy arrives.

She's wearing her black skirt and white blouse, her police uniform but without the insignia: she looks like a waitress. I stop, half-in and half-out of a chair, unable to move.

"Mandy!" says Ross, standing in surprise, "what happened to you?"

"Someone resisted arrest," she replies.

"You OK?" Ross asks.

"Fine, you should see the other bloke." And she smiles, lopsidedly, and looks lovely.

"It wasn't one of us," I say standing.

"No," she says, "it was one of them."

I grin too.

I put my pint down and move towards her. We take a long time because there's such a gap between us, a heap of events crammed into the last few days that need reinterpretation. It's like an archaeological expedition has dug up some new find, some impossible object, and theories need discarding like unsuitable cards and a fresh hand dealt from the deck. But we're OK, we're fine, we're in love.

"Guy, I'm so sorry..." she says. "When they... when you were..."

I put my arms around her, she does the same to me, and she cries, tiny sobs of relief, and I turn us slightly so that the others at the table can't see our faces.

We're still standing like that when the waiter returns for the second time to see if we're ready to order: Mandy goes for bolognese. I say the same. I'm so famished that anything would do. And we'd like more drinks. A bottle of wine is suggested.

We eat like an army that's marched. It's all just wolfed down with breadsticks, side orders, garlic bread and wine quaffed like ale.

"Trudie's been arrested," Mandy says. "He was at Stansted trying to catch a flight with a case of money."

"No way!" said Rabbie.

"With his mistress!"

"Och, what's some poncey Southern politician got to do with us?"

"Ross!" I say, "where have you been? He's only been trying to kill us."

"Has he?"

"Duh!"

"They've arrested some police officers," Mandy says and then she holds up her hands to make a plea: "But that's not official, just what's on the grapevine."

"Bad apples," I say.

"I was so scared I'd been discovered," Mandy says. "Vaughn was in the Observation Room. I set it up to record Trudie as evidence to put him away, but when I checked, the tape had disappeared. I was certain he'd found it and knew about me."

I fiddle out the evidence from my sporran and hold it aloft: "You mean this?"

"The tape!" Mandy says. "Where did you get it?"

"From the tape recorder, I was in the Observation Room when you..."

"Oh God!" She hugs me. "You star. We'll have to hand it in."

"Tomorrow."

"It's vital–"

"You're off duty."

I could see her hesitating, but I was firm.

"Tomorrow," she said. Phew. I put it back into my sporran as I realise that I'll have to find a cassette tape player to erase my yelling: 'bitch, bitch, bollocks, bollocks'. These are not words I want recorded for posterity or read out in some enquiry with my fiancée listening.

I won, so this is my history.

"What are we going to do next year?" Liam asks. "Re-run the Battle of Hastings, retrace Alexander the Great's footsteps, re-enact the Battle of Britain with kites?"

"I think I'll take a holiday," I say.

"Och, yer ken I've never walked the Pennine Way."

"Or seen Stonehenge," said Liam.

"Aye, and Dublin's got some nice pubs."

"When are we going then?" said Liam.

"I'm going on my honeymoon," I say.

"Too right," says Mandy. "Somewhere warm, somewhere romantic, somewhere–"

There's an intake of breath from Ross and Liam, and I interject: "On our own!"

"I'll need to get leave," says Mandy.

"Damn right!" I say.

And that's it really.

Most history is marked by the great battles, but the tide of time is made up of gradual developments. William the Conqueror won the Battle of Hastings, but the serfs tending the fields weren't affected one iota by the change of aristocracy: it was the creeping Norman tongue that developed into English that made a difference.

Afterwards, everyone's going to stop over at Kate's, except Mandy and I who are going to her new flat in East Ham. The plan is to take the tube, but I know we'll have drunk enough wine to realise we can afford a black cab just this once. And there, we'll hug, and wince from our injuries, and hopefully, take a bath together with bubbles and tea lights flickering on the side.

Or maybe bed first. I'll sleep for a week.

And slowly, the events of the past fortnight will fade away until they are anecdotes over a pint. Perhaps it'll be written about: who knows? It's all over Twitter already.

Tomorrow, we'll take the day off and I'll buy a toothbrush to leave at hers, and gradually, as the months pass, I'll add a shaving brush and a razor, we'll fight over space in the bathroom cabinet and struggle to adapt to living together in our London cupboard, fall out and make up, and that'll be living happily ever after.

The End

David Wake is growing more left-wing as he gets older or possibly the world is becoming more right-wing faster. This is his first political novel.

Thank you for buying and reading *Crossing the Bridge*. If you liked this novel, please take a few moments to write a review and help spread the word. Also, vote, protest, sign petitions and make your voice heard.

For more information, and to join the mailing list for news of forthcoming releases, see www.davidwake.com.

Many thanks to:–

Dawn Abigail, Helen Blenkinsop, Andy Conway, Tony Cooper, Guy Etchells, Tiffany Elliot, Mike Ibeji, Sebastian Melmouth, Smuzz, Mark Slater, Andrew Sparke, Mike Roberts, Jessica Rydill, Inspector Bob Hunter and the WPC in the local shop buying bread.

Mystery, clues and danger with tea and cake

The Vicar lies dead – Murdered!

Three budding Miss Marples, Pat, Diane and Annabelle, swing into action and they want answers: Why would anyone want to kill the vicar? Where does Mrs Entwistle go every night? What was Sir Victor up to at the warden's? And how will so many murders affect the circulation of the parish magazine?

The truth will be uncovered: once they've had a nice cup of tea and a biscuit.

Includes a FREE scone recipe.

"Enjoyed the whole thing and absolutely loved some of the touches both clever and amusing. No spoilers – no details. Read it yourself!"

"...all kinds of red herrings thrown in to confuse the reader. Unlike many crime thrillers or cosy crime stories when I have usually sussed out who the killer is, in this case I really hadn't a clue."

Available as an ebook and paperback.

A ripping yarn of cliff-hangers, desperate chases, romance and deadly danger.

Earnestine, Georgina and Charlotte are trapped in the Eden College for Young Ladies suffering deportment, etiquette and Latin. So, when the British Empire is threatened by an army of zombies, the Deering-Dolittle sisters are eager to save the day. Unfortunately, they are under strict instructions not to have any adventures...

...but when did that ever stop them?

"Think 'Indiana Jones pace'. It's fast and dangerous and does not involve embroidery!"

★ ★ ★ ★ ★

"A brilliant, fast paced steampunk adventure, trains zombies and zeppelins, what more could you want?"

★ ★ ★ ★ ★

THE DERRING-DO CLUB

Putting their best foot forward, without showing an ankle, since 1896.

The first novel in the adventure series
available as an ebook and a paperback.

A ripping yarn of time-travel, rocket-packs, conspiracy and *sword fighting!*

The plucky Deering-Dolittle sisters, Earnestine, Georgina and Charlotte, are put to the test as mysterious Time Travellers appear in Victorian London to avert the destruction of the world…

…but just whose side should they be on?

"Loved it! [...] Fast paced and exciting another great adventure for three Victorian Young Ladies."

★ ★ ★ ★ ★

*"…if I had been wearing a hat,
I would have taken it off to David Wake."*

★ ★ ★ ★ ★

THE DERRING-DO CLUB

Putting their best foot forward, without showing an ankle, since 1896.

The second novel in the adventure series available as an ebook and a paperback.

A ripping yarn of strange creatures, aerial dog-fights, espionage and *pirates!*

Strange lights hover over Dartmoor and alien beings abduct the unwary as the plucky Deering-Dolittle sisters, Earnestine, Georgina and Charlotte, race to discover the truth before the conquest begins...

...but betrayal is never far away.

"Well-written, fast-paced, and dangerously addictive – but with some extra thinking in there, too, should you choose to read it that way."

★ ★ ★ ★ ★

"As with previous adventures I really enjoyed the imaginative scene setting, building intrigue into unexpected twists and a spectacular ending."

★ ★ ★ ★ ★

THE DERRING-DO CLUB
Putting their best foot forward, without showing an ankle, since 1896.

The third novel in the adventure series available as an ebook and a paperback.

An Arabian tale of murder, Egyptian gods, mummies, temple raiding and *flying carpets!*

Nine suspects trapped on the SS *Karnak* with a killer! As the Deering-Dolittle sisters, Earnestine, Georgina and Charlotte investigate, mummies rise from the dead, ancient gods send messages and plots turn like cogs.

Their journey is far from straight even on the Suez Canal.

"Well-written and witty, this is a gloriously over the top pastiche of Agatha Christie's 'Death on the Nile' - and much, much more."

★ ★ ★ ★ ★

"You will not put this book down. [...] a quirky funny enjoyable Victorian tale and the last 300 pages fly by."

★ ★ ★ ★ ★

THE DERRING-DO CLUB

Putting their best foot forward, without showing an ankle, since 1896.

The fourth novel in the adventure series available as an ebook and a paperback.

A ripping yarn set in the British Raj with handsome officers, vile thuggees, diabolical plans, a terrifying death-goddess and *a fate worse than death!*

It's soon to be the happiest day of Miss Deering-Dolittle's life, but abandonment, betrayal and an old foe stand to ruin everything – and destroy the British Empire.

All roads lead to the temple of Kali and a desperate last stand against impossible odds.

Can our plucky young heroines, Earnestine, Georgina and Charlotte save the day?

"Think 'Indiana Jones pace'. It's fast and dangerous. My kind of Adventure! MORE PLEASE."
★ ★ ★ ★ ★

THE DERRING-DO CLUB
Putting their best foot forward, without showing an ankle, since 1896.

The fifth novel in the adventure series available as an ebook and a paperback.

Think *Black Mirror* with a Scandi-crime feel

Twenty years from now, everyone's thoughts are shared on social media: the Thinkersphere. Privacy is dead and buried. Pre-mediated crime is history. So who killed the woman in Chedding car park?

Detective Oliver Braddon is plunged into an investigation to track down the impossible: a murderer who can kill without thinking.

Hashtag is a gritty, dystopian neo-noir that poses uncomfortable questions about our obsession with social media and presents a mind-bending picture of what life might be like when our very thoughts are no longer our own.

"Superb futuristic scenario – good story and touches of dark humour."
★ ★ ★ ★ ★

"Oh my God what a fantastic concept!"
★ ★ ★ ★ ★

"...and suddenly you need to tell everyone else to go away and let you finish this book!"
★ ★ ★ ★ ★

Book One of the Thinkersphere series available as an ebook and a paperback.

The dark sequel to Hashtag

Black Mirror meets Scandi-crime in a mind-bending dystopia where 'likes' matter more than lives.

Detective Oliver Braddon's investigation into an apparent suicide leads him to a powerful media mogul. Is he the killer?

In this alarming vision of the near-future, everyone's thoughts are shared on social media. With privacy consigned to history, a new breed of celebrity influences billions.

But who controls who?

A gritty, neo-noir delving into a conflict between those connected and those with secrets to hide.

"Darker in tone than the previous book, which fits with our now slightly older Braddon's move from new and enthusiastic PC to somewhat more careworn Detective, there's a Scandi-noir feel to this one."

Book Two of the Thinkersphere series available as an ebook and a paperback.

The mind-bending future continues

Another mass suicide. Or is it murder?

The case drops into Inspector Oliver Braddon's inbox. The world demands answers. With everyone's thoughts shared, liked and monitored, why haven't the police solved the case in the usual 20 seconds?

Braddon's suspicions focus on a disturbing cult, the Church of the Transcendent Cloud, and tech-billionaire, Jacob Lamb, the creator of the Thinkersphere app, *After Life* – except that he's dead.

Plus Sign is a gritty, dystopian neo-noir.

> "...crackles with humour and tension as the reader is drawn into a world dominated by the all-embracing Thinkersphere and its tantalising app offering the promise of an After Life. Plus Sign is intriguing and alarming in equal measure [...] Thoroughly recommend."
> ★ ★ ★ ★ ★

Book Three of the Thinkersphere series available as an ebook and a paperback.

A tonic for the Xmas Spirit

Being Santa's daughter would be a dream come true for any child, but for Carol Christmas, the fairy tale is about to end. Evil forces threaten the festive season, and only Carol can save the day...

A grim fairy tale told as a children's book, but perhaps not just for children.

"This starts out as a delightfully childlike modern take on the Christmas myth – the kind of Pixar-esque story that can play to the kids and give the adults a knowing wink or two, but it gets dark. Very dark."

★ ★ ★ ★ ★

Available as an ebook, a paperback and an audiobook.

Do you fear technology? We have an App for that.

Your phone is your life. But what if it kept secrets from you? What if it accidentally framed you for murder? And what if it was the only thing that could save you?

In a world where phones are more intelligent than humans, but are still thrown away like yesterday's fashions, one particular piece of plastic lies helpless as its owner, Alice Wooster, is about to be murdered...

In this darkly comic near-future tale, a very smart phone tells its own story as events build to a climactic battle. Can it save all the virtual and augmented worlds? Can it save the real one? Can it order Alice some proper clothes?

"Excellent novel – by turns strikingly original, laugh-out-loud funny and thought provoking."
★ ★ ★ ★ ★

"Want to read it again soon..."
★ ★ ★ ★ ★

"A thoughtful, tense and funny look at a future that seems to be already upon us."
★ ★ ★ ★ ★

Available as an ebook and a paperback.

An epic tale set in Japan's Samurai era

In the days of the sword, a girl disguised as a boy turns killer to avenge her Samurai master, murdered by a brotherhood of ruthless and powerful men. Following the trail of blood, a brilliant detective – an Emperor's Watcher – searches for answers only to come face-to-face with an old enemy, a man honour dictates he must protect.

As the death toll rises, and the hunter closes in on the hunted, truth-seeker and ninja assassin find themselves at odds, not only with each other, but also with their fundamental beliefs: Honour or truth? Instinct or intellect? Justice or revenge?

Roninko is a bloody, action-packed revenge thriller steeped in ancient wisdom. A philosophical and breathtaking story of Bushido, 'the Way of the Warriors'.

"This is a beautifully written, atmospheric adventure through ancient Japan. Lovingly researched and with nuanced and interesting characters, I enjoyed this greatly."
★ ★ ★ ★ ★

Available as an ebook and paperback.